I0818160

Death of a Guru

DOUG GREENALL

Death of a Guru
Doug Greenall

Greenall, Doug
Death of a Guru
ISBN: 978-0-9908782-0-9

This book is a work of fiction. Names, characters, events and incidents are either the products of the author's imagination or used in a fictitious manner. Any similarity to persons, living or dead, or to actual events is purely coincidental.

Printed in the United States of America
February, 2015

Cover art by Glen Schroeder
Book design by John Zahlien

New York, New York

Contact: Zahlien Publishing / zahlienpublishing@outlook.com

DEATH OF A GURU

A brief word

I first set eyes on Devon Clarke on May 10, 1992 in Ao Lai, a small town on the Andaman coast of Thailand. Had someone told me then that I would spend two years of my life hunting this man down for the purpose of killing him, I would've found it absurd.

Most of what I know of Devon Clarke's extraordinary story came from his own mouth. Despite the man's prodigious cunning, I trust it to be true. Other sources have added considerably to my forays into his past, and in rare instances I have invented a detail or two, but always in a way that supports the integrity of the real events. If anything is amiss, the blame is mine.

Every once in a while a force as rare and brutal as a tsunami hits a human life. For me that force was Devon Clarke.

Magnus Larsen

Part One

Book of Devon 1

September 16, 1986

Massachusetts, somewhere south of Mohawk Trail State Forest.

Stands of white pine and northern hardwoods stretched into shadows over a twisting road. A copper-colored Porsche Carrera flashed like a spawning salmon as it darted through the broken sunlight.

A pair of gray-blue eyes followed the pavement through a winding descent. The driver maneuvered perfectly, yet he seemed vaguely disengaged, as if he was playing an arcade game that was too easy, or thinking about a speech that he needed to write. It was hard to tell. He was possessed of a strangely enigmatic quality.

The Porsche followed a bend where the road flattened out, feeding onto a two-lane highway. Sunshine hit the driver's profile. His eyes were slightly bloodshot, and the stubble on his face had dots of white. A green river to his right meandered gently with tones of blue and sunlit patches of yellow.

Smooth hands held the wheel and worked the stick shift. The man's thick brown hair was lightened with a hint of gray. His off-white shirt was a finely woven silk, and his only ornaments were a wedding band and a Rolex watch. He was inordinately handsome, but again it deferred to the enigmatic—he was neither pretty nor rugged. In the absence of wrinkles or the typical paunch of an aging male, most people would've been surprised to discover that he was the grand old age of fifty-two.

His appearance seemed to hint at a deeper element, always beyond the observer's reach. With the power of suggestion, it could've been nobility ... or sociopathy. Most of all, Devon Clarke was watchable. He was the kind of human that made other humans look.

Beyond the man himself, the other notable item inside the Porsche Carrera that day was on the passenger seat—a 9mm Glock handgun.

For three days Devon Clarke had been looking for a place to die. He had nowhere in mind—he just thought he would know the place when he saw it. He'd crisscrossed and zigzagged New England from Boston to Stockbridge, from Plattsburgh to Bridgeport. His only intake of food or drink had been orange juices, coffees, and mineral waters at service stations. In the deep of night he'd slept for an hour and twenty minutes on a grassy shoulder of I-91 south of Hartford, Vermont. A repeated rapping on his window broke into his slumber. After waking him up, a cheerful young state trooper had commended his decision to pull over rather than fall asleep at the wheel. The upbeat officer missed an item of commonality between them: a gun made by Glock.

The road was breathing in front of him. Leaves twinkled electrically in the afternoon sun. This was the special season, just after the Labor Day Weekend when the road was open and uncrowded, when he'd traveled with Olivia, taking trips up to the Hudson Valley, when trees were still green and time teetered between a fading summer and an impending fall. Memories struck deep chords of feeling in his sleep-and-calorie-deprived state.

A mountain of hay trembled in the rear of a truck; Devon blasted past. Reality frayed at the edges.

The river swirled south as it dropped into a dell. The Porsche diverged left, following an elevated plain with a vantage point of another highway below. Devon saw a white sedan crawling along the valley floor, and a good distance in front of it was a herd of motorcycles. He lost the view for a moment as the highway curved again.

A subtle shift occurred in Devon's face, as if the arcade game suddenly required a deeper level of focus, and the car picked up speed. A secondary road loomed to his right. Devon cranked the wheel, taking a wolf-like dive onto the artery that led to the lined road below.

A disintegration of the ordinary advanced on his mind. He hit the lower road with the sense that he was an alien being, riding within a strange shell that blasted him over his planet's terrain. Devon gained fast on the white sedan he had seen from the other road, passing it easily. The motorcycles were dots in his future. Distance closed and the dots grew. A deep growl of Harley Davidsons rose as he approached. There were about twenty bikers in all, give or take. The men wore leathers with their colors, a red and blue insignia that proclaimed them to be Satans Glory.

It was the insignia, amid the noise and the power, indeed the Glory of the chopped steel, that entranced Devon like a religious epiphany. In working-class bars it was told that, to become a full-patch member of Satans Glory, a man had to have taken a human life. At another place in time, Devon may have found himself skeptical of such a rumor—but today he believed it. Today, Fate had placed the disciples of Satan in front of him. These men were the Chosen Ones.

The copper-colored Porsche Carrera edged up behind them. The riders looked hard. Like investment bankers and new-age artists, their attire told the world who they were. This tribe chose leathers and bandanas, and colors on their skin. They were aware of him now. At least the men at the rear were.

Hogs and choppers filled the road in front of the Porsche, taking up a little of the left lane as well. The posted limit was 55—they were traveling just over 70. Passing these boys was a touch obnoxious but there was no oncoming traffic; the Carrera's 375 horsepower could've easily rocketed by them. Instead, Devon eased into the great roar of

Harleys. Several riders noticed him in their rear-view mirrors. One of the bikers glanced back—the Porsche showed no inclination to pass. Anger flashed through the rear of the pack. One or two tried to shout over the din of the motorcycles.

A rider dropped back, running his muscled chopper parallel to the driver's window. Devon saw a man with a bandana and tattooed hands shouting, and though he couldn't hear the words, he didn't need to be Helen Keller to get the gist. Clearer yet, the biker raised his middle finger.

Every man in the brotherhood now knew that some dumbass was way out of line. Other soldiers of Satans Glory moved into the left lane, to intimidate and box him in. Two of the tough guys near the front of the pack were withdrawing weapons as they rode. The finger was now a fist as the first soldier moved boldly close enough to pound on Devon's window. Devon smiled at him—it was neither warm nor malicious. Rage flared in the man's face. Devon veered easily to his left, smashing him to the pavement.

It happened so fast, none of the Satans Glory were expecting *this*. Adrenalin infected the herd. The accelerator pressed down and Devon surged, sending two more big bikes careening out of control. A deep screech of metal carved into his door as one machine twisted awkwardly—

Panicked riders shouted to each other as the Porsche blasted through the thundering Harleys, sending tattooed bodies helter-skelter across the pavement. Devon was now fully engaged.

Some tried to pull over to the shoulder, but Devon chased them down, inflicting carnage in every direction. Worse for the bikers, vehicles were now in the oncoming lane, forcing them into a narrower channel, which Devon exploited with violent, forceful speed. Cars began to pull over in anticipation of the madness in front of them, but Devon still banged a few more bikes, littering the highway with broken bones and bloody streaks of road-rash.

A canny rider near the front of the pack had managed to withdraw a handgun from some niche or saddlebag while moving at about 115 miles per hour—a respectable feat. But the would-be shooter had a problem: he couldn't turn around at this insane speed; it would be suicide to twist his body. There were still a few bikers between the malevolent Carrera and the gunman. The men in front of Devon were now riding for their lives.

Most of the Satans Glory behind Devon were strewn over the road; some of their unscathed comrades had stopped to help the wounded—but four focused soldiers followed Devon with wide open throttles.

Blind rage filled the air. Didn't this motherfucker know who Satans Glory were?

Devon blasted into the frontrunners, side-swiping two of the three bikers between himself and the man with the gun. The gunman's face floated like a white ball atop his large, inked body. His throttle was on the right hand side; letting go would've led to deadly assault from the violent Porsche behind him. Absolutely desperate, the rider began firing blindly over his shoulder with the gun in his left hand, inadvertently terrorizing his own pursuing brothers.

Devon drilled the Porsche into the man's s rear tire and the big hog jackknifed, smashing across the passenger-side windshield and tearing off the side-view mirror. A man's high scream ripped through the howl of engines as a large body flew through the air—

The carnage landed in front of Devon's pursuers—one bike couldn't avoid it, wiping out at a brutal speed.

Devon and the remaining posse blurred past an oncoming station wagon, leaving the driver agape. A fast-approaching sign indicated a turnoff to Rainbow Lake, left off the valley floor. A small service station with a convenience store was clearly visible about 100 yards off the junction. Devon cranked a hard left off the highway, his tire scraping against the metal of his freshly dented frame.

A kid in a ball-cap was pumping gas just as a man opening a bag of potato chips stepped out of the store. The heads turned in unison as three raging soldiers of the Satans Glory Motorcycle Club chased a banged-up sports car. In the conversation that followed, both agreed that they wouldn't want to be the guy in the orange Porsche.

The bikers blasted up a twisting road, leaning hard into corners, knowing that they now had an advantage over the Carrera, no matter how skillfully it was driven. Two leathered soldiers, neck and neck in the forefront, and another two hundred yards to their rear, rose over the crest of a bend...

...the road dropped into a slight depression, where the pavement gave way to gravel, and to their enraged delight, they could see that the Porsche had spun out of control and sat sideways, partially blocking the road. The driver was standing outside of his car. He must've known he was fucked.

Devon felt their fury washing over him like a wave. First off his machine, about forty yards away, was a man with long black hair. He was quick, the thick leather jacket with the blue and red logo of Satans Glory dropped from his shoulders, revealing arms that were tattooed and muscular. He efficiently withdrew a metal bar from a slot on his machine. The second rider had a scraggly beard and a mouthful of teeth that hadn't known the benefits of a dental plan. He too was fast off the hog, but he neatly folded his sunglasses and squatted to detach a hidden weapon.

Last to arrive, a large man skidded past his buddies, coming to a halt not fifteen yards from Devon. Mid-thirties, he was clean-cut with a full head of light brown hair, and his big hands were decorated with big rings. He might have been handsome if it weren't for his early gut and the tough history that life and prison had carved onto his face. He yanked his heavy bike onto its stand and shed his glasses by knocking them off his face. He stood at least 6 foot 5, and his demeanor was clear: he meant nasty business.

He went for Devon immediately, in front of the biker with the metal bar. Then stopped dead.

"*Tiny...*" was the single word of warning from the black-haired biker. But Tiny had stopped even before he saw the Glock sitting on the roof of the Porsche. Something was wrong—this piece of shit looked pleased—and not the kind of smug pleased that a cunning hit-man might be expected to show when his victim was getting taunted. No, he looked genuine, this guy—which was damn strange and just not right. Tiny felt the hairs on the back of his neck standing up.

Fury had made them morons. The black-haired soldier had a pronounced Adam's apple that bobbed as he swallowed. This motherfucker was waiting for them.

Devon spoke calmly. "*Tiny*—that's very clever." The hulk knew instinctually that Devon didn't think so. He flushed—how could they have been so fucking stupid?

The man with bad teeth rose with a machete that he'd finally extricated from his hog. Oblivious to the handgun, he said without joy, "Save me some cunt, Tiny Joe. I do sloppy seconds but not thirds."

Devon Clarke burst into laughter. "Your friend's got a real wit." It could not have been more brutal if he'd produced a semi-automatic machine gun. All three men were frozen.

The big man was good and scared but none of it showed. Tiny Joe wasn't born the day before yesterday and this wasn't his first ever confrontation with a shitbag. Even when he spoke lightly, there was something of a growl to his voice. "I'm figurin' you went and made friends with someone who just don't like us..."

"You're figuring incorrectly." Devon casually reached for the gun on the roof, and three hearts jumped. Tiny Joe lifted his hands as if to say, *Take it easy, pal...*

But Devon's demeanor wasn't threatening. Even with an unshaven face and fatigue coloring his eyes, he appeared ennobled. He addressed them with a certain formality, as if he were standing in an amphitheater.

"You've been chosen for a great honor. You wear my father's name on your persons ... and the time has come for you to honor that name." Devon paused, and then said, "My father awaits me. You will send me into his arms."

The man in the silk shirt was eerily calm. His way of speech had a tone like he was a fuckin' senator or something. Tiny never moved a muscle as the gray-blue eyes floated toward him—but Devon sensed his terror and committed the worst sacrilege of all: he began to speak *gently ... reassuringly.* "Don't be frightened, Tiny Joe ... I'm not going to kill you..." Devon held out the gun for him. "You're going to kill *me*."

Devon looked into the eyes of Tiny Joe, but they all heard his words. "My blood is your sacrament ... 'Satans Glory' will be manifest in the moment of my death. Send me home ... you will live in my father's blessing and bounty for the remainder of your natural life."

The big man could see the red capillaries in the whites of the pale eyes. The handle of the Glock was held up gently, offered—

Tiny Joe didn't blink—but neither did he take the gun. Dread ran through him like electricity. These guys had stood up to other men in barrooms, parking lots and prison yards, but this was not something that they could digest.

Devon's voice soothed, "Take the gun, Joe ... squeeze the trigger ... my father will reward you with heaven on earth ... he wants me home ... he wants *you* to honor his name." Tiny Joe was caught in the perfect madness of the gray-blue eyes in front of him. His stomach was queasy, and he felt his knees weakening. He couldn't move.

Then the man with the machete began quietly moving away toward his bike. Tiny Joe and the black-haired biker began backing up.

Devon's mood began to change. The world was falling out from under him. "What is this? You wear my father's name and you're going to disappoint him?"

The scraggly-bearded man with bad teeth had straddled his bike and was trying to kick it over. Something deeper and more painful flashed out of Devon, "Don't ... *don't* ... you disappoint my father!

You wear his name! Don't you fucking disappoint him!"

A motorcycle fired up, leaving a machete lying on the road as it roared off in the direction from which it came.

Tiny Joe was fighting to keep his hands steady as he pushed his machine off the kickstand. The devil in the silk shirt was at his side, and now more desperate. "Okay Joe..." Devon's tone dropped, "we did this the wrong way ... are you Catholic?"

The black-haired man lifted his leather from the ground, putting it back on with all the quiet dignity he could muster.

"Why do you fear killing me? It's not a sin," cooed Devon, fighting for his destiny. Tiny Joe was having none of it. Machines rumbled into life. The bloodshot eyes fought to be heard. "It's not a sin!" The heavy motorcycles began to go.

"For the sake of God, it's not a sin!"

Despondent, Devon wandered in circles, a pair of abandoned eyeglasses crunching under his foot. The gun was now a weapon, pressed to his head, his temple. *Why hadn't they killed him?* The defeat was agony.

A Winnebago appeared, cautiously circling around the Porsche. Devon lowered the gun. The occupants saw him and stared straight ahead, creeping by slowly as though it would make them less conspicuous.

Devon suddenly felt the depth of his exhaustion. The sun was dropping into the trees. He looked off into the forest and listened to it. He used to love this time of year.

Daylight was all but gone. Devon Clarke was doing something that, only a few hours earlier, he believed that he would never be doing again: showing his commuter card at Exit 14 off the Mass Pike. As he pulled his battered car away from the booth, a resonance of Septembers past stirred again; lying in the warm grass with Olivia ... the smell of schoolbooks and academia, of passion and ambition. How strange that those dead Septembers came back to him now.

Minutes later, Devon Clarke's drained body wandered out into a large, cultured garden. The air was still warm and sweetened by his neighbor's roses. Beyond the gentle hill of his home, a black mass of trees was cracked and Boston's skyline bled through.

A scientist may suggest, that what happened to Devon next could have resulted from a massive pituitary release of endogenous opioid peptides into his tired brain. A priest or a rabbi may have been inclined to see it differently. Whatever it was, Devon Clarke was suddenly in another world.

He was running along a riverbank with a boy called Magic. They each carried a small handgun; they were hunting. What a light, happy, beautiful place it was. The boy was eleven or twelve years old, and he had a rough shock of golden hair and a cherubic face. Devon loved him. The air smelled like soft, wet alders in autumn. Sunlight broke through light green leaves and the river shimmered silver.

Magic called to Devon as they frolicked along the river's bank, hunting God-knows-what creature with their handguns, but it didn't matter—this was a dream. And oh what beauty there was in the boy's face and what pleasure in Devon's heart as they joked and smiled. Then they came upon a clearing. Magic looked up at Devon and said, "It's time."

A sudden surge of panic constricted Devon's chest. He looked down at the boy he loved and said, "No ... no, it's not time."

The boy with the light hair and sweet face looked at him ever so lovingly and said it again, "It's time."

Devon's panic spread and turned to sadness. He knew the boy was right. His own gun fell from his hand. He dropped to his knees. Water from his heavy heart rolled down his cheeks.

And there in the enchanted forest by the river, Magic looked at him with love and compassion ... and raised his gun to Devon's head.

Olivia Clarke was frozen at the entrance of her grand home, staring with horror at the sight on her lawn. Her husband was on his knees, in the grip of some ... Olivia couldn't think of an explanation; it had to be insanity. At least he was alive. Thank God for that. She swallowed her own terrors and marched out.

"Devon..." Olivia couldn't have articulated what she saw in his eyes, and there were tears on his face. As they walked back toward the house, their housekeeper stood in the doorway. "You'd better say you were praying," Olivia said. Devon laughed, and it stabbed at the knot in her stomach.

A minute later, Devon was leaning over a kitchen counter, eating from a serving dish with the plastic wrap not fully removed. Filled with thoughts of the amazing vision, he consumed not with lust but automation. His body screamed for food—but he saw Magic, the boy with the angel's face.

He heard a melodic Mexican accent. "You can get a plate. I'll warm you chicken."

"This is fine, thanks." The world beyond himself was just noise.

Olivia said, "We're alright here ... thank you."

"Goodnight, Mrs. Clarke ... goodnight, Devon."

"Goodnight, Monica," was the mechanized response. The low voices of a delicate conspiracy crossed an unseen divide before a door closed.

There was a brief silence as Devon kept eating. Olivia was controlled. A handful of years younger than her husband, she looked the older, with large, intelligent eyes that contrasted the depth of her exhaustion. The monster inside of her was not to be detonated.

"What happened to the Porsche?"

Devon used his full mouth to delay an answer. "I hit a deer."

Olivia's tone dropped to something deeper.

"We don't do that."

Devon stopped eating. The words hung in silence. She hissed it again, "*We don't do that.*" He wouldn't look at her. Olivia couldn't contain all of her fragility. "We're Catholics."

"Are we," Devon said. There was another silence.

Olivia swallowed the monster. "I don't expect you to care that I've been out my mind—but understand—we have options. *You* have options, if that's what you prefer. I spoke with Father Ryan, he recommended an excellent counselor ... Father del Gado..."

Devon opened the refrigerator and searched.

"People come from New York to talk to this man—he works miracles."

Devon chose not to look at Olivia. He chose not to see her full brown eyes. He chose not to understand the lines that had come to her face, and he chose not to feel her pain. He poured a glass of juice.

Olivia whispered, "Or a psychiatrist ... if that's easier."

She watched the stranger swallow food and drink robotically, his thoughts God-knows-where. They both knew that Devon Clarke wasn't going to be going for any counseling.

He was consumed with Magic, the boy in his vision. The boy with the gun.

September 17, 1986 (a footnote)

At 10:15 a.m., an ambulance moved east along the Massachusetts Turnpike. Two paramedics and a nurse carefully monitored the patient in the rear of the vehicle. Robert Lechenier was connected to an IV drip and his body was locked into place by an extensive steel brace that held his torso slightly and awkwardly upward from a completely prone position. One of his ribs projected for several inches beyond a large, mostly purple tableau that was tattooed onto his chest. His right arm was twisted grotesquely behind his back.

The ambulance leaned into an exit that indicated Boston Liberty Hospital. Despite being pumped full of Demerol, Lechenier moaned at the slightest movement of the vehicle. "Almost there..." one of the paramedics reassured. Though the wound area was bandaged, the attendant could see that the rib had poked not only through Lechenier's chest but had also disfigured the bosom of a nude woman that had been inked onto his skin.

Lechenier was a member of the Satans Glory Motorcycle Club and was more commonly known as Purple Bob. He'd been involved in the largest mass motorcycle accident in Massachusetts State history. State troopers and insurance investigators were combing a stretch of rural highway northwest of Chicopee to figure out what the hell had gone on. The bizarre thing about the accident was that it wasn't one big pile-up; instead, the crash victims had been scattered over a two-mile stretch of road. Not surprisingly, the Satans Glory was a tight lipped pack. Other motorists who'd passed through the carnage were not volunteering to come forward. The only snippet of information that investigators could glean from an eyewitness was that the entire gang of bikers was harassing someone in a sports car.

Shortly thereafter, Purple Bob was attached to a gurney in a hospital room with overhead lighting and a cloth curtain for one wall. Nearby, he could hear a doctor who sounded like JFK saying something about consent forms. The Demerol clouded his head. His body hurt. Footsteps approached the gurney.

"Mr. Lechenier..." The doctor with the Ivy League accent appeared above him, filling his field of vision. "It turns out that you are one lucky son of a bitch..."

Purple Bob didn't feel like one lucky son of a bitch.

The upbeat doctor continued, "Devon Clarke has just agreed to head your surgical team. Dr. Clarke is the best orthopedic surgeon in the state ... maybe even the whole country. And he just got back from his holiday this morning."

Book of Devon 2

October 18, 1986

It was a late afternoon when Mark Lee spotted Devon Clarke in an alcove off of Boston Liberty's main cafeteria. Clarke had a white examining coat over his shirt and tie and was funneling coins into a vending machine. Lee, still in operating scrubs, decided that this was his chance.

"Hello, Devon..." The handsome doctor removed a cup of cappuccino from the machine's tray, his intense, pale eyes turning to Lee's eager face. Lee was shorter, in his late thirties with a youthful, slightly disheveled persona. "I'm Mark Lee, we've met before..."

"Mark Lee of obstetrics," Devon replied.

Lee laughed a little, as if he was chatting with a very pretty girl. "Excellent memory. I play tennis with John Perino. He always pays homage to your great prowess as a player."

"He's exaggerating." Clarke was as calm as Mark Lee was hyper.

Devon took a solid look at him, and Lee's feet found the ground. "I'm the Secretary of PAG for Massachusetts. I'm sure you've heard of us, Physicians Against Guns."

"I'm not interested."

"We were all devastated—"

"Say hi to John for me." Devon began moving away, and Lee followed him quickly.

"Please, Devon, give me just a moment ... I'm not trying to intrude on any personal pain here ... but we have an *opportunity...*" Clarke approached an elevator, Lee still chasing him. "With your voice, someone of your stature..."

Devon pushed the elevator's button, refusing to look at Lee.

"Politicians will listen to you. Something good can come out of your son's death."

The elevator doors opened and Devon moved inside. Lee continued, "I apologize if I'm hitting a nerve ... but do you know how many people die in handgun accidents every year?"

Lee stood helplessly as the elevator doors closed.

Book of Devon 3

Christmas Day, 1986

Devon pulled his bathrobe closed. He descended along a curving banister into the first glimpse of Christmas morning. Mary and the Child were hushed in a nativity scene worthy of a department store window. A great tree in a great room was shaped and adorned with professional perfection. Gifts were wrapped and placed with a decorator's eye.

Kneeling in front of the presents was a boy in pajama pants and an undershirt. He turned to Devon—it was Magic, his cherubic face aglow.

"Merry Christmas, Magic."

"Merry Christmas, Devon" said Magic, bursting with excitement. "Can I open one?"

Devon looked at him with all the love in the world. He moved under the tree and selected a package. "Here … try this one." Magic's smile filled the room. He tore off the bow and then the paper … he lifted the lid of a box. His eyes widened.

"Wow … holy wow…" Devon's heart felt every beat of Magic's joy. "Thank you, Devon … I love it ... Wow!"

Magic had a brand new handgun.

"I love you, Devon."

"I love you too, Magic." Devon's happiness was perfect.

Magic took a breath and looked up at Devon. "It's time."

For a moment Devon was silent. "No."

Magic looked at him with such affection. "Yeah, Devon … it's time."

"It can't be time." Love radiated from a round face framed with rough shocks of golden hair. Emotion began flooding into Devon. Magic waited for him. Devon knelt in front of the boy.

Magic lifted the gun and aimed it at Devon's temple.

Olivia Clarke was stopped dead on the stairs. She could see her husband on his knees, she could see his wet cheeks. But she couldn't see Magic or the gun.

Book of Devon 4

February 10, 1987

The nursing unit at the fourth floor ward of Boston Liberty Hospital.

At approximately 9:45 p.m., a ward clerk was relaying a message to a nurse on the other side of the counter. "Anna Schott in 428, cancel her 22:30."

Her colleague had a cart of assorted pills and needles. "Dr. McDonald has her scheduled for a shot every four hours, it's on the chart," replied the nurse.

"Dr. Clarke just called, he wants to examine her without sedation."

"Tonight?"

"That's what he said. No sedation."

The nurse with the cart gave her co-worker a long look. "That's different." As the nurse pushed off she said, "Get him to initial the chart."

Just after 1:00 a.m. elevator doors opened and Devon Clarke stepped onto the fourth floor ward. He approached the nursing unit counter, where a young black woman was now sitting with paperwork. "Good evening, Dr. Clarke."

"How are you?" Devon replied. The lights were dimmed and the ward was quiet. "Geoff McDonald has a patient up here, a woman named Anna Schott…"

The nurse glanced at a list. "She's in 428 … so sad, she's still so young…"

Devon nodded. "I'm going to take a look at her. I don't wish to be disturbed."

He moved through the subdued, pale light of the silent ward and entered room 428.

February 11, 1987

It was a terrible room to be in. Dark, rainy weather pawed at the window. A woman in her late fifties was flanked by her tall husband, about a decade older, and by a girl with light hair, about eleven, with the unmistakable tinge of Down's Syndrome. They were all standing. The family was nicely dressed; perhaps in clothes that lagged behind the latest fashions, but anywhere else they would have appeared dignified. But *here*, in this room, there was something in their helplessness that made them look like peasants.

In bleak contrast to the room's mood, a huge bloom of fruit and flowers was arranged in a basket on a bedside table. Two doctors, Geoff McDonald and Aron Epstein, sat in chairs next to a hospital bed. In front of them was a young woman, twenty-five years old, her bed adjusted to hold her body in an upright position.

Anna Schott was beautiful. Her dark, verdant eyes seemed to disintegrate into smaller shapes and shades of green like an exquisite work of abstract art, and they, along with her burgundy lips, contrasted the bleak pallor of her skin.

Dr. McDonald, a large redheaded man, was speaking to her softly. "...even if we repair the bone, we can't reconnect the nerves..."

Dr. Epstein interrupted gently, "Not at this time."

Anna's mother had to ask, "You—you said that another doctor would see the x-ray..."

McDonald turned to her. "I understand that Dr. Clarke has seen the x-ray. He should be here shortly. But ... you have to understand ... at this point it's a formality..."

McDonald continued with Anna. "I'm a bone doctor. Dr. Epstein is a nerve doctor ... and you cannot be in better hands. He will be taking over your principal care..."

Epstein began to speak—he was both realistic and positive; he talked about connecting her with a fantastic network of support from others with her condition. But all Anna Schott knew was that she would never dance again, she would never stroll through a wizened neighborhood looking for old books, she would never ski, she would never slap a lover's butt as she ran past him on a beach, she would never jump into a man's arms, she would never take tango lessons in Buenos Aires ... Epstein did the best he could. Now and then McDonald added a word of support.

Anna's face never moved a muscle, but the fragmented pieces of her green eyes filled with water that overflowed and dripped down her cheeks like blood from her screaming soul.

The standing Schotts turned as another doctor entered the room, extending his hand. "I'm Devon Clarke, I'm an orthopedic surgeon. How do you do."

"Have you seen the x-ray?" Anna's mother pleaded.

"Yes, I've seen the x-ray," Devon said, moving immediately beyond to the girl with the variant features. He spoke to her as if she were someone very special.

"I'm Devon ... what's your name?"

The girl was very shy. "Amy," she whispered.

"It's a pleasure to meet you, Amy." He smiled at her warmly.

As Devon turned away from Amy, something in his demeanor changed; the reverence was gone. "Okay let's see the patient..." With a gesture he indicated that Epstein and McDonald should clear out of his way.

Standing next to Anna, he looked plainly at her face. "So you can't feel your legs, huh." She shook her head ever so slightly.

McDonald wasn't entirely comfortable with Clarke's tone.

"Is it possible for you to move them at all?" Anna swallowed and again barely moved her head.

"So ever since the accident ... which was Saturday, you haven't been able to feel your legs?"

There was a hate-filled silence as Devon waited for Anna's answer.

"Not at all?" said Devon in a tone that bordered on nonchalance.

Anna finally said, "No."

Dr. McDonald couldn't wait for this to end.

"Well..." said Dr. Clarke, shrugging casually, "...if you can't feel your legs..."

McDonald and Epstein were ready to dive on him, but Devon, looking straight at Anna, finished his thought, "... then I guess it wouldn't bother you if I was to go like *this*—"

Devon drove his fingers into her thigh, and Anna screamed, ripping a jolt of electricity through every human heart in the room—her legs were moving!

Anna was gasping, crying in insane, unfathomable joy...

Devon gleefully continued to drive his fingers obnoxiously into her legs. "What's wrong, miss? Am I *bothering* you? I thought you couldn't feel that." Devon was laughing; Anna clutched his examining coat, gulping for air.

Shock stunned the others. A young nurse was frozen in the doorway.

"You faked this, didn't you," he accused her with delight. Anna mouthed 'no, no,' but she was choking with sobs. She hung on to Devon with an almost violent need. "You better have two insurance plans, because I charge malingerers double," he told her. Anna tried to laugh but was still gasping, gulping—

Devon called over to the younger girl. "Do you know what a malingerer is, Amy?"

She said, "No."

"In my old neighborhood they were called..." Devon's voice dropped to a confidential whisper, "*bullshitters*." Amy smiled. Both of her parents were crying.

"Geoff!" Devon exploded happily as he caught McDonald's face. "Look at him, Anna, you ruined his day. You were going to pay off his mortgage at the Cape."

Aron Epstein wasn't doing much better than Geoff McDonald.

"Let's get a picture," Devon declared. He called to the young nurse in the doorway; others were now congregating behind her. "Would you mind asking Nurse Ratchet there at the first unit if we can borrow her Polaroid?"

As the camera arrived, Devon squeezed onto the bed next to Anna, who was still hanging onto him. A crowd ogled from the doorway. "Come on, everybody, let's get in here ... come on, Geoff ... don't hide, Epstein," Devon enthused. The Schotts and two reluctant doctors crowded in around Anna's bed.

Just as the young nurse readied herself to take the picture, Devon cried, "Wait—"

"Amy, would you please pass me an apple, the red one?" Amy reached into the display of fruit and flowers and plucked a red apple, passing it across her parents. Devon bit into the apple and spat out a large chunk. He then hung the apple on his nose.

"Look! I'm Patch Adams!" he declared with joyous stupidity.

The Polaroid picture that developed revealed an unusual canvas: On one side, a happy, round-faced girl of eleven glowed like a jack-o-lantern with candles; next came her two aging parents, who, though they were smiling, looked strangely stunned, as if they had just seen the Virgin Mary and weren't really sure if it had happened. On the other side of the picture, a large red-haired man was peering out of the corner of his eye toward the scene at the center of the frame, and a smaller, dark-haired man looked as if he'd just seen a ghost. In the center of the picture, a woman's face was pressed hard against a man with mega-watt smile who was holding a red apple to his nose. The woman's arms were wrapped right around the man and she was hugging him desperately.

Fifteen minutes after the stewardship of Anna Schott had passed from McDonald and Epstein to Devon Clarke, the shell-shocked pair were glued to a light-box with a mounted transparency labeled *Schott, Anna J.*

Aron Epstein put on glasses and pushed his face close to the screen. "Clearly bone fragments ... coming right out of the incursion to L2..."

"Incursion? It's a fucking trench."

McDonald stood stoically as Epstein said, "I want another MRI."

Devon Clarke entered McDonald's office. "Please send Anna Schott's records down to me as soon as you get a chance. Including the x-rays."

"That's not her x-ray," said McDonald, referring to the light-box.

Devon responded, "At this point, I would say that's fairly obvious."

"We're taking more pictures."

"No. No more x-rays, no more MRIs."

Both men stared at Dr. Clarke, silently demanding some sort of elucidation. He responded, "Her parents own a bookstore. Be glad it's not a law firm. Or someone's insurance premiums might be going up." The chill of potential litigation hung in the air.

"Thank you both."

As Clarke turned to leave, Geoff's voice stopped him, "Devon..."

"Uh-huh?" he said.

Geoff McDonald's arms were open, palms up. "An explanation…?"

Devon paused for a moment, thinking. Then he shrugged. "I wish I had one." He smiled at his colleagues and continued on his way.

Book of Devon 5

April 14, 1987

A sliver of sunshine snuck past a blind, a hint of a much lighter universe outside the mezzanine-level meeting room at Boston Liberty Hospital. In here, a deep, slightly gravelly voice was reading out loud.

"...and the final item for the record, regards the repeated contravention of section 1410, articles 1a through 4a, the improper and illegal access of patient records..." Dr. Bailey took a slight pause. "Mr. Stanlow-Smith has indicated that the following also portends to violations of Massachusetts State law." A stenographer's fingers flew.

Charles Bailey was an endocrinologist in his late fifties with graying hair and glasses. Sitting to Bailey's right was an anesthesiologist, Janet Lynch, well-maintained, late forties with big glasses and added streaks of ruddy chestnut to her wavy hair. The one without glasses was Cabhan O'Brien, an oncologist in his early forties. He played with a pen. On the same side of the table, just off from the trio, was David Stanlow-Smith, the hospital's attorney. Typing the record was a young brunette who sat perpendicular to the group of three-plus-one.

On the far side of the table was Devon Clarke, alone.

When Bailey finished, he cleared his throat and lowered the papers. His demeanor carried a certain grim weight, as if it needed to convey the gravity of the task at hand. He took a moment before turning to the attorney. "Do you have anything to add before we hear from Dr. Clarke?"

Stanlow-Smith looked across the room at Devon. "I'd like to reiterate Dr. Bailey's concern that you've chosen to appear without counsel."

"Are you representing *me*, Mr. Stanlow-Smith?"

A brief pause. "It's clear I represent the hospital."

"Then save your advice for them."

A chill tickled the room, like a whiff of drama or blood to follow. The thrashing of the antelope before it succumbs to the lions. Stanlow-Smith shrank for the moment, like a clever virus that needed to hide before it returned, tougher than ever.

"Introduce yourself for the record, please," said Dr. Bailey.

"I'm Devon Clarke, you all know who I am." He faced the trio of interrogators. "I want to make one thing clear—I have never, ever said that I'm a faith-healer—or that I can miracle heal with my hands in any way. I have never made a claim to that effect. What other people say about me, I have no control over."

Charles Bailey made a notation as Devon Clarke continued. The others focused on the man with gray-blue eyes and a dark blue tie.

"Before I get into what I do at my clinic, and why it's my right to do it, I'm going to address the matter of the records." He looked directly at Bailey. "You stated that I could've accessed hundreds of them. I've accessed *thousands*." Across the divide, only the stenographer's fingers were still moving. "I've got five of them right here." Devon patted a short stack of file folders. "I want to tell you about a boy named Hector Gonzales. Hector's parents brought him down from Portsmouth—"

Dr. Bailey interrupted. "Excuse me, are we talking about a specific patient's records?"

"I'm talking about one of these five histories right here."

"I don't believe this context, as it's not medical, allows that." Bailey turned to counsel to support his opinion.

Janet Lynch spoke, "We're not treating the patient, Dr. Clarke..."

"Here." Devon held up a document. "I have written permission from Hector Gonzales' parents."

Stanlow-Smith said, "We'll enter that into the record."

Bailey frowned as Devon continued. "The Gonzales boy has no energy and his parents can't get a diagnosis from the family doctor. So they haul him down here to see a specialist—an endocrinologist..."

Bailey jumped in again. "I don't know what path we're on—we need some relevance to the charges at hand."

Stanlow-Smith asked, "Is there relevance, Dr. Clarke?"

"If I was represented by counsel, Mr. Stanlow-Smith, he or she would readily inform you that there is relevance. All shall be revealed."

Bailey began shaking his head. "These files have been misappropriated. He has no right to possess them."

Cabhan O'Brien said, "Can we not hear him out?" Janet Lynch looked to Bailey for reconsideration.

Bailey shook his head. "As chairman of this tribunal, I cannot allow this. I will not." Stanlow-Smith was looking curiously at Bailey.

Devon responded, "Let me suggest an alternative. I could head down to the ER and wait around until I see a man with a suit, a briefcase and a big bruise on his face. A man who got that big bruise because he was running full tilt behind an ambulance when the driver slammed on the brakes. And when I start to tell that man the story of Hector Gonzales, I think he's going to forget all about the throbbing in his face."

"Dr. Clarke, we're not going to allow this to stray..." Devon ignored Stanlow-Smith's directive and continued focusing upon Charles Bailey.

"When he hears about the big cheese doctor who misdiagnosed little Hector and performed an unnecessary thyroid operation I think he's going to light up like a ten-year-old on Christmas Day..."

Dr. Bailey looked to Stanlow-Smith. "We need to stop this."

Devon's tempo and passion rose. "When he gets wind of the pain that little Hector and his family have suffered … he's going to be dizzy with joy, just as I'm dizzy with disbelief."

Stanlow-Smith interjected, "This sounds like blackmail, Dr. Clarke."

Devon kept on Bailey. "But little does he know … his happiness is just beginning to blossom ... when he hears about Mary Lehman, a beloved grandmother, who died of a stroke because an endocrinologist didn't understand the contraindications of prescribing isradipine with an anti-coagulant—"

"Stop this right now. We are not reading this into the record." Bailey gestured to the steno—she stopped. "These references without context are absurd…"

"And the motive transparent," said Stanlow-Smith.

Devon was on Charles Bailey with a molten intensity. "And you—when your counsel asks me, 'What are you being compensated for your appearance here today, Dr. Clarke?' I'm going to tell the truth, the whole truth, and nothing but the truth when I say, '*Not a goddamn cent.* I'm here because I can't stand the pain and suffering that the Gonzales family went through at the hands of a greedy, incompetent quack who fattened his wallet to the tune of $78,000 with an unnecessary operation—and then abandoned the family when the boy got worse.'"

"You're not hearing me, Dr. Clarke," said the attorney, overlapped by Charles Bailey, "Devon, this is not a trial, we're here to ask questions…"

"It's 'Devon' now, is it?"

Stanlow-Smith kept trying to get his attention. "Dr. Clarke…"

Bailey was burning up inside. "There is no need to be ugly. We've convened to ask questions, not to attack each other."

Janet Lynch attempted to calm things down. "Dr. Clarke, you're not addressing the points we've tabled … if you have other concerns…"

"When you've offered someone a blowjob at a Christmas party, Dr. Lynch, shouldn't you recuse yourself from a committee such as this one?" Lynch withered. Devon's gaze hit the stenographer. "Why have you stopped typing?" The flustered young woman looked around for guidance. Cabhan O'Brien enjoyed a glance at Lynch's glowing face. His expression never betrayed him, but this beat hell out of telling some poor shmuck to get his affairs in order.

Stanlow-Smith said, "I'm going to end these proceedings. It's clear that this is an extortion attempt."

Devon spun on him. "I doubt that you were called to the bar yesterday—you don't get to pick and choose which part of my testimony is recorded and which isn't at the whim of the plaintiff." Devon regarded the motionless stenographer, and then asked with the utmost incredulity, "Why on earth, Mr. Stanlow-Smith, would you suspend the record during an extortion attempt?"

The attorney swallowed and continued as calmly as he could. "I'm afraid, Dr. Clarke, that this has devolved into something very ungentlemanly."

"Well then, please and thank you—you can tell your chairman here that the Gonzales boy was cured not with faith healing but with B12 shots and iodine. Unfortunately we found out about Mary Lehman's prescriptions too late."

Bailey was ashen.

Devon rose to his feet. "I don't give a shit how my patients think they got healed—they're still alive." Bailey twisted as Devon Clarke seared into him. "You accuse *me* of embarrassing this hospital? *You?*—you've got all the integrity of a fucking chiropractor!"

Silence hung. The stenographer's hands were on her lap. Charles Bailey's tail was tucked where it dared not wag. Janet Lynch's face flamed red. David Stanlow-Smith was not about to misstep now. Cabhan O'Brien was motionless, but of them all, he alone was thinking of how he could recount such vibrant drama over his dinner date later that evening.

"Are we done here?" Devon asked.

"Yes, Dr. Clarke, we're done," said Stanlow-Smith.

Bailey stood. “We meant no offense … we know it’s been very difficult since you lost your son.”

Devon’s cold eyes flashed with pure hatred.

Book of Devon 6

April 21, 1987

It was the end of a day. Devon Clarke was at his desk, finishing up some notes. Suddenly a pair of small hands covered his eyes. "Guess who?" A smile broke into his darkness as he reached up and felt the arms behind him.

"Hello, Magic," he said in a voice reserved for only the most beloved.

Magic marched in front of him. "Wassup, Devon?" Devon's heart soared. He felt an injection of that rare thing, happiness, as he looked at the boy.

After Magic's first appearance on his lawn in September, the boy usually came to him at night in vivid dreams, but every once in a while he would appear in broad daylight. Here he was again, about twelve years old, a ragged shock of flaxen hair surrounding an angel's face. Devon's heart was flooded with such joy it almost hurt his chest.

Then the vision continued as they always did. Magic looked at him lovingly and said, "It's time…"

Devon suddenly felt stricken with panic, sadness. "No, no, it's not time…"

Magic nodded compassionately. "It's time, Devon."

Tears welled in Devon's eyes. He knew the boy was right. He slowly left his chair and knelt before Magic. A desk drawer slid open and Magic removed a handgun. The boy's sweet face looked at Devon with all the love in the world. Magic then raised the gun up … and leveled it at Devon's forehead.

Chapter One

May 12, 1987

A nearly full moon followed us, riding above the black palms along the coast. I sat cross-legged on deck in a hot, gentle breeze. Easy waves rocked the boat as we shifted direction toward the shore. A small cluster of distant lights—yellow, red, orange—were nestled into the dark foliage ahead.

My friend and lab partner, Peter Weller, was a fellow student. We'd been traveling by fishing boat now for four nights and four days, coming up through the Malacca Strait to Thailand's Andaman coast. Because of our cargo we had decided to clear Thai customs creatively. That was back then, before I knew a thing about bribery and greasy palms.

I had just come off of the most grueling test of my soft life—four and a half months on Serapang, a lonely equatorial island in Indonesian waters. The project was an honors thesis. The brutality of insects, mud, vicious climate, cabin fever, and our often tedious routine had pretty much squeezed any romantic notions of the rainforest out of me. Starved for a woman, tortured by wasps and swollen with bites, more than once I had blasphemed against the precious jungle.

Peter and I waded back and forth in the waves, unloading the boat—taunted by our proximity to paradise. Music floated out of little bars and a sun-soaked populace bubbled over drinks and food. We'd lived on rice—here, open grills smoked with seafood; we'd lived on memories—here, real women strolled the beach. "Not too shabby," Peter deadpanned as some glorious flesh moved by. The palms were now above us, and the moon danced behind their fronds. It was actually cruel; we were starving men at a banquet that we couldn't touch.

We lifted box after box off the boat and onto a cart. Peter and I had put everything into this project—I'd made no greater commitment in my life, and it was going to earn us the cherry on our bachelor degrees. Otherwise, I'd have run screaming to one of those bars, downing beer and tequila to celebrate civilization and sing glorious praises to the human creatures of the tropical night. As it was, I dared not look at the nearby heaven. Our samples were sensitive to light and moisture, and they had to be in a lab in Bangkok by morning. Fucking up was not an option.

Peter and the boatman balanced the cart's load as I carefully and meticulously added the final weight. Then came the complication.

A group of partiers had considerately stepped out of one of the beach bars to light up some joints. Their trip to the sand was a little on the semantic side since the bar was in the open air and they were only a few feet away from it. A jubilant conversation wafted over the beach, first with a trace of tobacco, then weed...

The tobacco smoke hit me hard. "It's been three years, I doubt one smoke'll addict me," I told Peter.

He decently disagreed, but our attention was suddenly pulled to a female voice. "Hey what's all that?" The tokers were looking our way.

"It's drugs, man, they're fucking smugglers," responded a European voice. Peals of drunken laughter followed and someone called, "Shoot us a brick, dude!" A pretty girl began skipping over the beach toward us, a drink in one hand, a joint in the other. She was maybe twenty-two, maybe twenty-five ... maybe something else—it didn't matter.

She was sexy and obnoxious. My t-shirt was soaked from the labor. She fixated on me, maybe sensing the pent-up passion of a guy who'd been in the bush for four months. "What's in these boxes?" she demanded with the authority of a customs agent.

Peter jumped in. "Pleionogasters of the Megascolecidae family, twenty-three hundred of them." I loved the expression on her face.

"Worms," I translated.

"Oh my God," she squealed, calling back to her friends, "They've got *thousands* of worms!" A litany of worm jokes erupted in the alcohol-fueled troop.

Peter began shifting the cart, lifting its wheels out of the sand. As I moved to help, the pretty girl stepped in front of me. She emanated alcohol and perfume, an erotically deadly combo. Suddenly I was faced with a burning joint, and behind it, a woman who dripped sexuality. "Would Mr. Pleenofuckers like a toke?"

Time decided to stand still for a moment or two. A couple of potential answers sprang to mind, the first of which was *Fuck yeah*! Instead, I came back with a more Nancy Reagan-friendly, "We're working."

"Bummer," she said, backing away. Peter smiled ironically at my agony. We began to move the cart when she turned back to me. "When you're finished, come to the Luna Bar." She then lifted her top and showed me her breasts.

Now I don't mean to give the impression that I fall apart at the sight of a pair of tits. But those breasts and that woman combined hit my guts like some kind of an erotic bomb … I was momentarily incapacitated, and ready to follow her anywhere.

Later, in the truck to Bangkok, I lit my first cigarette in three years. As I inhaled, Peter said, "I thought we'd lost you."

When I recount this story, she's given the mythical proportions of the Unknown Soldier. I never saw her again, but I like to joke that it was the Unknown Woman who brought me back to Ao Lai.

Chapter Two

Five years later

The coming of the guru Dadaram to Ao Lai was prophesied by two things, the first of which was considerably less ominous than the second. It occurred the day I was running late.

There wasn't a hell of a lot of rush hour in my world but the pressure was on to get out to Wamathani Railway Station to fulfill my community service. A shipment of Western cigarettes and booze for the local expatriate community was arriving on the 18.20 from Bangkok. If I wasn't there to meet the train and pay my man, the degenerates would be jonesing. Imagine the poor fuckers stuck drinking Mekong and smoking cheap butts.

The first impediment to time had been a good one; a group of Japanese divers had filled my afternoon tour and we'd taken two spectacular plunges on a reef with electrically colored fish and sharks that circled indolently. Diving tours were 'on request' since I didn't maintain equipment in Ao Lai but rented it from a Finnish-run outfit in a small city forty miles south. Hauling the equipment was a pain in the ass but worth the fun. I hustled up and down the wharf, passing the gear to my sole employee, Mike, who was standing in the rear of a shared taxi, a little truck with long bench seats. Mike's real name was Molthisok-Ngman Emjaroen, which helps explain why he went by Mike.

The air was exceptionally humid, and in Ao Lai that's humid and then some. Droplets of sweat hit the dirt as I passed tanks and wetsuits up to Mike. I thought it may signal an early arrival of the monsoon this year, or at least a good torrent of rain. As the taxi departed Mike smiled with a bright, uniquely Thai innocence. Sometimes the notion of a deadline seemed a strange concept to the townsfolk of Ao Lai.

I stowed the *Zenobia*'s life jackets and was quickly rinsing her deck when I heard the wharf creaking with footsteps, followed by the friendliest of Thai tones. "Magnus..."

I cringed. The second impediment to time had showed up in the form of my dearest nemesis, General Pramana Bukit. The term 'general' should not be used to conjure an image of Douglas MacArthur or some other noble icon. I was facing a pot-bellied little badger whose territory was the *amphoe*, or Thai county, that I lived in. As far as corrupt, Vaseline-palmed extortionists went, Bukit was an okay guy and in a sense I considered him a friend. We needed each other—for him I was an excellent source of income; he never failed to instruct me on the high cost of 'protecting me' as a farang without a work visa. Despite his Muslim faith we had eaten and drunk together; most of Ao Lai's restaurants were in the open air and he never failed to obnoxiously call me over to a table of boozing cops if I happened to be passing by.

"Japan-people very wealthy," he salivated. There was something almost cartoon-like about the way he lit up whenever anything to do with money arose. His ears stuck out from under his 'general's' cap. It was a lousy moment to see him but I forced a friendly smile. Keeping up 'face' was important in Thai culture.

The local merchants charged a pecking order of prices based upon the buyer's nationality, with Thai people at the low end and Japanese tourists at the top. But with me, 'Japan-people' paid the same price as everyone else and I even ate the cost of transporting the tanks because I enjoyed the dives. I offered the general a cigarette.

"Why you don't smoke Marlboro?" he asked.

"I can't afford it," I told him and he laughed. We smoked and haggled over my taxes. I needed to pay homage to politeness and authority but the 18.20 from Bangkok was hanging over me. On that shipment there would be cartons of Marlboros, Camels, Dunhills—all for the degenerates, since as far as I was concerned, Krung Thep at thirty cents a pack was just as good.

Bukit noticed my sweat. "Hot," he said.

It felt good to finally be on the bike and pushing fast through the thick air. Moving north, I weaved along the coast then back into the trees in an undulating rhythm. The sky to my left was turning red. I passed other motorcycles and maneuvered around small trucks with dirty black exhausts. We were coming up on the bug hour, and hard-bodied little bastards smacked and stung my face. Coconut groves gave way to rougher jungle and I leaned right into a junction that split off inland. Bug deaths had begun to splatter my riding glasses, and I knew that for safety's sake I should stop soon and clean them. But time pressed me along harder than I ordinarily would've gone, and I weaved up into jungle-enclosed hills on a narrowing piece of third world pavement.

Bukit had lightened me of twenty-two hundred baht, which wasn't too bad considering the glow of 'Japan-people' that I first saw in his gleaming eyes. That was in the neighborhood of about seventy-five bucks in the good old USA, but here it was worth at least 400 bucks. Though I never asked the general himself, someone told me that policemen in Thailand made about 750 dollars a year. So even if Bukit made double that, it would never explain the easily middle class opulence of his home. He had even set up his son with a pharmacy. Bukit made a good buck nailing foreign tokers outside of certain beach bars. No white boy or dreadlocked white girl wanted to sit their ass in jail for even a few days when they could hand over 200 bucks to General Bukit and his boys. The irony was that if you went over to his house and wanted to smoke some Thai stick, his son Arnold would readily produce it. I once asked Arnold about the seeming contradiction, and he said proudly, “My dad’s a general, I do what I want to.”

My bike roared up into the hills. At this point I was counting on the 18.20 being late—otherwise I was humped. Or I should say, the degenerates were humped—I still had a good store of American bourbon, and I knew which Thai beer didn’t give you the bad hangover. The other small advantage I held over many of them was that I wasn’t a desperate alcoholic.

A rising bend first twisted up and then dropped sharply after the rise. Suddenly I hit the brakes—an accident scene with a crashed motorcycle lay in front of me. A couple of Thai boys and two foreigners were already there. The rider was a young tourist, painfully battered, with bloody scrapes on his face, arms and bare legs.

Quickly off my bike, I detached my first aid kit, noting the good luck since it was usually elsewhere when needed. The locals and the two farangs had helped the victim to his feet. He was a British boy, well shaken up. Trembling, we sat him on the bumper of the Thai boys’ truck. I began washing the worst of the wounds, getting the others to hold gauze while I taped it over. He needed to go to a clinic, which in Thailand would be painful due to their love of iodine and lack of freezing; I remembered my own road rash from a couple of years earlier.

The foreigners were male, white and black. They introduced themselves as Evan and Samuel. I hadn’t expected them to be Americans. As soon as they weren’t needed to hold bandages, they were organized and proactive. They moved the rented bike and its broken pieces off the road and began making a plan to get the British kid to a clinic in Ao Lai. There was something about them I couldn’t quite pigeonhole.

Despite his wounds and shaking body, the battered Briton stared at the damaged Honda. “I’ll be charged for that, won’t I?” I knew the dealer who rented them and promised to make sure that he didn't get ripped off.

From a distance, I'd expected Samuel to be an African; his face had an exotic tinge and his skin was a deep sinewy black. He could've been twenty-two or thirty-three, neither would've surprised me. I detected not a hint of a regional accent in his voice. Evan, his counterpart, was a clean-cut blond with a red hue to his newly acquired tan, somewhere in his early to mid-twenties. He tended to turn his *R*s into *Ah*s so I knew he was from somewhere along the northeast coast of the States.

They both stood out as healthy, strong, wholesome. Unlike my waiting friends, I could tell that they weren't late night drug and alcohol consumers, permeated with a lazy dose of ultraviolet. They seemed confident and at peace with themselves and yet … there was something else as well—they were just ever so subtly … remember the movie, *The Stepford Wives*, where all the women of Stepford took on a robot-like perfection? Samuel and Evan made me think of it.

The road-rubbed kid was now covered in a patchwork of gauze, and I shared some advice about avoiding infection. Swimming in salt water was something that I swore by for a fast recovery and natural disinfectant.

Then Samuel imparted his own solution: "When Dadaram comes he'll touch your skin. You'll heal like magic."

"When *who* comes?" I had to ask.

"Dadaram is our guru," said Evan.

Samuel held up his own palms. "Dadaram has power in his hands."

Well there it was. I gave myself credit; I could've said Mormon or Jehovah's Witness, or even dabbled with the possibility of Moonie, but I didn't—I went long on the Stepford Wives thing and nailed it.

"He's even raised a man from death," Evan added.

I found myself laughing. "Are you sure he wasn't just taking a nap?"

Samuel observed me with cold superiority. Evan said, "I would've laughed too if I'd heard that a year ago."

I handed the kid my best painkillers. “Careful with these, they’ll make you wish you were hurt more often.” Samuel and Evan had commandeered the Thai truck for ambulance service, so I offered the boys some gas money, but they refused it.

“It’s been a pleasure to meet you, Magnus,” Samuel said with an extended hand. Evan concurred and I shook with him as well. As the British kid was loaded into the truck, I resisted the urge to warn him not to join any cults.

The surrounding jungle was suddenly louder with blankets of cicadas and screeching monkeys. The foliage was near black against a sky with swirls of gray and deep purple. Hope of achieving my mission was all but lost. I wiped bug carcasses off my glasses and kicked the bike over. Despite the need for pace, a motorcycle accident always inspires a period of defensive driving in me. The British boy was lucky compared to some I’d seen. I swept over a winding potholed road with a renewed concentration. Not that I imagined it would make much difference at this point.

For those who may be noting negatively my spiritual insensitivity, I defer your wrath to my heathen parents, who raised me atheist. My mom in particular is notably intolerant toward any concept of God or to an afterlife. That’s not to say she encouraged my brother and I to be bigots—we were taught to respect people, regardless of the slobbering medieval nonsense that happened to be dribbling over their chins. I’ve always suspected my dad of having a secret streak of agnosticism, but he’s outwardly an atheist like Mom, just as some men are Christians because their wife happens to be a Christian.

At least with the big old religions like Christianity, Islam, Buddhism, et cetera, there’s a historical and cultural precedent for following the faith. It strikes me that some of these new or extreme offshoots are just out to exploit people. Look no further than the followers of the über-rich leader of the Unification Church, the grand Korean scumbag, Sun Myung Moon. Some of these folks, known as Moonies, found that trying to quit Moon's church was a good bit harder than trying to quit a mean pimp.

And let us not forget Bhagwan Shree Rajneesh, one of the most inglorious douchebags to ever set foot in my home state. This drug-polluted cockroach rolled through his commune in any one of his twenty-eight Jaguar cars while his devotees dropped their empty heads to the soil with each of his passings. One of his admirers once told me that his blatant materialism was simply a ploy to enrage Americans. Well, on that noble note, I could've headed off to India to enrage Hindus by slaughtering cows.

I recalled a weekend when, home from college, I was with my dad at the local feed store. Suddenly, in swept the White brothers as if they'd just seen ole Satan himself. Just back from Portland, Henry told of a scene stranger than any you could see, even on TV. Their pickup slowed by a little spot of congestion with a long line of Jaguar cars. Weirder-than-hippies in colorful clothes jammed the sidewalk. And lo and behold—from one of the Jags, out steps none other than the anti-Christ himself, His Holiness Bhagwan Shree Rajneesh. There he was, with a long white beard, a turban and flowing robes. I could just imagine the White brothers in their dirty old Ford—eyeballs bugged clean out—as the weirder-than-hippies all dropped to the sidewalk to kiss concrete. As Henry told it, they were so shocked, they plumb forgot the loaded 10-gauge in the rack. Then Bob, who was known to be the meaner of the two brothers, expressed an interest in an Indian rite called immolation—but Bob wasn't real good with multi-syllabic words and he put it more plainly when he said he wanted to soak the cunt in gas and light him on fire.

My father and I were the only two in Buckerfields that day who didn't break into spontaneous applause at Bob's forthright approach. Nevertheless, I was happy when the government finally booted his blood-sucking ass back to India.

Clouds of swirling insects buzzed around the fluorescent lights of

Wamathani Station as I approached. I expected walking inside to be nothing more than an empty exercise in completion. The lit platform was quiet with only a few settled bodies and their cargo—the 18.20 had obviously passed. But one of the food sellers began waving at me. Her smile lit mine as I saw that my man had left her the goods.

I rumbled through the hot humid night with saddle-bags bulging. The hard little bugs had returned to their invisible world, and I enjoyed the ride back. I smiled at thoughts of those who would twist a little tighter every ten minutes I was late. I could've swung by the Biting Monkey and relieved their agony but to hell with it, I was heading home to shower and change first. Maybe even grab a bite.

Over the past year, a small, gnawing terror had begun to grow inside me. It was something that I liked to ignore or tell myself that I was exaggerating, or even imagining, like a person who won't accept that an expanding lump might be a tumor. It was the feeling that I was sinking a little closer all the time to entrenchment in the social class at the Biting Monkey Bar & Restaurant.

Karol, the Thai owner, tolerated the perpetual presence of the degenerates. When other restaurants were empty, there was always one or more of life's dropouts having a late breakfast of beer, Mekong whiskey or coffee and marijuana, with something that resembled bread. Though sometimes they skipped the bread. For some folks, it took a couple of early shots to get the hand tremors to stop.

Don't get me wrong—I liked these people, they were my friends—but I could see it was a world ruled by addiction, and something worse, hopelessness. At least for some of them it was, the year-round core. And apart from Christmastime, that was me.

Chapter Three

The low rumble of my Triumph Bonneville heralded my arrival. "Du-uude…!" a happy voice shouted. A sign facing the street had been repaired, but I parked under one that still read 'Bitteeng Munkee Bar and Restooronte'. As I unpacked the saddle bags, eager faces gathered at the tavern's open-aired edge. These were the terrors of which I have spoken.

The loudest and nastiest expat was Franco, a Canadian once known as Frank Connelly, drifting ever deeper into his forties on a barstool in Ao Lai. An endless flow of quips, putdowns and opinions rasped out of a throat scarred from bombardments of alcohol, marijuana and cigarettes. During a short stint of factory work, an injury delivered to Franco what was likely his greatest achievement in life, a disability pension. Most of Franco's noise came from a deep and desperate feeling of failure.

Lester was another fixture, an aging queen with an addiction to alcohol. He'd migrated to Thailand from California but had grown up in some long-forgotten city of intolerance somewhere else. He was easygoing and fun but there was also a layer of sadness that reminded me of the decaying heroine in a Tennessee Williams play.

Then there was Arden, the parasite, a poet who bummed his beloved substances from the other expats. Sometimes he would sit at the bar and read his poems out loud. It gave him a good excuse to keep his Mekong glass topped up courtesy of others. Franco enjoyed telling him what none of the rest of us had the heart to: "A career in poetry is best left to those with a knack for it."

An intermittent expat, Charlene was in her mid-twenties and from Calgary, an oil-rich city on the Canadian prairies, where she would work as a cocktail waitress for a few months then proceed back to the beaches of Ao Lai for as long as her cash held out. I can't bestow upon Charlene full degenerate status because while she liked to drink and toke, as far as I knew, she wasn't truly addicted to anything but sex. And cigarettes. Call me a hardass but I'm not handing out a full degenerate badge for just those.

Robbin was Charlene's squeeze of the moment, and I had no trouble awarding him the highest honors for outstanding achievement in degeneracy. A full-time expat and one-time punk rocker from Stockholm, Robbin had an appetite for substance abuse that would've shocked Sid Vicious. Tanned and tattooed, he ran a small beach bar with his other hookup, a Thai woman named Pan. I always found it hilariously ironic that his passion for polluting his consciousness was never once dampened by the fact that he never seemed to have a good trip. Whether he'd just finished vomiting or was sweating in terror of his visions, he was not only *up* for another round—he was screaming for it. Who said drugs were supposed to be fun?

I also glimpsed William Stamp of England, aka The Lesbian. Hardly a true degenerate, he was working on a doctoral thesis of some sort. Stamp, however, was the kind of guy who made you not really care what he was up to. Excessively politically correct, he delivered his incantations in such a tedious monotone that even Noam Chomsky would've asked him to shut up. His speeches regarding the exploitation of Thai women in the bar culture earned him the wrath of a certain degenerate who lived on alcohol, joints and Thai pussy. It was Franco who nicknamed him 'The Lesbian'. In fairness to William though, he really did seem to care about exploited peoples, which is more than I could say about some of us.

Stamp's girlfriend was Beatrice, who came regularly from London to visit him. No one knew whether she refused to shave her legs because it would've demonstrated subservience to the oppressive patriarchy of Western civilization or if she just didn't give a shit about her appearance.

And there, in the tunnel of human darkness, was also a light. Making her seasonal debut was Sally-Sue Bronson, a charismatic blonde of about twenty-eight. An actress and performance artist, she was based mostly in Los Angeles. Such was her star power among the gossipy expats, that I already knew she'd returned with Lindy, an older, more masculine woman for the second time. Sally-Sue had danced with partners of both genders for as long as I'd known her. Her sexiness seemed fresh and wholesome—until you heard her blasting out a rough tampon joke. Once, when William, the other lesbian, showed up with a blob of sunscreen on his cheek, she asked him, "Who came on your face?" I have no idea what a psychologist would've made of it.

My arms laden, I approached the pack of hungry dogs. Franco's low rasp barked out, "How many times did you stop to whack off?" Eager hands cleared a spot on their table as I unloaded the precious cargo.

Like a damsel in distress from some old movie, Lester declared, "Not a moment too soon. I'm parched. I'm as dry and sear as a Saharan drought."

"What's that?" I said, pointing to his beer glass.

"A girl can't live by pilsner alone," he said sweetly, reaching amongst the other eager hands for the booty that would enrich his mood as it shortened his life. Cartons of Marlboros, Camels and Dunhills fuelled the frenzied feed among their glass-enclosed cousins. Sally-Sue was a modest drinker and didn't smoke at all, but her vulgar streak flashed when she announced that she'd walk a mile for a camel.

With the hope that springs eternal within the human breast, Arden the parasite hovered hungrily, knowing that tonight the scraps would be extra special. For Charlene it was Crown Royal and for Robbin it was a whole bunch of bottles. Knowing Robbin, far more than would ever reach his customers would be sucked down his gullet like the water in a flushing toilet.

Franco softened once an over-sized bottle of Canadian Club was firmly in his loving grasp. He looked at me gratefully and said in a much kinder rasp, "I'll give you a hint, Maggot … when you use your left hand, it feels like someone else is doing it."

I replied, "When I use my mouth, it feels like *you're* doing it."

The degenerates roared. To Franco's credit, he always made an attempt to laugh along whenever the tables were turned on him. Which with me was nearly always. I was among my friends and settling comfortably into my lower self.

Sally-Sue was a friend of sorts—we occasionally corresponded through letters while she was in LA, which was most of the year. After hugs and exclamations of delight, I told her how many Thai hookers I'd fucked since we last spoke. It was a running joke—when I'd first met her a few years earlier, I would gush with stories of how I'd rent four or five prostitutes at once. A look of horror gripped her face as I described wild sexual escapades with a room full of young cuties.

"Really?" she would ask, wide-eyed and unsettled. I never failed to enthusiastically invite her to my next sex party. She finally figured out that I was full of shit. In fact, I was probably the only guy in the Biting Monkey who almost never slept with local women, much less hookers. Okay, Lester never slept with local *women* either, but Thai boys were on his menu. Though I have no doubt that Sally-Sue was truly put off by the exploitational aspects of my stories, I wondered later if they didn't also titillate her a little. Just speculation on my part. She was, after all, at least part lesbian.

Then Franco demanded that I explain my lateness. Evan and Samuel, the Stepford Wives, made for a worthy enough topic. I discovered that almost everyone knew more about their cult than I did. The group was The Children of a Living God and run by a guru called Dadaram. Samuel, Evan and other devotees had introduced themselves around town over the past couple of days. They were building an ashram up by the estuary of the Ban Lam, a river to our north. With the stories of healing by Samuel and Evan, I knew it was some kind of bullshit and said so. Others rushed in to defend!

Whoever said that religion is not a good topic for a neighborly outing should have had their mouth washed out with soap. Nothing gets a crowd frothing into vigorous social intercourse like matters of the spirit. And I discovered that being a heathen put me in the minority.

Sally-Sue Bronson thought it was indeed possible that their guru could heal with his hands and implied that I should open my mind. Sadly, it didn't entirely surprise me—one night, as she'd held me in orbit with the fullness of her lip and the curve of her thigh, she'd told me about her own religion. It had to do with gods in other galaxies. She even had an alternate name, Solaria Andromedia or some similar nonsense. She was so goddamn sexy—how could she believe this shit? Eager to see the glass as half full, I quoted Einstein: "Imagination is more important than knowledge." She had looked at me askew, somewhat offended, I think.

It also surprised me that both Lester and Franco claimed to be Christians. Lester spoke of how Jesus had saved Mary Magdalene from being stoned by an intolerant mob and he saw no conflict in being both gay and Christian. Franco rasped, "If Jesus saw *you*, Lester, he'd be the first one to grab a rock."

Only a handful failed to find nourishment in organized spirituality. William Stamp's girlfriend, Beatrice, said that all churches institutionalized the oppression of women. Arden, the poet, tried to stick up for Buddhism but was quickly shouted down by Beatrice and William, who pointed out that in the Theravada practice of Thailand, a woman needed to be reborn as a man before enlightenment could be achieved.

For the rest of the night Arden was more acquiescent to the opinions of others, knowing that begging went better while siding with one's host.

Charlene from Calgary exhaled a cloud of marijuana smoke as she proclaimed herself a Buddhist. God knows she earned her good karma by never once turning away a young backpacker in need of sex. Robbin, already well on his way, slurred that all religions were cults.

Riding me for my skepticism in matters of the Divine, Sally-Sue asked what I believed in. I told her that I was an ardent follower of the TV evangelist and faith healer, America's own Ernest Angley. It warmed my heart when she replied, "I heard he likes to fuck a room full of hookers too."

As issues of the soul transitioned into shallower discourse, it concluded the first, and fairly inert, foreshadowing of the coming of Dadaram. Not that I gave it much thought at that point. A burning spliff moved around the table. The night progressed with predictable dynamics. Franco generously kept Arden afloat in whiskey, primarily so that he could subject him to an endless flurry of abuse over his mooching.

Sally-Sue was out on the town without her gal. In her last letter she'd alluded to challenges with Lindy. I had no idea if it was a hint for me or simply information. It was *kind of-sort of* a secret that she was a lesbian, maybe due to her career, but everyone seemed to know about it.

Lacking the essence of a true degenerate, she made her usual early exit, preserving the milk-fed glow of her Midwestern roots. I walked her to her bicycle and we made a date to have dinner and catch up on life—mostly hers, I imagined, since mine had stopped. Her parting gaze cracked with a glimmer of radiance: she'd gotten a grant and was writing her one-woman show in Ao Lai. I returned to my drink thinking that the complications of her personality were far outshone by the magnificence of her flesh.

Well into his bottle of CC, Franco became an expert on lesbians, opining that Sally-Sue was definitely 'curable.' Beatrice hissed at him, and even the tolerant Lester tsk-tsked a rebuke—but my lower self was with Franco on this one—when Sally-Sue went back on sausage, that was one barbeque I planned to attend. And I could already smell the charcoal smoking.

Chapter Four

With a morning tour, I was back at my bungalow by midnight, on my porch, smoking a joint. The ocean rolled and broke gently, not thirty yards away. I was tucked away from the expanding little tourist enclave of Ao Lai at the end of a dirt road that ran past a field of coconuts to the water. It felt secluded. There were so many great beaches along the Andaman coast that this one, split off from a rocky promontory on one side, was often mine alone.

The cicadas were subdued with the deeper hour of night, but an evolved symphony had arisen; owls and nightjars sang along with howling monkeys and other creaking, groaning insects that were black with mystery. The air was heavy and the heat relaxed me. After the joint I lit a cigarette. This had been so often my little nirvana, but something was invading paradise and it wasn't a parking lot. The ugly face of Truth leered at me, and this was no longer a place that I could hide. Truth fed the gnawing terror in my gut that I was no different from Franco or Lester or Arden, that I'd given up, that life had a speed limit and this was it. Truth told me that I was addicted to pot smoking and cigarettes. Truth told me that it was years since I'd gotten my degree and that I'd lost any momentum that might give it meaning. It told me that my family constantly worried about me and sensed that I was lost. I no longer invited them to come and visit me here. Perhaps there was a shame in what I had become. The problem wasn't that I knew these things—the problem was that I'd known them for years now.

Did it matter that I had turned thirty this year? It was, after all, just a number. Addict. A nasty little word. The irony was that I wasn't an all-day weed-smoker—rarely a wake-and-bake, except for my days off, which were one or two days each week. There were tourists who toked up morning, noon and night and weren't addicts. They dropped it all like a hot potato when they shined up for the return to work in Europe or America. I only needed it once a day, but I had the disease, as the alcoholics say. To look at me, you'd have seen a guy with a suntan who took care of himself with exercise, a guy with a healthy business in a beautiful part of the world. But here alone, Truth had invaded my little paradise and was pointing and jeering at the rot inside of me.

I was constantly telling myself that I was about to go home, about to pack up. But like some fucked-up gambler I always had another bet to place. What was it this time—Sally-Sue? When I'm really honest with myself, and that's not something I enjoy, my depressions began over two years ago.

During my second year I fell in love with Sorine. It was an affair of the heart that could've become a real commitment, at least for me. But distance took its toll, and when Sorine called me from Denmark to say goodbye, my sadness was normal and predictable. A few weeks later I dropped into a hellish pit of despair. My friends all said it was caused by the loss of Sorine, but I'm not so sure. My depression appeared with a flourish—as if an opiated veil of consciousness was suddenly torn away, revealing the true horror and ugliness of my world. I saw an endless unquenchable loneliness flickering through the bars along the beach; the same girls, the same drinkers with different faces, laughter that covered pain … it all came wrapped in a deep sadness that infected me for weeks.

Even then, buried in the horror was some small elusive hint of exquisite dark pleasure. Like a whiff of gasoline. It was as if I was living in the cruel bleak poem of some European madman.

Then the opiated veil returned and I could once again feel beauty in the spray of the blue sea, the songs of the night and in the smiles of women. For a time. During my second year I could rationalize: who needs to buy into the BS of the American Dream? Can someone please explain to me exactly what that is anyway? Two cars in the suburbs or some shit like that? I had a brilliant job in paradise. I only needed to have myself together for a few hours each day, and every informed traveler who set foot in Ao Lai knew that my tours were second to none; the scenery was better, the food was better, the drinks were better. Not to mention that without Sorine to hog my devotion, it was the perfect job to entertain the beauties of the world.

When did it become paradise lost? With Truth leering at the sores inside of me, I reached for the exalted memories of my first year in Ao Lai, the year I bought my boat, the *Zenobia*.

It was here I met the tropics that winked and twinkled in the dripping heat. Fruits with new tastes, exotic and delicious, came in bright hues and bold shapes. Eating was an adventure for the senses; I found a myriad of succulent dishes from coconut curries to the fish, prawn and shark pulled fresh from the sea and grilled with smoke and Thai spices. *Sanuk* was the Thai word for pleasure, and that it was.

The stretch of soft, blanched sand that fronted most of Ao Lai led to the great liquid delight of the Andaman Sea, with her shades of brilliant shimmering blue that exploded white on the beaches. This is where the hot sun sank into lazy flesh, and the coconut-oiled hands of Thai masseuses worked until all fight was gone from muscles. Most perfect of all, lying on their colored sheets, the beauties of the world decorated paradise.

Beneath the Andaman's pretty skin were coral reefs that dazzled with electric displays of color and exotic life. Adventure and discovery were in every plunge to the depths below. On land, a motorcycle ride was the perfect foil to the burning hot air of high summer, with the pungent smells of food carts and burning wood in little villages.

My finest rides were at night, dancing through the great shadows of the palms along the hot ocean with its seductive breath in my hair while white moonlight sparkled in the breaking waves and a lover's arms held my waist.

On nights of the full moon, my Scandinavian friends became hungry pagans who howled at the sky. We drank and drummed and danced into a trance that welcomed the dawn. And on occasion I bit the mushroom that opened a magic door to a place where one could see the world from a different and sometimes hysterically beautiful point of view. Even my heathen self knew that these were trips to the sacred pool, and I was smart enough not to go often.

There was the thirst that the Buddhists call *tanhá*, the delicious ache to know a woman's beauty, and the pleasure of consummation. Through the dark red hues of a sun sinking into the sea or the carnal pulse of dance music at night, Ao Lai was sensuality itself. Steamy nights became the substance of my life. My *raison d'être*. Yes, all that and more I discovered in Ao Lai—that was the heaven, the exalted paradise that drew me here.

But as any Hindu holy man will tell you, for an unenlightened being, every heaven eventually becomes a hell.

Chapter Five

My tours were canceled due to savage rains. I was alone and naked in a great gray afternoon ocean as buckets of water blasted down from a low, dark sky. The stretch of beach, a couple of hundred yards from my bungalow, was deserted. Wind drove the torrent of water through coconut palms behind the sand, and the air was so wet they were but occluded shapes bending in the storm.

Afloat in the big swells, the ocean exploded around me. I did the crawl, and then floated like a seal in my fierce paradise, avoiding the breaking waves that could smash you into the beach then suck you back out again in a powerful undertow. If I kept my face turned away from the stinging deluge it felt glorious, a majestic time to swim. That, however, was a minority opinion, because whenever it rained like this there was neither farang nor Thai to be found near a beach. The farangs would all be huddled damply, playing cards and drinking Ovaltine in little restaurants.

So I was surprised when I noticed an upright shape on the beach. As I shifted, I saw that it was two people under an umbrella, a lighter one and a darker one. It seemed that the Stepford Wives were watching me—or waiting for me.

I timed my way out of the sea and moved to the drowned spot of red that was my beach shorts, pulling them on for no other reason than propriety. Outside of the ocean's protection, the rain was like bullets on my skin. Samuel and Evan were hardly helped by the umbrella. I jogged up to them with a friendly greeting, but their faces were grave. We headed to my bungalow.

They had a taxi waiting in my dirt driveway. If this kept up, the road would be too muddy to leave. My place was small. I got them each a towel. They were very sincere and on a mission, electing for coffee instead of a beer.

Samuel began the business. "Two of our sisters have been arrested. They're being taken to jail in Bangkok."

For a moment I stood silently, awaiting more information.

"They are the family of Dadaram, and he wants them out immediately," Samuel added.

"These aren't the type of women who can be in a jail," Evan said. I wondered if there was a type of woman that jail was more suited to. But seeing how grim they looked, I kept my quips to myself.

"How would I be able to help with something like that?"

"Dadaram has chosen you," said Samuel. *Huh?*

Evan joined the campaign. "We need you to go to Bangkok and get them released."

The request was absurd. I was listed in travel guidebooks as a 'tour boat operator', not a Bangkok lawyer. Yet two damp, serious men stood before me, their eyes pleading. I felt a stab of compassion for the ridiculous position they were in.

I tried to explain. "Getting me to bust someone out of jail in Bangkok is like asking an auto mechanic to do heart surgery." And silently I determined that it didn't say much for their guru that he would believe otherwise.

"Dadaram is never wrong," was Samuel's resolute reply.

"Well, his winning streak just crapped out—he needs a lawyer."

Evan said, "Even with a lawyer, they won't be out for days. We need you, Magnus," as he produced a fat envelope. I had already launched my next protest when he withdrew a stack of U.S. dollars and laid it on the table.

"Two thousand for you, more in Bangkok for the authorities."

The money got my attention. Maybe in Florida or California it was reasonable for a short job, but here in Ao Lai it was considerable. My rent was about 140 dollars a month and it included twice weekly maid service. Two grand meant something. But it wasn't just the money—it was what it represented, the undercurrent of dire need that ran through Samuel and Evan, the intensity of the commitment to their sisters. Or was it commitment to their guru? In any case, my wheels started spinning. Maybe General Bukit could help me. If the big swells kept up my tours would be canceled anyway. Then I remembered my dinner date with Sally-Sue for the following night.

They watched me with bated breath as the heavens raged against the walls and windows. A coconut smashed my metal roof and they jumped.

"It's a sign!" I exclaimed with delight. "Dadaram has sent a sign!"

My humor failed to budge Evan but Samuel smiled just a little, amused by my ignorance.

Suddenly, time was of the essence if I was to be in Bangkok by morning. I had Evan take the taxi driver a coffee and a banana and ensure that his vehicle was pointed in the right direction. The road was so wet that it may have needed pushing.

Samuel wrote out all the details he had. I stuffed a small bag with a toothbrush and some respectable clothes for the morning, slipping in a toke as well. As we headed out, Samuel chased after me with the umbrella as if I were some kind of dignitary.

Packed into the little taxi we sloshed through the mud, windshield wipers grinding away.

"So what did your sisters do to get themselves busted?"

Evan stated, "The charge is for the illegal importation of a firearm.

The gun was in sister Amy's luggage."

I was surprised, intrigued. Samuel explained that the 'sisters,' who were sisters in the sibling sense as well as the cult sense, had arrived in Bangkok on a luxury cruise liner. One of their church brothers had engaged an 'agent' on the boat to bring the handgun through customs. I suspected that 'agent' was a euphemism for 'criminal.'

"What do you need a gun for?" I asked.

"It's the will of Dadaram and it hasn't been revealed to us," Evan said matter-of-factly. I wondered what kind of people I was working for.

We dipped through puddles. I was planning as we moved. I wanted to get the driver fed before we took off; my most efficient route to Bangkok was a taxi ride to Surithani, a city about four hours northeast of us, then to Bangkok on an overnight train. Unfortunately, the sisters would have to spend at least one night in jail. I became seriously committed to helping my deluded little gun smugglers. I asked if the hotel would have a fax machine. They assured me it would.

We stopped at the Biting Monkey so I could communicate my absence and cancel the following day's tours. The heavy rain had just abated and the bar was still packed with tourists. As we pulled up, Evan delivered the hard part.

"Dadaram wants the gun retrieved."

I assured him, "That ain't gonna happen. Some general already has it in his private collection."

"Dadaram has full faith in you," said Samuel with smug confidence.

I pushed through the throng in the Biting Monkey and lifted the phone to try to reach General Bukit. The line was dead. Not atypical after a storm. I wrote a note for my Thai man, Mike, and shoved some baht at Karol, the owner, to ensure that he got it.

Evan and Samuel shadowed me, watching as I hustled. I turned to them. "Where are you staying?"

They mentioned Ao Lai's best hotel.

"Good. I'll be sending you a fax from Surithani—you're going to get the body of it retyped on your church's letterhead and faxed to me in Bangkok." I went into deeper detail and they both looked pleased. I had no idea whether or not I could pull this off.

A drunken rasp rose out of the crowded bar, "Maggot … you've joined a cult!"

Franco, the good Christian, was chortling at my association with the Stepford Wives. The other good Christian, Lester, was admonishing him, though not entirely unamused by the comment himself.

I decided to stop thinking of Samuel and Evan as the Stepford Wives. They were weird but … so were all my other friends. They had met Sally-Sue, and I made them promise to explain my absence. They agreed, emphasizing that the gun charge required discretion. I wondered if she'd still be soft on these kooks if she knew they were sneaking a gun around.

My driver and I took off to General Bukit's house. The late sun burned a rising mist out of the soaked ground. With the taxi waiting, I crossed a courtyard where a shiny new jeep and some motorcycles were parked. I marveled at how well my greedy friend was doing. As I approached the house I could hear his son, Arnold, eating. I had never in my life heard anyone crunching and smacking his way through a meal as brutally and happily as Arnold Bukit. His teeth broke bones and then loudly sucked the marrow from every joint. He cared not that food covered his chubby face in a greasy halo around his mouth. For Arnold, each meal was an orgy. I always found it hysterical that he had the same name as the Ziffels' son, the pig on the TV show *Green Acres*. The Bukits were Muslim, and I wondered how the poor fucker ever made it through Ramadan, the traditional period of fasting.

"Hey Arnold…" I called through the open door.

He lit up magnanimously, gesturing me inside. "Magnus, come on! Come eat!"

"I can't, my friend, I need to see your dad."

"You want beer?"

"No thank you, I've got a taxi waiting." I nodded at Arnold's wife as he barked at her in Thai. She left the room. "Is there any possibility of seeing your father?"

"He is having a nap, we do not disturb him," Arnold said more soberly.

"How long will he sleep?" I asked.

"Come on, let's drink some beer, maybe he will wake up," said the gracious host. His wife returned with a bottle of Singha and a glass for me.

I felt the pressure of time. I needed to be on that overnight train in Surithani. Arnold didn't care. "We go to disco some night, you and me, we can get chickie-chickie in disco," he beamed. His wife said something in Thai. Arnold's fat, greasy face shook with laughter. "She wants to know what chickie-chickie is!"

I drank the beer out of politeness. After all the socializing I could bear, I produced a thousand baht and suggested that I would pay it to anyone who may be inclined to wake the general. With the money lying on the table, Arnold looked to his wife.

I was happy to see that she returned without a black eye, and Arnold translated that his father would see me.

Bukit was gracious. He sat in a sleeveless undershirt rather than his usual uniform. I was at my very politest, thanking him and apologizing for the intrusion. I told him, "We are friends, and it would please me to give you a gift." I wasn't screwing around—I dropped 200 bucks on his table. The general was surprised; usually I bargained on my own behalf.

There are tricky subtleties to bribery, and I didn't want to cross any lines into disrespect. "Even the smallest help will be greatly appreciated."

I continued by revealing my own ignorance; it was a necessary part of Thai culture so that the person subjected to the inquiry didn't lose face if they couldn't answer the question. "I don't know anyone in Bangkok," I said humbly. "No one who is important who could help me."

Basically I was asking Bukit for his very best connection in the police department, the highest-ranking person in Bangkok that he could recommend to me, and also recommend me to them. I explained that the people that I was trying to help would be generous.

General Pramana Bukit was rarely mute. It disturbed me. In the uneasy silence, I began to realize that a Muslim general from the south might be persona non grata in an old boys club of Bangkok officers. Bukit was the product of an Indonesian father and a Thai mother. In the far south and other enclaves of Thailand, Muslims prevailed, but most of the country, including Bangkok, was Buddhist. Relations between the two groups were not always cordial and there were violent clashes in the south. I sincerely hoped I wasn't touching a wound.

Putting the money on the table may have made things worse. The room was air-conditioned but I felt myself beginning to sweat.

Bukit finally moved. He produced a pen and began writing on the back of his business card in Thai script and then in English.

I was off like a rocket. The taxi banged and bounced over a potholed road as I rehearsed my game plan. I poked at a draft of the letter that would be faxed to Bukit's contact in Bangkok until it was too dark to see. Four hours later, I arranged my scraps of paper at a hotel near the Surithani train station and dictated to Evan over the phone. I infused the letter with a formality that I hoped, in the cultural translation, would impart some authority.

> *Dear Sir:*
>
> *We are grateful for your esteemed attention in the matter of two American citizens. Amy Schott and Anna Schott are members of our religious society who are currently housed in Bang Khen Prison. Our agent in Thailand, Mr. Magnus Larsen, will be pleased to furnish the details that exonerate both persons from the charges that currently detain them. You will find that these two women were misled by an*

unscrupulous person who falsely represented himself as a recognized authority in the Kingdom of Thailand.

We have the utmost respect that your time is valuable. For your immediate assistance in this pressing matter, our agent, Mr. Larsen, is prepared to cover all necessary fees, and be generous with our gratitude in any way that you deem is appropriate.

Once again we reiterate that the women in question are law-abiding citizens that would never intentionally break the laws of Thailand. We trust that a man of your office is as interested in the pursuit of justice as we are.

We thank you kindly.

On behalf of The Children of a Living God,

Evan R. Williams

It was to be signed and faxed immediately to a Niran Choonhavan at the Phahon Yothin Police Station in the Chatochak district of Bangkok. Bukit's friend wasn't the biggest cheese, but he worked for a colonel in the jurisdiction of Bang Khen Prison. Bukit had assured me that his friend would place the letter under the colonel's nose with discretion but not delay. Especially since he'd be in for a piece of the action.

Evan said that ten thousand dollars cash would be waiting for me at my hotel and that they were scrambling for more. I didn't think they needed to; I tried to impress upon him that ten grand is a small fortune in Thailand.

"Getting our sisters out is an absolute priority," Evan said.

"The colonel will either take money or he won't," I replied. Through the phone line I felt Evan shiver. "Do you doubt the choice of Dadaram?" I smiled through a brief pause.

"They had to pay for the privilege of not being split up. They have no cash." Evan sounded sincerely desperate. I requested that any permit or gun license be faxed to my hotel in Bangkok. Evan had no idea if such a thing existed.

When I was certain that I had a sleeper berth on the 22.40, I released my Ao Lai taxi. As we groaned out of Surithani Station, I banished all thoughts about the morality, or even the weirdness of what I was doing. One thing struck me though—if only one of the devotees had a gun in her luggage, why were both of them in prison? Were Evan and Samuel telling me the full truth?

There was another issue as well that worried me more than whether or not a Thai cop would take money—and that was whether or not he could effect their release. Corruption was endemic within the bureaucratic structure of Thailand. Nevertheless, officials needed to maintain 'face' and not appear corrupt. The man would likely need an 'excuse' to overturn the internment.

The importance of 'face' in Thai culture is not to be underestimated. It's the difference between making love to a woman and then giving her a hundred dollars—or making love to a woman and then giving her an antique purse that cost a hundred dollars. If you don't know which one will get you kissed and which one will get you smacked, you might not want to try bribery in Thailand.

As the train chugged northward I smoked a joint out the window of the sleeper with a Dutch backpacker, depressed to be heading home. *Funny,* I thought, *I'm depressed to still be here.*

Chapter Six

At 8:45 a.m. I checked into a four-star colossus called the Grand Lullaby Resort, chosen by The Children of a Living God for its proximity to Bang Khen Prison. Garish décor encircled me as I signed for ten thousand dollars in cash. The desk clerk then handed me a manila envelope. As I withdrew the contents, my spirits rose—lo and behold, it was the facsimile of a gun license. A 9mm Glock handgun was registered in the Commonwealth of Massachusetts to a Devon Clarke of Boston. *Hot damn.* This was the prop I was hoping for.

My winning streak ended shortly thereafter when I was on the phone in my room with Niran Choonhavan, the contact of General Bukit. The man struggled with English as I struggled with Thai. I needed clear communication with his superior, the colonel. There was no way that this man could possibly understand the nuances of the letter that Evan had faxed him. I managed to explain that I was coming over immediately and that I needed an audience with the colonel. Suddenly *What the fuck am I doing?* seemed to be a recurring thought. I swallowed it repeatedly.

I freshened up quickly and put on a clean shirt. In the lobby of the Grand Lullaby I collected two more items, a leather briefcase and a translator. I offered one of the young desk clerks fifty dollars for a short stint of assistance. A kid who made only a few bucks a shift, he jumped. Behind the front desk, I saw the Bangkok Yellow Pages and had an inspiration that would serve me later.

The translator's name was Som. I began filling him in as our taxi maneuvered through the clogged streets. When he learned we were headed to a police station, Som suddenly looked grave. "Outstanding warrants?" I joked. He shook his head seriously.

Nerves fluttered in my stomach as we pulled up to the Phahon Yothin Police Station. The fact that I was about to attempt to bribe officers of the law stared me straight in the face. General Bukit was a small-town operator who reached into my pocket on his own accord. Suddenly it seemed like I was taking a helluva risk for people that I didn't even know. What if this colonel had scruples? I banished the horrible thought from my head as Som and I entered the building.

I emphasized to Som that it was necessary to impart the respect and also the formality of the letter that I had faxed. I would ask that he be furnished with the actual copy of it when we met the colonel. "Anything I say to the sergeant or the colonel, you repeat it, please." Som nodded gravely. Again, I wondered what was wrong with him.

Metal fans buzzed and twisted on the wall behind the reception desk at Phahon Yothin Police Station. Even with the moving air it was hot. Nerves tickled me again as I informed a clerk that Sergeant Niran Choonhavan was expecting us. I wondered if I was about to find *myself* in a Bangkok prison.

Upstairs, I exchanged warm greetings with Niran Choonhavan, telling him that he was spoken of highly by my friend General Bukit. I preferred to file those comments under 'good manners' rather than 'phony bullshit.' I looked to Som for a translation. Thai people are good at keeping up 'face' but Som was struggling. He looked strained speaking to Choonhavan.

"This is Som, my translator," I said buoyantly, hoping to impart some confidence in him.

Choonhavan uttered something ever so briefly in Thai. I ensured that he received an envelope with my appreciation.

Som watched the passing of the money like someone was sticking a knife in his guts. I asked if Som could see the copy of our letter. Som shyly managed to translate the request. He was sweating. *I* sweat in that heat—Thai people don't. I wasn't sure if Som was rattled by authority or if he believed he was part of a crime. I sure as hell didn't want to give the latter impression to the colonel. As for the letter, Choonhavan said it was already with his boss. He lifted his phone.

We were shuffled in to meet Colonel Thanarat, a serious man well into middle age with a broad, jowly face. He struck me immediately as no lightweight. Pictures of the Thai king and royal family decorated the wall behind his desk. There was a well-known case of an Englishman serving thirty years in prison for having spray-painted nasty graffiti about the king. I hoped a conviction for bribery would be less severe.

After the formalities, we took our seats. "I trust that you've received my church's letter?" asked the heathen of the colonel. Som began to translate, but Thanarat waved to indicate it wasn't necessary. The office was air-conditioned, and I hoped that it was assisting Som.

"Allow me to provide you with a brief history of what happened," I began. As I started to speak, I opened my briefcase and withdrew the permit for the gun. I held it as a piece of evidence to be revealed as I explained that a crew member on the Royal Danish Cruise Line had falsely informed the Schott sisters that he was a legal broker for bringing firearms into Thailand. The devious man had received his fee and then returned the firearm to one of the women's suitcases without her knowledge. *Christ, I hoped they hadn't made a statement contradicting any of this.* I had no idea if that part of the story was even true—that's what Evan and Samuel had told me.

Silence ensued.

"My translator, Som, is here to help us all."

The colonel ignored Som. "How much for fee?" He was referring to the 'gun agent.'

"I don't know, they paid it on the boat," I said.

"Why they bring gun to Thailand?"

"One of the sisters was the victim of a horrible sexual assault. For a time she couldn't even leave her own house, she was so frightened. She had to see a psychiatrist, that's a doctor of the mind." The colonel nodded.

"Her doctor applied for a handgun on her behalf." After a slight pause, I added, "She is terrified without it." I handed over the sheet of paper with the Massachusetts registration, adding, "She can possess the gun legally in the United States."

The colonel handled the document, making a small show of looking at it.

The gun license may have been real in Massachusetts but here it was a piece of nonsense. It wasn't even registered to one of the Schott sisters. The whole point of it was to make the bribery possible. It was like a little emperor that we could all agree was wearing clothes. It allowed us all to maintain 'face.'

In my last-minute inspiration at the Grand Lullaby, I had obtained the name of one of Bangkok's prominent law firms from the Yellow Pages. I perused the hotel stationary, reading my own (invented) notes. "We have a quote from Mr. Nung Palat of Songkhla International." My story continued. "Mr. Palat is confident the sisters will get bail. He's quoted us 82,500 baht to effect their release. That's the fee for Songkhla International." My notes looked realistic, as if I'd taken them while chatting on the phone. The 'quote' of 82,500 baht was circled. I passed the paper to Thanarat as I continued. "Obviously we prefer that the charges be dropped. These people are not criminals."

I played the big card. "If they can be released immediately—*today*—the church would be willing to pay fees to match Mr. Nulat's quote." There was a brief pause. "I can obtain U.S. dollar cash immediately if such a fee is appropriate."

It would've been nice to get some encouragement from someone but we sat in silence. I glanced at Choonhavan—he wasn't meeting my eyes. I could feel Som sweating behind me. Had I said something wrong? Then Thanarat asked if I was willing to write out a declaration that I knew these women personally and that I could vouch for their good character. I didn't hesitate in agreeing. He spoke in Thai to Choonhavan, who hustled off immediately.

Thanarat seemed oblivious to the fact that Thailand is known as the 'Land of Smiles' as he sat gravely stoic during the sergeant's absence. The stress of it all had me jonesing for a smoke. An ashtray lay on Thanarat's desk, but all I had were Krung Theps and such cheap butts would've lowered my status like a stain on my shirt.

A piece of letter-headed paper returned with Choonhavan. A pen was passed across the desk by Colonel Thanarat. As I placed the paper on my briefcase, I became acutely aware that if any of this went wrong, I could be arrested. I wished to hell that Som would mellow out. *Why was he so fucking uptight?* The subtleties of the English language would likely be lost in translation so I expressed that I 'knew of' their good character and raved on positively about two cult members that I'd never met. A scenario in which my own lawyer was explaining the distinction between knowing them and knowing *of* them to a Thai judge flashed unpleasantly through my head.

Beads of sweat tickled my forehead. Since I had banished all thoughts of the morality of what I was doing, I now wondered about these women. Why did they need a gun? Why was it registered in a man's name? And once again the question flared, why were two women charged when only one had a gun? Maybe this wasn't the best time to think about this shit. Beneath my glowing account of the sisters Schott, I wrote my name, and underneath that, I indicated 'The Church of a Living God.' I handed the signed paper to Choonhavan with all the confidence in the world. He in turn passed it to Thanarat.

The colonel's eyes perused it. When he spoke I heard my name in a jumble of Thai. I felt Som rise behind me, then he and Choonhavan left the room. I waited for Thanarat to speak.

A fly landed on his desk. I waited.

"How much you pay for Choonhavan?"

My fate was nigh. If I admitted passing money to Choonhavan and the colonel was an honest cop, I would be in handcuffs very quickly. But I'd already jumped off the cliff—all I could do was pray for a soft landing.

"Three thousand baht," I said.

The colonel then wrote on the hotel paper with my phony legal firm notes. He passed it back. He had written '110,000 baht.' *Hallelujah, he was bargaining!*

Emboldened, it was my turn to be cool. "I'm not the boss. I'm authorized for 3,400 dollars if our sisters are released today. It's possible … that they will authorize this … *maybe*," I said, referring to his amount.

"Tomorrow can be released, one hundred ten thousand baht. U.S. dollar okay."

"I will ask for four thousand dollars—better than 100,000 baht—but only if they're released today. If they can't be released today, it's *possible* that we will accept the offer tomorrow … but I will go visit Mr. Nulat, the lawyer, first. I want to know how long it will take him to get them out."

"He cannot get them out tomorrow," said Thanarat, showing signs of life.

"You are my first choice, Colonel … let's get them out *now*. I'll tell my boss to pay you."

"Maybe not possible. Tomorrow for sure. Pay me today, maybe today."

There are a couple of notable points about Thai culture: one, 'tomorrow' can be a long time in coming; and two, the person with the most money has the most status. I decided to give myself a further elevation. "I'm going to get eight thousand dollars in cash—*200 hundred thousand baht,*" I emphasized. "The sisters out today and the gun returned today." There's no way Thanarat made more than thirty-five hundred bucks a year in salary.

I repeated it slowly. "Eight thousand dollars cash—the sisters out today and the gun returned today."

Now Thanarat was closer to speechless than silent. I launched into a story about how the traumatized sister couldn't live without the gun...

Thanarat didn't care; we were talking about eight grand in Thailand in 1992. The old dog was slobbering. Hell, the previous day I'd had my own little slobber over a mere two thousand.

"My favorite uncle is a policeman," I invented. "I'd much rather give the money to you than to a lawyer."

Things were becoming possible very rapidly.

In the taxi I was jubilant. Until Som began trying to give me back the fifty dollars. "You were great," I insisted. "Just having you there gave me status." He started telling me how much he hates the police and their dishonesty. Som came from a small town in the northeast where the police acted as thugs for local politicians who needed to reclaim land from poor farmers for business projects that stuffed their own pockets. They used violence and even burned homes when necessary. The corruption began in Bangkok and spread like tentacles of disease throughout the country. In Som's village, some farmers ended up so poor that they sold their daughters to Bangkok brothels. *Jesus.* Som knew how to rain on a guy's parade.

In my room at the Grand Lullaby, I sucked back Krung Theps as I flipped channels between a Bangkok soap opera and a rerun of *MacGyver* in which all the actors were dubbed into Thai. Despite my faith in Thanarat's lust for the cult's cash, I couldn't relax until I knew for sure that the sisters would be released. If the gun came through, it would be icing on the cake. Expensive icing, but it wasn't my money, and maybe these nutty cult girls really were scared without it. At least half of my hometown drove around with gun racks so I didn't see it as a huge deal. Although … I had to admit, most folks didn't take their piece traveling with them.

The phone rang and I jumped for it. Instead of the colonel it was Evan, twisting on the other end of the line. The cult was sweating and ready to arrange truly massive amounts of cash; Dadaram wanted them out no matter what the cost. I was impressed by the deep pockets of this little pseudo-religion. Another thing I noticed was that if this Dadaram wanted to poke at his nuts with a sharp stick, then Evan and Samuel would also want to poke at their own nuts with a sharp stick.

Evan's strained voice emphasized that the sisters would be without cash and traumatized. He begged me to go to the jail immediately to reassure them—but I couldn't go anywhere while I waited for Thanarat's call. I got him off the phone to free up the line.

It was now just after 1:00 p.m. The time was beginning to drift over the deadline I'd given the colonel before I went to see Mr. Nulat at Songkhla International. Of course that was a bluff; I'd never even spoken to a lawyer—but if Thanarat couldn't come through, we'd have to call one. I knew the colonel wanted our deal to happen as badly as I did. I reflected on the fact that I did not know these women at all and I had precious little reason to care deeply about their fate. Was it the challenge?

Stepping into the burning smog on my balcony, I searched the hazy view for a glimpse of Bang Khen Prison. I didn't know where it was except that it was supposed to be on Nonthaburi Road in the same district as the hotel. A ringing phone yanked me back inside like a dog on a chain.

I prayed as I lifted the receiver.

"Mistar Lahrsen, you can bring me fee at once okay." *Hot damn.*

"Four thousand or eight?" I asked.

"Eight," he said. *Yes!*

I had the front desk call Bang Khen Prison just to make sure he wasn't bullshitting me and the release of the Schott sisters was confirmed. I tried to pass on a message to the sisters that I would be coming down to get them but I wasn't sure that they'd ever get it.

As Thanarat had requested, I arrived back at the police station with some 'documents' for him. He had the gun, I had the money. After we'd counted the cash, he lifted the Glock, examining it with such admiration that I hoped I wouldn't have to wrest it out of his hands.

Before I left the colonel's office, he asked me about my church. I explained that we were called The Children of a Living God, and that our guru Dadaram teaches us to open our hearts to love. I had no idea what this Dadaram preached but I figured he was probably a pretty sleazy motherfucker. As I headed back to my hotel to ditch the gun, I thought of Som and could've said the same about myself.

Chapter Seven

My taxi crawled. Horns beeped in an endless cacophony. Evan was right—even a single night in a third world jail would be traumatic. I determined that the Schott sisters wouldn't suffer a second longer than they had to. The truth was, it felt good to be concerned about someone other than my own wretched self.

We turned onto Nonthaburi Road and I strained through the sun and haze to see a guard tower several blocks away. When the traffic choked to a standstill, I told the driver to wait for me outside the jail—I was running ahead. On the sidewalk, nasty yellow heat was saturated with exhaust from tuk-tuks, trucks and motorcycles. Thai rock blared from little buses. I ducked and dodged quickly through ambling humanity and street carts despite not knowing if the sisters would still be there. Once released, they may have been inclined to bolt. Had they gotten the message that I was coming?

Sweating, I came to the bars, wire and steel doors of a large institution with multi-lingual signs indicating 'No Photograph.' Bang Khen is part of a larger prison system called Klong Prem. It took me a while to figure out which part was Bang Khen, the women's prison. I was scrambling, asking people on the street, but sometimes Thai help is the opposite of helpful. And just to make things extra stupid, Bang Khen Prison was also called Lard Yao, which I didn't know. People didn't have a clue what I meant when I said Bang Khen. And Thai people will never tell you when they don't have a clue, because then they lose face.

When I finally found Bang Khen, I ended up in a frustrating little set of missteps that included being sent to the wrong section with the general visitors. Jails are horrible and fascinating places but I was in no mood for a tour.

My tail-chase came to an end when a woman guard with a mass of clinking keys led me through various security gates and hallways. The concrete with faded paint was clean everywhere, perhaps a benefit of free labor. She brought me to an administrative wing of the prison and referred me to a final corridor.

This was where it all changed.

About fifteen yards into the hallway, light from an opposing office bathed the faces of two white females on a bench. They sat next to some luggage, almost formally, the first with her hands folded on her lap. The image struck me as an inspired classical painting; saintly women maintaining their holy dignity amidst a great sacrilege. I was flooded with intense and unexpected compassion. The closest had brown hair that fell to her shoulders with a slither of sensuality, and her full, dark lips played against a light suntan. The other was a teenaged girl with sandy hair that framed her round face and pale blue eyes that slanted slightly upward. She had Down's Syndrome. As different as they looked from one another, each seemed to possess a certain sublime quality.

As I approached, it became even stranger … I felt a sense of reverence. They turned to see me—and the full force of the elder sister's beauty struck.

"Mr. Larsen, I presume."

I replied, "The sisters Schott, I presume." The shorter girl had presence and dignity in her round face. I smiled at her and she looked away.

"I'm Anna," said the exquisite creature as she rose, "...and this is Her Royal Highness, Amy Schott, the Princess of Massachusetts." The younger one looked at her with amused tolerance. Anna continued, "She's been wrongfully imprisoned and thanks you for your assistance."

"My sister is telling stories. I'm just Amy."

"With all respect Your Majesty, I think you are more than 'just Amy.'"

She smiled shyly. "Thank you for helping us," she said, a slight thickness to her speech.

I hoisted the bigger pieces of luggage. Whatever I had been expecting, this wasn't it.

We loaded up my waiting taxi. It must have been glorious for them to step into the loud, dirty heat after a night in Bang Khen. But as we rolled away, Anna expressed that they wanted to return to the prison before visiting hours were over. *Say what?* I twisted to look at them in the backseat. They were worried about a foreigner who had been going through various trials for five months, still wasn't convicted, and hadn't had a single letter returned from her home. Anna said that at the very least, they could arrange for some fruit in her diet and get her a little money. I couldn't believe it—for all their composure, I knew damn well that place had been a nightmare for them. The puffed up sense of accomplishment I felt at having bribed the colonel was replaced with a second poke of humility.

My job was over; they were out of jail. Once I handed them their gun and the leftover cash from the bribery money, I could hop the night train south. Anna asked if I would mind going back to Bang Khen with them; visitation ended at 6 p.m. I didn't mind at all but as the taxi inched through rush hour, returning that night didn't seem practical, not if they wanted to shop for the woman. There was some private conversation among the sisters in the rear. Anna said, "Amy wants to know if you can come tomorrow." The question caught me off guard.

"I'd like to know as well," Anna said.

As we turned off of Nonthaburi Road a low sun filtered through the smog into the backseat. Anna Schott's eyes were broken into pieces of green that came in various shades from different depths. After a second of suffering her beauty, I looked over at Amy's adorable face. "Her Highness is too mighty to speak for herself, huh. I didn't know Massachusetts was that grand of a state." She squirmed with embarrassment and laughed with her sister. Despite the Down's, Amy was not ugly. Some people can be ugly and still adorable the way an ugly little dog can be adorable. But that wasn't Amy. Nor did she look vacuous. She looked … dignified. And a little vulnerable. Even when she was embarrassed she was like a teenage girl who felt the pressure of the spotlight.

It turned out that Samuel and Evan had told me the truth—the 'agent' who was to bring the gun in turned out to be scum. Anna had taken equal responsibility when it was found in Amy's luggage, for obvious reasons.

"So … why do you need a gun?" I asked.

"I don't know … Dada hasn't told us that."

I noted the affectionate shortening of the guru's name and took a sober breath. Despite the charm and empathy that the Schott sisters held, I reminded myself that they were cult members. Their guru had asked them to babysit a gun, and they never even asked why. I found it disturbing.

Anna's voice floated like dark oily liquid. "What do I sense, Magnus … skepticism, concern?"

"You just spent the night in a Southeast Asian jail. How was it?"

"That wasn't his fault."

As we approached the hotel, I brought up the logistics of the following day. If Anna and Amy wanted to travel south with me after the prison visit, we could take the train or perhaps share a taxi. Anna began to explain that Dadaram had ordered them to sell some incense before they headed south. A feeling of disgust rose inside of me and I turned to face Anna in the back. A smile broke gloriously across her face, sparkling her abstract eyes. Sadly, the pleasure of my gullibility didn't stop there—the Princess of Massachusetts was laughing too.

Dusk had settled into Bangkok's thick air. All was good, the Schotts had risen from the hard floor of Bang Khen Prison to the cheap grandeur of the Grand Lullaby Resort. I'd stuffed the remainder of the cult's ten thousand bucks and their gun into my briefcase and handed it over to them. At a nearby street market, I picked up a fresh shirt for dinner with the sisters. It had been a day out of days. I reflected upon the bizarre turn of events that had me bribing a colonel. Despite my nerves, it was really no great achievement—in Thai jails you'll find foreigners in for drugs, not bribery. The strangest thing of all was the sense of reverence I felt upon my first sight of Anna and Amy.

But the day wasn't over, and something much stranger was yet to arrive.

The night held a hot, humid caress. Anna and Amy dragged me through the fluorescent lights of cheesy, pulsing markets with their stacks of designer rip-offs, pirated music, cheap electronics and hustling voices. In the gentler light beyond, brown bodies were languid and reposed. Anna had a quality that seemed to whisper softly underneath the music and bustle of the booths. Her waist and breasts were small and she moved with a lithe grace. Even when I chose not to look at her, I could hear a voice that was rich and intelligent. It seemed somehow incongruent with her bargaining skills, which were pathetic. I had to step in a couple of times.

They shopped mostly for their incarcerated friend. Anna became captivated by some fabric, and I teased Amy about what we'd be eating for dinner, listing a myriad of delicacies from smoked rat to worms to fried beetles. Amy's laugh was joyous, squeezing her almond-shaped eyes as if some divine intervention was taking momentary possession of her earthly self. Still, it could be tricky with her—when I told her that beetles were just as tasty as cockroaches, she yelled, "I won't eat that!"

"Calm down, he's just teasing you," said Anna, holding up a blouse for inspection. But I didn't need defending. Amy had a hint of a smile when she growled at me.

We found a crowded restaurant on the open-air top floor of a warehouse. The Chaophraya River below was kindled with the moving orange lights of boat traffic. Over dinner, I learned about a cruise that had begun in Singapore, come up through the Gulf of Thailand, and ended with a terrifying night in a Bangkok prison. One of their church brothers had indeed been taken in by a sleazy 'agent' who had promised to import the gun. I declined to offer my observation that if you can let some guru take you in, you can be taken in by anyone. I was still choking back the fact that these two charming creatures were members of a cult. Contradicting my earlier observation on religious discourse, the one topic I hoped to avoid was their spiritual beliefs. Despite my affection for the Schotts, I was dedicated to keeping some distance between us.

Amy poked at her *laab gai*. I wondered if we'd have to stop at Khao San Road after dinner to get her a piece of pizza. Anna sensed the culinary challenge as well—she called the waiter for some *phad thai* and chicken with peanut sauce. Amy slurped the bottom of a fruit smoothie. "One more please," she said.

A pair of variegated green eyes looked across at me. "You live in Thailand…"

"Yes," I said.

"And what do you do … when you're not saving women from prison?"

It was Anna's question but Amy's blue eyes looked at me with such innocent curiosity that I smiled. "I give boat tours to islands in the

Andaman Sea. Down where you're building an ashram."

Anna looked at me for a long beat. Time twisted as she broke ever so slowly into a subtle smile. "I read your essay—about the worms."

I was stunned. Speech eluded me long enough for Amy to ask if it was about worms I'd eaten. Anna laughed. "No, dear, these are evolving worms. He compared them to human culture."

"You read that?"

Anna nodded. Her lips found the straw in her gin and tonic and she took a drawn-out sip.

"How…?"

She was enjoying my shock, making me work for information.

"Dadaram asked me to read it. He wanted my opinion."

The essay was published in a university journal the summer after I'd done my honors thesis. It wasn't really about worms. It was about how human culture has dominant and recessive characteristics that work with a striking parallel to the mechanics and mathematical probabilities inherent in reproducing genes. The piece had won me a science prize and a bit of money. It seemed like a million years ago, another world away now. My stomach twisted uncomfortably. This was bizarre—and Anna knew that I was waiting for her opinion.

I wasn't about to ask for it. But Amy did. "Well, Anna?" she demanded on my behalf, or so it felt to me.

Anna took a long look at her sister. "It was brilliant." Amy beamed as if she was terribly proud of me. The guy who'd busted her out of prison had been validated.

Anna smiled at me softly. Again my stomach danced. I didn't know what the hell was going on.

&

Back at the Grand Lullaby Resort, I broke open a carton of Krung Thep and tore into a package of smokes. I'd been invited (or was it summoned?) to room 704, the temporary home of Anna and Amy Schott. I had offered them a moment to get settled before I came down. But as I drew in smoke almost unconsciously, I wondered if it wasn't me that needed the moment.

Who were these people that held fragments of my former life?

Anna welcomed me into their happy chaos. Her Highness was on the phone with Evan, and clothes were laid out everywhere. The suite was infused with the feeling of relief and jubilation that comes at the end of a stressful episode. Amy interrupted her conversation to ask about a lemonade. "It's been ordered," Anna said. She smiled at me in reference to her sister.

Their balcony had a better view than mine. Bangkok's lights twinkled in the humidity. Looking west, I could see the bigger boats moving on the Chaophraya. Anna came outside, handing me a beer. She smelled delicious. Something in her persona threatened to smash through my defenses like a slippery running back.

I tasted a mouthful of cold beer. "We're so grateful, Magnus … if there's anything I can do for you, I'd like to do it."

This is where my lower self malfunctioned. There are a couple of things that I should have been suggesting for a woman as compelling as Anna Schott. Instead I told her that it had been my honor.

"Oh," she said, remembering, "I asked Dada what the gun was for…" I looked at her. Just then Amy called me; she had Samuel on the line. Anna nodded subtly to indicate that I should take the call first.

Inside, Amy was holding out the receiver to me. My curiosity about the gun's purpose was like an itch that I couldn't scratch as I listened to Samuel gloat that Dadaram was right again; I had indeed been the man for the job. Amy's lemonade was ushered into the room, and I was forced into a stint with Evan as well.

When I was finally free, the sisters were waiting for me.

"So … what's the gun for?"

Amy stood in front of me with a mischievous smile. She was holding my former briefcase flat like a tray. I looked to Anna for a clue.

"Do you enjoy ironies, Mr. Larsen?"

I smiled. "I love them." Amy proudly lifted the lid of the briefcase.

I was silent. There was something askew, incomprehensible, about the image in front of me.

"We brought the gun for *you*," Anna said.

A strange little snake of terror shifted in my stomach—lying on a folded towel in between two orchids was the 9mm Glock handgun.

Amy smiled radiantly. "It's a gift from Dadaram."

Chapter Eight

A great buzz of chattering Thai women filled Bang Khen's morning visiting hours. An open room was the size of a gymnasium. We were divided from the inmates by a low wall that allowed communication. Bodies two and three deep crowded up to the barrier. Indigenous people from hill tribes like the Hmong and the Akha were disproportionately represented in the prison population. Just like in America, I thought, where in some states Native Americans were disproportionately incarcerated. I also saw a few rough white faces. Anna and Amy were fish out of water.

A large black woman stood out in the brown crowd. Unlike the women around her, she was alone, isolated by language, and you could feel her despair from a distance. Edwige Gbagbo was an Ivorian. She showed a flash of light when she saw Anna and Amy. As was the protocol, the sisters passed their bags of food and other supplies to a guard, who then gave it to Edwige. I faded to the rear of the grand scene and watched as Anna Schott spoke to a warden. The Thai warden was not only cognizant of Edwige's unique troubles but compassionate as well. Anna's donation enabled her to have fruit on a daily basis. Amy was as proactively loving as her older sibling. The Schotts had a communal quality as well as their individual attributes.

Jails are depressing. This place was horrible for them. It took guts to return to the scene of their sacrilege. Once again, I felt the strange sense of reverence.

For a moment I wondered if my exaltation of them wasn't simply a comparison to the degenerate company I kept in Ao Lai. But that theory didn't hold up—the degenerates weren't the only people I associated with. On my tours I met many wonderful folks with the relaxed glow of being on holiday.

Watching them that morning, I faced something else, something that seemed incongruous with awe and reverence: they struck a vaguely ominous chord within me. It had nothing to do with their characters—it was just a feeling that poked at me now and then, a cousin of the snake that had uncoiled in my stomach when I saw the gun. And I'm not scared of guns. Whatever that concern was, I couldn't articulate it. Little internal voices like that are hard to read; sometimes they end up meaning something, other times they mean nothing.

When the baleful feeling arose, I thought of my new gun, a non sequitur I still hadn't processed. How could they possibly have been bringing it for *me*? It didn't connect—*read a guy's essay, give him a gun?* Uh … no. I suspected Dadaram had invented that idea after the fact. Anna and Amy didn't question it. Which explained why they were in a cult and I wasn't.

I had a business waiting in Ao Lai, and despite the leanings of my lower self, I attended to it with discipline and respect. Thinking in that vein, we should've hopped the first train south. At least I should've. Instead I suggested the night train. I knew of a place in the *klongs*, the little canals off of the Chaophraya River, where farangs rarely went. We could get a boatman to give us a tour if they were up for it.

It was burning hot with drenched humid air as our little boat motored up the *klong*. Rundown junks and houseboats crowded the banks, and tightly packed slums overhung the waterway with multitudes of humanity, old and young. Garbage floated past islands of water-plants. For some stretches it was unpleasantly pungent. People were washing their clothes and their bodies in the filthy water. Dwellings were built of anything that worked, often corrugated scrap metal for roofs. Naked children wandered next to laundry that hung in lines of faded color.

Anna and Amy struck an image of colonial aristocracy as they floated through the rough squalor in their light clothes and wide-brimmed hats—but there was not a hint of condescension. They were transfixed by the pulsing, impoverished humanity, just as I'd been the first time I saw it. We shared the brown water with small boats so overloaded with bananas, sacks of rice and people that they were barely above water. This was not the colorful floating market in the tourist brochures, and there was no danger of confusion.

A teenage boy held his breath and dove underneath a boat in the putrid water to effect some repair. Anna gasped and said something about cholera. At one point, the rotting, bloated carcass of a dead pig floated past our boat. "That's why I never order fish in Bangkok," I told them. To Amy I added, "It's why I stick to rat."

Black plumes billowed into a blood orange sky as we chugged south through the smokestacks of industrial Bangkok. "It's pretty," Amy said, ignoring the poison.

The car wasn't crowded, and Anna and Amy could sit with me in 2nd class. The Thai trains segregated farangs from locals in 2nd class, and we were among a few low budget travelers. Anna wanted to know why I'd booked them a 1st class, air-conditioned sleeper while I'd chosen a lesser berth for myself. Truthfully, I preferred an open window to air conditioning. I declined to add that the pull of my lower self required that I toke up at least once a day; it was easier to be discreet in 2nd class. Anna told me that in future she would be traveling 2nd class as well. It seemed like a directive to *me*, though I couldn't see what future would find us traveling together again.

I refused to ask a single question about Dadaram. But he was a concept that was beginning to linger at the edge of my consciousness. He was out there, somewhere, a force in the unseen world. I didn't know if Dadaram was a name or a title. I knew nothing of what he preached. I didn't know if he was a brown man, a white man or a black man. I didn't know if he was Indian, American or Hungarian. Or Mongolian or Pakistani. I really only knew two firm facts about this entity. I knew his followers believed that he had magical healing powers, and I knew that he had given an essay I had written to Anna. The first fact indicated that he was a charlatan, the second was more mysterious. And harder to shake from my head. Oh yeah, there was something else I didn't know—whether or not Anna Schott was fucking him. I remembered Samuel's words, *They are the family of Dadaram.*

Anna peeled a banana. "Did you tell him about SUDS, Elf?"

Amy scowled and crossed a whining noise with a growl. I laughed; no word or phrase could have expressed a feeling so precisely.

"I'm sorry … I forgot." Anna explained, "She's too old to be called Elf." Amy chose to isolate herself from us by staring at the ground. Anna chose to ignore it.

"What's suds?"

SUDS (short for Stepping Up with Down's Syndrome), Anna explained, was an intensive four-month program for families with a high-functioning DS member; it taught a practical framework for people like Amy to live healthy, fulfilling lives.

"We were the poor cousins in that group," Anna said. Insurance and bursaries didn't begin to cover the hefty price tag, and I thought of my mom, a lifelong campaigner for public health care. She would've chafed at the program's limited availability.

"Without Dadaram's help, we never could've gone," Anna said.

There he was again … I had a momentary awareness of a 9mm

Glock pistol, wrapped in a towel, buried in a bag next to my smokes.

As our train chugged into a dark rural night, I lit a cigarette and began my lesson in trisomy 21, also known as Down's Syndrome. The chance of the mutation increases dramatically with older mothers. Anna was a first child when her mother was thirty. I'd taken some genetics. I should've remembered that Down's people have an extra 21st chromosome. Anna teased her sister sweetly. "Better one too many than not enough."

Amy seemed younger than her sixteen years and had a subtle speech impediment but otherwise communicated well. Anna attributed her exceptionally high function to their passionate and loving parents. Amy soon forgot the shame of being called Elf and was bubbling with memories of the SUDS program. She told of a boy named Richard Corrigan who had come in drunk and bitten a boy named Richard Rosenblatt. "He had to get a shot," Amy gushed.

Anna recalled it. "The poor kid had no support…"

"Richard the biter or Richard the bitten?" I asked.

"The biter," Anna laughed.

"Magnus, this is how he looked when he was mad." Amy was referring to the biter as she displayed a heck of a mean expression.

"The program was for the whole family, but his parents were some breed of nouveau gazillionaires with not a moment for their kids…"

Amy said, "I still have the shoes his parents bought me."

Anna explained, "The one day they showed, they took all the kids into Manhattan and bought them shoes." She shook her head at the weirdness of it.

Amy giggled. "When Richard got in the van…" She stopped her sentence short and plugged her nose. "Booze and marijuana," she said.

I started laughing. Anna gave me a deep look, not entirely kind.

"I know a bar in Ao Lai where this guy would fit right in," I said, trying to explain the flash of my lower self. I wasn't about to admit it here, but I kind of liked this Richard the biter. Of course, I'd have taken a rabies shot before I went drinking with him.

Heathen though I am, I decided to tear a commandment from the Bible and honor my mother and father. "I would like to inquire of Her Royal Highness, Amy Schott, the Princess of Massachusetts, as to whether or not this SUDS program accepts donations?"

Amy paused with a grin, and then looked to Anna who nodded.

"Yeah," Amy relayed.

"I wish to further inquire, Your Highness, as to whether I could place the donation with yourself?" Anna nodded again.

"Yes!" Amy echoed, her round face bursting with joy. The tax receipt was to be addressed to a Bill and Ingrid Larsen of Copper Creek, Oregon. The sisters were gracious and thankful as I wrote out the address.

The brawl broke out in the dining car when Anna discovered I was donating about fifteen hundred bucks, the remainder of the fee I'd gotten from their church.

We disembarked at Wamathani Station. Forty-five minutes later our taxi pulled up at the Montien Plaza Hotel in Ao Lai, the temporary home of The Children of a Living God. As soon as one devotee saw Anna and Amy, signals were beamed out, and the rest came pouring forth like ants from a hill, greeting them in a great happy lovefest. Samuel and Evan shook my hand and others thanked me as well. I figured I'd better scram before they started trying to convert me. I called goodbye to Anna and Amy, the great stars of the moment.

Anna extricated herself from the throng and Amy followed her. She faced me and said the simplest of goodbyes. Mine was no more complicated. "Goodbye, Anna."

Before I could say a word to Amy, she clutched her sister, pulling her into a whispered conversation. I waited for their private *téte-á-téte* to end. Anna looked at her sister. “Why don’t you ask him yourself?” Amy’s head turned down and away as she stared at the ground, reminding me of her moment on the train. I waited, but she didn’t move.

Finally, Anna did it for her. “She’s a little shy … she wants to know if she can have a hug.”

It was no ritual of politeness—Amy hugged the way she laughed, possessed by the moment, and I succumbed to the sweetness of genuine affection. I straightened up with an expectation that an embrace with Anna would follow. But she had chosen to be swallowed by her crowd. I touched Amy’s cheek, and her smile burned beautifully before I ducked back into the cab.

As I pulled away in the taxi, I reached over to my small canvas bag and discerned the shape of a gun.

I wasn’t offended, but I felt the sting of Anna’s choice.

Chapter Nine

"Magnus … what the fuck?"

I was down in the *Zenobia*'s galley when I smiled at the incredulous voice above. Kurt was a Californian about my age, just back from his tour of love duty. His days were filled with pot smoking and Thai girlfriends.

I rose to the deck with two beers. "Open the magazine, it holds seventeen."

Kurt shrugged, "I don't know a thing about..." He took a beer. "Great, alcohol and firearms, thank you."

Glancing around to ensure we were alone, I opened the clip, pointing out, "It's loaded."

Kurt couldn't take his eyes off the Glock. "Dude, this is *insane* … how did this guru even know who you are?"

I grinned. "I'm in all the guidebooks."

"What, he read in the *Lonely Planet* that a handgun makes a nice gift for a tour operator?"

Kurt was an extremely intelligent bum, and though our tastes in women diverged, we agreed on issues of human rights, individual liberty and U.S. foreign policy. We never went deep with personal stuff. Once, when I made some reference to the struggles within me,

Kurt said, "You're not as fucked up as I am." I sensed that there was a depth to that statement but we took it no further.

For the moment, I tucked the gun away in an alcove for lifejackets. He watched it go as if it was a piece of radioactive material.

"And what about this cult? Worth joining?"

I laughed. "We didn't go there. I'm not ready to give up earthly pleasures."

"Fuck no," said Kurt, pulling out a package of Thai stick. "You've got to be the *leader* of the cult—then it's all the peons you can bless and all the pussy you can eat."

I found myself vaguely disturbed by the notion of Anna being romantic with her guru, Dadaram. I banished the thought quickly—it was none of my business.

The following days

The change had come. Going home was no longer a concept or a dysfunctional imperative; it was now a plan, a fact. I would sell the *Zenobia* after the monsoon and return to America. When the seas became too violent for tours, I would face the cold turkey of quitting weed and cigarettes. I couldn't articulate the mechanics of my change of psyche, but I knew it had something to do with the experience of the Schott sisters.

Though tourists were beginning to thin out in Ao Lai, my Thai man, Mike, was still booking me two full tours a day. I planned to work like a dog until the storms came. A fierce need for sex burned and I ended up with a twenty-two-year old Londoner named Barbara I'd met on my boat. Like my early time in Ao Lai, I went days with little sleep, dancing at the Luna Bar, and then going to bed with Barbara. Physically it was great, but there was some part of my need, the bigger portion, that still hungered. With no disrespect to Barbara, I was glad when she left.

Guilt nagged at me for dropping my dinner date with Sally-Sue and not making amends or even communicating. My disappearance into the world of Barbara and the Luna Bar required more than a note. One late afternoon I dropped by the bungalow that she shared with Lindy, a little warily because I knew they were splitting up. The grapevine at the Biting Monkey had informed me that Lindy was soon headed back to LA.

Laundry hung roughly; *A Prayer for Owen Meany* was splayed open on a wooden table. We all sat on the porch, Lindy and I smoking; an odor of emotional fatigue lingered from inside the bungalow. It was such a small town, especially for expats—my fling with the English girl was common knowledge.

My feelings for Sally-Sue had shifted. The pure lust she evoked had somehow been diluted by the reality that we might really touch each other, really talk to each other. The fantasy was now flesh and blood, and she was no light undertaking—despite the vulgar quips and woman-of-the-world vibe, all her fragility was sitting next to me. My desire to fuck her brains out was now a desire to … maybe talk a little first.

If there was any other reason that my hunger for Sally-Sue had tempered, I wasn't about to acknowledge it. We agreed to find time for dinner soon.

I dropped into the Biting Monkey with partiers from my day tours. The drinks went down easily but I couldn't quite access my lower self. Bits and pieces of the ambience were like scenes from a living movie that I was walking through. The old boys—Lester, Franco, Arden, Stamp—were settled into their characters like seasoned actors. Charlene's latest boytoy slipped his tongue into her mouth. The short-lived ex, Robbin, was reeling under the weight of his drunkenness.

In another vignette, a Thai woman was telling her date, "You have drink, I have drink. You no drink, I no drink."

A vibrant scene at the bar showed Arnold Bukit, roaring like a lion, accompanied by two hookers, one with massive pump shoes that pulsed with battery-powered red lights. I bought bottles of whiskey and to Arden's delight kept all the glasses full, as if I was fueling up the great circus show around me.

A show with an expiration date.

Chapter Ten

Early light flooded the vast blue of a surprisingly calm sea. Birds and insects sang harmonies in warm, sweet air. It was the kind of day that pretended the monsoon wasn't coming. I squeaked down the gangplank to a nearly empty wharf; the fishing boats had left before dawn and were already mere dots on the horizon. As I hit the dock I saw it—

A great white colossus of a yacht was anchored less than a mile and a half north, offshore of the estuary of the Ban Lam River. Scrambling onto my boat, I got my binoculars. I was transfixed like a loinclothed primitive at his first sight of a great European armada. It screamed of luxury and insane wealth. It was not the type of vessel that ever came to Ao Lai. Phuket *maybe* … Bangkok Harbor *maybe* … but not here.

Later that night, the buzz in the Biting Monkey confirmed my suspicion: the guru Dadaram had arrived. Perhaps the yacht was his version of the twenty-eight Jaguars owned by the Bhagwan Shree Rajneesh.

Days went by and there was much talk but no celebrity sightings. It seemed that Dadaram did not deign to walk the streets of our humble town. There were no flashes of robes with regal divinity, no signs of a long rabbinical beard, nary a bejeweled turban—no one to thank for my new handgun.

The devotees had disappeared from the town itself. All that remained of them in the hot streets was the occasional ghost of an inspired hug, or a sublime burst of green eyes, or the fleeting recollection of a feeling of reverence.

As I went about my routine in those days I carried the sense that I was being observed. Like some kind of a laboratory specimen. Of course it was nonsense; if I looked around I would see that I was by myself or notice that there were no invading eyes. It was just a feeling.

Something about that great white boat sat in the pit of my stomach. Tourists and locals clustered on the shore to ogle it. I sensed some religious metaphor. Was it easier to be sold an idea when one had an iconic image? I thought of the great Catholic churches that the conquistadors had built in the Americas. How could the Indians not convert? Anna and Amy were connected to that boat. *They are the family of Dadaram.* I tried not to look. Who was I kidding? My curiosity was desperate.

I altered one of my tours to include the estuary of the Ban Lam River. As we passed by at a respectable distance, my heart pounded harder than was logical. She was called the *Aceso* and she was art, the kind that inspires awe. My tour group that afternoon was two German families comprised of three generations. The children squealed, the grandparents gushed. The parents gasped and babbled, and I knew the essence of everything that was said, though I don't speak the Deutsche. As they shared the binoculars I allowed myself glances. She was about 160 feet long and had svelte lines that represented her decks and the hull below. Next to this jewel, my sweet old converted fishing boat was a flea on a queen's leg. The Bhagwan's twenty-eight Jaguars were but a blip on the *Aceso*'s radar.

As we motored into the mouth of the Ban Lam, land was being cleared and a building erected. I saw Thai people and devotees. Happy and glowing. They were The Children of a Living God. I recognized some of them and waved as we passed.

May 10, 1992

One day after my tour, I was securing the last of the life jackets under the deck seats when the sensation of being watched arose again. I was learning to ignore it, but this time I felt vividly aware that I was not alone. Perhaps I'd heard footsteps on the dock, and when they ceased it triggered my awareness. If so, it was completely subconscious because the powerful feeling seemed to arise from nothing.

I turned around and there was a man on the dock, a white man, not six yards away. He had a potent physical presence and gray-blue eyes that were locked on me. But the strangest thing was the look on his face—as if he was trying to choke back the emotion of some incredible joy.

He said, "I'll be damned … it's Magic Larsen."

Part Two

Chapter Eleven

I laughed. "*Magic* Larsen … been a while since I've heard that."

I tried to place the man—he must've known me from my boyhood. I remembered all of my own teachers so I wondered if he wasn't one of my brother's. "I go by Magnus now," I said, drawn down onto the dock.

He extended his hand. "I'm Devon Clarke. It's a great pleasure to meet you, Magnus."

His grip was firm but the skin on his hand was soft and smooth. He sounded like he was from Massachusetts. I would've guessed early middle age but it was hard to tell. His clothes were as loose and casual as if he'd bought them in an open-air shop just off the beach in Phuket, but they had a quality that betrayed their origins. And there was something else … something that sat just beyond the realm of physical description: he looked *extraordinary*. As in a rare human being—as in someone that you don't encounter every day, someone with a light within himself. Or maybe it was a fire. And when I stood in his presence, I felt more present myself.

"No one calls you Magic anymore?"

"Not for a lifetime. 'Magic' lasted about five years. I switched back to Magnus when I was sixteen."

"I'm curious, I could ask why you switched to Magnus, or perhaps it's more telling why you went by Magic."

"I grew up in a rural county. Magnus was a little too exotic for some of the local bumpkins. And a girl in fifth grade started calling me Maggot."

"A girl with an overly creative mind. An early menstruator perhaps." He smiled. So did I. The air crackled with energy.

"How'd you know I was called Magic?"

"I dreamt it," he said.

I laughed. "So that's how it's gonna be, huh."

"Grant me a little mystery, Magnus." To that I had no reply. I felt Devon Clarke's eyes holding me center stage.

"I'm here to hire you. How should I go about that?"

"I'm booking till the weather changes."

"I've already got a boat. I need an advisor, someone to help out."

"I'm not sure what that means. But I'm busy until the monsoon."

"It means you come on board my boat for four or five hours a day and we find something for you to do. It pays 200 dollars a shift. Is that okay?"

I tried to process what I was hearing. Clarke read my confusion and smiled. Suddenly I had a dozen questions. I began with, "Where's your boat?" Devon Clarke gestured up the coast—to the *Aceso*.

I looked first at the great white yacht—then back to Devon. I was now struggling to digest something else.

"My parishioners speak very highly of you," he said.

"Your parishioners?"

"We're extremely grateful for what you did for us in Bangkok."

This guy *is the guru? It can't be,* I thought.

Devon read my face. "I've really got to get a dot. Right there." He tapped his forehead.

"You're the man? You're Dadaram?"

"Maybe when you're advising me you can help pick out a robe … something that says 'Holy Man.'" He was teasing me. This guru, faith healer, Devon Clarke, Dadaram, was teasing me.

I couldn't help myself. "You're the *faith healer*?"

"I've never said I was a faith healer."

"Your followers think so."

"They call me Dadaram, you call me Devon."

"I'm not religious. I don't join faiths or any groups."

Clarke stared at me plainly. "There's a couple of things you need to know: number one, I'm not a homosexual. Number two, this isn't Amway or the Moonies. I have nothing to sell and I don't proselytize."

"Your offer is awfully generous," I said, explaining my wariness.

"Are you a communist? A peasant? Each shift you can earn either 200 dollars or a bag of rice. Your choice."

He was both ominous and exhilarating. I began seeing him as Anna's lover… He was attractive. He was disturbing. I liked him. I could see why he had followers. But what was it? What was that *something else*? Where was the booby prize hidden?

As I agreed to work for him, his gray-blue eyes lit with an intense joy. A trickle of excitement moved through me. Not that I was about to sign up for any of the hocus-pocus. A dynamic force seemed to run through his hand as we locked on our new agreement.

By the time he'd left the dock, I realized that I'd forgotten to mention the handgun.

Chapter Twelve

On my first morning off, I met Devon Clarke amid the bustle of construction on the banks of the Ban Lam River. Here, he was the guru Dadaram, a living god who had descended from his great white floating palace to walk among mortals. His charisma was fierce. Again I felt the smoothness of his hand as he welcomed me.

I could see nothing immediately phony about Dadaram, just that the persona was different from that of Devon Clarke. Alone with me, he was all Devon. He laid out the tough ground rules of my employment. "There's nothing you can do to get fired."

"Nothing?"

"That's right, Magnus. Nothing. You can say anything you want to me, no censorship or deference is required."

"And you're not gay?"

"You're fired, asshole."

A guru with a sense of humor. Intrigued, I still had no idea what this so-called job was about. Devon, or rather Dadaram, assigned Mariel as the guide for my morning tour, a kind of meet-and-greet around the rapidly developing ashram. She was about forty and dressed in the loose, breezy clothes you might see in a yoga retreat.

I found myself pleasantly aware. Mariel led me through lush foliage accented with translucent greens as it filtered the sun. Birds chirped and hollered, unwilling to take second position to the noise of human toil. Most of the work was applied to the main structure of the ashram. "If we leave," Mariel explained, "the building will convert easily into a local school."

I was introduced to all of the devotees that I hadn't met. They varied in age; a few had children, and some could've passed as Mormons. Others, like Mariel, had a new-age look. Had they been geographically separated, I never would've guessed they were all in the same religious order. Seeing them together, it was clear they were bonded by joy and by their labor. Here among their brethren, even Samuel and Evan looked looser and happier. These were The Children of a Living God.

In my mind I humorously compared them to my friends at the Biting Monkey, whose beings were battered by day's early light. I could see Lester's shaking hands as he poured whiskey into his coffee, Franco lining up his shots at the bar and Arden yearning like a hungry dog for *anything* to forget his pain. Here, there was light and joy and energy in working muscles.

I knew that Anna Schott could appear before me at any time. Each time the thought flashed, I felt a rip of excitement that I found totally annoying. As a mental exercise, I practiced substituting Sally-Sue immediately when Anna's image arose. As it turned out, neither of the Schott sisters appeared to be on the construction side of things. Likely a benefit of being *the family of Dadaram,* as Samuel had once described them.

The most fascinating and disturbing observation I had that morning was of Devon Clarke himself. I found myself drawn to him even from a distance. He mingled with devotees who broke from their tasks to share a moment with him, always deferentially I noticed, often with heads slightly bowed. I saw no arrogance in their guru; rather he seemed to reflect their joy, come to life in their happiness for the moment that he faced them. And vice versa; they glowed in the light of their leader.

It was like a chemical process where both parts were required for a reaction to take place. When the meeting broke, the devotees seemed charged up with joy—but alone, Devon looked empty.

Mariel caught me staring at him from a distance and gently tried to pull me along. I didn't budge. Devon performed a couple of simple tasks, jotting something in a small notebook, and then going to a basin of water, where he splashed his face. He looked more than sad ... more than empty ... his darkness was vivid. As if the very light around his face had changed. As if some holocaust had eaten out his guts. I was seeing a negative, the inverted image of the man I had met on the wharf. I was gripped, frozen—staring without concern for politeness.

Suddenly Devon looked up from his basin, straight into my eyes—and a joyous, electrifying smile jolted me. The other Devon was back. I felt my heart pound. Yes, it was that weird.

The day deepened into a hot blue sky.

Devon Clarke took me through all three levels of the *Aceso*. The class and elegance before me squelched out all other thoughts. She was completed in 1966, and Devon said that her design had never since been improved upon. Agape at rich floors of tropical hardwood, the high ceilings of the staterooms and the sensuality of the decks, I was in no position to argue. The rooms could easily accommodate all forty-five members of the little cult. There was a spa with a Jacuzzi on the second level. The kitchens were made for chefs. The *Aceso* was one sexy girl.

Each of the previous three owners had put their stamp on her. The grand wine cellar of the original French family had survived every renovation. Perhaps the most apropos contribution of the founder of The Children of a Living God was a spacious ashram on the middle deck. She was called *Diana* when Devon obtained her at an auction; a Taiwanese businessman had fallen on hard times.

Devon took great pleasure in telling me about the sacrilege that the second owner, a Saudi prince, had inflicted upon the boat. "He painted the logo of the Miami Dolphins on each side of the hull." I shook my head in disbelief. "What a prick," Devon said, adding, "I can see the Patriots, but the fucking *Dolphins*?"

I howled.

Devon introduced me to a devotee cleaning one of the observation decks. John was a white-haired Englishman, wearing a sarong, with a smear of Hindu blessing on his forehead. I referenced Devon's fun with me on the dock, remarking that Dadaram could do with a more spiritual appearance himself. John looked at me squarely. "*You* call him 'Devon,' don't you?" It was an odd moment. It wasn't so much a question as a reprimand. They already knew about me. Huh. Imagine that...

The potent energy of Devon Clarke felt like a wind next to me. We ascended the stairway to the highest deck like the breath of a yogi into the upper chakras.

The guru led me into his lair. A crescent moon of a living room, slightly sunken, was surrounded by decks. I stepped down into art that seemed plundered from the great galleries of the world. Rich furniture was stolen from the pictures of a magazine, except for the coffee cups, clothes and the towel that lay uncollected, the stuff you don't see in *Better Homes and Gardens.*

Outside, each vast space luxuriated with its own personality; one was sheltered by a garden fortress of exotic trees and cultured plants, twisting and bursting with color and shape. Another was naked and open to the sky, save for the umbrellas on the deck chairs that fringed the turquoise swimming pool and the red tile of a hot tub. Here, one could cool off in the tropics or bubble in hot mineral water under cold stars on the Baltic Sea.

The ship's bridge was masterfully integrated so as not to disturb the higher residents.

Devon spoke little as we stood by the pool. He watched as my eyes swept beyond the circular shape of the living room to French doors that connected the hedonism of the decks to bedrooms. I'm not often awed by displays of wealth, but I stood amid an exception. This wasn't showing off—it was a triumph of art and design. Of human endeavor. A glory.

Back inside, Devon and I discussed my schedule. Such was the power of the *Aceso* that I was caught off guard by a voice I'd heard before. "Guess who's back in your life, Princess?"

From somewhere more distant, I heard Amy say, "Who?"

Despite the annoying tickle of adrenalin, my smile opened easily as I turned around. The simmering splendor that was Anna Schott dropped a stack of books onto a dining room table just above us. She was barefoot in a slinky burgundy dress.

Devon said, "He's back in your life too, Anna." They seemed to share a beat of something between them—a communication that was not necessarily pleasant, or perhaps just complicated. I found it vaguely disturbing.

The feeling quickly passed with the arrival of Her Royal Highness, Amy Schott, the Princess of Massachusetts. Her face lit up as she squealed with delight, and lucky me, I got a hug without anyone having to ask for it.

Anna and I exchanged warm pleasantries. Humans really do survive on bullshit. Oceans of passion roar within us and we filter it down to friendly chat with just the right amount of warmth. At that point in time, Amy was the most honest person in the room. Devon hadn't revealed an inkling of what he was really up to, I wasn't about to tell Anna what exactly she did to me or what exactly I'd like to do to her, and she wasn't about to spill her frightened guts onto the expensive floor. Instead, we all discussed a book that Anna and Amy were reading together for the second time. Anna asked Amy to tell me the theme. Amy recited that it was about how Love can conquer. It was *A Wrinkle in Time* by Madeleine L'Engle, and I remembered reading it as a seventh grade assignment. Even then the buds of my cynicism were starting to show. I had told Mr. Doyle that the book was good but the ending—which was about Love—was sucky.

Amy was schooled by Anna, Dadaram and others who could contribute to her formal and artistic education. It was decided that I would help Amy out with science lessons. "Proper science," Devon instructed. "Don't start telling her about worms and their cultural attributes."

I knew I was taking the bait. "Excuse me, what I expressed, is that human culture has dominant and recessive characteristics that are similar to genes." Devon smiled, delighted that he'd pulled my chain. Anna seemed to enjoy it as well. Amy was smiling too, probably just because they were.

That pretty much concluded my first day's orientation. Samuel piloted the small boat that ferried me out of the *Aceso*'s grand shadow and back to the shore. A tough day at the office, I thought. A job that I couldn't get fired from. Hanging with the sisters Schott. Two hundred bucks a day for sweet fuck-all. That in itself should've been a red flag.

Chapter Thirteen

Devon had chosen the upper deck garden as our meeting place. A large standing fan spun in near silence, moving air through our section of furniture and gently vibrating the large leaves of the garden's plants. The eyes of my new employer were upon me.

"Start from the beginning. Start with your birth."

"You're kidding."

"Actually, begin before your birth. What were your parents up to? Who are they?"

"Let me explain something ... when someone starts jabbering on about their life, you say, 'Don't give me your life story.' As in, quit boring me."

A smile grew on Devon's face. "I'm astounded at what a godsend you are. I even get tips in social etiquette." I shook my head. Devon called into the open doors of the suite. "Anna ... can you get Amy? Magnus is about to begin his life story..."

I asked—again with disbelief, "So you want to hear, 'I was born in a small town in northern California, about nine days prematurely, to a Bill and Ingrid Larsen...?'"

"Save it," Devon commanded. "Our ladies aren't here yet." As if they would miss the beginning of a great film.

Anna arrived with a pitcher of lemonade and the bright smile of her little sister. As they settled, Anna poured a glass for Amy.

"Do you remember the book Daddy read to you from at home, *Tales of the Arabian Nights*?"

Amy searched.

"The storyteller, Scheherazade?" Anna prompted.

"Oh yes," Amy chirped.

"Magnus is our Scheherazade," said Anna.

The concept was as sweet to Amy as it was sadistic to me.

"Go back to that part you just said," Devon instructed.

Three sets of eyes focused in on me. Anna said, "Popcorn would be perfect." I looked into her dark sunshine, not sure if she was intending to torment me.

It turned out that the beginning of my life wasn't that boring after all. The audience of three asked questions, which led to discussions, then to anecdotes, and sometimes humor. A story about my dad pulling me on a sled, one of my earliest memories, had Amy and Anna reminiscing about their past as well. It's amazing how large the pool of memories can be when you get into them. By the time we reached the third year of my life, it was really more of a structured discussion than my own story.

Devon hung on my every word. It was ironic, because he was the one that was fascinating.

I was back in my familiar world by the hour that Dadaram and The Children of a Living God gathered for 'temple.'

On my porch, my cigarette was accompanied by a cold beer. I wrote a long, positive letter to my mom and dad. My decision to leave Thailand was laid out; I expected to see them in September. I knew they'd be thrilled.

I went through some practical issues in my head—even the nasty one—picking a date to begin cold turkey.

Evolution is not always the gradual process documented by Darwin; modern observation has shown us that it's often long, even periods punctuated with sudden and massive change, wherein natural selection is augmented by the steroidal effect of mutation. And that's what I could sense on my porch that late afternoon—the massive transformation that was about to hit my life. I'd been a tour operator for five years. I'd smoked cigarettes and marijuana daily for nearly six. Whether I found myself in a classroom, or behind a desk with a tie on, or living at my parents' unemployed, change was a comin'.

Of course, the change that was really coming to me was unimaginable at that point.

I would miss my porch. I lit a joint and sank into my chair. The great sky turned purple and orange, and flashes of white pulsed into the horizon. The guru's image gripped me. I replayed the strange moment where he'd looked up from the basin. It twisted my stomach. I couldn't stop thinking about Devon Clarke.

It frustrated my Thai man, Mike, that I wouldn't book two tours daily as the season was winding down. I was the only operator in Ao Lai who could pull that off. But each afternoon I would race over to the wan, sweaty jungle at the estuary of the Ban Lam River, where a new ashram was developing like a Polaroid picture. The Children of a Living God applied paint and finishing touches. The humidity wilted bodies but their resilience glowed.

Usually Samuel would ferry me out to the *Aceso*. His smile was white against his shiny black skin, and my association with Dadaram had given me an unearned credibility.

Devon's charisma burned. I climbed the hanging walkway to the deck, and he loomed above me in his white Panama hat like a seasoned star from old Hollywood. As we rose to his private quarters I felt as if his arm was around me. "We've been discussing your life, Magnus."

"Oh Jesus," I said, laughing.

As the days progressed, my life story continued, leading to ever more boisterous discussions. We sat in plush chairs shaded by the dripping opulence of the *Aceso*'s gardens. Intermittently, a devotee brought refreshments to Dadaram and his family and emptied my ashtrays. I jabbered on about my childhood as chronologically as I could. Devon's gray-blue eyes felt like a spotlight. His focus bolstered me and put me on stage as a storyteller.

Amy's questions were bold and innocent. Why was my third grade teacher, Miss Smithson, the only person with colored skin in my home town? After I'd looked for a simple answer, she wanted to know, "Was Miss Smithson pretty?" I recalled that her teeth were big. "Why do you smoke so much?"

"I'm addicted to tobacco. I don't feel good when I don't smoke."

Amy was on a tear. "Do you think Anna is pretty?"

"She's more than pretty," I said with factual dryness.

"Thank you," Anna said quietly, probably because politeness required it. Devon and Amy were both beaming. As the princess leapt into her next query, Anna cut it short. "That's enough, let him talk."

Anna was reserved with me, as I was with her. Most of our communication was filtered through Devon or Amy. I felt the élan that pulsed under her skin. Sometimes I sensed she was studying me, seeking a clue to something. I wondered, was the green-eyed consort of the guru Dadaram a wife or a concubine? What was her story? I could see Devon's attractiveness as a man, his obvious success ... but didn't one need to offload some of their gray matter to become a devotee?

Rather than becoming inured to the charm of my new friends, I fell deeper under their spell. The first four days were so dense that they felt like a month of my life.

As discussions bubbled and flowed, I yearned to know more of Devon Clarke. I had only the most cursory details: he'd been a surgeon and married for twenty-three years. I wanted more. Every time I inquired, I was reminded that my own story wasn't yet told.

Devon and I couldn't take our eyes off each other. I knew what I saw in him—but what did he see in me? It was awful rich fun—but what was it *really* about? Why my life story? Was he looking for a way to convert me? Trying to find that crack of vulnerability that would bring me to my knees at the altar of The Children of a Living God? Was I that kind of a challenge?

Even early on, I knew there was something he wasn't telling me.

And always lurking nearby was an image that was seared into me—it was of the other Devon, the man I saw at the water basin that first day—the being who looked every inch the walking dead.

My curiosity was rising like a hot sun in the east.

During my nights away from the *Aceso*, I was frustrated not to find Kurt; the guy was once again gone like a ghost. Of my friends in Ao Lai, he was the only one with whom I could process intellectually. I craved to chew through the mystery of my perplexing new job with someone. I dared not ask any of the local girls about him lest they burst into tears with a broken heart.

Chapter Fourteen

Afternoon on the *Aceso* began with an examination of Amy Schott's art papers. Her almond-shaped eyes followed me as I circled the dining room table, layered and strewn with her creations of chalk and acrylic. Mariel, the woman who had shown me around on my first morning, was her teacher, and she was watching me as well. I adjusted each piece individually and appraised it from different angles.

Amy was bursting, waiting for me to say something, and I think Mariel was too. So I took my sweet time. Amy began to make her horrible little noise—the whine-growl I'd heard on the train when Anna called her 'Elf.' I started to laugh.

"You don't like them!" was the accusation that was hurled. But I knew that there was still hope in her heart.

"I find that they have the simplicity of Chagall and the richness of Van Gogh." (I hoped they were both painters.) "Is that what you were trying to achieve?" I asked the young artist with the rounded cheeks.

For a second, she held her breath like she wasn't sure. Mariel told her it was a wonderful review. Amy lit up. I'd earned myself an original artwork. I chose a woman whose brightly colored hair resembled the leaves of a potted plant in the same canvas.

Anna swept into our presence. "Mommy's on the line, princess."

Amy rushed off. "I just cut a deal with my parents—she's mine till September," Anna tossed out lightly. Mariel was gathering up Amy's art. When she left, Anna took a breath and asked cheerily, "Would you like to see our bedroom?"

A crass person might've said, "Why the hell would I want to see the place where you fuck someone you call Dada? So I can imagine you naked on the bed?" But I'm not crass, so instead I replied in a neutral voice with a hint of pleasantness, "No, thank you."

Unfortunately, Anna reacted as if I'd said the first one. There was a moment of silence. "Did I say something wrong?"

"Not at all," I said. I was getting to know my way around and I moved into the kitchen for a glass.

Anna stood in the dining room. "I'm sorry, I thought you liked architecture ... Dada said you enjoyed some of the design he showed you."

"I do. I just don't feel like it right now." I dropped ice cubes into my glass. I could feel Anna staring at me.

"It seems like I said something wrong."

"No … I hope I didn't project that," I said calmly, pouring water over my ice.

Anna again took a long assessment of me. "I'll tell Dada you're here."

"He knows … I'll be in the garden." I moved past her politely and went outside. A moment later, she was with me.

"If it's ... *inappropriate* ... to offer to show you our bedroom, please tell me."

"Who said *that*?" I asked, aware of how ridiculous our conversation had become.

"It's a beautiful room. That's why I suggested it." My guilty pleasure was to enjoy the fire in her fractured eyes.

"Okay … let's go look," I said.

"I thought you didn't want to."

"You're not willing to let go of that fact, so let's go look."

There was a moment of silence. With Anna there was always the danger of feeling something deeper and more intense than I wanted to.

"No … not like that."

I looked at her a moment too long. I felt chastised. It wasn't just her beauty; that was savage enough—but a fragile essence of her being stood delicately before me.

"Dada wants us to be friends."

The words hung in the air. "Why would he want that?"

She looked vulnerable, even ashamed. "He hasn't said."

Book of Devon 7

April 27, 1986

It was a sunny Sunday morning. Alicia Fitzroy was on her knees preening her prize roses when she heard a *pop!*—or was it a *bang?* She lifted the brim of her wide hat and looked toward the Clarke house just beyond her own. It wasn't the loudest noise in the world but it made her uneasy. For a moment she wondered if she shouldn't walk over and knock on the door. But no more hard sounds breached the gentle day, and she turned back to her roses.

Minutes later, Alicia heard sirens rising in the distance. It wasn't long before she stood gripping her shears as emergency vehicles pulled onto the grounds next door. She saw the Clarkes' maid open the door to the police and paramedics.

They found the surgeon in his den, on the floor, his five-year-old son's head in his lap, the mouth slack and open, a tiny single-shot Flobert pistol, an antique, lying nearby. Dr. Clarke looked catatonic. There was hardly a drop of blood.

The little boy's name had been Roger Justin Clarke. Roger was wearing a shirt with a picture of Mickey Mouse that his grandmother had given him.

Chapter Fifteen

One afternoon in mid-May, Anna declined to join us and Amy had classes. Her words, *Dada wants us to be friends,* echoed inside of me. My stack of questions grew, but with Devon there was a potency to the present. I wanted to talk about the gun he'd given me—he wanted to talk about Magic Larsen.

And it was here, while we were alone, that yet another layer of his personality emerged. Bathed in the spotlight of Devon Clarke's attention, I was eleven-year-old 'Magic.' Amy may have giggled when Cindy Bergen first called me Maggot—but when I was alone with Devon, he dug into my socio-economic roots.

I came from a family farm in a small Oregon community. My dad was elected to local agricultural boards, and he was known as a man who could be trusted. As a little league coach, he was at least part of the reason why my younger brother, Jason, went to George Fox University on a baseball scholarship. Intelligence based upon common sense—that was my dad.

Then there was Mom, the political dynamo. Though she always said she was a farmer first, during my childhood she often worked as a nurse. She could've been a teacher but figured it was easier to jump in and out of hospitals than schools. A left-wing Democrat, she believed in an

America with equal opportunity for all, and that included socialized medicine. My audience of one reacted. It was as if I'd rubbed a magic lamp and an American businessman suddenly appeared.

With the sisters away, Devon's persona was furthest from Dadaram. At this point, I knew very little about Dr. Clarke. I hadn't a clue that he was connected to the national chain of Clarke Surgical Centers, much less the co-founder. I was subjected to an eloquent speech about how and why socialized medicine would degrade healthcare in America. I could just see my parents cringing.

Arguing with Devon's words was one thing, but he had a rhythm and bearing to the way he spoke that implied credibility, *correctness*, a kind of Ivy League lilt that made him seem learned. Even when he was full of shit.

Our little farm went through tough times in the late 1970s, and we probably couldn't have kept it if Mom hadn't worked. Today she was an administrator at a private hospital.

"A *private* hospital?" Devon asked, enjoying the horror of a socialist in such a place. It wasn't always easy coming from a rabidly Democratic family in a Republican county, but I respected my parents and they'd passed on many of their values. In our home, *Roe vs. Wade* was a triumph and a woman's right to choose was sacrosanct.

"In a future with ultrasound and abortion rights, people like Amy won't exist. Are you in favor of that?" Before I could respond to that poke in the eye, he jumped in with, "Is your mother in favor of that?"

"Let's leave my mom out of it."

"That's what you get when you cross socialism with abortion rights," he stated as if he was addressing a class at Harvard.

My mom's brain would've popped if she could hear this guy. We flared into debates and arguments all afternoon. Sometimes Devon was clear and eloquent, other times I think he was just trying to rile me up. On a wide-ranging trip through my family's political background, we found a spot of mutual relief—at my mother's expense.

I recounted a time when my mom had found a poli-sci essay among my things and was thrilled to see I'd gotten 100 percent on it. She had no permission to touch it, much less read it. But beaming with pride at my stellar mark, she took it upon herself to ... have a little peek. The basic gist of it was that the policies of Margaret Thatcher and Ronald Reagan toward the Soviet Union were banging away at the iron curtain, and if sustained, could lead to the end of the Cold War. Well, I can assure you that by the end of that essay her pride had turned to horror.

"It served her right!" Devon laughed.

"She couldn't believe I was her son. She wanted to go to the campus and face off with the professor." I recalled how royally pissed I was. Devon's delight was irrepressible.

But mostly we argued. Social programs were anathema to Devon Clarke. And he caught me completely off-guard when he referenced Franco, the rasping alcoholic at the Biting Monkey.

"Take your friend, Mr. Connelly ... courtesy of Canadian taxpayers he's in a bar getting drunk all day..."

Something was amiss. "You know him?"

Devon continued, "It's a two-part question: are the taxpayers getting their money's worth, and is Mr. Connelly getting value from his life?"

"It's a one-part question—how do you know him?"

Light was leaving the air. Devon's face was grayer. For the second time in a day I was at a moment that I was struggling to process. "I don't know him personally," Devon said. "People tell me…"

I rose with concerns that wouldn't articulate. I guess it wasn't a big deal that he knew of Franco. Or was it?

"Magnus … what's wrong?"

"How did you know I was called Magic? How did you find my essay?"

"Your essay is published."

I took a breath. "Tell me about the gun."

"What's there to tell?" Devon shrugged. "We brought you a gun."

"You were not bringing that gun for me," I said forcefully.

The powerful presence replied calmly, "You're welcome to believe what you like."

I felt an unease that teetered on panic. "Why am I here, Devon?"

"You're here for the same reason that Anna and Amy are here—you're extraordinary." *Extraordinary.* That was a word I could've used about Devon. I had trouble applying it to myself. I didn't know what to say.

"You're obviously concerned—have we tried to draw you into our fold? Drag you to temple?" He attempted humor. "Have we breached your atheism with our vulgar spirituality?"

"There's something you're not telling me."

"You have a destiny that's not related to tour-guiding."

His words were a kick in my guts. "You're speaking guru, Devon. Feel free to be less evasive."

He knew I was wounded. "You're not ready to understand," he said as kindly as he could.

As daylight faded, Devon walked me to the hanging stairs, where I met Samuel with the skiff.

"There are no chains here, Magnus. We're a family. I know I speak for Anna and Amy as well when I say we all love you." He hugged me for the first time. As I embraced him I was careful not to wrinkle the picture that Amy had given me.

Samuel pointed out a ravishing sunset as he ran me back to the shore. Devon's words played back in my head. "*You're not ready to understand...*"

I should have told him to go fuck himself.

Chapter Sixteen

I moved like a foreign invader through the hallways of the *Aceso*'s private luxury. It was quiet and eerie, removed from the world beyond. Where was Anna? I wanted to find her before Devon and I resumed our verbal stances. I didn't want to leave any open wounds between us, certainly not for her.

I finally found her outside, tucked away in a little alcove, reading. She was stretched on a chair, her hair dripping onto her summery fabric. She glanced at me from a distance and immediately returned to her book. I swallowed my nerves and approached. Humility was mustered.

"Any chance for a tour of the bedroom?" She glanced at me coolly before turning back to her pages. "Please," I said.

She gestured back toward the interior. "Follow the tile to the wood and turn left." I watched her for a moment as she ignored me.

"I think Dadaram would prefer if you showed it to me yourself."

Anna responded at once, dropping her book. "Come on." She was already in motion. Immediately, I regretted what I'd said. I chased her inside, down a hallway.

"Anna ... stop."

She stopped on the tile, barefoot under a skylight. She stood open and scared without a hint of complaint about her position. "People can't be ordered to be friends."

"Dada is very, very special. You don't seem to know that."

Actually I did. The one thing that kicked you right in the face when you met Devon Clarke was that he was special. Sunshine from above hit her sun-streaked hair, warming her cheek and shoulders. It was so easy to imagine kissing her, sliding her dress up over hips... Then she moved, sashayed—I followed her lithe form through double doors of carved black teak.

A slight descent brought us into a sumptuous room. Anna's dress was a muddy green, casual as a rag, and yet … with her hair and eyes … it was too perfect. I noticed she was speaking. "See ... it's the design I wanted to show you..."

The room was a sublime integration of shape and sensuality, a royal bed the starring feature (non-human feature, that is). Anna pushed a wall covered in art; it parted to reveal a great tiled bath that looked out over the sea. She showed me sophisticated lighting, with choices to delight the moods of lovers, and the lovers of moods.

She fell into her role and began discussing the art on the walls as if she were a curator in a fine gallery. Her voice felt like a sip of rich coffee. She spoke of 'art deco' and 'cubism,' of Paris in the twenties. Suddenly she turned on me: had I heard of Paul Klee or Tamara de Lempicka? Uh … couldn't say I had.

The room had a stillness. A radiance seemed to flicker from within her cheeks, around her eyes. Time slowed down. "Have you heard of *Pablo Picasso*?"

"Didn't he used to play for the Boston Bruins?"

She assessed me for long a moment. Her irises fractured into verdant tiles—noticeable when light hit them. Her lips were dark and luxuriant. An undercurrent of vulnerability and excitement charged the distance between us. Finally, she smiled ever so slightly. "You're a fool," she said. "He played for the Celtics."

I felt her studying me. The spotlight was both harsh and pleasing.

I wondered what she was looking for. "You're a worm expert … of all things." I was being teased, provoked I think. We both laughed.

Her bare legs were two feet from the bed. "See," she said. "I haven't attacked you."

There were a dozen witty responses. "No," I said.

It would be an understatement to say that I was uncomfortable with just how attractive I found Anna. Beyond any logistics of becoming her lover, there was the moral issue. She was Devon's love, Devon's woman. I was his invited guest. And just because I felt a sparkle between us, it didn't mean that there was for her. I had a very clear sense that she worshipped Devon, or *Dada* as she preferred. I decided the best course of action would be to avoid her. Not rudely, but just to find a little distance. You can't burn your eyes if you don't stare at the sun. That was my thinking.

Another element to buffering myself from her would be found away from the *Aceso*, back in my own world. I decided to take the following day off.

I was in the upper deck garden when the wizened devil appeared, holding hands with Amy Schott. They blasted me with smiles. I was thrilled to be there. My little panic attack of the day before was over. I thought *Really—who gives a shit why I'm here? If Devon wants to play his little game of intrigue, let him.* I knew that part of being a guru was being a conman. As Devon said, there were no chains—I could leave anytime I wanted to. Our conflicts had drawn us closer together.

Anna joined us briefly then left with Amy. I'd come to a point in Magic Larsen's life that wasn't always family entertainment. Devon drew me deeper into my sometimes troubled teenaged history. As always, our sessions terminated when Devon needed to become Dadaram and conduct 'temple' for The Children of a Living God. This day I agreed to hang around and join the entire family afterward for dinner.

We ate at long tables on the banks of the Ban Lam with citronella torches burning to keep the insects at bay. Amy's idea of fun was to open her mouth after she'd chewed her food, giving me a look inside. An elbow from Anna ended the practice, and Amy giggled at her own evil. They all looked so happy in the flickering light.

Chapter Seventeen

Phase two of my plan to inure myself to the charms of Anna Schott was not going well.

I was ready to kill Sally-Sue Bronson. Yes, I was laughing, but killing her was still an option. There I was only moments earlier, sitting outside amid her hanging underwear when she'd delivered my good news. "You're going to be famous!"

"How so?" I asked calmly, allowing her to hog the thrill of my success.

"You're in my show!"

Remember Sally-Sue's one-woman show—the work she was developing for the fringe festivals of the world? The masterpiece-in-progress wherein she compared her life in Ao Lai with her life in LA? The one in which her cultural statement would shine from Edinburgh to Los Angeles? That one.

She was reading from a clutch of papers that she had snatched from the disarray of her bungalow. She flipped her hair back in a horrible approximation of yours truly. Her voice had changed. "Imagine this, Sally-Sue—my drink is in one hand, my smoke in the other ... one girl is sucking my dick while the others are dyking out on the bed..."

I was dying with laughter but my protests never stopped as Sally-Sue continued doing *me*. "You haven't lived until you've fucked five girls at once ... you've gotta come join my next party ... you like pussy, don't you?"

When I imitate someone, I have the decency to do a good job of it. I rose from my seat on her porch, pushing past a piece of hanging laundry to inform her, "We're doing a little editing, Sally-Sue."

She shook her head, aglow with her power over me. Her hair was wild, her shorts and top didn't match.

I protested, "People will think I was serious..."

"You didn't care if *I* thought you were serious, did you?" she shrieked with delight.

"I'll have to sue you."

"Good! I need the publicity!"

I chased her into her room. A tussle ensued as I tried to take the script. She retreated to a bed in which the sheets shared space with a sarong, a blouse, two books, bug lotion, skin cream, sunglasses, notebooks, pens and a fruit called mangosteen. We came to an impasse as her body protected her work. My face touched her skin by her shoulder.

"I've got everything on this bed but a banana." She giggled suddenly. When she stopped, I moved into her lips and kissed her lightly. She knew that I was going to do it again.

Chapter Eighteen

I found yet a new mood in Devon as I moved deeper into my teen years. He watched me with such intensity that it felt like a probe inside my body. Each time I lit a cigarette, he was a mirror that reflected my weakness, my inferiority as a human being. Dislike it as I did, it never stopped me from lighting up. I was addicted, and in the presence of stimulation like Devon, putting them down didn't seem achievable. I always felt a sense of judgment. Whether it was coming from him or me, I didn't know.

Mike began scheduling my daily tour for the afternoon as often as possible.

Mornings were steeped in the light, rich wonder of life at the ashram. The building was raised to survive the rising river that the monsoon would bring. The Children of a Living God decorated their new temple with color and artistry. Though I was only an observer, I felt a vicarious pleasure in their joy.

I wanted to understand their beliefs. We stood by the river amid the buzz and sizzle of cicadas when I assured Devon that I wasn't trying to sign up for anything. His face lit with amusement. "Of course not. You're a scientist." Mariel was assigned to speak with me. Was this the recruitment routine?

Mariel explained that the essence of their practice was to celebrate, honor and enrich the human spirit, or soul. They recognized an individual aspect to spirituality, in which each person required a unique framework to reach their spirit and bring it into their lives. It mattered not if one was Christian or Hindu—what was important was touching the essence within, the eternal, the soul, and living each moment with its joy.

The parallel value held that there was a communal element to spirituality; in this they sang and chanted and honored and shared each other's path. Mariel spoke of Dadaram as a divine being. She had seen him heal. She had once suffered from a skin condition that disappeared in his presence. Each devotee had been drawn to the guru through unique circumstances that could not be explained by mere coincidence. Dadaram had an ability to reach inside a person and help them find a path, *their* path. That's what they believed.

Once, after a night of rain, I arrived at the river as a soft fog filtered up through the jungle. Devon Clarke stood on the patio of the new ashram amid the rising mist, a noble figure shrouded in all the mystery of a Buddhist temple high upon a mountain. Beheld by the devotees, their movements spoke of awe, devotion.

For several days I'd seen Devon, or Dadaram, working with a new devotee. He was French, in his early thirties, and he seemed a bit lost. He reminded me of Arden, my friend the broke poet. I watched from a distance as they spoke intimately. I witnessed Dadaram's support and affection. I'd become used to seeing them together, strolling along the river or sitting outside the ashram with tea.

When the sunshine burned away the mist, the foliage behind Devon and the new recruit burned with a light green translucence. My head twisted:

The man was on his feet, looking skyward, wracked and contorted in some kind of rapture. His guru held his elbow lightly as tears rolled down his cheeks. He was speaking in French. Other devotees became aware of the Event and poured in around them to offer support.

Devon's gaze crossed the divide and he saw me watching them.

When I returned to the *Aceso* after my tour it was a starless night, oppressive with humidity. Devon and I were alone on deck. His eyes had lost their blue in the low light. We were sipping scotch. My lighter flashed as I lit another cigarette.

"There's no way that you can heal with your hands. Not without a scalpel."

I sensed an underlying rise in tension. Then he shrugged. "If you're seeking a debate, there's nothing to say—I've never made any claims."

"There's an incident that happened when I was sixteen." Devon nodded for me to continue.

"My parents were out and they'd left a note saying that I wasn't to take the truck anywhere. When they found out later that I'd gone out with the truck, I told them that I hadn't seen the note. Literally, it was fact—but my brother had told me about the note and I knew I wasn't supposed to take the truck. When they found out about that, my ass got hauled onto the carpet. For lying. Bill and Ingrid didn't give a shit that I hadn't seen the note."

"You have a gift for parables."

"Since I'm not ready to know why I'm here," I said with a note of sarcasm, "there's something I should emphasize—"

He watched me with open interest. Confronting Devon wasn't easy but this needed to be said. "I'm not going to fall for the shit that other people—other people here, fall for. Your devotees see miracles—I see a scam. Just so you know—I don't get sucked into that shit."

He watched me silently. "There won't ever come a day," I said, "that I join your…"

He looked at me for a second, then completed my sentence. "Cult?"

I nodded. I exhaled. It was a difficult conversation. Devon continued it.

"You think I'm a charlatan?"

"Yes, I do."

He was silent, possibly hurt, and it stung me. He drained his scotch and lowered the glass. He turned to me and spoke quietly. "One day, you may find ... it's not that simple..."

"So why do you do this?"

"Do what?"

"Pretend to have special powers."

"I don't pretend anything..."

"No?"

An intensity rose in Devon—I was deep in tender territory. "They endow me. These people have chosen me. They *want* to believe..."

"They're getting sucked in."

There was fury underneath the words. "You think that I seek people out to con them? No, no ... they seek *me* because they want to believe—and they want to believe so they can *transform*—I facilitate that for them. They endow me with the power to do that." Devon stared into me. "They give it to me. I don't have to ask for it or beg. They give it. *Generously*."

I felt the force in the gray eyes across from me. "You saw Benoit today..."

I nodded.

"You think he's being *conned*? He was *transformed*."

"Devon, no offense to the guy—but you can see he's weak. He's a male bimbo."

Devon's voice softened, whispering, floating above the fire below. "I would trade everything ... my intelligence, my possessions, *my life* ... *everything* ... to *feel* what he felt today." The words were spoken with such force that I was unsettled. Devon's energy stayed on me, holding me inert like a wrestling move. When he finally relaxed, I could breathe, as though an elbow was lifted off my neck.

Devon stared into an empty glass. "You ... and he ... have something I don't. You've got a soul."

For a moment that stopped me. Devon was obviously serious—what a bizarre thing to say.

"I don't believe in a soul."

"You don't have to believe in oxygen either—but if you ever find yourself without it, you'll know something's not right."

We sat in silence. I sensed something unseen moving inside of him, like the monster in a child's bedroom, shifting in the dark. The man drew many emotions from me, but the strangest of all was the feeling that I loved him.

After the intensity of our conversation the night before, I approached my afternoon on board the *Aceso* with some trepidation. I needn't have. Devon crossed his crescent-shaped living room and embraced me. "I appreciate your honesty," he said. "I value your friendship."

The ocean rocked the *Aceso* with swells. After surveying the sky for impending fury, we decided upon our usual spot, the garden. The only lingering note from the night before occurred when Devon told me, "I don't have a soul. I was serious when I told you that."

How the hell does one respond to a statement like *that*?

I didn't. We continued into my teenage years like the good adversaries we were. I was at a point where Magic had once again become

Magnus. At sixteen I was dropping acid and reading Carlos Castaneda with a crowd I considered enlightened.

I'd shared some rough patches with Devon but today I was into lighter stuff. It was Sally-Sue's imitation of me that had me remembering a high school pal. Alfie Bonici had once told me, "You're smarter than me, but I've got a higher consciousness." Devon watched me chuckle at the memory.

Apart from being an all-round sweet guy, Alfie had a couple of memorable traits; he was gifted at taking tubes and beakers that he'd swiped from the school's science lab and turning them into water pipes. He was also a huge fan of Al Pacino. His bedroom walls were plastered with movie posters from *Dog Day Afternoon*, *Serpico*, *Panic in Needle Park*, et cetera. It drove him nuts that I could do dead-on imitations of his hero, Al, and he couldn't. "In between bong hits I would do these blurbs from *Dog Day Afternoon* or whatever. Then he would try and it would come out miserably." I was laughing as I recalled Alfie's frustration.

Something in Devon's gaze had become more personal. "Where the fuck were your parents when you were doing this shit?"

"Relax," I said, absorbing his intensity. Devon and I had tussled many times over politics and ideology but this was the first time that I really felt it was personal.

"That's how you spent your high school years? Taking drugs and reading garbage?"

"Devon—welcome to America—kids smoke dope."

"Carlos Castaneda?"

"I know, he's a fraud." The word 'fraud' resonated between us for just a second. "Still, it's creative."

"Anna's your age, she didn't waste her time polluting her head. You can see the quality that proper discipline, proper education, has instilled in her."

"And conversely, the lack of quality in me," I observed.

"You gave up sports to be with druggies."

"Devon, for fuck's sake, you've got a limited view of the world."

"What do you think your friends at the Biting Monkey are? You're attracted to these people."

I squirmed under his gaze.

"Amy was in a program where one of the boys smoked marijuana before breakfast—he was biting people by lunch."

I broke out laughing. I recalled the boy that Amy and Anna had told me about on the train, but it was Devon Clarke's *Reefer Madness* ignorance that was funny.

"I know, to people from Oregon it's a fucking vitamin."

When my mirth subsided, I began to explain my philosophy: that education isn't always academic. "There's an experiential element to knowledge," I told him.

Devon stared at me for a moment. "I just heard my wife's voice, '*Now you're killing me*'—that's what Olivia used to say whenever she thought something was ridiculous."

"Heard it quite a few times, did you."

Devon smiled. "You're funny. Magnus Larsen is a very funny guy."

It was on the surface a light moment—but it was also significant for something else; it was the first time that Devon had brought his other life into our discussions. His wife had a name: Olivia.

Chapter Nineteen

Gray began creeping into the bright blue days. In past years it had always held a hint of melancholy for me as it signaled the end of the tourist season. It was still mostly sunny but it heralded the coming of storms, the wet winds called monsoons. This year I welcomed the end and enjoyed the moods of the sky.

At night, Sally-Sue and I burned incense in her bungalow and took turns massaging each other. She acted out pieces of her developing play. I often tried to decompress from the intensity of Devon Clarke by talking about the man. When I dove into his inscrutable contradictions, she asked if I had seen him heal. I was on my own when it came to Devon. And since she had never met him, when I did my imitation, the sheer brilliance of Dadaram's mannerisms and cadences were lost on her.

I enjoyed her beauty and her warmth, and her rough, childlike humor. I cringed only when she spoke of her own beliefs—the astral spirits that traveled through galaxies seemed a cross between Native American Indian mythology and a *Star Trek* episode. There was a tinge of guilt in my affection. She was my amulet, warding of the charms of Anna Schott.

&

The glories of my Dadaram imitation might have been lost on Sally-Sue—but here on the banks of the Bam Lam River, The Children of a Living God were agog. Ready to kiss my shoes. What started out as just a couple of pie-eyed faces had become a throng.

I explained that Dadaram and I had been practicing teleporting his spirit so that it could enter my body at a distance. If I wanted, I could summon it; Dadaram would feel my request and beam it over to me. *Just like Captain Kirk on Star Trek,* I thought as I enjoyed their stupid faces.

As Dadaram, I reached out and touched the devotee, Benoit, the man who had experienced the rapture. "We each have a journey that is unique ... each of our souls has its own sacred path..." Holy shit. I thought Benoit might start crying again.

"I knew you were special," Evan said in utter awe. The others chimed in. I was the chosen one.

"All doubt is gone," said Samuel, his eyes shining in his dark face.

"There was never doubt," said Mariel, the glow in her cheeks lit by the magic (not intended) in front of her. I couldn't believe how gullible these people were. It was fun though, fun as hell.

I was begged to call Dadaram's spirit again, and I obliged, this time making more of a show of reaching into myself and summoning the spirit. Devon's voice emanated from me, "My friends ... your brother Magnus ... has come among us bringing love and light. He is a rough stone but with work..." I carried Devon's Dadaram cadence perfectly, "...with work, we will find the gem within ... and he will join our altar." I snapped out of it, smiling at the nutjobs surrounding me. Their faces told me that one day I could have my very own cult.

My upbeat mood continued onto the *Aceso*'s upper deck. It was here that I violated one of my own rules. Anna faced a counter, slicing fruit; she'd just popped a piece of pineapple into her mouth when I began speaking as Devon. "When Magnus arrives today, I thought it would be nice if you could prepare something special for him…"

"Umm…" Anna nodded with her full mouth, and turned to her lover behind her. Her hand moved sensually on my leg before she saw it was me. I continued as Devon, looking right at her, "I find he's an extraordinary person, don't you?" Suddenly she gasped, her fractured eyes frozen wide.

"You have food on your face," I laughed.

She licked a piece of pineapple off her lip. "How do you do that?" she asked, still aghast.

"Oh grow up," I said, "haven't you ever seen an imitation before?"

"You're like … Rich Little?"

"Rich Little? Don't insult me," I huffed.

I heard movement in a corridor and called down as Dadaram, "Have your lessons been done, Amy?" The princess was reeled into the kitchen like a fish on a line. She couldn't stop giggling. "Magnus will be your new science teacher. You must always do as he says. If he tells you to extend your finger and poke your sister with it, you must obey." Amy was biting her lip; she sensed her chuckles were a naughty pleasure as she glanced nervously at Anna.

I turned back on Anna with Devon's mannerisms. "It's clear that Magnus is a very special person…" I looked into the cold green of her eyes. "It would warm my heart if you and he were friends."

She stepped forward and slapped me. Her stare broke as she left the room. I was stunned.

"*What the—?*" I looked over at Amy who, suddenly sobered, shared my look of confusion.

I had decided to stay for dinner after my session with Devon. I hadn't discussed my encounter with Anna, and it still sat uneasily with me.

As Devon and the devotees prepared for 'temple,' I browsed through the music collection in the living room. The cruel, lovely apparition of Anna Schott appeared.

"Ignorance is a condition, not a sin," she explained. I nodded. "I'm apologizing," she added.

"Accepted."

"Please don't disrespect Dadaram in front of me. I find that very difficult."

"That was hardly my intention—but I get it. Disrespect for Dadaram is disrespect for you."

Anna stared at me as if controlling her fury. "There's so much … you don't know…"

"Do you enjoy ironies?" I asked, the identical query she'd once posed to me in her Bangkok hotel room. Her mood broke a little as she acknowledged the question. "Don't you think it's funny that the only person without an idiotic response to my imitation … was a girl with a triplicated chromosome?"

She regarded me for a long moment that ended with a hint of warmth. It wasn't so much of a reaction as it felt like she was mining me for information, for clues. I thought of Devon, again unsettled by the perception I was being studied. *Klhai khlai tae mai meuan* is a Thai expression that means, 'same same but different.' What were they looking for?

After she left for 'temple' I went back to the music, grateful that at least she didn't get the religious tickle like my friends outside of the ashram.

Devon's welcoming smile was the brightest feature in the *Aceso*'s garden of discontent.

"I've heard it's very good." He paused for a second, his bright, arrogant eyes on me. I put my cigarettes and lighter on the table. "Let's see it," he said.

"See what?"

He remained fixated upon me, his open expression like the casual tone of a man with a knife behind his back. The nickel dropped—Devon's eyes were the headlights that freeze a deer—

I was trapped in a déjà vu, sitting before a vice-principal, reliving an ancient crime—

A dangerous talent

I was expelled for ten school days—two full weeks—and everyone said it could've been a lot worse. Mr. Williams, the vice-principal, told my parents he was shocked that a student like me, one of his favorites he claimed, could do such a thing. My mother was horrified; she went on and on about how she thought she'd taught me to respect women. A failure again, Dad pointed out what a dismal example I was for Jason. I had to write a letter of apology to Mr. Conway and also to Marilyn Lemon. Worse, I had to go the Lemon house in person and apologize to Marilyn in front of her entire grim-faced family. And every Wednesday for six weeks I would have a counseling session with Mr. Hargreaves. I was the very picture of humility and regret, telling everyone how sorry I was and cursing my own poor judgment.

But deep down inside I wondered … if God didn't want me to imitate Eric Conway, why had He given me such a talent for it?

Mr. Conway taught Social Studies to sophomores. Marilyn sat near the front of his class, and like the deceased movie star she was probably named for, she preferred a top that showed her cleavage. The lisping Mr. Conway moved back and forth as rhythmically as he lectured. His furtive and sometimes not so furtive glances at Marilyn's chest indicated that despite a lisp, he wasn't gay.

The first telephone conversation went like this:

Marilyn, it'th Eric Conway, your thocialth teacher…

Oh. Hi, Mr. Conway…

You know you're my favorite thtudent, Marilyn…

Uh, oh thanks…

I have a thmall favor to athk, Marilyn.

(pause) *Okay…*

I have trouble conthentrating when I thee your breastth, Marilyn. I get terribly arouthed. (pause) *Would it trouble you to wear a thweater in clath?*

Mike Hillier and Alfie Bonici were behind me killing themselves; they'd just smoked a bowl of sinsemilla. By the time I'd got done with Marilyn, Alfie was doubled over and Mike was crying on the couch. To add glory to triumph, the very next day in socials class, Marilyn was wearing a sweater. "Chilly, Marilyn?" I asked innocently.

But I didn't stop there. Bolstered by a troupe of friends behind me, the calls got kinkier and kinkier, until Marilyn wouldn't answer or come to the phone. But one Saturday afternoon, I caught her.

It'th Eric Conway, Marilyn.

Sir, I can't talk now, Mom's in the car, we're going shopping…

Thith'll only take a thecond, Marilyn. It'th about your mark.

(pause) *Yes?*

'll give you an A if you thit with your pantieth on my fathe.

As the Buddhists instruct us, nothing is permanent, and I ended up a victim of my own excellence. Once it got out that Conway was perving on Marilyn Lemon, he was hauled onto the carpet. Apparently he made a good case for his own innocence, and the sleuthing began. On the street it was well known that one Magnus Larsen did a perfect imitation of Eric Conway. Yours truly: busted!

There was a big meeting up at the school with me, my parents and all the wounded parties. I gave a speech about how sorry I was and thanked Mr. Conway for not pressing charges. Our vice-principal, Mr. Williams, presided; he was the picture of gravity. At the end he said, "I'll have a word with Magnus in my office."

I was seated across from Williams behind his desk. He scribbled something down, and then looked up at me. "So let's see your imitation."

I said, "Oh no, sir … I've learned my lesson, it was wrong of me to imitate Mr. Conway."

"Tell you what," Williams said, "show me your imitation and I'll transfer you into Mrs. Gein's class with a good word. You won't have to suffer any lingering prejudice from Eric."

I replied, "If you thay tho, Mithter Williamth … that woould be nithe, almotht as nithe as thucking Marilyn'th titth and licking her puthy." Mr. Williams hadn't smoked anything at all, but it wasn't long before I had him weeping on his desk.

Back in the garden with Devon

I threw him the anecdote as a bone and he smiled with dissatisfaction. He wanted to see me doing *him*. I refused. He insisted. I squirmed and held my ground. Devon Clarke was a hard man to say no to. But he never should've told me that I couldn't be fired.

The request turned out to be a precursor to something deeper. A lazy breeze penetrated the foliage. We were standing. Devon's face was clouded.

"You've been very clear in sharing your belief that I'm a charlatan." He paused. "Please don't tell Anna that."

I felt ashamed. There seemed a raw layer of vulnerability in the man before me. For a moment there was only the sound of birds in the garden, an ocean beyond. He wasn't pleading, just asking, but there was a depth to the need, the importance. "Wait until I'm dead. For our friendship, please save your opinions until I'm dead. I won't be here forever."

How could I not honor such a request? He never even reprimanded me—that came from myself. After all Devon's hospitality, after everything I gained from his presence, how could I not honor it?

Chapter Twenty

I did a good job of avoiding Anna. There was nothing blatant about it. If she joined Devon and I, either alone or with Amy, I shared with her as I shared with them. She got my respect. I sensed her rhythms in the living quarters, at the swimming pool and in the dining room, and found ways to stay away. When I put forth a suggested curriculum for Amy's science lessons, I made sure that Devon was with us.

Unseen, she was never invisible. She moved through the periphery of my world like a dense sun, pushing and pulling me with a cruel gravity. It helped that I was making love to Sally-Sue. All in all, it gave me a little distance, a buffer.

I warned myself not to fall prey to the mystique of occasional flashes, like the day I glimpsed her kicking off her dungarees at the swimming pool. For a second my heart stood still, like a Catholic catching a glimpse of the Virgin. I cursed her beauty as it boiled inside me for the rest of the afternoon. But it wasn't just beauty—it was the sublime current that ran through her brain just as it ran through her skin. It was that which couldn't be smelled or heard or tasted and yet sat within all the senses. A believer may have called it her spirit.

&

As we moved through my 'life story' I looked forward to its completion. I was left with a pattern that I couldn't escape. I often felt a sense of failing my parents, or myself. It was a feeling that persisted into the present.

Devon challenged my choices in life. When the smoke of our battles cleared, I often had to accept that he was right. I liked him immensely. The more I knew of him, the more I understood his power over people. Every single one of his devotees would've done anything for him. They'd have cast out their own eyes on Dadaram's command.

The problem was, I understood it all too well. To me he was 'Devon,' and I had all the religious devotion of a goateed Russian communist. And yet I sensed his growing power over me. I sensed him inside of me. It wasn't just the power that affection fosters—it was a power I was wary of. It was the power of cocaine whispering to a budding addict.

The word I couldn't escape was 'control.' The ache to know him was growing. I loved him, but my guard was up.

&

Afternoon on board the *Aceso* fit my pattern; I contrived to miss Anna's lunch hour. Devon called from the kitchen. "A drink? Or too early?"

"Maybe a beer," I said.

He rummaged in the fridge. "Whatever happens between you and Anna is fine. She's not my wife." Air wouldn't move in my chest. Devon turned to me. "She thinks you avoid her. I hope that's not true, you'd be doing yourself a disservice."

The casualness in his offering was agonizing. "She's very attractive," I said sedately as I accepted a beer.

Devon smiled as he looked through me. "Religious differences aside, I think you'd complement each other." The bottle felt cold and wet in my hand; my face felt hot. I was naked in front of Devon and he was enjoying it.

A phrase echoed violently in my chest: *He wants us to be friends.* Now I knew why Anna had slapped me.

Chapter Twenty-One

The *Zenobia* set out into open water with a morning tour group despite weather that was hard to read. Sally-Sue had found me 'distant' the night before. The fresh gray air was a reprieve from the intensity of life.

Backpackers and other wanderers filled the deck, bantering happily. I always enjoyed the *ooh*s and *ah*s that the massive yacht up the coast elicited. At my group's excited bequest, I detoured so that we could swing by the *Aceso* for a titillating ogle. This morning, however, the questions were not directed at me. An American woman had read a magazine article, and she knew all about the guru Dadaram. His real name was Devon Clarke, she chattered, and he'd been a prominent Boston surgeon—*yeah, I was listening*—and the co-founder of Clarke Surgical Centers, a national chain of clinics, she explained, for the sake of those not from America. She moved into the sordid facts like she was sharing the plot of a movie: Dr. Clarke had gone through some kind of a breakdown after his little boy had died in a gun accident.

His little boy died in a gun accident. I was whirling; by now Devon Clarke was someone that I cared about, *loved.*

The woman bubbled with *Vanity Fair* details; he had been accused of fraud by some, exalted by others as a faith healer, and had founded a group called The Children of a Living God.

Circling the *Aceso* now felt lurid. The chattering woman was running out of facts that she could recall. But the big one was wide open. *Devon ... the little boy...*

Birds twittered in a sky that seemed to suck light from the air. I felt really sad.

That afternoon I climbed the *Aceso*'s ramp with Devon's wound bleeding inside of me.

I looked for Anna. She was on the second deck, preparing for dinner with other devotees, inside due to the threat of rain. She noted the obvious: I wasn't ducking her.

She honored me with a private audience. "You seem humble, Magnus. I'm not sure it suits you." She smiled. I settled my chair closer to our little table.

"What was Devon's little boy's name?"

Anna paused. "Roger." She was quiet for a moment. "You know what happened?"

"I heard there was an accident with a gun."

Anna nodded softly. "Roger was five … he had Lejeune's Syndrome."

Suddenly I was hearing Devon's story. It was the weekend after the Boston Marathon; Olivia and Devon had hosted an afternoon party for two of Boston Liberty Hospital's staff that had survived Heartbreak Hill the weekend before.

Anna spoke simply, but her voice had deepened and I could feel her proximity to 'Dada's tragedy.' "One of the finishers was a young doctor who'd grown up in the south like Dada had ... they began to reminisce about hunting as southern boys…"

Devon had taken the doctor into his den to show him an old collectible pistol. Anna said it looked like a toy; it was tiny. They were suddenly called back into the party, and Dada left the gun on his desk with a shell still in the chamber. The following day, Roger picked it up and pointed it at his face.

Emotion welled in Anna's eyes. I reached over and took her hand.

During their 'temple,' I was alone in a crescent-shaped opulence as hymns rose in waves from the ashram deck. I couldn't stop thinking about the guru who'd smuggled a gun into Thailand after his little boy's death. I'd never want to see another gun as long as I lived after something like that. I recalled the empty being, the glimpse of the holocaust I'd seen on my first day. In my ignorance, I thought I now understood it.

Dinner was inside, on the lower deck. I watched the strange light of a man shine among his people. Even for the lone heathen, he was becoming a shrine. I felt a level of compassion and empathy for him that was never before conscious in me. Later, I yearned to ask about Roger but I just couldn't wade into that pain.

Rain dripped down the windows of the convex room that enclosed my new family in luxury. Just before midnight, one of the devotees arrived to take Amy Schott, Her Royal Highness indeed, to her quarters. For Devon and I, Anna played Italian operas. The words were meaningless. The trembling passion of divas ascended into the night like they were reaching for the dawn; shattered souls screamed in arias that gasped for the heavens.

I was vividly aware of the way we all sat in the living room that night, each apart and together. It was late when the music played out. Anna said, "Sleep here."

Devon added, "We have everything to take care of you." I never brought weed to the *Aceso* and my body needed it. I would twist and turn and fail to sleep a wink without it. Without THC, my brain would punish me by telling my muscles to tighten. No, I was hungry for a toke.

Anna hugged me. At my own peril, I was no longer avoiding her. Devon's words from the other day played in my head. "*Whatever happens between you and Anna is fine. She's not my wife.*" Time on board the *Aceso* was tricky—I realized it was only yesterday that he'd said it.

Devon took me to the skiff, this time rowing me ashore himself. I bailed rainwater as his oars dipped in the sea. A breeze blew wet onto our faces. I spoke my request, friend to friend, man to man, student to master. Prey to hunter.

"Will you tell me your story?"

Chapter Twenty-Two

Devon began with facts that were relatively bloodless compared to my own recital. His father, a marine manager at the port authority in Charleston, South Carolina, died in an automobile accident when Devon was eight. His resilient, energetic mother had remarried by the time he was ten. In 1948 his stepfather took a job selling business machines with a company in Boston.

I wasn't about to sit there like Sigmund Freud, asking how he felt at his father's funeral. Plain as the facts were, I found them striking. And disturbing.

By age fifteen, it seemed that he had done more academically and athletically, than I had in my whole life. A force of industry and endeavor, he rose early on cold, dark mornings, running through a paper route, bagging groceries after school, attending wrestling practice after dinner… His innate drive earned him trophies on the mat and *As* on the honor roll. For me, it was a rough comparison. Yeah, I worked on our family farm but it wasn't without substantial coercion. I was never one to trade a warm bed for a chilly morning without a push and a harsh word from Bill and Ingrid. His achievements continued into his twenties, thirties ... beyond. I was choking on what he'd accomplished. It was a mirror that reflected my mediocrity.

&

After lunch I found myself in Devon's office with him and Anna. His shelves were stuffed with scholarly tomes on everything from hypnotism to cytology. Framed photographs gave glimpses into a life that existed before the *Aceso* arrived in Ao Lai. It included pictures of Anna, Amy and Dadaram at the ashram in Boston.

Here, Anna commandeered the narrative of Devon's life. She injected passion and presented his feats with the honor that they deserved when she spoke of the celebrated surgeon, his medical patents and innovations, his coast-to-coast franchise of surgical centers. Devon protested that it was his wife Olivia who deserved the credit for Clarke Surgical Centers, but blind to his modesty, Anna carried on with an agonizing reverence about the man who had scaled Mt. Everest, lectured in America and Europe … and so on. Processed through her sublime intelligence and expression, man and deity merged.

I felt diminished as a human. Diminished as a man. What was *I* worthy of?

Even when Devon Clarke finally dropped out, he was no ordinary bum: he was the guru Dadaram, a man whose devoted flock would drink the deadly Kool-Aid at his bequest, an aging supernova whose lover drank Truth from his lips and offered Obedience.

And here I sat at his altar, yearning to know more—my self-esteem pounded and blistered with each revelation. The über-successful are rare; it's part of their fascination. Devon was the male who was imprinted for Success, a man beyond impulses for alcohol and escapism, a man with an instinct for knowing the easiest path from A to B. A man who was excellence personified in everything he did. A man who didn't need a birthright to take what was his.

I escaped early that day, carrying the weight of my ego to shore. At home, Sally-Sue was camped on my porch. Nice hug, casual kiss. I sketched out a couple of science lessons for Amy. With Sally-Sue I relaxed into my lower self, the self that had held me in Ao Lai. The self that compared itself to Devon Clarke. The self that was under siege.

There was so much I couldn't share about my life on board the *Aceso*, the biggest part of my existence. If I tried to express my fears of that abnormal culture, or its magnetism, not only was she oblivious to my wavelength, she began to hint that she'd like to attend 'temple' and hear Dadaram speak. I couldn't very well tell her about Devon suggesting that I sleep with Anna. Or how it had pounded my heart. So while our bodies touched, she dwelled in her little world and I dwelled in mine.

Was it the paranoia that sometimes comes from smoking a joint? Once again the question flared: *What does Devon want with me?* But tonight the concept came with pulses of terror that I couldn't comprehend.

One thing I knew for certain: I couldn't succumb to control. I *wouldn't* succumb to control. Not from Devon.

Book of Devon 8

Christmas Eve, 1964

It would become a magical moment in Devon's life.

The bustle of the day had waned. Devon navigated a slushy sidewalk past rows of brownstones, their festive lights rising as dusk settled. Whenever he passed someone, he said 'Merry Christmas.' He reflected upon how relaxing it was to have missed his flight. Frank Sinatra was crooning 'I'll be Home for Christmas' from a neighborhood house, and Devon walked slowly to drag it out.

He was in his third year of specialty as he walked the eight blocks to Olivia's apartment. His mom and stepdad had already gone to his grandmother's in Charleston for Christmas. Tonight, Olivia was his only family. Tomorrow she was flying home to Montreal.

She'd put up a small living Christmas tree in her tiny bachelorette. Devon found her chicken dinner surprisingly competent, an adequate substitute for the feast he would have found at his grandmother's. The only fault that one could find with the other, was that Devon had forgotten to bring his Christmas present from Olivia to her place so they could open their gifts together.

It was Olivia's idea to attend Midnight Mass. Devon didn't resist.

It wasn't terribly cold but Olivia wore a large fur hat as they walked through a neighborhood twinkling with Christmas lights. About her fur hat, he inquired, "Is that a toque?"

Olivia laughed, shaking her head. It was a running joke; Olivia couldn't believe that Devon had never heard of a toque—everyone in Montreal, whether English or French, knew what a toque was. So whether Devon saw a baseball cap or a fedora, he asked Olivia if it was a toque. It was a hokey joke but they always enjoyed it. "No, Devon, this is a Stetson." Olivia glowed that night—Devon had never seen her so beautiful.

He knelt beside her, reciting the Lord's Prayer. The stained glass that reached high around them was exquisite. He felt a sense of himself as a Catholic that he'd never known before. Catholicism had been a part of his upbringing and culture—not his personal faith. Before that night, Devon would've said that he didn't have much use for religion. That night, he felt a sense of history and belonging. A history that he shared with the beautiful woman beside him. This was *their* faith.

Even more than that, Devon felt a sense of knowing God ... as if the Holy Spirit had settled upon the congregation.

Devon and Olivia made love when they got back to her apartment. She'd been a girlfriend for some time. They'd said 'I love you,' and for Devon it wasn't false but it never stopped him from seeing other women when the opportunity arose, which for him was not infrequent. But something changed that Christmas Eve. It wasn't a wedding night, but for Devon it was *the night*—the night where they bonded for life. Olivia Laronge became the only woman that he would sleep with for the next twenty-three years.

It was the beginning of a partnership of passion and ambition, in which two driven people filled the holes in each other's DNA to become a single potent force.

It was rare when Devon and Olivia had time to talk, *really talk*. They talked all night. They made love, they talked—they made love, they talked.

Years later, Devon couldn't recall a single word they said, but he never forgot how beautiful it was to talk to Olivia all night long under the colored lights of the tiny Christmas tree.

Book of Devon 9

May 12, 1987

Olivia Clarke knew something was wrong shortly after landing at Logan Airport in the early afternoon. She'd been in Houston, where they'd moved the head offices of Clarke Surgical Centers. The move had been made for tax reasons as well as low-priced office space after Houston's real estate bust, but Olivia harbored a hope that she and Devon could find a new start there; that they would leave behind the poison of their son's death and the insanity that had stricken her husband. Not that they had even discussed it, but she'd played out the possibility of it in her head, imagining the conversation with Devon. Things had not been well with them for a long time. Olivia had suffered through rumors and tales of her husband's bizarre behavior, and Devon himself never spoke to her outside of the most mundane things. A tough blow came while she was in Houston—she learned secondhand that Devon was closing his private practice and tendering his resignation as a fellow at Boston Liberty.

On the way back from the airport she took Devon's call on the car phone. Would she be home soon, he asked, he wanted to see her. When she lowered the phone, her stomach battled with her mind. *He wants to talk to me about the resignation*, she thought, a good sign. But her stomach said something else.

Devon had an agenda. Olivia was upstairs when he entered the house. He moved past Roger's old room as he approached the bedroom, where Olivia was going through the actions of unpacking clothes. "Can we sit somewhere and talk?" he asked. It was odd in a big, beautiful home to find a moment of struggle in searching for a place to sit and talk. They finally settled on the bedroom. Olivia sat on the bed. Devon chose a chair, moving it for just the right amount of physical distance.

His speech was simple. "Three things, Olivia. Number one, I don't blame you. Not one tiny little bit—not one iota. Guilt belongs to me—and me alone." Olivia didn't want emotion, not the kind that was starting to rise in her chest. She knew it was bullshit; Devon was not the only one entitled to self-hatred. "Secondly, I will never love another woman like I've loved you." Devon paused, controlling his own emotion. Olivia was dying, and it was about to get worse. "I can't imagine what my life would've been without you." Another pause. Olivia dared not speak for fear of hysteria. "It's over. Please forgive me for not being strong enough to touch you." Devon rose.

And that was how Devon Clarke ended the partnership that had begun twenty-two and a half years earlier under the lights of a tiny Christmas tree. Olivia would later tell a psychiatrist that during the most profound emotional devastation of her life, she noticed that Devon's accent had lost all its southern twang.

Chapter Twenty-Three

It was a cloudy morning. Devon and I walked a trail that ran along the banks of the Ban Lam. It took us through thickets of cicadas and small Thai villages with wood fires and sprawling gardens. Despite having lived in Ao Lai for five years, the route was new to me. It was nice to be with Devon in a fresh and peaceful environment. My recent knowledge of the man's tragedy, and his stratospheric achievements could be set aside for a moment. We paused inside a clearing, where a meander bent around us. Insects sizzled against the gentler sound of moving water.

Devon smiled as I lit a cigarette. "How will you survive without those things?" I must've told him I planned to quit but I didn't remember it. He smelled the air. There was a light mist on his forehead. He removed his Panama hat and watched the river, robbed of its green by the gray sky.

He knew that I knew about Roger. Anna would've told him.

Devon's approach to Olivia began tepidly; her prettiness, her smarts, how they met ... the usual boy-meets-girl. Rather than making her seem a benign topic, Devon's restraint had the opposite effect, shading her with power and mystery. It was as if, once we entered the world of Olivia, there would be no turning back. *Innocence lost.* The superficial details ensured that I could still retreat to my safe and blissful ignorance if the road got too rough. Or maybe it was Devon who would need to retreat—Olivia the memory, the life recorded inside of him, was a part of his great tragedy.

It was here that Devon's tale really began. His resume had been revealing—but this—*this* was the flesh and blood below the facts, a drama of Shakespearean proportions—a story that Devon needed to tell.

For the next days, only work and sleep drew me away. The marriage of Devon and Olivia Clarke unfolded like a fairy tale in reverse, starting with them living happily ever after, and ending with their dragons destroying them.

When the deeper, rougher parts of his marriage came, Devon spoke of his former wife with delicate and sometimes hushed respect. At one point, he took me down a dark, twisting stairway into the childhood of Olivia Clarke (née Laronge), a childhood that included a savage betrayal. It left me raw and breathless—but its telling would comprise a tome unto itself. I mention it only to remind us that there are forces beyond the present, pulling and pushing with their unseen gravity.

I can't speak of all the images that held me spellbound. But one piece of Devon's history is vital in illuminating the man who arrived at Ao Lai on a great white yacht. And this I will present skeletally—because the truth of Devon Clarke's transmutation from a successful, well-functioning man to a being without a soul, can't be fully known without it.

The first simple fact was that Olivia was incapable of loving their son.

Roger Justin Clarke was born on November 7, 1980. His little head had wide-set eyes; the scream that escaped his throat was that of a kitten in pain. Although Anna had used the alternate term, Lejeune's Syndrome, the condition was more commonly called Cri du chat,

French for 'call of the cat,' due to the distinctive sound of early crying.

There was much that Devon didn't say. An unspoken blackness was defined by the picture around it. I saw Olivia on the hospital bed, great bouquets of flowers darkened by the pain of a cat-like howl in the nurse's arms. I saw a woman whose fortune had known no rebuke in the eyes of the world—until now.

Devon would never speak of Olivia as being depressed or ashamed, but in a seemingly unconnected reference he would say that she liked the drapes drawn, the blinds closed. When visitors were present the little boy was always tucked away, unless brought downstairs by someone else, a relative or loving guest. The smell of shame and withdrawal weaved into my images.

Days passed and I fell deeper into Devon's years with Olivia. At times it seemed as if he was speaking of someone else, a third person; it wasn't always easy to reconcile the doctor in the story with the Devon Clarke in front of me, much less the guru Dadaram. Whether we were in the living room, or on the deck, or by the river, he spoke with a steadiness. But I could feel bigger rhythms stirring inside him—this was tender territory. As time went on, the connection strengthened between the man in front of me, the Boston surgeon, and the boy from South Carolina.

Though I sensed Devon had a need to tell his story, I was honored to receive it. Honored that he'd chosen me to listen.

Images of a life stabbed me like sharp pieces of poetry:

> *Olivia, the hostess, as a woman tells an anecdote of her eight-year-old son one-upping his geography teacher at school. Parents laughing … Olivia finding it amusing a moment too late … Roger Clarke nowhere to be seen among the other children…*
>
> *Olivia, alone with her humiliation, her husband a handsome, celebrated surgeon. Roger, the shame of her womb.*

A little boy dressed by a maid, screaming for love.

Devon seeing the papers for a committal, an interment that he can't sign.

No, Devon didn't speak *all* of these things but I saw—

Flashes of arguments; Devon pleading their wealth, feeling his bond with the small boy…

Two people beginning to break…

I was rapt.

Chapter Twenty-Four

It was afternoon when I found the guru in his office with the *Aceso*'s pilot, discussing moving the ship for the monsoon.

As they spoke, I was drawn to a picture of Devon as a young man. He was flanked by two friends and they all held up drinks in a toast to the camera. The same guys could be seen in solo frames as well. One had longish hair and was laughing at a party; the other was seen in a football uniform. The captain left, and I asked about them.

When Devon talked about Haskell Grund and Harvey Cook, a lightness and playfulness came into his eyes and voice. Devon revered Harvey; they were competitors from the get-go. Devon spoke of him as a great mind, a man who got things done. Harvey was an orthopedic surgeon like Devon and an avid lifelong athlete who'd won the over-forty hundred-yard dash in ten seconds flat at the 1975 Corporate Games. Despite coming from a pile of money, he went to school on academic and football scholarships. "'Course you remember John Riggins, the Redskins' running back … Harvey could've been that, if not more." Devon had a twinkle in his eye. "I always beat him in push-ups though, contest after contest."

His delight was infectious and certainly a relief from the dark days of his marriage. Glancing at the corridor, he pushed the door mostly closed, as if we were fifteen-year-olds sharing a dirty joke.

"One night we scared the living shit out these new students. Harvey and I were in our third year and we'd been working with our classmates on a cadaver in the operating theater. Which was separate from the morgue. So it's after midnight, and it's the job of the pre-meds to take the gurney with the body back to the morgue, which went outside through a dark area with trees on one side. Before we called them in, Harvey decided that instead of the corpse under the sheet, he'd go under there himself. So there's these two pimple-faces right in darkest part of the route when up comes the sheet with a moan!" Devon was laughing like a teenager. "We could hear them screaming from inside the building."

With Haskell, he was equally elated. "Look at this." Devon had pulled down a large hardcover book titled *Faith*. "Haskell and Annette, that's his girlfriend, go all over the world every Christmas and celebrate with different faiths, different cultures. Annette takes pictures. They write about it." The book's cover had a dynamic picture of a smiling child in an ethnic costume holding a box. "He's completely insane," said Devon with affection.

I handled the book, perusing images that held a potent simplicity and grace. "Are they religious themselves?"

"Haskell's from a family of Jewish intellectuals."

"Which means they're not religious."

Devon sighed with weary amusement. "You're such a fucking snob, aren't you." I shrugged innocently. "God and higher thought are not mutually exclusive," he instructed.

"I thought you weren't going to proselytize."

"I'm offering a concept—that's not fucking proselytizing."

The debate that ensued was the closest I ever came to discussing religion with him. Devon culminated his assault on my apparent snobbery with, "Don't judge God by the scriptures of the world. They're tools, merely tools, to help some people access the Divine. If you don't need a Bible, don't use one."

"I don't need God at all," I said.

"Not you. You've got marijuana and socialism. The Oregon State religion." Devon lit with pleasure as he described a future of legalized grass with a picture of Karl Marx on each package of joints, and a slogan: *If you smoke enough, you can understand socialism.* He taunted me with a smile so radiantly obnoxious, that I think, for a moment, he forgot he didn't have a soul.

Chapter Twenty-Five

Lightning fractured a black sky. The *Aceso* rolled as rain pounded her decks and thunder bellowed. It was the second storm in four days and I decided that by the end of the week, I would put the *Zenobia* away.

I was outside on the lower deck, covered but still wet. As the rain subsided, chanting emanated from the ashram within. It was eerily beautiful—an accompaniment to the dark, shifting sea.

Piercing images from Devon's marriage flickered through me. I knew we were coming up to Roger's death, and part of me was relieved that we'd stopped. I wanted to know and yet ... it was like being a kid at the creepiest part of a horror movie, where you covered your eyes and tried to look away. At least part of the tension was not knowing *when* Devon would continue—when he would walk into a room and find his child dead.

For all Devon's strength in the telling of his past, it was with his wife that I saw for the first time his fragility. Underneath all the excellence, all the luminance, he was just as human as we all are. I felt compassion for both him and Olivia; they'd suffered like dumb animals, lacking the skills to alleviate their pain.

When 'temple' was over some of the devotees came outside. Anna loomed like a dark angel as she approached the bench where I sat. The boat rocked. "We have dry clothes for you."

"As nice as these?" I asked, referring to my shorts and t-shirt.

"You can stay here tonight. No one wants to take the skiff in rough water." She hesitated for a second. "We have everything you like to smoke..."

I was speechless. They'd figured out that weed was the reason I needed to leave each night. *But*, I wondered, *how did they figure that out?* My paranoia flared, mingling with humiliation.

Anna read my distress. "The point is ... we can make you comfortable."

"The point is that some people know a fuck of a lot about me."

I realized clearly at that moment that I had never told Devon I planned to quit smoking, either dope or cigarettes. "He spies on me," I spat out. "What's his problem?"

Anna was uncomfortable. I recalled my promise not to disrespect Dadaram in her presence.

"Sorry."

"Shall we get our friend into some dry duds for dinner?"

She stood above me, the *Aceso*'s warm lights behind her, the mysterious hue of the expended sky shading her face. The memory of her fingers in my hand flooded back. I surrendered to my humiliation.

On the upper deck, Anna showed me into a guest room. I hadn't actually agreed to spend the night. With a hint of trepidation, Anna lifted the lid of a little box with buds and Thai stick.

I smiled. "Got any methadone?"

She gave me a look. "Addict humor," I said.

"Honestly ... I don't know why you're so sensitive."

My sensitivity was no doubt intensified by my recent comparison to Devon Clarke. I felt like a bum. I surprised myself with a naked reply: "I'm ashamed of how much of my soul is in the Biting Monkey."

Anna appraised me. "Atheists don't have souls."

The dry clothes were on the bed. Anna moved to let me change.

But my paranoia had been piqued. "Anna…" She paused at the door. "What does Devon want me for?"

Anna was dead still. She swallowed. It had the effect of making the question seem complicated, scary even.

"I don't know..." she finally said.

"Should I be worried?"

"*Noo*," she whispered. She collected herself. "It's very difficult to discuss *trust* with *you*, Magnus … you're not someone who trusts easily."

"So this is about trust?" Silence. "I should trust Dadaram?"

Anna nodded. "Yes." I watched her. "*Yes*," she said more emphatically. She tried to leave.

"Does it frighten *you*? ... not knowing why I'm here…" It struck a nerve. She wasn't looking at me but I could see her eyes, dark and searching.

Finally she said, "The dinner prayer starts soon, you should join us." Then she slipped out.

There I sat, a rich pauper in borrowed clothes, holding hands with devotees on either side of me. Our heads were bowed as Evan led the blessing in his own words. My sense of violation, humiliation and distress had drained away. It was pleasing to be among them, as though the blessing was manifested as it was spoken.

We passed dishes of fresh, bright, meatless food. The guru Dadaram looked at me so warmly that he could be forgiven for any invasion of my privacy. In fact, in the presence of such familial closeness, one could wonder if such a thing as personal privacy even existed. I loved the people around me. When I looked at Amy, she knew she was the teacher's pet. Her loving glow echoed back. The only person who never met my eyes was Anna.

&

A bottle of scotch, old and venerated, shared a tray with mineral water and glasses. Anna entered the crescent-shaped room as I lifted the scotch, examining the label.

"My dad knows his scotch … but we're not the aristocracy."

"I know it, you could feed a Thai family for a year for what that costs." Anna took the bottle from me. "Still want some?"

"Yep." She poured golden red liquid into tumblers. There were only two of them.

"You're not joining us?" I asked.

"Dada's not joining *us*. You're stuck with me."

An electric tickle moved through my stomach and loins. "Is that bearable?" she asked as if it might be a real question.

"I'll tough it out," I said. We touched glasses. The smooth scotch went down my throat to the inner storm.

We sat on the same couch and Anna lifted her knees to face me. We had a moment of shyness. She took a large swig of scotch.

"A month's food for a Thai family in that swallow." She laughed, still shy.

"How about *your* life story?" I asked.

"No … I like yours."

"I'm finished."

"Impossible," she smiled. "A life story is infinite."

In the silence, her beauty roared and screamed. A sublime essence whispered under her skin, burned in the fractured perfection of her eyes. I imagined my hand on her leg, her waist … my cheek on her hair, my lips on her skin… My heart pounded. I wanted Anna to make the first move. I still wasn't absolutely certain that she was there to seduce me. To be wrong would've been classless.

"What was so funny this afternoon?" she asked.

"Oh. Devon telling me stories about his old friends..." We'd been laughing in the garden before the storm as Devon continued with the escapades of Harvey and Haskell.

"He doesn't tell *me* those stories."

A terrible irony shot through me—one of Devon's anecdotes had involved a man suggesting that Haskell sleep with his wife one night when they were both young waiters at a Boston restaurant. Suddenly his words were back: *"Anything that happens between you and Anna is fine. She's not my wife."* How much clearer could it get? It was my turn to swallow a girl's dowry worth of scotch.

We moved outside so I could smoke a joint. Anna was nervous. I was hardly calm myself. I exhaled a pungent cloud and stubbed the joint. Anna was at the deck rail, looking out over the sea. I lifted a glass and tasted the slight carbonization of mineral water in my mouth. Until I touched her, every action would seem self-conscious and lengthy.

I joined her at the railing. Across the water, a living jungle sang and screeched. Her eyes were black without light. I took her hand. It trembled. Her breath deepened, and she turned into me. My hand found her waist ... my cheek and mouth touched her hair ... she moaned softly, "Dada loves you ..."

I stopped moving. "Does he want you to love me, Anna?"

"He wants us to love each other."

I was in a sudden and ugly awakening.

Anna searched my face. "Magnus...?"

I swallowed. The *Aceso*'s glow hit half of her face, making one of her eyes green, the other black. For a disturbed moment, I couldn't move.

"What's wrong?"

I broke for my room. Anna ran after me. I stripped off Devon's clothes. "Hey, stop this..." she whispered. I put my own damp clothes back on.

"I want to be here," she hissed. My head throbbed with blood, my torso with panic.

"I need to go."

"Magnus—I *want* to be with you."

I secured my keys in my shorts. Ridiculously, I felt close to tears.

"You're making me feel like a whore."

Anna chased me down to the lower deck. I descended the ramp where the skiff was moored. "There's no one to take you!" I kicked off my shoes and dove into the ocean. My head bobbed through the dark swells. Behind me, I heard her voice cracking, "Magnus!"

Three hundred yards later I breathed heavily as my feet found the shore. I followed a muddy path to my motorcycle and was reminded of an incident from my boyhood.

Once, when I was 'Magic,' I'd seen a horror movie at Billy Hogg's place. Going home was terrifying. The tree-lined trail I romped by day was now the domain of the movie's monster, a green-skinned alien. I was a full twelve years old, and running back to the Hogg household like a little pussy to get a ride was not an option. I knew that the green-skinned alien blood-drinker did not exist at all, much less in the woods just beyond our farm. But her bloodthirsty leer lurked in every rustle of leaves, and every creaking branch jolted me. Once I saw the lights of our farm, I ran like hell from that dark forest.

I approached my motorcycle, sweating—was I running from a green-skinned alien? Or something real?

Rain had begun to spit again as I rode home. Shivering and barefoot, I went inside and took a shower. I didn't have hot water, but I got the sweat and mud off. Crawling into bed, I was unable to sleep. Another storm rose outside, picking up fury, ripping fronds from palms, and rumbling with thunder. Lightning pulsed behind my curtains.

I tossed, trying to find comfort under my cover. The storm smashed through the trees. It stirred images of Devon and Anna. It birthed ideas that would not complete. I smoked in bed. Branches and coconuts pounded my metal roof. Before dawn the ruckus had subsided to rivulets of dripping water.

I tumbled into a dream where Anna Schott had died and I was chasing her soul through other worlds and dimensions, never able to catch up to her. At one point I came to a planet with a wine-dark sun hanging over an ocean of placid red. I stood on the shore—and Anna floated above the sea in the perfect peace of death, her hair hanging below her.

It was an image that I would hold on to after she was gone.

Chapter Twenty-Six

"Dude, no one is narcing on you."

I had raged through the bar, castigating those who had spoken of me to members of The Children of a Living God. Kurt and his latest girlfriend were among the throng.

"You're quitting weed and butts? Gee, I sure wouldn't want *that* to get out," rasped Franco.

"What's the big fucking deal?" said Lester, adding, "I thought you joined that cult."

That sent the degenerates into a little chuckle. Robbin lifted his glass to slur, "He's fucking his way to God..."

I smiled as another wave of fun rippled through the low-lifes. My fury was spent. I knew they were right. I mean, why *shouldn't* they tell someone that I planned to quit smoking when I put my boat away? I'd announced it publicly enough several weeks ago—much to the jeers and derision of the degenerates. Some of them could understand cigarettes, but *weed?*

There was no way I could explain about Devon Clarke and the strange sense of foreboding I sometimes felt. Hell, I couldn't even explain it to myself.

Arden flinched as a bat darted past his head and into the night. It was a pared down squad. Charlene, the horny waitress, had returned to the Canadian north, and William Stamp had departed for England, taking his hairy-legged girlfriend and doctoral thesis with him.

I swallowed whiskey, that unlike Devon's, burned my throat. It felt good. I was among friends. I reached for my lower self, hoping it was still there.

"Who wants to check out the Luna Bar tonight?" I asked.

"Where you been, amigo?" smiled Kurt; his latest girlfriend was running her fingers through his ample chest hair. "Luna Bar closed last week. Tourist season is over."

Man, I'd been out of the loop. Lester looked at me coyly, knowing that a trip to the Luna Bar generally meant one thing. "I thought you were fucking Sally-Sue."

"I thought you thought I'd joined a cult, Lester." There was laughter, but Lester had piqued my guilt. Sally-Sue wasn't really my *girlfriend*, but I wondered if *she* knew that.

It was good to be back among the degenerates. I needed a break from the intensity of the *Aceso*. My community service runs for booze and smokes had lapsed and I took some shit. But they were happy to see me.

I was well lubricated by the time I rolled up to Sally-Sue's that night.

Chapter Twenty-Seven

The sky was angel blue, a reprieve from the gray. Waiting for my afternoon group, I stooped to the wharf to retie one of the boat's hanging fenders. Mike had sold all twelve seats, the maximum tour size I would take. For some reason, one that probably involved bribery, the little bastard failed to mention that they'd all been sold to just one person.

"Do you enjoy ironies, Mr. Larsen?" The silky voice sent a wave of cruel pleasure through me.

I rose from the dock, so happy to see her. Anna Schott was in a tank top, a wrap-around skirt, flip-flops, a wide hat, sunglasses, and a canvas bag hung off her shoulder. Not that I noticed. I awaited my 'irony.' She removed her sunglasses. Her green eyes twinkled above an evil smile.

"What kind of a *fool* ... names a sea-going vessel the *Zenobia* ... when she was in fact a *desert* queen!"

"Well..." I struggled, "you know how they call a camel the *ship* of the desert...?"

Anna was laughing. "Please, Magnus ... don't tell me you didn't even know who she was!"

"Give me some credit."

"You thought she played for the Boston Bruins!" Anna was chortling at my expense! I couldn't believe the mood this woman was in. What a departure from our last encounter.

Anna produced twelve tickets. Here her insecurity shone through. She stood precariously as if waiting to be banished.

Christ, she tore me apart. My brain said, *No—send Devon's offering back. The poor woman is a whore. Her lover is playing a game with me. She's not here to please me, she's here to please Dadaram. Don't be a part of this. Send her back. Send her AWAY.* My heart thumped as I looked at her.

"Twelve tickets does not buy a piece of ass with Magnus Larsen."

Her eyes widened. "What grand conclusions we jump to..."

"Unlike your erudite self, I might not know how many quarts of semen Queen Zenobia's boys had to pump out for her royal skin massage each morning, but I do know this: Devon sent you to seduce me."

"I—I don't even know *how* to seduce a man..." she sputtered, adding, "I think that was fairly clear a few nights ago."

"Of course you don't, you don't need to. Look at yourself in a mirror sometime. You can slap your leg and men will come running like dogs."

"You're crazy ... I've made love to five men in my entire life ... I'm not a ... *seductress.*"

She stared at me for a moment, then slapped her leg and used a dog-calling voice. "Come on, come on ... let's make love..." I laughed. "*See?* It didn't work," she said.

"That's because it's Devon calling me."

Anna extended her tickets, needing me to take them. The wharf rocked gently in the hot sun. Whether it was my innate weakness, or because moths fly as close to a flame as they can, I said, "What the hell ... let's give Dr. Clarke his money's worth."

The namesake of an ancient desert queen sliced through the great blue of the Andaman Sea like she was a virgin. On her modest deck, Anna was settled deliciously into a soft chair. I had locked off the wheel for a dip into the galley. I ascended with the queen's offering,

fresh lime and pineapple juices, ice and gin. I sat down next to her. "Mmm..." she said, tasting it.

"My love for you today will be platonic. Hope your guru's okay with that." Her hair had sun-lightened pieces that fell on her shoulders and arms. Her breasts were small and beautiful. Her lips had a color I could taste.

Anna's hand reached out and caressed my face. "Am I allowed to touch you?"

I was playing with fire. "It won't lead to satisfaction for your guru," I said. She looked at me darkly. I rose for the wheel to adjust our course.

The glow of my halo was the light of a false prophet, for I, one Magnus Larsen, had formulated a plan, both brilliant and diabolical. Though my words bear the playfulness of a sun-drenched day, the message I planned to send Devon Clarke was a serious one: You don't control me.

You CAN'T control me.

It was going to be my great pleasure to send his girlfriend back to him, tortured with lust, diseased and crippled with desire—and completely unsatisfied. To stretch a metaphor: hymen intact.

I threw anchor in the shallow bay of a black sand beach. Anna rose on deck, sliding her toes into her flip-flops. There was a hot burn to the late afternoon. Water swished gently into the sand. Birds were distant, subdued by the heat. Dragonflies flitted in and out of the shade. A leaning fringe of palms variegated the dark sand with even blacker shadows. The blue of the ocean was deep here.

Anna stood transfixed by the beach. I recalled my first time here—the feeling of being saturated with beauty, like a sponge, unable to absorb any more. The sensuality of walking into the water was so rich, it was erotic.

I held Anna's hand as I helped her off the deck into knee-deep water. She reached for the beach gear I'd assembled. "When you've bought twelve tickets, madam, it means you don't carry things."

"I can help."

"Carry your flip-flops." Anna waded through the burning blue water, agog at paradise. I was agog at the way she moved.

I set up our colored sheets in the sand. Anna watched me as I threw down the coconut oil and put the cooler in the shade. She dropped her skirt and tank top in anticipation of the water.

"Should I take everything off?"

A beat of time flickered past like a dragonfly in the shadows. "I'm not a Muslim."

Her smile thrilled me. Her eyes thrilled me, her mouth thrilled me.

Anna unhooked her bikini bra. Her panties dropped onto the blanket. I threw off my t-shirt and shorts. I looked at the water. The voice beside me said, "Should we hold hands?" I took a deep breath then held out my hand, finding her fingers. A glimpse of her beauty was agonizing. Hand in hand, we walked toward the sea.

"We're Adam and Eve."

"More like Mary and Joseph," I said, "where you're getting fucked by a higher power and I'm hanging out with God's girlfriend."

Her laugh bubbled. "Another religious metaphor from Magic the atheist."

We moved into the liquid blue. I could feel her hips beside me. I wanted to touch more than her hand. I wanted her neck, her hair, her waist. I wanted to kiss. I wanted to taste the color of her lips. I wanted to taste inside her wet mouth. I wanted to kneel and put my cheek on her mons venus. I wanted to put my mouth between her legs.

Jesus, what the hell are you doing to yourself? I asked silently. We swam, we frolicked. I was no longer playing with fire, I was pretty much roasting in it.

Back on the blanket, coconut oil drizzled over Anna's back. A light sheet covered the part of her body I wasn't touching—protecting it from the sun, protecting *me* from the full force of her eroticism. My fingers slid into her skin and muscles, hot and slow and deep. She moaned and softened and purred.

I worked beyond her waist, sliding the sheet from her buttocks and legs, up her back. "My professional detachment is taking a shit-kicking, Ms. Schott."

She sighed, "Fuck … fuck your detachment…"

Oil dripped over her sexy ass and down each leg to her heels. It was such sweet torment. By the time hot oil fell on her foot and between her toes, she was gasping with pleasure. One might say things were going as planned. But a problem had arisen (innuendo not intended).

There was a lesson that I should've learned in childhood. I had even recounted the particular incident to Devon and the Schotts while I was telling my 'life story.' My little brother and I were sleeping in a dead relative's room in Minnesota, some great-uncle that we had never met. I was nine, Jason was six. I decided, just for the fun of it, to scare the crap out of him with a good ghost story. Well, I told him such a creepy tale, that by the end of it, not only was he terrified, but so was I! Even though I was the one who'd made it up. Some may call it poetic justice—I call it a lesson that came back to haunt me on a beach with Anna Schott.

The torture peaked while Anna was on her back, twisting, gasping as I massaged each nipple simultaneously … I was at the point of insanity. I held her breasts in my hands and shifted my body to kiss her. Never in my life—or in the event of reincarnation, in any other life—had I felt anything so madly beautiful as necking with Anna on that beach. A line of saliva broke as I lifted my lips, moving my body over hers. She tried to pull me into her, gasping, "Please, please..."

Oh to be inside of her—

"Leave Devon and I'll fuck you."

She moaned again with an element of pain. I was face-to-face with the monster. She writhed and one of her fingers slid between her legs. I lifted her arm above her head so she couldn't touch herself.

"Will you leave him?" I whispered, begged.

"Oh Magnus, *please...*" I saw the gasping beauty of her lips, the perfection in her cheeks, the cracked green pools of her pleading irises ... *oh to be inside of her...*

"Leave Devon, Anna..."

"C'mon, make love..."

Oh to be inside of her—

The excruciating loveliness beneath me was Devon Clarke's finest weapon—a wrestling move beyond all others. If I succumbed, I wasn't worthy of her. How brilliant is that?

Above Anna's imploring eyes, I shook my head. Suddenly she was crying. I released her and headed for the water.

I plunged under the surface. Was I clinging desperately to control like an anorexic refusing food? Did Devon make me feel so diminished as a man that I needed to do that? Or was the green alien real? I couldn't see Devon's motive for conquering me—but I *felt* his need, his buried hunger. He wasn't just offering me his loving consort like a friendly Eskimo offers his wife, he was seducing, *insisting...*

I walked proudly out of the water, a beast unconquered. Anna sat up on the blanket, smoking one of my cigarettes. "How many women have you made love to?"

I shrugged. "More than five."

Her eyes followed me accusingly. "A lot more," she said. I took the cigarette. "Who's the whore, Magnus?"

I slipped the sheet over her shoulders, tucking it around her.

The sun dropped in the sky. Under the great fronds of palm trees, Anna sipped a drink. In our little paradise of black sand and sexual frustration, she watched me finish rolling her a joint. I lit it for her, careful not to inhale. She reached to take it and the sheet fell off of her breasts. I readjusted it as her lips drew smoke. She stroked my leg as if I was her lover. She coughed a little. Her hair hung in pieces on her shoulder where the sheet had slipped again.

I'd warned Anna that I wasn't about to indulge in anything that might weaken my resolve. Ignoring the distant hope of success, she offered me the joint.

I shook my head. "I'd be fucking your sweet brains out."

"Let's smoke together!" The green eyes lit, her cheeks flickered with pleasure. There was never a moment or an angle or a mood in which Anna Schott wasn't compelling.

"No," I laughed.

I drank water from a bottle. Anna coughed again and spoke seriously.

"Dada loves you. Why is it so hard for you to trust?"

"Why do you trust so blindly?"

She assessed the question, or the best way to answer it. She began telling me about an accident; riding home from a dance class when a bus smashed into her passenger van, driving a piece of metal from the rear seat into her back. She awoke at a Boston hospital, unable to feel her legs or wiggle her toes. "It felt ... not as if I had changed ... but as if the world had changed ... I went from a life of choice and privilege, and most of all, hope ... to a life without hope." Anna sat silently for a moment, and then added, "My life had been plundered."

"They took x-rays and MRIs and said I'd never walk again. Every doctor said it. Then Dadaram walked into the room and in front of..." Anna paused, controlling her emotion. "In front of my family and the doctors, he started saying I was faking it. He grabbed my legs ... violently ... it was like jolts of electricity were going through them..." She was smiling as a tear rolled down her cheek. I too was moved by the intensity of her memory.

Nevertheless, there was a part of me that was quick and eager to look deeper at the incident. Behind the questions swirling through my head was Devon's voice: *Please don't tell Anna I'm a charlatan.*

She stubbed out the joint. "When something like that happens, you have to ... readjust mentally. You've found a new truth. It's not about 'abandoning your intelligence', as Magnus Larsen says, it's about being blessed with experience and insight. Dada teaches us to build our beliefs and values around what's been revealed."

I lay beside her, absorbing her soft, rich voice. The issue of Devon's control over me was something I couldn't articulate. Yet I knew for certain that Anna was his tool, his method. She belonged to him. Despite the affection between us, all she offered me was her body.

"That was the nicest kiss I've ever had."

"Same," I said.

"I almost came."

"Enough, Anna!" Her eyes flashed with delicious evil. "Fuuck!" I expressed, while she laughed. Rising to escape her eroticism, I put on my t-shirt and shorts.

The *Zenobia* carried us back to Ao Lai. The plan was to have a quick shower then a bite on the beach. I wondered if I was insane. What if that afternoon was the only chance I'd ever get to make love to Anna? I stood at the wheel; she reclined in a deck chair, her languishing body pulling me. A descending sun blazed color into the fabric on her skin and lit her hair, aflutter in the breeze. She met my eyes, and I inhaled her savage beauty into the pit of my stomach. I imagined how delicious it would be to take her at my bungalow.

I yelled at myself: *Stop it!* Silently, I reaffirmed my commitment to resist Devon's gift with every fiber of my being. And that's pretty much what it was taking.

My bike bounced up to my bungalow with Anna's arms around my waist. Through a cluster of trees we could see the broken dance of the sun on a silvery sea. "This is lovely," she said, obviously referring to the location. My porch was in front and we had to walk along the side to get to it. Anna still hadn't given up hope of pleasing Dadaram. She smacked my butt. "You're going to get your tip in the shower." Laughing, I turned around to face her effervescent mischief. Suddenly her expression changed; she was staring beyond me…

Sally-Sue was on my porch and looking as if she'd rather be anywhere else in the world. "I came here to write ... didn't mean to interrupt..."

She began collecting papers that were strewn out on my table.

"You're not interrupting," I said. "This is Anna Schott, she's Dadaram's girlfriend." Anna was very polite, but she knew she'd been busted. Both she and Sally-Sue were eager to leave. Anna insisted that I take her back to the ashram.

"Didn't you want a shower first?" Sally-Sue asked sweetly. I opened my home for Sally-Sue while I ran Anna up to the Ban Lam.

I dropped Anna at the trailhead where I usually secured my motorcycle, giving her the option of discretion if she required it. She got off my bike with the vibe of a woman leaving a bad date. "Amy and Dada miss you," she said, then added, "You have a beautiful girlfriend." She turned hard and began walking away.

"That is so classless."

Anna stopped, taking a slow look back at me. I shook my head in apparent disgust.

"When a woman calls another woman 'beautiful'— and it's obvious that she's more beautiful than the woman she's talking about—it comes across as cheap."

Anna's hard look relaxed. "Oh, Magnus…" she exclaimed, the light sparkling off her face.

Back at my bungalow, Sally-Sue's vulgar streak was raging. I smoked cigarettes and asked nicely how her script was coming. She speculated on how I might've taken my tip in the shower, pairing up various objects with coconut oil. That night, when her offensive subsided, we made intense, sweet love. The moans that rose in the dark were Sally-Sue's, but I was tasting and feeling and seeing a green-eyed woman on a beach.

Chapter Twenty-Eight

The loving tentacles of the *Aceso* had reached out and carried me back. Devon shone from above as I scaled the hanging ramp. We embraced under a moody sky, and for a moment afterwards, his smooth hands touched my face as he surveyed me. His gray-blue eyes stood out in the dull air. I felt a buoyant sense of power—we both knew I hadn't slept with Anna.

The crescent room of the highest deck was nirvana in the clouds. My prize pupil charged at me with bubbly excitement. I shared a deep gaze with her onlooking sister, infusing it with just a hint of a grin, a reminder that she hadn't managed to tint the virtue of Magnus Larsen.

I felt more relaxed with Anna than ever, and I loved her more than ever.

Ice tinkled in a glass. A man whose story needed telling handed me a drink. I'd only been away a few days but it seemed much longer. Home sweet home. There was not a green alien in sight.

That evening we were in the garden. Clouds were adrift, sometimes revealing, sometimes occluding a large, waxing moon. Devotees emptied my ashtray and refilled our glasses with the black silence of ninjas. More than once I saw Anna beyond the foliage, a moat of tension keeping her at bay.

Devon soldiered on through gut-wrenching memories of his cracking marriage.

The night that Olivia spoke her ultimatum…

For all Devon's strength, he wasn't Abraham—he couldn't lift the pen to sacrifice his son.

Devon couldn't live without Olivia—Olivia couldn't live with Roger.

Devon's voice had dropped into a deeper, slower octave. He seemed to become a different being, one that existed over a core that was molten and painful. I was gripped, not for just the words, but for something that was intertwined, underneath, a kernel as invisible and deadly as a black hole with its imploding gravity.

Each moment seemed as if we were about to enter a room with a little dead boy, but that was part of the agony; I felt so close to that point of horror but never quite reached it. The ordinary scenes of their lives; an afternoon party for finishers of the Boston Marathon, intermingled with the private, invisible hell of Devon and Olivia and Roger Clarke.

At the very crux of it, Devon knew that with their extreme wealth, there was no reason to inter Roger. They could've hired a small army of caregivers—they could've even bought love. Devon never told me that he had loved Roger. But I knew that he had.

Words and tone and nuance burned images like flares. I saw the night Devon left his house with Olivia's ultimatum inside of him. I saw Dr. Devon Clarke, a man with nowhere to turn, grasping for light, for help, for transcendence, for deliverance—like Anna's trembling-voiced opera singers reaching for the dawn.

Devon stopped. There was more. There was something more. I could feel it in the air between me and Devon.

"What time can I expect you tomorrow?"

"I'm putting my boat away." I added, "I can come late."

Devon's weight shifted slightly. "I want to tell you the rest in daytime. I want you to see me in the light of day."

I was tense enough already. It was an unsettling comment.

Book of Devon 10

June 27, 1992

Anna awoke next to the man she loved, the man who had saved her, the beautiful man—the man who could awaken a human soul. The birds outside seemed more distant than usual, the air a little darker. Something was shifting in her stomach; her nerves felt raw.

She had looked deep and hard at Magnus, as Dada had asked. And yes, beyond the infuriating arrogance, the pride and the atheism, she saw the quality of spirit, the diamond in the mist. But why was it her job to love him? Why did he feel so dangerous? Why was Dada's love for him so terrifying?

She moved against Dada, craving comfort. He responded with affection and intimacy. But after they'd made love, Anna lay on her back, again feeling the fear that couldn't be breathed out.

Obedience was effortless. Not the task, but the obedience to perform the task. Her obedience to Dadaram was Abraham's obedience to God.

Ever since Magnus had come to them, and even before, the fear had been inside of her. Why would Dadaram want her to make love to another man? She recalled the days when she retired to her plush bedroom to complete her task—to think of Magnus while she gave herself pleasure. In some way that she couldn't articulate, Magnus was a threat to everything she had.

Amy chattered at breakfast, mostly about Magnus; she was making him another picture and wanted input on this color and that idea. She and Dadaram brainstormed happily. Anna had trouble concentrating. Just because she was thinking about Magnus didn't mean she wanted to hear about him.

The day was overcast until late afternoon. After lunch, Dadaram took her face in his hands with all the warmth in the world. "You *know*, don't you..." he said, and Anna felt flushed with a feeling that moved through her chest, her stomach, her loins...

"No, Dada, I don't," she said softly.

The feeling stayed with Anna all day. An inexplicable sickness in her stomach. It had been with her for weeks, but not like this. Anna watched a pink sun sink into a gray sea.

Just after sunset, 'temple' convened in the new ashram. At the request of the guru, none of the children or young people or hangers-on were present. The congregation chanted the chants that held them together—they sang the songs that made them soar. That evening, Dadaram was riveting before them. He was both light and elegance. His voice resonated inside of each changed life. They loved him, and it was easy to see why. Most of The Children of a Living God were seated on benches, chairs and little risers all designed to make the space an amphitheater, a church. A couple of large standing fans moved the air. Anna was on her feet at the rear of the audience; one hand touched a post of the structure so she could lean a little.

Dadaram spoke of the 'voyages of spirit' that he saw taking place among the flock. Then he began to speak about the rarest of subjects: himself. "I've given everything I can to your personal journeys. Now I stand before you all ... asking for your trust and support with my own path. For some of you, it won't be easy..." Anna watched her lover aglow with light and humility. He was such a beautiful man.

Dadaram moved on the slightly elevated stage. The congregation hung on his every word. "At least part of life is about coming to a place where you can accept your own death. My own path ... has been revealed to me in visions…" Anna felt Dada's voice inside her. "I can embrace my own death ... by following what God has shown me..."

The man made eye contact—heart contact—with his followers.

"You've all met my friend, Magnus..."

Anna's breath stopped. Here, the guru's pause was longer, allowing the thought of Magnus to settle upon them.

"I've chosen Magnus to take my life ... with violence."

Anna felt her legs, her knees collapsing...

The beautiful man continued. "It will not be an assisted suicide ... or a murder." The flock was frozen.

"It will be an execution."

Anna was now seated, covering her mouth as the sobs shook her.

Chapter Twenty-Nine

After lunch, I was teaching Amy. I was impressed to find that she'd brought up a previous lesson on evolution with some of the other devotees. I didn't agree with their premise that both the Bible *and* the theory of evolution were correct, but I was happy to see Amy captivated to the point that she'd gone beyond our classroom.

Today, I felt a connection to Devon that I couldn't break, a pull to our unfinished business, his unsettling words. The previous day had consumed me with thoughts of his marriage, the loss of his son, Olivia's pain, and how they were all intertwined.

Anna arrived at our small classroom. "Dada's ready for you." It seemed oddly formal, like she was a receptionist at a dentist's office. Her shape in the doorway provoked a stab of lust.

I stepped into the sunshine of the upper deck. Devotees were towel-drying furniture in the garden, still wet from the morning rain. The devotion struck me as feudal.

"Would you like a drink?" I turned to Suvita. She was Chilean; her name had been Paulina.

"Just water, please," I said, a grind of nerves in my gut. I tried to return her smile.

Devon came outside hatless in a pale yellow shirt. We settled, alone. Goddamn if it wasn't intense. I concentrated on some birds that had come to dart through the branches of garden foliage, chirping in high-pitched pulses as frantic as their movements.

"Consider something," he said. "It's an old cliché but let's give it fresh life." He looked at me plainly. "If you could go back in time and kill Adolf Hitler before he was the chancellor of Germany ... would you do it?"

"You mean right now, go back in time and snuff him?"

"Yes. Imagine him as a little boy petting a dog. Could you do it?"

"Probably not."

"You could save twenty million lives, you wouldn't do that?"

"No ... because I'd also be wiping out General Patton's achievements, his career. I'd be wiping out the heroism and humanity that went hand in hand with the horror. I'd be wiping out what we've learned as a human race from fascism, I'd be wiping out the children of love affairs, I'd be changing history. I might not exist. My brother wouldn't exist."

"Okay, okay." Devon cleared his throat. "Let's say it's not now, it was back then ... and you're a Jew, your mom and dad are Jews. Let's say it's 1945 and you've survived the war—but think of your mother and father, think of *Bill and Ingrid*—they died in Nazi death camps." Devon paused for effect. "Would you go back in time and kill Hitler before he committed a crime?"

"Yeah ... putting it that way ... yeah, I would."

"You would avenge your parents. Pre-avenge them, because you love them, because you can imagine them. They're not a nameless soldier, a faceless family." Devon repeated the information like he was absorbing it. "That's very honorable." He looked into me. "It's honorable ... it's the right thing to do."

Where this was going, I had no idea.

"No one else knows what I'm about to tell you. Just me and God." There was the briefest beat and the bomb was exploding. "I killed Roger. I killed my son. I shot him."

The air in me was gone. His words were plain and simple with just a bit of pace, as if to get through the horror like a fire-walker on coals.

"I walked into the den and he had the gun in his hand. Nothing was planned. I did not leave the gun out on purpose. It was an oversight. Possibly fatigue. I took his little hand in mine and lifted it to the right spot under his chin and squeezed. It happened that quickly. I lost my soul."

Then Devon paused. His eyes were upon me the entire time. "Can you see me, Magnus?"

I didn't answer. This time Devon's voice shook with the hell below it. "I betrayed my own son. I murdered my boy."

After a silence, he spoke again. The present was crushing the air out of my lungs, but my past with Devon was playing back simultaneously. "I've never actually denied killing him. I said I walked in and found him. Literally true. I found him alive. No one asked. If we'd been a family from Dorchester, social services and police would've crawled all over it. But Olivia and I were above inquisition."

There was another silence, the air still too thick to breathe.

"There's a point to what I'm telling you." He continued gently. "When someone has no soul ... it's not a sin to kill them."

Then he abandoned me. There was no escape. I was alone in the garden with a giant burden of knowledge. Solace was nowhere. Not with Anna or Amy or the devotees or a hard swim in the ocean or a motorcycle ride. So I sat. Me and the birds. Me and the knowledge. Me and my lost innocence.

After Dadaram and The Children of a Living God had shared 'temple,' in the new ashram, we gathered for dinner at long tables outside. Amid the flickering torches, the screeching jungle, the happiness of the others, I ate alone, I barely ate. Anna glanced toward me now and then but made no attempt to breach my solitude. Nor did the devotees. Amy was the sole exception, when after dinner she informed me in a whisper that she had completed another picture for me.

Devon shot his little boy. That'll rain on the party, that'll piss on the parade.

And it was our little secret, mine and his.

&

The moon was full. Late that night I was in the garden again with Anna and Devon. Anna felt the weight I carried. The secret she wasn't privy to. They spoke of this and that, and Devon in particular did not acknowledge my leaden silence. When Anna left, she embraced and kissed me warmly but chastely.

Alone with me, Devon said, "It will strike again."

He was a huge presence in front of me. A huge force. He leaned forward to explain, as if to a child, something very serious. "It's inside of me, Magnus ... the same disease that's in a Hitler, a serial killer..."

Now my stomach was twisting. I felt the depth of Devon's gaze. "It struck with Roger ... it will strike again."

I was face to face with Devon's insanity, his breakdown.

"You have a gun, you can stop me." Speech wasn't coming to me. "There will be no repercussions. I can arrange that very easily." He continued. "I would never make you a murderer. You mentioned General Patton—do you think he was a murderer? Of course not."

"I'm not going to kill you, Devon."

"It's your duty."

I rose, my heart pounding. Suddenly I understood my role; the gun, the easy money... "Can I get a boat?"

"You listen to me—" Devon left his chair, facing me like a street fighter. An element of southern twang worked roughly into his voice. "Your guts will hang to your knees the next time I go off. You have a legacy to claim, like George Patton. Don't be a coward."

Shadows and crevices had appeared around the gray-blue eyes. His force was confrontational. I wondered if I'd have to fight him. I knew he'd been a star wrestler.

"Why don't you do it yourself?"

"Suicide is not God's will. Not for me."

"Can I get a boat, or do I have to swim?"

Devon piloted the skiff. The full moon was bright on the water and on his flesh. The jungle howled at us. My heart was breaking. This was the end. The green alien had finally appeared.

Devon followed me to my motorcycle. We walked a rough road in white moonlight. I felt the enormity of his madness. His pain.

"If you don't stop me, I will never stop. The guilt will be yours. I killed my son. I shot Roger. I won't stop."

"You need therapy. Go back to the States and turn yourself in."

"I'm turning myself in to you, Magnus." I forced myself to keep walking.

"I'm begging you ... I'm fucking begging ... please don't let me do it. It's so horrible ... it's so horrible..."

I stopped and stared at him. His eyes had a lupine glow in the moonlight. I'd never seen him so vulnerable or demented. "What is it you plan to do? What can I stop?"

A low whisper slithered out of him. "It's unspeakable."

A wave of pure terror washed through me. I began backing up unconsciously, then moving again, moving to escape ... my feet hit the dark red dirt. Devon Clarke, the new face of insanity, followed me. He hissed, "I'm giving you Anna."

That stopped me. "You are not giving me Anna. Fuck you."

"You have to earn her, Magnus—are you worthy?"

I burned. Instead of exploding on a madman, I kept moving on to my motorcycle. I began unlocking my bike.

"Do you think Jim Jones had more power than me—when he asked his followers to join him in death?”

A flash of the mass suicide in Guyana chilled me. Devon saw it. He moved in seductively. “A squeeze of the trigger and it’s done. It’s no sin to take a life without a soul...”

I fought terror and inertia. “I won’t kill you.”

Devon Clarke fell to his knees. “Magic, I love you. It’s got to be you. I’m begging you...”

There was the mighty guru, Dadaram ... the exalted surgeon, Devon Clarke ... on his knees in the dirt, tears glistening on his pale cheeks. Even there he was a potent force, an inverted icon bathed in the white lunar light. I felt a sudden rush of compassion.

“I’m so sorry about Roger...”

As soon as I could tear my eyes away from the man in the dirt, I pulled my bike off its stand and straddled it.

“If you don’t kill me…”

My foot slipped off the bike’s starter.

“You’ll carry the same guilt I do...”

It took me several kicks to fire the bike. I rumbled into the night feeling the image of the man in the dirt behind me, even when I couldn’t see him.

I tore through the night aflame with my plundered innocence. I leaned into corners and blasted up hills, my bike growling and screaming beneath me. His voice kept replaying in my head: “*It’s inside me, Magnus, the same disease that’s in a Hitler or a serial killer...*”—“*I’m giving you Anna*”—”*You’ll carry the same guilt I do...*”

But I saw just one image—the man in the dirt, begging for death.

&

Before dawn, I ended up at Ao La Ngu, an inlet fifteen miles south, where I'd sheltered my boat. I kept the 9mm Glock on the *Zenobia*, and for no reason decided to look at it, to touch it. I sat on deck as light entered the air. I consumed cigarettes until I ran out. It was light for over an hour before I even thought to smoke a joint. I had a toke and finally slept.

Chapter Thirty

Morning crept into Sally-Sue's snug, cluttered bungalow. I gently lifted her warm swirl of blonde off of my chest. I'd slept poorly again. The evil spirits of marijuana and cigarettes had poked and taunted me all night. They wailed in a hundred horrible voices: *We've given you so much pleasure, Magnus—how can you just abandon us? Don't be so cruel!* They danced on my shoulders, they screeched in the birdcalls outside, they hissed under the blanket of insects. In my mind I hissed right back: *Fuck you, you little pricks, if I can resist Anna Schott, I can resist you.*

It was six days now. Sally-Sue had been wonderfully supportive. I swallowed my growl each time she suggested that I do yoga or channel extraterrestrial gods. I'd relax my own way, goddamn it. Grrr.

There was an ache in my chest that I couldn't share with her. It wasn't just the substances; I missed Anna, Amy, Devon, and the devotees. I missed my life aboard the *Aceso*. I was grieving.

I summoned some sweetness—actually, I faked it a bit—and kissed my sleepy friend goodbye. What was I doing later? she asked.

When I got home, I saw footsteps in the muddy ground. Someone had been by. I opened my door and found an envelope on the floor. Stuffed with U.S. dollars, it was my 'pay' from the *Aceso*. It seemed absurd.

I hit the road in laced-up sneakers; my strategy was to exercise until the pain of exhaustion obliterated all the other pain. I began at my house, running up and down the long dirt driveway, along the road, then the beach. I ran and ran and sprinted until I staggered, then I dropped and did push-ups until I could do no more. I repeated the cycle until I lay panting on the ground, drenched and expended, my pulse pounding hot in my cheeks … staring at the blue sky, marbled with white cloud. No, it didn't kill all the sadness but the little demons of nicotine and THC were silenced—at least for a while.

The monsoons were upon us. Most days were a combination of sunshine and torrential storms that came and went.

I put out the word that the *Zenobia* was for sale as a boat or a business. I traveled up to Phuket with stacks of ads, doing a couple days of legwork, promising a commission to any hotel or business that got me a sale. Where I come from, everyone knows that it's easier to sell a convertible in the spring than in the fall—I didn't expect any hits on the *Zenobia* until the monsoon was over in September.

I was generally miserable. Sally-Sue was my only friend as I still needed to avoid encounters with booze and weed. This meant the Biting Monkey was off-limits, and so was Kurt. For a while.

Amy had given me a beautiful acrylic painting and I'd left it when I fled the *Aceso*. Details like that bothered me.

When I returned from Phuket, the *Aceso* was missing from her mooring at the mouth of the Ban Lam River. The coastline looked bleak and naked without her. It somehow represented the loss of Anna and Amy.

I knew that she'd be sheltered at Ao La Ngu for the monsoons.

My addictions had eased to occasional bouts of sharp hunger. My sadness for the people of the *Aceso* was more resilient. An internal movie played back Anna, effervescing like an exploding wave as she teased me; Amy Schott giggling, her squeezed features oozing joy. Other times I saw Devon's shadowed face, sharing his insanity, or kneeling in the moonlight, begging me to kill him. And also pictures that were warmer.

Without a job, I expected the next couple of months to be long ones.

Timo prowled the *Zenobia*'s deck, shaking chairs and life preservers as if they might not be secure. Right off the bat he was low-balling me. He and his brother Jari ran a scuba-diving shop in a town to our south. The Finns wanted to move up to Ao Lai, expanding their business. With lovely beaches and pristine offshore islands, this was where they saw their future. Sadly, I agreed, knowing that one day I'd never recognize the place.

We were in the same inlet as the *Aceso*. I kept my back turned to the big yacht but I could feel her intense presence in my stomach. Timo's smile featured a space between his front teeth. "Look at that fucking thing," he said.

His offer was an unexpected bird in the hand, but I balked at the low dough. To compensate, he offered me a job; they'd pay me to teach them my tour business, the basics of the *Zenobia*'s diesel engine, how to deal with General Bukit, maintenance on their two other boats, et cetera. I choked when I heard the pay—sixteen bucks a day for twelve-hour days.

I couldn't wait to get out of the *Aceso*'s shadow. I said goodbye to Timo off the wharf. He said he'd talk to Jari, see if they couldn't do a little better. His rhythmic voice lectured me, "It's not Manhattan, Magnus. Our Thai guys get *six* for twelve hours, resorts pay their girls thirty for the fucking month."

"I wondered why they were all hookers."

Timo showed me the space between his teeth and we left it at that.

Chapter Thirty-One

It was a sunny respite from the wet winds. I left Sally-Sue's after a lazy morning. My growly old Triumph Bonneville sloshed through mud as I approached my home. Before I could even stop, I saw Amy Schott's face poking around from my porch.

I was off my bike like a crazy thrilled dog, tail-wagging berserk as he greets his family back from vacation. She ran up shouting, "Magnus!"

"Hello, princess!" I hugged her, held her face. A brilliant smile squinted her almond eyes.

"I'm thirsty," she said.

Anna had stepped off the porch and was watching us. Something was up. I held Amy's hand as I approached her sister. "My mouth is dry," Amy informed me. "It was dark when we came this morning." Suddenly I realized that she might not have had water for eight hours or more. "I wanted to drink from the ground."

I rushed past Anna, stumbling over a pile of luggage on my porch. My door opened and seconds later Amy was guzzling water from a cup I kept refilling. Anna drank more sedately but I could feel her intensity. I was so happy to see her. She avoided looking at me.

I figured they needed my help to get to a train or something.

"There's a pineapple in there," Amy grinned coyly, referring to my fridge.

Anna sat down at my small table as I sliced pineapple. “We’re on holiday with you,” Amy chattered happily.

“That’s wonderful,” I said, shocked but sincere.

Anna drew a dark breath, staring away outside.

“Look!” Amy gasped as she saw her artwork on my wall. I couldn’t stop smiling.

We left the princess on the porch eating peanuts and pineapple as Anna led me away for a private talk. We stopped under some trees near the beach. Birds and insects buzzed and hollered in the abatement of the monsoon. Anna swallowed, not knowing how to begin. “Amy knows none of this—” I could feel the intensity of her distress.

“None of what?” I forced myself to stop smiling, lest Anna think I was enjoying her suffering.

“We’ve been sent away. We have no money...” This was hellish for her. “There’s rules ... I can’t take support from anyone but you...” *What?* Devon still hadn’t given up.

“Will you take us back to America with you?”

“Yeah, I will,” I said without hesitation. I was still caught on the thought, *He throws her out and she’s got* rules *to follow?*

Waves broke onto the beach. Nature sang, oblivious to any human pain. “Where’s your questions? Admonitions?” she asked.

“Don’t look so grim, Anna Schott—it hurts my feelings.”

Anna laughed the laugh of someone in a dark mood. “It’s got nothing to do with you.”

She was in naked agony. “Amy doesn’t know that we won’t see Dada alive again.”

I was stopped dead, silent.

“I need you to take her for the afternoon.” As she started to crack, she turned away, toward the ocean. I watched her for a moment, still unable to speak. I looked back toward my home and waved at Amy on the porch. Then I moved into Anna from behind, “Mi casa, su casa

... there's lots of time to talk."

Anna stared out at the sea. Sunrays broke through the branches above us. Her hair sat lazily on her shoulders. "Dada said you'd take us."

Amy a got tour of the coast on my motorcycle, then we walked up to a waterfall that fell into a natural pool. I told Amy that as the monsoons continued there would be many natural pools to swim in. We lazed by the waterfall with some Thai families who knew me casually. They were fascinated by and friendly with Amy. She had impressive swimming skills and had been on a team back home. Thai people aren't generally good swimmers and I was entertained by watching *them* watch *her* as she backstroked around. Later we were driven out by hordes of mosquitoes that we joked were mini-vampires.

There were moments when I felt real sadness with Amy. We ate grilled shark and chips on the main beach in Ao Lai and she babbled on about Dadaram with such affection, telling me things he'd taught her, showing me the way he liked to tickle her ... she really loved him. It was heartbreaking. The poor girl hadn't a clue that she'd been banished from his life so that her sister could have sex with some guy who was supposed to kill him. She had no idea that her sweet 'Dada' was insane.

"New girlfriend, Maggot?" I'd stepped away from our table to pick up a couple of fruit shakes when I turned to Franco's smirk.

"Fuck off," I growled with a look that warned him to shut up. He backed down appropriately and immediately began lamenting the Thai rum he carried.

"This shit carries a mean hangover. Even Arden won't mooch it." When was my community service going to resume? he begged. Instead of a firm answer, I invited him to meet Amy with a stern warning about bad humor.

I put a papaya shake in front of Amy. "This is Franco. He's from Canada."

"Hi," Amy said. "I've been to Canada."

Franco sat down across from us. "Hi Amy..." he rasped. I pushed my leftover dinner to him. "Are you with the group, the uh ... The Children of a Living God?" he asked nicely.

"Yes, I am," Amy beamed. My heart twisted.

Amy was abuzz with her adventure when we got home around 9:30. Anna talked lightly about settling in, but I could see she'd been suffering. "We're not taking your bedroom," she said.

"As a matter of fact, you *are* taking the bedroom," I told her, adding, "Sissy girls from Massachusetts need their comfort."

Despite all my concerns about Devon Clarke's control over Anna, or rather her submission to that control, and the practical challenges dumped on my lap, I was ecstatic to have Anna and Amy Schott stuffed into my little home with me. They taught me a card game that we played until bedtime. It was really fun, like the kind you had when you were a kid, though I sensed Anna's sadness. I expressed just how happy I was to have them. It lit Amy up, and Anna was humble and gracious, but darkness shadowed her.

I could have gone to Sally-Sue's for my customary welcome but I decided to sleep on the living room couch. It was really nice to have them in the other room.

It was over two weeks since I'd quit weed and cigarettes and I still craved both. I woke up in the dark, wide awake. I drew some deep breaths as I thought about a cigarette, and hell, a joint would've been nice too. Not nice, fucking *lovely*. Instead I poured myself a dram of bourbon and stepped quietly onto my porch. I could tell it was deep night as the symphony of creatures was subdued. The bourbon was fine in my mouth but it made me ache for a cigarette. Waves broke in a gentle rhythm.

Then I heard the horrible noise: it was crying, moaning—I listened hard—I heard it rise and fall—it was wracking sobs—it was human agony—

It was *Anna*—somewhere in the distance—alone.

I'd never heard such human pain. It ripped through my guts. It made me weak—

She was crying for Devon Clarke.

Anna came quietly inside just before dawn. I pretended to be asleep on the couch. I hadn't gotten a wink.

My place was pretty cozy for three people, but it was only for a couple of months. I hoped it wouldn't be too rough on girls used to the *Aceso*'s luxury. I figured it was probably nicer than Bang Khen Prison. I gave the sisters a stack of cash and warned Anna not to be grateful. "Your guru overpaid me, remember?" The reality was, I had plenty of money. For years I'd made more than I could spend. I could easily fly us all home. A decent offer on the *Zenobia* would be icing on the cake.

Despite having a kitchen, I almost never cooked real meals. I packed the sisters onto my bike and we headed to Ao Lai for breakfast and shopping. It was coming up to the season where you could get stuck indoors for days at a time. I hoped we could keep Amy engaged.

I decided to be proactive in telling Sally-Sue; better than her dropping by or hearing about them. You didn't need to be the Amazing Kreskin to predict her reaction. I assured her that I slept on the couch. I felt guilty. Couldn't I rent them their own place? she demanded.

A low sun had broken through clouds after a wet day. Amy was napping inside. Anna was next to me on the porch with a glass of bourbon. The sun warmed her face. She was still grieving. It was very personal and I left it alone.

"If he says it's not a sin … it's not a sin."

I was stunned, silent. She continued, "He knows things that we don't."

"You know what he wants me to do?"

She turned to face me. Away from the sun, her fractured eyes were black green. "Yes."

I stared at her for a moment. "Holy fuck, woman, you need to be deprogrammed."

"You need to do what he asks..." I was numb. "He gave you a gun."

I searched for a response to the insanity sitting next to me. Anna spoke again. "I know it feels impossible … it's not."

"Why don't you do it?"

"If I could, I would. It has to be you."

Fear filled my chest. "And why the fuck is that?"

"I don't know, Magnus, it's what he wants."

I was chilled. I left the porch and splashed cold water on my face. I spent the night at Sally-Sue's.

The wind blew rain that soaked me to the bone. A shared taxi followed my bike down my long, mud-slush driveway. The driver wisely stopped part way. Provisions were slogged down to my house. Anna came outside to help—I laughed at her expression when she saw my new mattress, wrapped in polyurethane.

The power went out for a while as I rearranged the living room to accommodate my new mattress. "We stole your bed," Anna said guiltily. When the rain stopped, Amy and I burned garbage outside. The humbleness of my shack was offset by the glory of the nature around it, and by the twice-weekly arrival of Oi and her cousin whose name I could never remember. I told Anna they were hookers but I think their cleaning supplies gave them away.

A part of Anna made me shudder—it was her connection to Dadaram. The untempered love and obedience. Along with her mystery as woman, there was *that*. Our conversation from a few days earlier was not repeated or referred to again. But it was there. Dadaram still burned in my life. I no longer had the friend, Devon Clarke, who could look at me with all the love in the world—no, I had the cruel madness that lived in the woman I loved. That was very much alive. I was jealous of his power.

I spent the rainy portion of a day inside with the sisters. We played cards, we joked, we ate by candlelight when the power went out. Anna's spirit was getting lighter.

Timo and Jari increased their offer for the *Zenobia*. I would work for twenty days for marginally better money than what was offered before. At the end of my toil, the brothers would buy the boat for cash. I didn't realize it then, but when I think back, I know I took the job so that I could live with Anna and Amy. The reality was, I could've sold the boat and gone home. It was going to cost me more than my wages to support them for the extra time.

I wanted to be with them, crammed into my little place.

That night I went to Sally-Sue's after an absence of several days. She knew that I'd been in town with the sisters, at restaurants, at the local market. She accused, she cried. Though I had not sinned of the flesh, my heart was guilty. I held her. I left.

At home I paused outside, looking at the moon. It had been over a month since I'd seen Devon on his knees, begging me to kill him.

The lights were off. Anna was at the sink, bathed in the pale light of a window. I closed the door gently.

"You're home," she said, a little surprised. She was in a tank top and panties, as if she'd just gotten up for a glass of water. She filled a glass and was momentarily illuminated when she opened the fridge, putting away a water bottle. I set my keys on the dining room table.

She moved toward the bedroom.

"Where are you going?"

Anna stopped and looked at me. In the gray moonlight her skin was pale, her lips were black. I could see the shape of her breasts and hips. She took a deep breath and put her glass on the counter. I moved into her…

Kissing her was a wild, hungry, madly beautiful rush. We gasped and moaned. It was unhinged and rabid. Ecstatic and sublime.

Later, we lay on the living room floor, crying, tangled on my new mattress. We kissed, whispered, tasted each other's tears.

In a quiet moment I began to laugh. "Looks like Devon finally got laid." Anna jabbed me playfully, but it wasn't quite as humorous to her.

Chapter Thirty-Two

The fierce storms had arrived, bringing days without sunlight. I went for daily swims in the massive swells but most of my time was spent indoors with Anna and Amy. We talked and cooked, played cards, giggled at silly jokes, and did art with Amy. When the power was out we lived by candlelight and watched great light shows exploding in gray-black skies. At the apex, thunder boomed like artillery, as if the air itself was being ripped apart just beyond our walls. Debris hammered the roof. At night, light strobed across the sisters' faces. Amy had such joy inside of her. Anna's pain seemed to have dissipated. It was lovely. I couldn't imagine a more exquisite little prison.

Invaded by the sisters Schott, my house had never felt more like a home. They maintained the practice of speaking a blessing before each meal. Our hands were joined and Anna and Amy took turns speaking words of thanks, sometimes embarrassing me with their gratitude. One evening Anna asked if I would like to speak the blessing. With all four eyes on me, I did. Bizarrely, it felt really good.

At night, Anna lay in my arms and we talked about our lives, our loves, our families back home, Amy's unique challenges. We talked long and deep—but the one subject that we never broached, day or night, was 'Devon Clarke, aka Dadaram.' Unless Amy brought it up, we never spoke of life on board the *Aceso*.

Anna's grace was something I'd known from the first moment at Bang Khen Prison. Here it gained depth and clarity. It demanded that I honor her. My devotion was effortless.

My long driveway was a river of mud. I traversed the perimeter by foot from the shared taxi to the house. When I got inside, I shed my dripping rain poncho and Anna took my backpack. Like two nosy bears, Anna and Amy looked inside at the meager results of my shopping trip.

"Will this last us?" Anna asked. "Pack your sunscreen, ladies, we're going on holiday," I announced. Resort islands in the Gulf of Thailand didn't get a monsoon until September and even then it was tepid compared to the Andaman coast.

"You can't afford that," Anna told me. I could see that Amy was delighted.

"How do you know what I can afford?" It was only an overnight train ride and a ferry away—and a lot cheaper than taking them somewhere back in the States. Especially if they were in Boston and I was in Oregon.

Amy was given some baht to pass along to the boy who carried our bags to our bungalow. It wasn't the *Aceso* but it was a hell of a lot more upscale than our home in Ao Lai. Wicker furniture adorned a balcony overlooking a pretty cove. Anna jabbed me in the ribs. "You've been holding out on us, Magnus!" I was laughing as her pretty eyes flashed wickedly.

Before I knew it, I was in a brawl with two Schotts. Anna's evil infected her little sister, who echoed, "You've been holding out!" as she attacked me. I was laughing too hard to muster the strength to defend myself.

If Anna was still in mourning for Dadaram, she kept it to herself. There was a lightness about her, as if she was a sparkler of joy. We snorkeled and enjoyed a variety of food at our resort's excellent restaurant, of which Ao Lai had no rival.

Coral Cove was a snorkeler's paradise and it was something that we could all enjoy together. Every single time we went out among the ubiquitous schools of electrically colored fish we saw new sea creatures, sometimes with grotesque allure, like the puffer fish with its deadly spines, and the small sharks we scared. The enchantment in the eyes of the sisters excited me. There was such pleasure in seeing them happy.

Anna wasn't the only one transforming. Yes, I had to draw a few deep breaths when a waft of weed or tobacco caught me by surprise. But I was shedding old skin and looking to a new frontier. The pleasure of the now and the hope of the future glowed within me.

Though I've been faithful to certain girlfriends in the past, I'm naturally polygamous. It's always been a trade-off, love and sex for multiple partners. But with Anna next to me on the beach, reading or arguing with Amy, there was no further lust. I occasionally looked up from the pages of my own book and saw the beauty of topless sunbathers—but it held no hunger, no mystique. I felt the freedom of a Buddhist monk who had conquered desire. Though all the credit was due to the quality of Anna Schott.

One night at the bungalow there was some crying and drama. Anna needed to explain to Amy about her apparent relationship with Dadaram, and now with me. It must've been confusing. I left them alone. Later we went to one of the big beaches for dinner, and Amy got to taste our cocktails.

It was a near-perfect four-day adventure bookended by a travel day on either side. One other milestone sent a flutter of excitement through me. I came out of a travel agent's office with three airline tickets in my hand. On September 10 we would fly together from Bangkok to Los Angeles, then on to Portland for me, Boston for them. How it loomed. I doubted that Anna and I would stay on opposite sides of our country for long.

The peak of the monsoon season had passed, and sunny days were beginning to creep back.

Every day I commuted by motorcycle down to a town called Pak Kaen and put in ten-plus hours a day. I was scraping and sanding hulls with Timo and his helpers. Both of their dive boats in were in dry dock. Jari stayed in their shop, *thinking*—which I figured was a lot more fun than sanding. I realized how cushy I'd had it. I suffered the work, Timo suffered my jokes, most of which had to do with him being a slave-driver.

I arrived home with aching muscles, thrilled to see Anna and Amy. Amy's face never failed to light up when I returned. Dirty though I was, I got hugged and hogged by the princess. Anna was an angel, my friend and lover extraordinaire, ready with a massage and clean clothes when I stepped out of the shower, laying out dinner as if she was a housewife.

Holding their hands at the table had become a simple, rich part of my day. I loved saying the blessing, and loved hearing them say it. "I thank God for being with Magnus … this is our best holiday…"

Sometimes at night, after we'd made love, Anna and I discussed what we would do at home. I still didn't know—I could go back to school or get a job. Anna said she'd work, support me if I came out to Boston; I could go to a *good* school, she teased.

Conversations that I'd had with Devon came back to me, in which he pressed me on my past plans and urged me to follow through. In particular, I had an idea for starting a company that makes science accessible for average folks. One thing I learned as a student on the Indonesian island of Serapang is that I need to communicate; it's part of who I am. I never brought up Devon though. Life was too good to mention my nemesis. Being unfamiliar with happiness, I feared it was tenuous—not to be shaken by a reference to Anna's former lover and guru.

A mysterious weightless cloud settled in my cells and beyond me. I felt it tingle around my chest. I breathed its white ethereal beauty in the air; I smelled its essence in the wet plants of the jungle. It wasn't just in the richness of Anna's face as she watched the setting sun dance on a vast transmuting sea, or in the taste of her skin at night, or in the frolicking joy of Amy when I came home … it was there when I hauled heavy gear and scraped barnacles at Timo's; it was there when rain blasted me on my motorcycle and when my muscles ached and when I wished there were more hours in a day.

For all the rich, wonderful and exhilarating times in my life, I'd never known anything like it. I was floating.

Chapter Thirty-Three

In the black of night, Amy began screaming and crying. Anna and I were awake and rising at once. Anna turned on the bedroom light; she was hugging and comforting her sister as I came in.

Amy had seen someone at the window. First she heard them, and then she saw the body pass. "Are you sure it wasn't a dream, Elf?"

"No!" Amy insisted.

I assured her that it was safe here. "I'll go take a look."

I grabbed a flashlight. Anna tried to stop me. "No..." she said.

I shrugged. "If someone's out there, let's see who it is." I slipped her grasp and went outside. I stepped off the porch. The moon was a sliver.

I kept my flashlight off. Looking for an intruder in the dark is a little creepy but I didn't think it would amount to much. At this point, the potential villain was nowhere near as frightening as the green-skinned alien I'd once seen at Billy Hogg's house. Even a subdued jungle at night holds a layer of sound, so I wouldn't hear much if someone was at a distance. I followed the tree line set back from the beach. I saw nothing. Maybe Amy's scream scared them off. Maybe she imagined it.

I turned on the flashlight outside Amy's window—my heart picked up pace—there were sneaker prints in the moist ground. "That you, sweet?" Anna asked through the wall.

"It's me," I assured her. I followed the tracks until I lost them, which wasn't far. I walked up to the road. It was desolate in both directions. But when I walked back down my long driveway, I saw the sneaker prints again. I examined them with the light. They were size eleven or twelve, most likely belonging to a farang. I switched off the flashlight. I wondered if the owner of the tracks could see me.

I'd never known any problems with crime in Ao Lai, and I wondered who might want to stake my home out. My gun from Devon was still on board the *Zenobia*. The bad weather was by no means finished—I could get stuck down in Pak Kaen on any given night. I thought I'd bring the gun home for Anna.

On my way back to Ao Lai after work, I stopped at the *Zenobia* and retrieved the gun from its hiding place in the galley. The *Aceso*'s great shape glowed offshore. I paused on deck as a melodic chant carried over the water. I felt a stab of auld lang syne, as if my time there was long ago.

Should auld acquaintance be forgot, and never brought to mind?

Not all my memories of Devon were cruel.

At home it was my instinct to hide the gun from Amy as she came at me with her usual rambunctious charm. Then I recalled that she was the one who had presented it to me. "*It's a gift from Dadaram.*" At the time, *I* was the one who was unnerved. Now Anna seemed more uncomfortable with the gun than she had been in Bangkok.

I removed the magazine, showed them both the safety latch and how to replace the magazine. Of course they wouldn't need to use it but … with someone creeping around outside…

Chapter Thirty-Four

My days with Timo and Jari got shorter. America towered in our future.

One late afternoon Anna wanted to talk. She contrived to keep Amy busy, setting her up with acrylic paints while we went for a walk. I knew immediately that it wasn't to seduce me. I felt the dark current in my lover. We sat on some driftwood up the beach. Unsettled, I waited for her to speak.

The night before, I'd tumbled into her essence, *I love you, I love you*, pouring out of me.

Nothing could soften what she was saying. "You have to understand, I'm loyal to Dadaram." She was gentle but firm as if explaining to a child. "If he asked me to come back to him, I would go."

I felt my chest collapsing.

She tried to console me. "It doesn't mean I don't love you. You know I do." She whispered, "You know how much."

Devastated, I looked at the sand.

"Killing Dada is an act of love."

I couldn't believe my ears. She repeated, "*Love.*"

&

I aggressively volunteered for the worst jobs. My hands blistered with lifting, my knuckles rubbed raw with scraping. I worked late.

I cursed my naivety. Of course, she'd been sent by her guru. *Of course.* I knew that. Out of his shadow, I'd relented. Her belief that I should kill Devon as an 'act of love' was beyond ridiculous. I questioned everything that had happened between us.

When she washed my back, she performed the will of Dadaram. When we walked the beach in moonlight, she performed the will of Dadaram. When her tongue found mine, she performed the will of Dadaram. When she listened to me saying *I love you*, she performed the will of Dadaram.

I was humiliated—humiliated to know that I'd never loved like I loved her, humiliated to know that I would love her even if she returned to Devon. There was an element of choice in my addictions to cigarettes and cannabis. With Anna I was powerless. If it was to end, she'd have to end it.

Despite trying to simply accept what was, her pronouncement festered in me. It burned. I wanted my paradise back. She tried to comfort me; if I was standing by the sink, she'd slide her arms around me and lay her cheek on my back. At night she held me tight, but she was alone and she knew it.

Lying in the dark, I heard Devon's words: "*I'm giving you Anna.*"

At work I reflected on Anna's miraculous healing and wondered what that was all about. Is it possible, I wondered, that Devon Clarke could truly possess some power that allowed him to defy the known laws of nature? I didn't think so. Who knew what had *really* happened in that Boston hospital room? I suspected that Devon had used some combination of hypnotism and deception to pull it off. I would've liked to get my hands on the magazine article that the woman on my boat had referenced. But at home, 'Dadaram' was a subject I avoided.

I was trapped between resentment and helplessness. I knew I had to just let it go.

Work was done. The brothers had obtained a space in Ao Lai, and I'd agreed to help them bring one of their dive boats up the coast. Then I'd sign the *Zenobia* over to them and collect my wages.

Chapter Thirty-Five

With time in Ao Lai winding down, it looked unlikely that Anna's apparent loyalty to her lover-guru would amount to anything. When we made love after several days, it was mad and hungry. The sweet scent of her hair mingled with sex. It mattered not that she was tinged with insanity. For one glorious moment she lay gasping in bed, completely mine. With my barrier broken, she poured into me as if love was a warm liquid.

Anna lit a candle and straddled me, once again her conquered beast. She searched and caressed me with the fissured abstraction of her eyes and tasted me with lips blackened by night. Only in sex was I dominant; here I was naked and vulnerable, open to whatever cruelty she held. When she breathed, "I love you," I'd never heard sound so excruciatingly beautiful.

The cloud had lifted and happiness once again mingled with conjugal pleasure.

Amy wanted to start a new acrylic. "We can't take them all home," Anna told her. How I loved my little family, on loan from Dadaram though they might be. When I kissed Anna, nearly all was forgotten. Sunshine was back, literally and figuratively.

Finished working for the Finns, I took a day to touch base with the folks of Ao Lai. I took Molthisok-Ngman Emjaroen, aka Mike, out to lunch and gave him a good tip for his years of help. Plus I'd talked him up to Jari and Timo—they'd be fools not to use him for bookings.

A dinner feast was reserved for Pramana and Arnold, the Bukits. The general and his boy loaded their plates with every meat but pork—Allah's delight at their omission was quickly canceled out as our whiskey bottles drained.

My alcohol poisoning continued into the night. The denizens of the Biting Monkey poured beer over my head in their particular version of a soiree. Franco railed against my country like an Iranian terrorist—how could I possibly want to go back? "He'll miss you terribly," said Lester, as if I needed consoling. Sally-Sue dropped in as well to say goodbye. She thanked me for helping with her performance piece. I held her hand tenderly, alcohol fueling my sentiment. But before long we were all bellowing out old songs in drunken ecstasy, even the theme songs of TV shows. When I finally stumbled along, I promised the degenerates they hadn't seen the last of me.

We got a titillating thrill the day after my hangover. After breakfast, I'd taken the sisters up to the waterfall that Amy and I had visited on her first day. The park was pulsing and alive with filtered sunlight and rushing water. Many more natural pools had filled for swimming after the heavy rains. But as we undressed for our dip on the rocks, Anna gasped and Amy screamed. The longest snake I'd ever seen in Ao Lai slithered energetically out of our would-be swimming hole and attempted to climb a bamboo tree. It must've been eight feet long. It got onto some lower branches, bringing down the foliage with its weight.

Chances are that the monster snake was harmless and just as frightened of us. We bubbled and babbled, with me suggesting that Amy should test the water first. "No!" she hollered. "Just dip your foot in—see if you get a bite." A second "No!" was hollered. Then the sisters got mean and tried to push me in. It was a wonderfully goofy morning.

We ended up swimming off the beach by our house. I took turns with Anna and Amy, playing in big waves, frolicking carefully.

Just after lunch, I straddled my bike with transfer papers for the *Zenobia* tucked into my daypack. Anna and Amy came chasing after me, laden with fruit. They stuffed bananas and mangosteens into my bag. I was hugged and kissed. Affection for the road.

I began rumbling up the driveway when I stopped. For no reason at all, I looked back toward the house. Anna's arm was around Amy, and they were watching me lovingly. Anna's sunny beauty and Amy's radiant joy. I lifted my goggles and returned their gaze in kind with a wave and a blown kiss. Then off I went.

Chapter Thirty-Six

The plan was to ditch my bike at the wharf closest to Ao Lai, taxi down to Pak Kaen, complete the sale for the *Zenobia*, collect my wages, help Timo and Jari load up their dive boat, bring it up the coast to Ao Lai, unload the diving gear into their new shop, have a beer and call it a good day.

I was at the wheel, on deck, at 9 p.m. Timo, Jari and their two men made five of us. Everything had gone pretty much as expected and we were working our way along the coast to Ao Lai. It was slower than Timo had hoped for but I elected for safety, choosing to zigzag into and away from the waves rather than getting hit broadside. Their boat had no radar and we took turns with a searchlight off the bow.

We'd passed Ao La Ngu, the sheltered cove, and were still miles from home. I could see a dull blush of lights; in the off-season, Ao Lai was more like a fishing village than a resort town. The boat rose and fell in the swells. As we leaned into a turn, I caught sight of something else—up the coast, just beyond Ao Lai, there was a sharp orange glow. As our trajectory zigzagged back toward the shore, the view was lost by a jutting promontory. Right away I was disturbed.

I had to wait until our cycle of zigzag turns had us moving away from the coast. As we cleared the obscuring land mass, it returned, a hot orange glow, the color and size of Mars. Precise calculation was impossible—but it seemed to be coming from where my home would be, a couple of miles north of Ao Lai.

Each time I saw it, terror crept into my stomach. It made no sense, but it did. Even if I figured the distance correctly, someone could be burning coconut fronds, the debris of the monsoons.

I asked Jari to take the wheel. The Finns noticed something was wrong with me. I showed them the incandescent point of orange. Timo looked at me. "Jee-zus, that can be anything." He was right. But it didn't quell my rising panic.

A pleasant night on the sea had become a nightmare. We lost all sight of the tiny glow as our trajectory along the coast shifted. I ached to be docked in Ao Lai. The hour and a half seemed a hellish eternity.

The brothers thought I'd lost my mind. I was poised to jump off the deck as we drifted toward the wharf. "Don't forget your money." Timo handed me my daypack. I slipped it on automatically.

I tore up the dock to my motorcycle. Goggles forgotten, I squinted as I flew over the swath of road overhung by black trees and jungle. Panic pushed in my chest … maybe it was all okay ... but I had to see … see all was okay … I was desperate to see…

I leaned hard through a bend … at distance, a police jeep was atop my driveway, and some motorcycles … I approached fast…

A policeman faced an elderly Thai woman who was speaking in agitated excitement. I tried to turn down my driveway … a cop stepped out to block me … I slid, the bike ending on its side in roadside gravel … I was running, legs pounding dark ground … smoke in the air…

The black silhouette of a crowd grew in front of me … light beams swung through murky air … my house wasn't there … people, arms and hands, General Bukit, were holding me back—I was choking in panic, terror—bodies pressed against mine—

My tin roof was pulled back … a whisper of smoke drifted from the ashes…

The saintly women that had shone at me in Bang Khen Prison were now charred skeletons. Sculptures that told of their final agony. Black and frozen and destroyed amid a little smoke that still rose. Anna's longer body lay over Amy—she was facing upwards, perhaps inhaling death.

Gone was the flicker behind Anna's fractured green eyes and the exquisite radiance of Amy's smile. Ash and bone was all that remained of the two members of the religious order, The Children of a Living God. Asleep forever without a dream. A memory. Ashes to ashes, dust to dust.

Anna and Amy were gone.

An atheist named Magnus Larsen woke up in hell.

Part Three

Chapter Thirty-Seven

I was on Sally-Sue's bed in a semi-fetal position, the pain in my chest radiating through my entire being. The knowledge that Anna and Amy were dead screamed through space. Bits and pieces of the night and morning came back to me; I recalled several of the boys from the bar coming down to my beach in the daylight. Robbin had brought a box of coffees, and someone said, "You tried to throw your money away," as they handed me my small backpack. Other stretches of time were more occluded; my body was bruised, my knee was sore. I had no idea how it had happened, nor did I care. I didn't know if I'd slept at all, or what time of day it was.

The most horrible gash of memory—seeing the girls in the ashes—was nakedly accessible.

Something else was present … pressing against the walls, too big for the room. I'd felt it earlier, in the dawn and morning, on the beach by my home. Former home. *Our* former home. There, it was distant and sinister, vague even. But now it was pressing into my grief. Every time I asked the question *Why couldn't they get out?* it pushed me. No matter how dumbly or rhetorically or pointlessly *Why couldn't they get out?* played through my head, the un-nameable thing hovered.

I heard Sally-Sue moving behind me. I needed to *function*; I needed to perform the tasks that honor the dead and help the living, claiming the remains, contacting their family, the house owner's insurance claim, et cetera. I just wanted to lie a little longer … half an hour maybe. Then I would face the world. I would rise and *function*. After all the functioning, I could collapse. Collapse and grieve.

Then the monster in the room introduced itself with a bolt of lightning that shook my body—

Devon killed them.

My feet swung onto the floor, the malignant truth sloshing inside of me. I sat on the bed, facing the door, the cloud of stupidity gone.

"Devon killed them," I said out loud.

Into the air behind me came a sigh of sympathy, of pity. Sally-Sue believed in her gods from other galaxies, but she wasn't about to believe that Devon Clarke had killed Anna Schott and Amy Schott. *That* was far-fetched.

Moments later I was on my bike, roaring down to the burn site, violently awake. Devon's threats, taunts wailed at me. I recalled asking him what he planned to do. *"It's unspeakable."* My every cell was screaming. *"You'll carry the same guilt I do."*

Down my driveway the local poor were scavenging in the ashes. My furious arrival scattered them. They retreated with spoils of twisted cutlery, misshapen glasses, containers that had been in the fridge. I waded into the ashes—searching for what?

The fire had taken nearly all of the upper walls right up to the metal roof. An exception was the bathroom; comprised of brick and tile, it didn't burn easily and had a high window. It was blackened but still intact. I lifted it from the ashes and saw that a sheet of metal had been riveted into the brick. I stared at it, aghast. The window had had a bug screen.

Had all the doors and windows been boarded up? Had they been sentenced to die, imprisoned? *Trapped inside.* The thought of it had the power to sentence me to madness. I fought to focus on facts, hunting for the frames of doors and windows to see if they'd been blocked off. But the frames were so completely destroyed, they gave no clue.

I dove into the ashes, searching for the gun, not that I expected it to be functional after an inferno—but its existence and location might have provided a clue to Anna and Amy's final moments. It was not near its hiding place—and what did that mean?—things could've gotten pushed and moved when the metal roof was pulled off. The scavengers could've found it. Perhaps the killers of the sisters had taken it. I searched and searched.

Part of me wanted to fall into the fire pit and die with them, but I refused to go down.

There were doors to my subconscious that were shut tight to me then. When I forced myself to search for the gun where their bodies had been, I didn't understand the terror I felt. That revelation came to me later.

The horrible truth was, I knew very little about their actual death. The horrible truth was, I knew everything about who was responsible.

Twenty minutes later I was in the courtyard of General Bukit's home. There I stood covered in soot, passionately explaining to Pramana Bukit that Devon had told me he would kill them. No, not in those words—but close enough. Arnold stepped out of the house a little timidly, hovering behind his father, maybe unsure of the look in my eyes. I wanted Devon Clarke charged with the murders of Anna and Amy Schott. And though I didn't say it out loud, I wanted to see him in front of a firing squad, the method of execution in the Kingdom of Thailand.

Bukit's reaction was a different version of Sally-Sue's. He understood that I was suffering. "Very big hurting," he said.

I explained about the bathroom window, blocked off with riveted steel. "Why couldn't they leave the house?" I asked rhetorically.

"Dadaram big man—big evidence needed for big man. You very hurting."

Bukit was telling me that my grief was manufacturing a case against Devon Clarke.

"I swear to you he killed them." I floundered on passionately and desperately and hopelessly, knowing full well that there would never be a forensic study of the ashes, that Devon Clarke would never even be questioned. I knew that even in the United States, the case against him would likely be unprovable. I must've looked every inch the lunatic, clothes and body covered in soot, proclaiming the guru Dadaram to be a murderer. It was probably the only time I ever saw Arnold Bukit quiet.

I can't begin to express the weight I felt that day. A sense of defeat pounded me as if I was trying to knock down a brick building with my shoulder. The screaming agony of loss was all around me and in every fiber of my being. I had to rise and take it—I had to keep standing. I wanted to claim the remains of my loved ones, scant though they may have been. I wanted dignity for Anna and Amy Schott. I asked where their remains had been taken. I expected the answer to be either a local mosque or a nearby temple, both of which had morgues attached. Neither the general nor his son responded. I stared at them while dead air burned. Arnold wouldn't meet my eyes, Pramana looked at a spot on the ground as though locked in thought.

"Where … are … the sk—skeletons?"

Pramana had to answer. "The church, Magnus … they have … accepted the bodies."

The 'church' did not mean the mosque and it did not mean the Buddhist temple.

I was still standing. The Bukits were silent. Birds were black, fluttering shapes in my peripheral vision, the jungle hissed and hollered as the day crept a moment closer to dusk, a moment closer to the end of time.

I learned something that day. Whatever insanity may befall me in life, it will not be a sudden snapping of my psyche—it will not be an explosive catapult into blissful nonsense. For me, madness will have to creep in quietly, taking gentle possession. Because if it were to come, where the atom of my being was split, that moment was *the* moment—when I was twisted into an impossible hell that was more than I could bear—and I was still standing.

There, in front of the Bukits, at the worst moment of the worst day of my entire life, I was still standing.

&

Sally-Sue washed me. I stood in her shower stall as a cloth moved over my face, my ears, my neck… Her fingers squeezed a drizzle of dark, gray soot from the rag, then she rinsed it and began again, following the contours of my torso. I felt her eyes, her breath, her sweetness. I'd never been more aware of loving her. Or felt so humble in her presence. I had no right to receive the comfort and care she gave me—not after using her to save me from Anna and then ending it.

She was casual to the point of unkempt. She never seemed to care if her top matched her shorts or if a swirl of hair was knotting up on the back of her head. But she had a radiance, a natural freshness, and when she decided to dress up and dazzle, dazzle she did.

Numbingly potent horror pressed me on all sides but for a small tunnel of comfort that was Sally-Sue.

Though we'd both grown up on family farms, our experiences couldn't have been more different. In Nebraska, she'd been an honors student from an angry home. My teen years had often brought out the wrath in my parents, but she came from a background that left a deeper, more traumatic scar. My folks were atheist lefties, hers the religious right. She'd been with men and women, women and men. She seemed contradictory and complicated but maybe it was all very simple. She was my friend and I knew how damned lucky I was. I couldn't, and wouldn't, make love to her—but I loved her.

She was next to me, listening, as I lay on my back upon her bed, the exterior light dimming, a dark symphony of insects rising as I searched for a way forward, a direction. A search I could barely articulate, barely comprehend.

"Just grieve…" she said softly.

There were things I wouldn't tell her. I desperately wanted to claim Anna and Amy as my own, *my* family. But were they? No, not with what Anna had told me before her death. She was loyal to the man who had taken her life. Our time together had been short but Anna had felt like a wife. For her … it may have been quite different. Would she have wanted their bodies to go to the cult? Christ, I hoped not … but how could I not doubt after what she'd told me?

Anna was an experience that my life would never again duplicate. One day, when the mad, howling pain ended, I hoped I could look back with gratitude upon the magical hour of time that I'd spent among the sisters Schott. But now I reached into the dark, knowing that something was required of me before I could grieve. Thinking was dangerous, knowledge had a crushing brutality. Devon Clarke's transformation from a man I loved to a man who did the unspeakable, I dared not contemplate. I dared not contemplate the final moments of Anna and Amy Schott. I dared not contemplate my own complicity, my guilt, in failing to heed the warning of Devon Clarke. I just wanted a path, a way forward; I wanted to phone the sisters' parents and cry with them.

But it wasn't dead simple. The sisters' ID had been destroyed in the fire. The path to their parents, the easy path, was to go to the cult for a phone number. In a million years of hell, I wasn't about to go hat-in-hand to the sociopath that took their lives. As that thought crossed my mind, a knock arrived on Sally-Sue's door.

Do you enjoy ironies, Mr. Larsen?

Sally-Sue opened her door to reveal a small delegation from The Church of a Living God. It was me they wanted. The only clothes I owned were hanging on the line outside, so I wrapped a sheet around my waist and moved into the dusk. They pushed back a little at my presence, which was distinctly unbending. Sally-Sue stood near me on the porch, exchanging condolences with the cult members. A throng of faces included Samuel, Evan and Mariel. Dusk had settled into the shadows.

They spoke of sadness, our shared sorrow. They all contributed pieces but I didn't participate. Then Evan came out with it; Dadaram would like me to join their service tomorrow, their funeral. Evan said his piece and I moved forward again, closer to them, violating the rules of distance between unfriendly people.

"The man's name is Devon Clarke." I looked around at them. "Are you aware that he killed the sisters? That he killed Anna and Amy. Did you all know that?" I realized my question was sincere—did they know? Noises and movements of denial began. I moved among them. "Devon Clarke is a fraud. He can't heal with his hands any more than anyone else. He tricks people. Sometimes it's all very simple, other times it's complex subterfuge. He had a little boy named Roger. He killed him." It was obvious that no one was buying any of it, not even Sally-Sue, though I wasn't looking at her.

The day's last gasp of light shadowed the bleak faces of believers. Mariel said, "Our hearts are broken. Please reconsider, Magnus. Dadaram is love. He welcomes you."

"Dadaram is the invention of a conman named Devon Clarke." With that I went back inside. Seconds later, Sally-Sue closed the door. I sat on the bed and couldn't escape the pain that dripped out of my eyes and onto the floor.

I forced myself to function with focus. I greased my way through some bureaucracy to get a death certificate for Anna and Amy, the airline's requirement for a full refund. A few thousand dollars had been lost in the fire, a comparable amount to what was in my backpack. If I was staying in Thailand, and I was, refunds for our airline tickets would be meaningful.

I drifted down the coast like a black cloud on my Triumph, to Ao La Ngu. I found a spot on the shore with a vantage point of the *Aceso*. I stared at her for a long time. Devotees moved on deck. I ignored them. I seemed to think about nothing. As usual, the skiff was tethered to the hanging ramp. I examined the great yacht coldly; her shape, the height of her lower deck from the water. The steel of the deck rails was patterned with open spaces. I noticed the differences between the hull, bow and port side.

A gray sky suddenly descended and blasted buckets of rain. The only creature, flying, crawling or warm-blooded without a place to hide was me, and I sat numbly through a twenty-minute soaking. When the sun returned, the heavy air cooked. Then the melody came—a choir singing one of their regular hymns, familiar to me from my time with the cult. But this wasn't the usual hour for temple. Sadness saturated the voices, and the expanse of water between me and the *Aceso* carried the sound into my heart like a knife. I screamed and burned with jealousy and sadness and pure hatred as they held their service to celebrate the lives of Anna and Amy Schott.

I don't believe literally in the devil, but the thought of Devon Clarke conducting their service was close enough.

My lugubrious mass rode back to Ao Lai. I stopped on the way to cut and pick wild flowers and blossoms. At the site of my former home, I laid two bouquets. There, alone, I jabbered naked words, pieces of my bleeding heart, and cried a torrent.

The 'crying a torrent' part was completely against my will. I was here to honor them, not to grieve or heal myself. For a while I looked out at the ocean. I imagined shedding my clothes and swimming out into the blue eternity until I could swim no more. It was a peaceful, seductive fantasy.

That night, I found an incredible comfort lying next to Sally-Sue.

It didn't really ease the pain but it kept me connected to something human. I felt guilty that I'd never asked her more questions, gotten to know her in a deeper way. On the other hand, that wouldn't have been fair to her either. I was already tethered to Anna when our friendship became physical.

During those horrible days after the deaths, my consciousness was layered like an artfully presented latte. The top layer remained sharp amid the screaming pain—this was the part of me that was down-to-business, searching for options to ensure justice for the girls, *my* girls. This was the part of me that salvaged the riveted window of my burned home (as evidence of foul play) and the part of me that spoke to General Bukit yet again, fully aware of my virtually non-existent chance of a criminal investigation. It was the part of me that dealt with all the practical issues of my shattered life, from buying new clothes to meeting with the owner of my former home.

It was 10 a.m. when I sat down with Tongsai at the Biting Monkey. Wafts of cannabis and tobacco circled my grief like vultures circle dying flesh. I resisted their allure with a belligerent masochism.

Tongsai was a sweet man who offered warm condolences. I believed our meeting would be about the deductible on his insurance claim. I began pledging my motorcycle to cover it, a generous offer for him, and it saved me trouble of selling it before I left town. Tongsai stopped me. The Church (yes, *that* Church) had already paid it. The information caught me off-guard and I choked with resentment. It felt invasive and ugly—was there anywhere that Devon Clarke didn't have his fucking tentacles?

There I sat, churning, as Tongsai spoke of the leader of The Children of a Living God.

"Guru Dadaram is very big heart, yes, I think," the kind man said innocently.

My reply, "He's a sociopathic piece of shit," was never spoken.

The second layer of my psycho-latte was the part of me that wanted to go to bed and hide from the pain, to close my eyes and never wake up. It was the part of me that had stood at the ocean's edge and dreamed of swimming out to sea until I could swim no more. I felt the fierce pull of this layer several times a day. I was resolved not to succumb.

But it was the third layer that was mysterious. It was like an iceberg, wherein most of the mass was submerged and invisible. Within that layer was an instinct that told me not to grieve, to keep the agony of Anna and Amy's deaths inside of me. Yes, I'd cried buckets at the site of our former home—but grieving was a process that was bigger than that, as Sally-Sue so lovingly instructed me. I knew I needed the pain, that I couldn't let go of it. The reason for that was neither apparent, nor unknown—it simply existed in the submerged portion of the iceberg.

I didn't look at my history with Devon, not beyond knowing that he had killed his son and virtually informed me that he was going to murder again. During those first days I did not psychoanalyze. It was apparent that Devon's madness was driven by guilt and his own twisted grief, but I didn't look for a hypothesis that could explain the unexplainable. I didn't ruminate. I didn't face my own guilt. I knew that Devon Clarke had killed them, not me—but somewhere in that vast submerged iceberg there was more to it than just that. But I didn't go there. Not then.

Late that afternoon, I walked next to Sally-Sue, her Birkenstocks padding the red dirt on one of Ao Lai's old roads. It was more like a trail with its rough uneven width. The sounds were vibrant and pulsing, the sky spinning with birds, and the air alive with the mist of plants and flowers. The weight never left my chest and the world's colors seemed saturated with melancholy. It reminded me of my depressions but this was much worse. The smells more than anything threatened to dredge uncontrollable sadness from my depths. I inhaled Anna Schott and her little sister Amy in the sweet redolence. I fought the emotion hard.

I felt Sally-Sue observing me. When I was sure I had conquered my feelings, I informed her that I was going to Bangkok the following day, but I wasn't leaving Thailand, I wasn't going home. Not yet. She stopped walking and looked at me, stunned.

"No..."

Her kindness had been magnanimous and she had earned her right to disapprove.

"Go home, honey—now's your chance," she said emphatically. "Really, what's here?" Her eyes demanded an answer. "What's in Bangkok of all horrible places?"

"Our embassy."

"You can't function in the state you're in. You'll end up with a needle in your arm." Sally-Sue started to cry. "Come home with *me*..."

She was leaving on the fifteenth, and it wasn't the first time she had suggested we fly home together. I couldn't bear the thought of *doing nothing* in Ao Lai even if it was only for a few days.

"Hey..." I soothed. "If I don't feel like I've done my best, I'll never leave this behind, it'll always be with me, like a disability."

"What'll the embassy do? They don't solve crimes in foreign countries," she sniffed, adding, "If there *was* a crime."

I fell into a long embrace with the woman who couldn't believe that Devon Clarke was a murderer. There was a rush of sweet recognition in the smell and feel of her body—but that comfort also defined the pain outside of it.

At the end of our walk, we approached her bungalow, and I recognized a devotee named Margaret sitting on the railing of her porch. Even from a hundred yards away, I sensed an odd vibe from her. "Your friends are back," said Sally-Sue, though Margaret was alone. I didn't know her well; she was an acquaintance from the cult.

As we walked up, warm light hit the young woman's dirty blonde hair. A sarong glowed on a clothesline behind her. She remained seated on the railing; the normal social instinct would've been for her to stand, greeting us as we approached.

"Hello..." said Sally-Sue sociably.

Margaret grinned. "The man's name is Devon Clarke. Are you aware that he killed the sisters?"

Fear stopped Sally-Sue dead as my words from the previous night were spat back at me. Margaret's smile played against the abrasiveness of the quotation, like a dissonant chord in music.

It was Sally-Sue's bungalow, yet the devotee's presence seemed to hold ownership of the space.

"What brings you by, Margaret?"

"I am the emissary of a divine being. A message has been placed inside of me." She swung off the railing and onto her feet. Again she smiled, possibly just because Dadaram had chosen her for such an honor—but it came across as nasty. Sally-Sue hated her, that much I could tell. A question was directed at me. "Can we walk?"

Suddenly I was faced with a choice—did I want a message from Devon Clarke? Sally-Sue broke the silence with a hint of sarcasm. "Is it a *secret* message?"

"It's for Magnus," Margaret said pleasantly.

Somewhere in the submerged iceberg, a decision was formulated. I nodded at Sally-Sue, who went inside, passing the devotee with wary distaste.

A short distance from the bungalow, Margaret stopped and faced me, adjusting herself to speak. I took a breath, steeling myself to show no emotion. I still hadn't dared to ask questions like *Why? Why did he kill them?* and I felt my heart pounding.

"From Dadaram." She swallowed and began. "'You are the revelation of God's will, Magnus, whether you believe it or not. Your lack of action has allowed me to know God's endowment for myself; I have been blessed with the ability to take life—or save it—without guilt. It is an honor that has lifted the shroud of *guilt* from me. You know what I'm talking about.'"

I followed the cadence of the memorized speech and wondered, *How could I have not seen such madness until the very end? How could I have loved this man?* I listened without moving a muscle.

It was Margaret's face and voice, but I heard the man speaking underneath her performance, just as I was meant to. "'It is not God's will that I should die—but only by begging you for my release would I ever come to know that. Forgive me for taking your gun. The death of my son once made me irrational. The death of the sisters will for a time hurt.'"

Devon feared me—or he would've come himself.

"'You were God's instrument. Your choice to allow me to kill was the perfect choice. Take solace in the fact that Anna and Amy were partners in their final moments. No such thing as 'murder' took place—'"

Suddenly my guts were locked. *They were NOT partners—*

"'Magnus, you came to me in visions from the other side of the world; I loved you in my dreams and I love you now. How can I not love what God has sent me?'"

My resolve to show no emotion was being tested in fire. A silent scream inside me wouldn't stop. *They were not complicit! Complicity was impossible, impossible, impossible—*

I feared it was *possible—*

Margaret's lips were still moving. "'You are the book that has taught the teacher. Call yourself a heathen but I think not. You are a pagan, and I shall celebrate you. You have earned your glory. With love, Dadaram.'" Margaret's tone changed. "That's it."

My inner screams were coming from the iceberg, the submerged layer of consciousness.

"You can come back." Her eyes seemed large and innocent; the sense of evil from before was gone. Shock must've shown in my frozen body.

Finally I managed to feed her hungry gaze with an answer. "I was never really there."

But the truth was, I *had* been there, present and accounted for.

"Is there a message for Dadaram?" she asked eagerly. I shook my head and turned away from her wide eyes and open face and started for Sally-Sue's.

"Are you angry?" she called. "Magnus, are you angry?"

She got no reply. I was flooded by the horrible concept of *complicity*. Why would the bathroom window have been riveted shut if they were complicit? If there was an answer to that question that was reasonable, I didn't want to hear it. And how on earth could Amy have possibly consented to suicide? Anna… Here I stopped for a breath. Anna never would've allowed it. Not for Amy. That's what I was choosing to believe. *They were not complicit.*

I stood outside the bungalow door for several moments, just decompressing, letting the poison escape. *They were not complicit.* I turned and Margaret was still watching me from her distance. Our eyes met for a moment, and then she turned and left, like a wolf that wanders onto your property, sees you, and then goes.

As the door shut behind me, I had Sally-Sue's immediate attention. She stood outside the bathroom holding a towel. She had just seen the creepy side of the cult, or sensed it.

"*And…*"

"Devon Clarke believes he has the right to kill."

The normally warm disarray of her room felt cooled. I saw her as she considered for the very first time, the possibility that something *was* skanky in Denmark. For Sally-Sue the performance artist, it was not her brain that unsettled her, but something she felt.

And that was how the light faded for me in Ao Lai. There were no goodbyes to my friends at the Biting Monkey or to the Bukits, just a final moment of comfort with the sweetest of friends.

The following day, I left for Bangkok.

Chapter Thirty-Eight

It was now Day 3 of my bludgeoning in the Worldwide Overseas Phone Office, and my patience was being battered yet again. I'd been squeezed into the dingy, stifling little booth for hours and was hearing a familiar version of my frustration. A female American voice emanated from the handset.

"Sir, please listen to me, you want an overseas operator, *I am not* the overseas operator…"

"I understand that, believe me I do, but whenever I dial the number they give for the overseas operator it connects me to you…"

"I'll give you another number to try, sir…"

I had suffered through the clusterfuck of invisible electrons and radio waves to get through to Boston directory assistance a grand total of four times. There were over eighty Schotts listed and no operator was willing to give me all of them at once. My memory said that their father's name was Hans so I started with the *H*s. That produced no results—it could've been under their mom's name, which I didn't know, or unlisted. I'd tried over thirty Schotts when I decided to change strategies. Their parents owned a bookstore that had 'scribe' in the name.

This time, the Boston operator quickly found 'Scribe's Lane.' I gasped with relief—yeah, that was it. It would be the middle of the night in Boston, so I gratefully copied the number and escaped the cubicle.

My mood had changed since the first couple of days after the deaths. Then, I had a desire to connect with the elder Schotts, a yearning to mourn with them. Now, the call had become an obligation—and one I wasn't going to shirk. Honoring Anna and Amy meant contacting their parents, but I was now doing it for them, not me.

My lack of sociability extended to meeting Sally-Sue Bronson at the train station. I was determined that she would never see a hint of my preference to be alone. *That* she didn't deserve. When her train pulled into platform 5 at Hua Lamphong Station, I was waiting with all the 'face' I could muster. We had a big hug, and I relieved her of her pack. Moving through the hustle and bustle of the station, she seemed to be assessing me. "Are you sleeping?" she asked.

"Yeah, I'm somnambulating," I said. "Wake me up when we get to the hotel." She showed no sign of amusement at my little joke.

At the Siam Riverview Hotel, I tried to keep the conversation away from *me*. Sally-Sue was out of the shower and brushing her hair out under the ceiling fan. I told her how wonderful her performance piece was and that she should stop picking at it. That was quite sincere. Her piece, still untitled, was dynamic and unique; it flared with imagination and instinct. Yeah, her parody of me was still in there but names were changed to protect the innocent.

Sally-Sue wandered over to a bureau and plucked a piece of paper, a message I'd received from the front desk. I knew what she was reading. The English script was a scrawl but the information was discernible—a Brian Morski at the U.S. Embassy had agreed to meet me tomorrow at 2:30 p.m. She settled the note back down and didn't refer to it. When Sally-Sue was quiet, I sensed I was being judged. When she spoke, I *knew* I was being judged.

"Have you called your parents?"

Stab. "I'm writing them a letter."

"Aren't they expecting you about this time?" Stab.

"For chrissake, Magnus, call them."

"What the hell am I going to say?"

Sally-Sue spun on me, suddenly agape. "You tell them about the fire, about losing Anna and Amy." She stared at me. "That's what people do—they share pain."

I dreaded calling home. My mother was going to freak; there'd be tears, remonstrations … and how the hell could I ever explain about Devon Clarke? And my belief they were murdered? There were things I didn't even speak out loud to myself, much less to others, much less to my parents who would never understand.

"You will call, won't you, Magnus?"

"Yes." Yes, I would. I took the brush from her and finished combing out her hair, working on a knot at the back. It struck me that Sal had more respect for my parents than she did for her own.

Before dinner, I headed out to the hateful little booths that comprised the Worldwide Overseas Phone Office. When I reached Scribe's Lane, a woman answered the phone. Neither of the Schotts were there.

"They've taken some time off," the woman said.

"That's understandable," I replied. A delay on the line was lengthened with a short pause.

"May *I* help with anything?" the voice asked.

"I'm Magnus Larsen, I lived with Anna and Amy in Thailand. Would you please tell them I called?"

"Yes, of course. It's Magnus *Larsen*?"

"Yes."

"Do you have a number?"

"No, I don't."

The deed was done. Though I'd told the clerk I would call again in October, I wasn't sure I would. Sally-Sue had kicked my ass about calling my parents, and I knew I'd bite the bullet and do it.

We were in bed early on account of her morning flight. The room was mostly dark. I lay near naked under the fan, staring at the blur of gray movement as Sally-Sue spoke. She lay on her shoulder, facing me.

"I've had my good fill of therapy ... and ... I've learned ... you never can resolve everything. Some things ... you let go." There was a pause. "Moving on is healing. The past can't always be repaired." Her hand touched my chest, moved on my skin. "I know you've cried a little. Cry more." A dog barked on the street. The fan whirred. "*Cry more.*"

I could've succumbed. I could've rolled over and sobbed into Sally-Sue until dawn. But it wasn't the right time. Not for me. Not then.

Her hand moved down onto my stomach. "What's in here, Magnus? I don't recognize it." Her breath whispered under the fan's purr. "It frightens me."

I didn't know then what she felt incubating under my skin. It would be two more weeks before I recognized the assassin.

I ascended the stairs to the U.S. Embassy's grand foyer in the early afternoon heat. Outside the entrance a black Marine stood resiliently crisp and tall.

"How you doin', sir?"

"Good as gold," I lied. "How 'bout you?"

Inside, I indicated that Brian Morski was expecting me. The clerk at the counter ran a finger down a paper list.

"Mr. Larsen?"

It was my second visit to the building flying the Stars and Stripes on Wireless Road. Last time I had struggled with a terrible dilemma; to lie or not to lie, that was the question. Devon had not told me that he was going to kill Amy and Anna. He said he would do something 'unspeakable,' which after the fire took on a crystal clear meaning. What could possibly be more unspeakable than that? A parent deliberately murdering his own children to spite the other parent would be in the ballpark.

However, to an outside observer, the term 'unspeakable' did not translate into, "I will kill Anna and Amy Schott." To me it did, in retrospect, of course. General Bukit had no faith in my certainty, and even opening Sally-Sue's mind a crack or two did not mean that she was a juror voting 'guilty.'

Therefore, two weeks ago, I had seriously considered lying. I hate dishonesty, but compared to Devon Clarke getting away with murder, it was a minor evil. Why didn't I just say that he told me that he planned to kill them?

The night before my first meeting, when Sally-Sue had finally slept, I'd spent hours deliberating that course of action. The problem was they would certainly check with General Bukit. And then they would ask why I hadn't reported it, or even told anyone when he made the threat. If I could get Devon Clarke prosecuted, I didn't want any lies coming back to haunt me. In the end I was shackled with honesty.

Today, I wasn't about to make the same mistake I had nearly two weeks ago when my exhaustion and fervor must've looked like the ranting of a madman. In fact, I know it did; I could see it in the eyes of Morski and his aide. The more passionately I pleaded that Devon Clarke was a murderer, the more deluded I looked.

This time things were different. With the help of a pill, I'd slept. Both my linen slacks and silk shirt were new, and my leather shoes and briefcase completed a picture of affluence. Or at the very least of professionalism.

Morski was director of the Transnational Crimes Section of the embassy. He had spent our last meeting explaining that it was their job to *help* U.S. citizens abroad, not get them criminally indicted. He enjoyed the phrase, 'outside of our purview.' I managed to point out that I too was a U.S. citizen, as were Anna and Amy Schott. They'd finally agreed to make some inquiries.

I never considered that to be much of a victory, because I had the uneasy feeling that they were savoring me as a piece of drama—to put it bluntly, a nutjob. This time I was determined to make a different impression.

The crux of my request of the embassy was simple: to officially ask the Thai authorities for an investigation into the deaths of Anna Schott and Amy Schott, with a focus on Devon Clarke. And here I was again.

A security gate buzzed and I made my way to a second tier of offices. Morski met me at his door.

"Come on in, Magnus ... you remember Bevan Smith…"

We settled into the meeting. Morski was in his mid-thirties, and the air conditioning allowed him to wear a jacket over his shirt and tie. Bevan Smith looked late twenties and she had the vibe of someone who'd done a stint in the Peace Corps. Their career-bureaucrat faces were on, but these were people I may have liked in another context.

I wasn't being completely dismissed—a folder was open on Morski's desk. My heart shifted gears uneasily. I had a partial glimpse of facsimiles that were death certificates for the sisters. Ironically, I had my own as well.

Morski was explaining, "The bottom line here isn't what you're looking for … but we did send an inquiry to the church's office in Boston."

"For what purpose?"

"Well … you've made some very serious allegations."

"What was the inquiry about? That's not what I asked for."

"We asked if they'd like a chance to respond to what you're say—"

"Sorry, but I'll tell you what you got back—an intelligent, measured explanation about a deluded … unbalanced … man suffering from grief. Or maybe not—maybe I was threatening the cult, stalking someone. Was that it?"

Morski took a breath. "May I see the letter?" I asked.

"Unfortunately not, they have the right to respond in confidence." He looked at me squarely. "I've shown your file to the ambassador. It's simply not enough to ask for an investigation."

I swallowed. I'd expected nothing else. I knew I was hanging by my last strand of DNA. For me, the very essence of my certainty of Devon's guilt was in what he said to me the night he begged to die. They'd heard it all last time. It was my word against Devon's. And I probably looked as crazy as Devon when I told it.

I spoke. "Every fire in America is investigated. We do forensics." I leaned forward. "There was a piece of metal riveted over my bathroom window. It wasn't there when I left that day."

For a moment I couldn't speak. They watched me, respectful of my surge of emotion. When my breath returned, I said, "Devon Clarke was communicating with me."

"Your allegations are—" The diplomat in Morski struggled for words.

"Go ahead, say it."

"Provocative—and I don't mean that in any way that demeans what you're going through." I nodded. "Since we met you, two weeks ago I think it was—I've thought quite a bit about Dr. Clarke."

"You haven't been ignored," Bevan added. "I have a friend outside of Boston … she Fedexed me everything she could get. Dr. Clarke and Dadaram are well known in some circles."

Morski dipped into the folder on his desk, below the death certificates. "Have you seen this?" He passed me a periodical called *The New Englander*. A fresh, vital picture of Devon Clarke, a tad younger, shone on the cover; he looked like a yachtsman, his gray-blue eyes a compliment to an azure background. The headline had a grade-B tinge: *The Strange Case of Doctor Clarke*. "They don't know half of it," I said.

Bevan Smith laughed politely. Maybe that's why I was still here—they were attracted to Devon Clarke's celebrity. I wondered if this Ms. Smith of The Peace Corps didn't get a little tickle of excitement from Dr. Clarke—the rich, handsome persona emanating from the cover of a magazine. I too had had my own non-sexual infatuation with the man. But unlike Ms. Smith, I'd seen the lunatic in his eyes; the night that he'd knelt in the dirt, begging me to kill him, was branded into me.

Despite the sliver of empathy, or maybe just curiosity, it wasn't translating into results. I played my final card, for what it was worth.

"What if ... I was willing to swear an affidavit about Devon telling me that he murdered his son..." I made eye contact with each of them. "Would that change anything?"

After a beat, Morski replied, "It might, Magnus ... if you swore out the complaint in Boston. Not here."

I was sinking. Sunk. I wondered what I was doing here. For a moment it felt surreal. The cool room had an austerity about it, a very un-Thai-like vibe with its high ceilings and clean, nearly naked walls. A portrait of President Clinton was displayed next to another photo of Clinton in a semi-circle of dignitaries that I assumed included the ambassador to Thailand. Another wall had a large calendar.

"May I ... be the devil's advocate and ask you a couple of questions? It's not official but you've certainly piqued our curiosity..." I nodded at Morski.

"Why on earth would Devon Clarke confess this to you?" He was referring to him killing his son, Roger.

"I don't know. I think it was somehow tied into him wanting me to kill him."

"It's difficult to understand that. If he's wracked with all the guilt you say he was, why didn't he just turn himself in, or commit suicide?"

"I don't have an answer. He told me on more than one occasion that he'd had visions—even before he'd ever met me, long before—of me killing him. Before I even met him he gave me a handgun."

I looked at their faces and shrugged, to concur that it didn't make sense to me either. No, it didn't.

"If I was going to lie I'd make up something intelligent." A beat. "The man is insane. Absolutely diabolical." Bevan Smith brushed a lock of hair behind her ear. I finished, "And he's a murderer. He now has three victims, and two are premeditated."

Our meeting ended with them wishing me the best, the usual slobber of condolences. Bevan Smith asked if I was going to be in Bangkok for awhile and gave me a calendar of events for the embassy. As a U.S. citizen I was entitled to join the ambassador for a visit to an AIDS hospice for children and a fundraising picnic afterward. She believed that 'getting out' would be good for me.

The security gate buzzed and I moved through the foyer to the steps outside. I exchanged a parting pleasantry with the Marine guard as I headed for the gate. Even before my feet hit the street, I was fully aware for the very first time that I was going to kill Devon Clarke.

As I moved down the busy boulevard that intersected Wireless Road, the vivid intensity of Bangkok seemed to recess. The people, the noise, the heat, all seemed to clear a little space around me. I walked without objective, aware of a huge new body of ideas and feelings inside of me. Raw memories of Devon Clarke accused me of failure, of weakness, of complicity in the sisters' deaths. *"You'll carry the same guilt I do."* The submerged iceberg had melted.

My decision to kill Devon seemed to arrive suddenly but no, it had been there for a while. Early on I had known that General Bukit wouldn't order a forensic review of the burn site or an interrogation of the guru. I knew that based on the flimsy evidence I had to offer there was no way my embassy would request an investigation, if indeed, as Morski said, it was even within their purview. I had survived in that building on the sensation of my allegation and the notoriety of Dr. Clarke.

There was the vaguest sense of peace, or resolution, in accepting that I would kill Devon—I say vague because it also carried new arteries of terror. Taking another man's life, if I didn't do it right, could cost me my own. I was surprised at the level of fear that held for me.

A screech of brakes penetrated my little enclave and I passed through a belch of diesel to board a city bus moving west. The clunker's seats were designed for people smaller than me so I stood and let the inner world take me over again. As the bus bumped and jiggled, I saw Margaret, the devotee, reciting Devon's message to me outside of Sally-Sue's bungalow. Maybe that was when I decided to kill him. Really, I don't know. Various pieces of the past played back, each with their own emotions and ideas.

I got off the bus twenty minutes later and walked to the Chaophraya River, where I waited with nameless masses of Thai people for a commuter boat. Rage that had been frozen in the submerged iceberg now circulated freely, intermingling with grief. Armchair psychologists may say that because those factors were present, I was driven by vengeance. I say I was not.

Had I been able to see Devon Clarke standing trial in front of a jury of his peers and seen him convicted, death penalty or no death penalty, that would've sufficed as justice. Not healing, but justice—and for me, justice would be the first part of moving on.

So my clear new objective had nothing to do with pain, rage or the taking of revenge. It was an undertaking of justice. Justice. Plain and simple. Healing, that was an ancillary benefit; this was about honoring the lives of Anna and Amy Schott. If I allowed that atrocity to go unanswered—then what did it mean to be human? I had never before floated with happiness or been so nakedly willing to surrender to a woman as I had to Anna. The sisters had touched me in a way that no other people ever had. God, how I loved them. God, how this world was empty without them.

They had brought a joy that I would never seek to find again. Its scarcity made it a fool's errand. No, whatever riches or poverty my future may bring, it would never again bring me Anna and Amy.

If I didn't honor those lives with justice, I could never be fully human.

And maybe I did want to blow his fucking brains out.

The riverboat carried me up to the Banglampoo district. After Sally-Sue had departed Bangkok, I'd moved to a cheap guesthouse at the end of an alley, well off of Khao San Road. The growl of buses and bumper-to-bumper beeping tuk-tuks were muffled by distance as I climbed the stairs to my room. Inside, I closed the door and felt a comfortable sense of isolation.

I moved to a small desk, where two meticulously crafted handwritten letters were laid out; one was addressed to the Boston Police Department, the other to *Vanity Fair* magazine. I reached into my slacks for a lighter I'd picked up on my way here—and page by page, burned the letters.

If Devon was to die by my hand, I didn't want to leave a trail of evidence for police or scandal-hungry journalists eager to create a portrait of a Lee Harvey Oswald-type nutjob lying in wait to assassinate a great man. The fact that I'd been to see General Bukit and the embassy was bad enough. Certainly on my first visit, Morski and his aide would've seen the fervor in my sleep-deprived eyes.

I had a vision of Bevan Smith, the former Peace Corps volunteer, in the thrill of the limelight as she raised her hand and swore to tell the truth, the whole truth and nothing but the truth at the first-degree murder trial of Magnus Larsen.

It was really just my racing mind; I didn't know a thing about the Thai justice system or even if Ms. Smith had been in the Peace Corps.

Light black ash from the letters settled down to the concrete floor. When the last page was burned, I was stuck for a moment. I literally didn't know my next move. Then it hit my stomach. I lunged for the bathroom—my heart thumped as I stared down into a squat toilet, ejecting wet strings of terror.

Chapter Thirty-Nine

In a dark restaurant below street level, my food and beer were largely neglected. I played with my pen next to a list of possible sources for a gun. It could've stayed in my head but I was fidgeting.

Occasionally the environment poked through my thoughts. Music blended awkwardly with another beat from next door. At a nearby table a woman was telling a hawker, "I have forty-sree Buddhas in my house in Germany—I don't take more…" The tables by the street were crowded with travelers in pairs and small groups. Deeper inside, short-skirted, pump-heeled Thai girls and lady-boys intermingled with single men. None of it concerned me.

I sneered at the list. For every 'pro' next to a name there was also a con. Both General Bukit and his son were out of the question; they knew that I had a hate-on for Dadaram and what I'd accused him of. My old connections, Sergeant Choonhavan and Colonel Thanarat, were on there as well. But did I really want to buy a gun from a cop when I planned to take the law into my own hands? And that's assuming I could invent a story that would trigger their assistance.

I also wondered what a fistful of dollars might shake loose in one of the refugee camps up along the Thai-Burmese border. Along with displaced families there were ethnic fighters from the various hill tribes, and also student fighters, some of whom were armed.

The final item on my list was inspired by an aging Aussie expat I'd once met on a train. The jabbering old ruffian seemed to live a spectacularly seedy life somewhere in the untouristed bowels of Bangkok. Amongst his tales of infidelities and vendettas was a piece of unsolicited knowledge: if I ever needed to kill someone, I could hire an assassin in the meat-packing district. The men who smashed through flesh for a living were either Christian or Muslim—never Buddhist, he told me. It could've been urban myth or outright bullshit. That afternoon I had no idea where the 'meat-packing district' was, if such a place even existed.

I swigged on my beer. There was a lot to think about. I figured that killing Devon would be easy—getting out of the country before I was charged with it was the challenge. And really, circumstance would determine the best way to kill him; it didn't have to be with a gun. But showing up without one would be like going to work on a construction site without a hammer in my belt.

The big storms were finished on the Andaman coast, and the *Aceso* would be back at the estuary of the Ban Lam, where the ashram now stood. I began to fantasize about meeting Devon with the gun when—

A thin male body dropped into the seat across from me. I barely looked at the dark flash of skin that I knew would be a hustler.

"I'm not looking for company," I said. I turned to my piece of paper, trying to avoid his presence.

"Why not?" was the reply that made me want to throttle him. He was a skinny, skinny little Indian, obviously a junkie. Shoulder-length black hair framed his boney face, a face riddled with drug sores.

"Not interested."

"You be with me?" I focused on my paper, as he badgered. "Why not?" And then again, "Why not?"

"Would you mind fucking off?"

"Why? Why you don't be with me? Why not?"

Planning to kill Devon had me on edge, and I felt a rising urge to jab a fork into his heroin sores and twist it while I thumped his head on the table. Instead, I took a breath and faced him.

I froze. *His eyes.* Black orbs were set in bloody yellow. The hair on my skin was up—I'd seen them before … but that wasn't possible … they weren't exactly cataracts—*what was it?*

I was staring—trapped—searching for the source of familiarity, my stomach twisting. Then it came. I recalled the day I'd seen Devon by the ashram, the Devon with the dead eyes. You could only catch it once in a rare while with Devon, but the frail Indian junkie was naked, artless and gone. Devon's eyes were pale and healthy, the junkie's eyes were black and jaundiced. But they were the same. He had no soul—this little junkie had *no soul.*

Man, I was losing it. I gave myself a mental slap, a reminder that there's no such thing as a soul.

He kept speaking to me. I pushed my plate of spicy cashews and rice over to him, but despite a dire need for nutrition he took no interest in it. I still didn't like him. I felt plainly belligerent and anti-social. A tourista at a nearby table kept peering past her partner to ogle us. I guess a white man and his same-sex prostitute were more interesting than her tie-dye wearing boyfriend.

The room had a clutter of music and voices. I didn't care what the desperate little zombie was saying. I leaned forward and interrupted him.

"Where can I buy a gun?"

He stopped talking, his mouth hung open.

"A gun," I repeated. I mimed a bang-bang with my fingers.

"Money," he said.

I wasn't naïve enough to think that this wastrel was actually going to be of assistance. And God knows I wouldn't have trusted him any farther than I could spit him across the room. But I continued the charade.

"Gun, then money."

He asked for money again and I shook my head. Then his hand hit the table, chopped it. Chop, chop. He leaned forward, his mouth moving under his dead eyes. "Cutting animal."

"What?" I said.

"You get gun where animal is cutting."

"Like cutting *meat*?"

"Cutting meat," he said. He chopped again.

Strange how things work. I opened my billfold and passed him a couple hundred baht. Out of the corner of my eye I saw the white woman following our transaction. I swallowed my beer and took another look at the creepy little fucker. He made an 'O' with his mouth and stabbed his finger at it—his quaint way of offering to suck me off.

The curious woman's eyes followed us as I headed for the street with what had to be the mangiest hustler in all Bangkok.

We stepped into the ruptured innocence of Khao San Road, a density of people and commerce. Beat-driven music pumped, hawkers and hookers proliferated. Among the goods and services at my immediate disposal were a happy hour cocktail, a fake student card, a discounted train ticket bought with my fake student card, phony press credentials, a bag of weed from the pool hall next to the police station, a custom suit from turbaned tailors, an oil massage, or a blowjob from an addict with facial lesions. The one thing I couldn't get on Khao San Road was the one thing my heart desired: a handgun.

The little guy's name was Aroo.

When the famed strip had turned to neon and all hope of Aroo showing up was lost, I returned to my guesthouse. I'd expected nothing else. My first mistake was in giving him money up front. Of course he had to go and fix. For all I knew, his soulless body had stopped moving. That much cash traded for heroin would be lethal in a single dose. This I knew from a girl I'd once encountered who smoked heroin. In Thailand she could chase the dragon all day long for fifty dollars a month.

I sat bleakly in the garden of my guest house, thinking. Unlike the foggy days in Ao Lai after the fire, my brain now burned like a flare. I was invaded by a guy with a gray ponytail and a Singha beer who plopped down to roll a joint. He couldn't 'fuckin' believe' what had happened to Khao San Road. He waxed sentimental for the old days of sleepy guesthouses and orange-robed monks. Earlier, his horror of commerce had been piqued when someone tried to sell him tickets to a 'ping-pong ball show,' an event that involved naked girls doing more tricks with little white balls than trained seals can do with large, colored ones. In another time, another headspace, I would've liked him. As it was, I could barely respond when he asked, "So what ya up to, mate? Headed south?"

"Uh, no," I said. "Headed home actually. I lost my uncle…"

"Aw shit, mate, that's a bummer," he said sympathetically as he offered me the joint.

"No worries," I said, waving off the spliff, "he had a good life."

I hated the lie. Damn, I wanted get this over with.

I awoke in the dark to a cacophony of barking dogs and the knowledge that Anna and Amy were dead. My chest felt crushed.

When I got back to imagining, planning the specifics of Devon's death, time felt urgent. It was as if a big ticking clock loomed over me. For whatever reason, I wasn't sure. Maybe I sensed the danger of circumstance changing the longer I took to execute my task. More likely though, it was the ache, the pull, to collapse—to lie down and scream and cry. The urge I buried again and again. I often visualized a period of retreat and mourning in Thailand, but in reality I would have to do it in America. After I killed Devon, my ass would need to be gone fast, back to American soil. Though I hadn't actually checked, I doubted that my country had an extradition agreement with Thailand for murder. And even if we did, I doubted that the Thais could produce any evidence compelling enough for my extradition. That was if I went about things correctly.

I was well aware that the best-laid plans can go awry, and now and then I was shaken by a wave of sheer terror. Fierce determination wrestled it down—I sensed it wanted to evolve into an excuse not to kill Devon, not to go through with justice. My forefathers had fought in wars for their countries, a vaguer concept than fighting for one's family. They had faced death and dismemberment—I said *I can face this*. No, I wouldn't succumb—I would complete my task regardless of whether it scared the shit out of me. The fact was, the terror of eternal incarceration exceeded the fear of death.

No one who spoke English knew where a 'meat-packing' district was. I wasn't about to go asking Thai people on the street, because they would've just made something up—that's the 'face' thing, and it would've wasted my time as it twisted my brain. With little hope of finding Aroo, I headed for a place that I knew had English language Yellow Pages for Bangkok.

I entered the air-conditioned décor of The Grand Lullaby Resort in my linen slacks and mask of respectability. I recognized Som, my one-time translator, in a jacket and tie behind the desk. I greeted him politely and offered a tip as he passed me the directory. He replied in clear English, "Money isn't necessary," no doubt remembering me as the cop-bribing piece of shit who had contributed to Thailand's deep and endless cycle of corruption.

Basically, I struck out. No one expected English-speaking tourists to be looking for meat plants. Or maybe—another vivid possibility—there *was* no 'meat-packing' factory or district. I felt the big clock ticking.

The closest thing I could find was two seafood wholesalers, one that looked Thai, the other with a Japanese name.

I jumped a taxi and headed down to the Klong Toey district, where the Chaophraya River enters the Gulf of Thailand. I found both of the wholesalers and a ripe stench of fish rot, but nowhere that looked as if it may have a stash of handguns.

That evening I wandered the Khao San Road neighborhood looking for Aroo.

I made the decision to head for a refugee camp in the Kanchanaburi district bordering Burma. On Khao San Road I waited as my press credentials were created. I was Magnus Larsen, a writer for a Washington State publication called *The Chinook Journal*. With a press card and a little cash, I didn't see how I'd be denied a visit to a camp. After all, the Burmese military were the bad guys, and there was no love lost between Burmese and Thai soldiers.

I was no sooner in the street with my new identity when lifeless eyes stopped me in my tracks. Lo and behold, the dead chicken still walked—it was Aroo.

Forty-five minutes later our taxi weaved through a district bustling with industry amid roughly worn buildings, where men with muscles pushed and pulled carts of goods to trucks and tuk-tuks. We turned toward a sliver of ocean with an industrial shoreline and a flotilla of junks beyond. Aroo and the driver spoke in Thai. The taxi twisted again through narrow streets. The deeper we went, the slummier it got.

This time Aroo got no cash advance. The details of our transaction were clearly defined up front—if I bought a gun, he got paid; if I didn't buy a gun, he didn't get paid. Despite that, his most constant comment was, "Money." Sometimes he got downright Shakespearean with lines like, "Why you no be with me?" The sores on his face were disgusting.

The driver spoke again and Aroo answered. The taxi slowed, and suddenly we were amid a putrid stench. Bangkok, like most of the third world, has its share of ripe sewers, but this was odious. I covered my nose and mouth with my shirt. We stopped outside a building the size of a big barn with cracking paint and wooden boards. Men were pulling massive ice blocks up a conveyor belt into the structure.

I instructed the taxi to wait as I got outside with Aroo. It was indeed a place where chickens and pigs saw their last glimmer of consciousness. Aroo wanted to go in alone. Fine by me; I was dying of stink poisoning. But despite all the information I had imparted to him, I couldn't get him to understand what a silencer was. Finally, I borrowed a strip of newspaper from the taxi-driver and drew a picture of a handgun, then added a silencer. The zombie gazed at it and was on his way. "And bullets!" I shouted after him.

Back in the taxi, the driver laughed at the sight of my shirt over my face.

I was no gun expert. We had rifles on the farm, and when I was twelve years old I'd taken a one-day course on the safe use and storage of firearms, and earned a certificate. I'd done some target practicing with my dad and even plugged a couple of grouse for dinner. One thing I'd noticed as a kid, was that kids from Republican families had better guns than kids from Democrat families. My good buddy, Mike Hillier, had access to a stash of handguns, and once in a while we'd sneak a .38 Smith & Wesson revolver out to shoot at tin cans and food cartons. The last time I'd actually fired a gun I was blowing a hole through Aunt Jemima's head like she was a vicious punk in a *Dirty Harry* movie. And silencers were known to me only from films and TV.

The big clock hanging over me ticked ever so slowly in the insufferable stench. My fingers were crossed. Finally Aroo appeared, as empty-handed and alone as when he'd gone in. I watched him eagerly, refusing to abandon faint hope.

Back in the cab, Aroo managed to convey that we had a rendezvous of some sort later that night.

"They have a gun?" I asked hopefully as taxi rolled to better air.

"Have gun," Aroo said. Then added, "Money."

"I'm not coming back here with money," I told him. "I see the gun first—if it's good, then we'll get some money."

"Must take money."

"I'm not taking any fucking money," I replied.

It was hours before our 'meeting' but I wasn't letting him out of my sight. We left the district, to the great relief of my nostrils. It was late afternoon, I hadn't eaten since breakfast. At a street side eatery, I ordered us orange juice and skewers of smoked chicken. Aroo was the most calorie-adverse person I'd ever seen. The irony was, if anyone needed food, it was him. He drank some orange juice but swallowed nothing else. Who knows what his tiny body was running on. It wasn't food and it wasn't love, that I could see.

That night we returned to the stench but kept going past the slaughterhouse. Aroo gave orders to the taxi driver until the streets narrowed to a point where cars couldn't pass. We continued on foot.

A jagged path cut through a slum. I followed Aroo over patches of cement cracked with weeds as he melded into the night. Dogs with a scabrous mange came to life, snarling as we moved through their world. I was the farang, the alien—they may not have barked at all at just Aroo.

Odors hung like weightless plumes in the soupy air. Cooking coals and candles glowed in the hovels surrounding us, some with no privacy at all. Bodies reposed, the young and the ancient. Some squatted and ate. Our physical vicinity would've been invasive in the West. I got a sweet whiff of burning opium. There was a mystique about the lives that existed amid squalor. Eyes poked out of their borrowed shells like a colony of hermit crabs as we passed—a farang in pale linen pants following a black skeleton…

The cluster of dilapidation broke as we passed over narrow *klongs*, barely wide enough for a canoe. Here, I could see the ocean, only a block or two away. A large orange moon hung just above its own distorting reflection, adorning Aroo's pitch-black hair with a sheen of light that I wasn't about to mistake for a halo.

We came to an area that opened into narrow lanes that dissected old rundown buildings, mostly dark. Amid the many ripe smells a stench arose. Here the ocean view was blocked by buildings, and as I followed the frail spook we twisted through lanes and alleys, and I lost all sense of direction. I didn't like feeling dependent upon Aroo—but what choice was there?

It seemed like we'd walked a long way. Couldn't we have taken a taxi here, come another way?

The streets opened up into a mostly lightless rectangle surrounded by decaying buildings. The dark shapes of bodies moved along the street, appearing and disappearing from doors and alleys made secret by night. Aroo advanced toward a subdued glow emanating from the third floor of a box about five stories high. The destination whispered uneasily in my guts.

We trod up a narrow staircase, twisting through total blackness until we came to the third floor.

Thick with smoke, a dainty place it was not. Tables of card players and dice throwers packed in around bottles of Mekong and Thai rum. A clutter of girls lurked with their captured men like a colony of sea anemones in the dark red light of an alcove. I was the only one of my kind in the place. I stepped up to the bar with Aroo, where he indicated that I should wait.

The barman's first assumption was that I wanted a girl. I didn't want anything, but I ordered a beer, mostly to keep my mind off the fact that I alone was white and wearing linen slacks. The beer was insanely expensive, about six dollars, maybe a price just for me, or maybe it included a lady's fifteen minutes of service. I watched the barman closely as he opened my beer. I didn't need to wake up in an alley stripped of my clothes and belongings.

Aroo returned shortly with a young man of smooth skin and full lip, not as rough-cut as I'd expected. I greeted him in Thai, and we returned to the black stairs and ascended to the next level. I was led down a dingy hallway with claustrophobic walls and a pungent cloud of opium. The Thai boy knocked lightly on a door with peeling layer of green paint. A voice barked from within and the door was pushed open to a stained floor.

The two characters in this room more than compensated for the first man's façade of innocence. A tall, lanky man with a hard face was in charge. His eyes and mouth seemed scarred with hate. Maybe this was what became of children who were beaten and burned with cigarettes. He rose from behind a small table. The second man stayed seated; an apparent aristocrat, he was smoking a Marlboro.

I don't speak Thai but I can get through basic greetings and numbers, often helpful in negotiation. The lanky man with the vicious face had some English. "What you need?" was followed by, "What you look for?" Both sentences came out as a sort of a bark.

"A good handgun with ammunition—bullets—and a silencer."

"You look," he said, pulling up a ragged briefcase. It opened and he unwrapped a cloth, revealing two guns and a few loose bullets. From somewhere deep in the building's entrails, I thought I could hear someone screaming.

Neither of the guns looked anywhere near as solid or classy (if 'classy' is a word you can use for little machines that kill) as the Glock that Devon had given me. I examined the better-looking of the two. It was a Korean job called a Daewoo and it looked like a Luger. I opened the clip to find it empty. I turned to the dog of war for an indication about bullets. His face told me I was luckless. I hoisted the other. It looked older, more worn—it was called a Type 77 pistol. The magazine was full with seven bullets and there were three more outside the gun.

I wasn't impressed—one gun had no ammo and the other was … Chinese-made. The crap from China you could buy in the street markets didn't exactly inspire confidence. But damned if I wanted to be goose-chasing around for bullets for the Daewoo, the nicer-looking Korean gun. If they could demonstrate that the Type 77 pistol worked, I'd take it. Hopefully the Chinese put more into their guns than they put into their flashlights and alarm clocks.

As far as a silencer went, I was shit outta luck.

In Thai, I asked what he wanted for the gun. The price was exorbitant. I danced around his growls, insisting I wasn't going to pay 800 dollars for a Chinese gun.

"Why you want gun?" he sneered. "You wanting to kill—or you frightened?"

"I'm frightened," I said.

He looked into me, as deeply as Anna used to, but it was a much uglier probe. "You no lady-boy, you wanting to kill."

I couldn't wait to get this done with. We finally agreed on 300 dollars, a good price for him, not me. But we weren't done yet. When he found that I didn't have the cash on me, he took it out on Aroo in a rough barrage of Thai that I couldn't follow. But that wasn't the hard part. I needed to see that the gun worked.

"This looks old," I said, "I need to know it shoots."

"It shoot, okay," he said with a fury.

"Let's go somewhere and you can show me."

"Where we go? Nowhere to go! Gun shoot, okay!"

"Okay," I said. "You can show me."

His eyes were murderous. "You no trust? I am liar to you?"

"Not at all," I said calmly, my heart beginning to race. "Please," I added politely, "let's go somewhere and you can show me."

"You no trust me…" he growled. "I show you gun work." His arm rose with the loaded pistol until it was leveled right at Aroo's head. "You tell me, show you—I show you." His voice shook with the threat. Aroo leaned back as far from the barrel of the gun as he could.

"You say, shoot! You say, show me!" the thug yelled. I searched madly for a response when suddenly the arm spun and a blast detonated—

I cursed myself for jumping. There was a moment of quiet shock in the aftermath. I crossed the stained floor to the wall where the slug had entered. I found a pen in my pocket and took it apart, sliding the plastic ink cartridge into the bullet hole as far as it would go. It wasn't a large caliber slug, but it had gone deep.

"You happy?"

I turned back to the salesman of the year and nodded. Our final obstacle was, or so I thought, completing the transaction. I wanted to do it in a bar on Khao San Road, where it was unlikely that they would simply shoot me and take my money.

Aroo explained the problem. "Polices is chasing him."

'Polices is chasing him.' As far as I was concerned they couldn't have picked a better guy to be chasing.

"I shoot for you. Now trusting okay?"

In the end I acquiesced. I would go get the money. I couldn't wait to get out of the horrible room with its anger, its stains and its bullet hole. But they weren't done with me yet. I was about to meet the real ugliness. The real horror.

"Hey, you look," said the tough. He spoke in Thai to the seated smoker. "Yes, you can look okay," he said to me. I watched the seated man place a photo album on a chair. They wanted to show me something. I moved over to look. A scarred, smoke-stained hand opened the book. It was an image of what looked like a dead woman. The page turned. Naked people were lying on beds, dead. Women, girls, boys … some of them tied and bruised.

As my stomach turned, the thug's voice whispered, "You want to kill … you angry can kill … ten thousand dollar, you fuck and kill …

boy, girl," he hissed. "You rich man, you can enjoy to kill…"

Seconds later I was moving down the black stairs alone. It felt as someone had broken a bag of wet poison inside of me. My God, life was horrible.

I walked for blocks before I found a tuk-tuk to take me out of the slum. I told myself it was a scam. It had to be. The photos were fakes. Some piece of shit shows up with ten thousand bucks and they rob him and kick the shit out of him. That had to be it. God I hoped so. My hands were on my stomach. For an atheist, I was invoking God quite a bit.

I had to believe that. Or I wouldn't have gone back for the gun. The clock was ticking. The pain in my guts ached to be heard, to be screamed. Detonated. I needed that gun. Yeah, I went back and dealt with the devil.

I left the sleazy warehouse with a Chinese handgun hidden in a small daypack and a junkie in tow. We taxied back to Khao San Road. This time when he said, "Money," I passed him a stack of baht. Maybe I should've been grateful, but between his dead eyes and his greasy friends, I felt sick and unsettled. Whoever said 'parting is such sweet sorrow' hadn't spent time with Aroo.

I wandered away from the colored lights and clog of people, up the emptier lanes to my guesthouse. As I approached my room I could see a throng of travelers in the communal garden, buzzing with talk, drinking beers. They had a glow of happiness, enjoyment. "Hey, mate, come and join us!" called the guy with the gray ponytail to the guy with the gun in his little daypack.

I tried to dredge a piece of humanness out of myself. All I could mutter was, "G'night."

I closed the door on the voices in the garden. I removed the gun from my pack and placed it on a dresser. And there it sat, a symbol of triumph and disgust.

I took a long shower, trying to wash the psychic filth off of me.

Chapter Forty

I awoke to a thrill of fear. Today I would head south to kill Devon. I was under no illusion that my plan didn't have risks. I intended to take every possible precaution. When my train rolled out later in the day, I planned to disembark at the stop just north of Wamathani Station, minimizing the chance that I'd be recognized—after all, I'd lived in Ao Lai for five years.

I'd run through vision after vision of shooting Devon, plan after plan; killing him near the ashram, killing him on board the *Aceso*. I was leaning toward a kill that would not be discovered for a period of time, twelve, fourteen hours or longer. What if I killed him and weighted his body, or got on board the *Aceso* and hid it? Or got into his room and shot him, then put the gun in his hand as if it was his own act. I wondered if it would be possible to close all the doors and windows in his room and wrap the gun in a towel to silence it, or at least muffle it from the decks below. What if Devon slept with a new lover? Then what?

The *Aceso* did not post guards at night; it wasn't necessary. At least it hadn't been before. I believed I could get on board, and I knew my way around the upper deck.

To make matters more challenging, I would need to be completely invisible in Ao Lai—everyone knew me. With every plan, a problem, but with every will, a way. With no major stops I could make it to Bangkok in ten hours with a taxi and a focused driver. Hired outside of Ao Lai of course, someone who didn't know me. Straight to the Bangkok airport, where I would be standing by for the first flight to America. Or Canada. Or London.

I'd be suspect number one in Devon Clarke's death. I'd be foremost on the mind of every devotee—and when the U.S. Embassy got word of Devon Clarke's killing, Brian Morski would take a breath and recall the passion in my eyes, and Bevan Smith would feel the tickle of her proximity to infamy.

But with a little luck I'd be back in the United States of America, the land of the free.

I had a quick breakfast and returned to my room to pack. As I tucked the Type 77 pistol into my luggage, I was struck by a rebellious thought. It occurred to me that Anna, regardless of the circumstances of her and Amy's deaths, would never approve of me killing Devon. Not now. Not after he'd changed his mind. I smiled.

Do you enjoy ironies, Ms. Schott?

Devastation came quickly. I'd snuck around like a ghost's shadow to discover the plain fact: the *Aceso* was neither by the mouth of the Ban Lam River nor in the sheltered cove, Ao Ngu La. The great white palace had pulled anchor, and The Children of a Living God and their leader had vanished.

I clung to distant hope. After my initial letdown, I thought it may be possible that the boat had gone for maintenance; with all the devotees living on board, the fresh water supply would need to be replenished more often, the heads flushed, et cetera. But when I saw the ashram in the light of day, it had become a schoolhouse; local children and teachers filtered in and out. My heart sank—they weren't coming back.

I had a dilemma: Should I step out of the shadows and start asking where the boat had gone, thus revealing myself as someone stalking the *Aceso*? At that point I still had an instinct for self-preservation. But how else would I find her?

I chose to ask the teachers at the new school. The Children of a Living God had given them a building; perhaps they had a forwarding address. They knew me, I was Magnus, the guy who did boat tours. I spoke to a young woman teacher outside the ashram—the joy in her eyes reminded me of the devotees that had been there before her. Yes, she told me eagerly and kindly, they had gone to Penang in Malaysia, part of a big tour, she said. Her bright eyes were the opposite of Aroo's, and she couldn't say enough about Dadaram's greatness.

For all the stress and frustration their departure had caused, it was maybe a blessing in disguise. Malaysia was due south of Thailand. If I could sneak in and kill Devon, and then get back to Thailand with no Malaysian customs stamps in my passport, it would be a pretty fine alibi. I would have to maintain a presence, such as a rented room, somewhere in Thailand. An illegal entry would also save me the risk of clearing customs with a handgun in my possession. I recalled what had happened to the sisters Schott when they unwittingly tried it. There would be no record of me ever having been in Malaysia. Unless they caught me down there.

It was well after midnight and moonless. We were at least a mile offshore, one of a long line of bright lights that were squid boats. We rocked gently, almost serenely, but there was an undercurrent of anticipation, danger. I was tucked away, out of the sight of the other fishing craft. We weren't in that tight of a line but the skipper had a healthy dose of paranoia.

Huge lanterns hung from each boat, penetrating into the ocean depths. Cephalopods rose to the light like they were being called home by God. In a sense they were—teenaged boys hooked them, filling the ship's hold with squid. The skipper grunted in my direction, extending a rough hand, and I passed him my binoculars, not for the first time. He stared out hard in several directions.

I respected his diligence, though it was probably more for his own sake than mine. I'd been to Malaysia legitimately on previous occasions. Foreigners living in Thailand need to leave the country every three months for a fresh visa stamp; many land at Langkawi Island just offshore.

Clearing Malaysian customs at Langkawi, the Jewel of Kedah, is unforgettable. Signs indicate that possession of drugs carries the death penalty, and there are large, lurid photos of backs and buttocks beaten bloody and purple by rattan canes. With a special consideration for the illiterate, there are no 'keep out' signs on restricted areas but rather a silhouette of a man with a rifle shooting a man without a rifle. Malaysia's no-nonsense approach to outlaws would make an Arizona sheriff proud. It made *me* pay attention.

The captain spoke to the boys, and the lantern's gas was turned off; light ebbed as its hiss died out. I came out under the stars. The golden hue of fishing lamps extended north and south until the line faded into thick air.

The Malaysian boat was as dark as we were. Our port sides bumped together, and I climbed from one vessel into the other.

Penang Island is a Chinese enclave in the Strait of Malacca. At 11:30

a.m., my ferry, bound for the port city of Georgetown, was packed with tourists. The trip from the mainland had been just over thirty minutes, and we were almost there. Sightseers crowded around the windows as the city left over from Malaysia's days under British rule came into view.

I alone remained seated and looking at the floor, holding the daypack that contained, among other things, a gun. Amid the chatter of voices, I was drawn to a particular conversation; an English couple was looking out a starboard window.

"See … that's a garden ... those are trees..." The woman's British voice held a good dose of awe.

Her male counterpart agreed, "It really is lovely ... makes the others look like baby yachts ... for baby tycoons." The woman laughed lightly as I rose to my feet.

I pushed into the throng for a starboard view. Less than a mile away was the unmistakable beauty of my prey's floating palace, docked at a marina. A flush moved through my head. *That was easy*, I thought. I wondered if it was a good omen or bad to find it so easily, then reprimanded myself for thinking superstitiously.

I checked into a cheap hotel in a neighborhood that seemed exclusively Chinese. No one asked to see my passport and I called myself 'James Douglas' in the register. I hid my gun in a room that had a whiff of mothballs. It was hot and I was excited. My binoculars were in my daypack as I headed out.

I approached the Tanjong City Marina, the resting spot of the *Aceso*, walking distance from Georgetown. I was nervous about being spotted by a devotee—were they out roaming the streets? My eyes were wide open.

I didn't much stand out and that was a good thing. High-end tourists and backpackers dotted the streets of the old colonial city. I found a restaurant with a view of the marina and ordered some food with my binocs on the table. I kept tabs on the entrance to the pier.

There was a security gate but it was open, and those who moved past the guard house (or office or whatever it was) weren't being checked.

As the afternoon deepened, I grew bolder, moving closer and closer until individuals would've been recognizable at the pier, at least with my binocs. Then I started to see people I knew: Mariel, Suvita, then Samuel and others were returning to the ship … this revved my pulse. I was absolutely determined never to hurt anyone but Devon, even if it meant fucking up my mission. Hurting innocent people would not have honored Anna and Amy.

I kept creeping closer to the wharf. I bought a white hat from a shop that catered to visitors. I figured it would help disguise me, at least from a distance.

I got within a block of the Tanjong City Marina. The security gate was open and there was indeed a guard standing by. The trickle of devotees had ended. I was frozen—do I go forward, or is it enough for now? *Is it safe?* I turned in a circle and looked hard for anyone who may know me. Then I moved for the gate. The guard watched me intently as I approached. "I'm with the *Aceso*," I said casually as I passed. He nodded with cursory politeness. My heart thumping, I headed down onto the wharf.

I made a point of looking at things through my binoculars so it would seem in character when I assessed the *Aceso* from a distance. Really, it was pointless paranoia—no one would even be noticing a white guy dressed like me. When my glasses swept over the *Aceso*, I saw no one on deck. I was searching for a plan when a familiar sound hit me—they were chanting in the ashram. Before I knew it, I was headed toward the *Aceso*'s mooring. I kept my eyes sharply on her decks—Dadaram and the devotees would all be in 'temple,' but the ship's pilot was not one of The Children of a Living God. My new hat was on, and I was ready to drop my eyes quickly and turn around if anyone popped up. The dock squeaked below me. The *Aceso*'s shadow loomed like Goliath.

Tied up to the pier, there was now a different kind of ramp up to her second deck than the hanging ramp I knew. Sweat ran out of my hat, over my forehead, down my cheeks; my shirt was damp with wet stains on my chest. I ascended the gangway. I tried to find comfort in the hymns emanating from the ashram. *What the hell was I up to?* I rose to the upper deck in what seemed like slow motion, though my legs moved with purpose.

Devon's quarters were unlocked. A stab of sadness shook my fear. The crescent room felt different but there was a ghost of Anna and Amy. A ghost of beauty and happiness.

I was thinking, thinking … my mind felt hot like a flare and sharp like a razor. I moved down to the master bedroom … then into the luxurious ensuite. I opened the medicine cabinet, looked on the counters—there were no signs of a female presence, no pink razors or tampons or womanly skin cream. I hoped that meant that Devon slept alone.

I looked at the shower curtain. It struck me that if I pulled it just slightly across, I could hide behind it. If Devon came in and turned on the sink, I'd shoot him with the gun wrapped in a towel. If he took a shit, I'd turn on the water and shoot him. If he opened the shower curtain, I'd just shoot him. I found a tremor in my hands. That wasn't acceptable. Even within this room, even wrapped in a towel, I worried about the noise of a gunshot, one or more. I'd seen in movies where they wrap the gun in a towel—that's what made me think of it, but I didn't trust movies. From where I was I could barely hear the singing from the ashram—but I could still discern a hint of it. They would probably hear the gunshot on the second deck; they'd hear *something*.

Then my best thought came: I had Devon's voice. I could do him perfectly. I heard his cadence in my head: "I'm alright, thank you. A little privacy, please. I'd like to be alone." What if the devotee kept speaking? More speech from Devon: "Tell them not to worry. I'm perfectly alright."

I could do it. I'd put Devon's corpse behind the shower curtain. I'd clean up the blood. He wouldn't be discovered until the following morning, maybe later if they only took a quick look around his room. If I left the *Aceso* at 2 a.m., I'd have a five-or-six hour head start. A private boat from the island and a taxi north. Potentially I could be on a boat back to Thailand before they even found him. My Chinese gun would be in the bottom of the ocean. My passport would have no Malaysian stamps.

Could I imitate Devon under extreme stress? I could if my life depended upon it. And it would.

Heart pounding, I moved outside where hymns from the ashram grew louder. My knees were shaking. I moved down to the lower deck as quickly and casually as I could. *Relax, I belong here*—that's what I told myself. That was the image I wanted to project if anyone saw me. I looked around—the lower deck was empty.

I crossed the gangway as silently as I could without being stealthy—that may have drawn attention. My shoes squeaked on the wood below me. I was dripping wet. As I approached the security gate, I made a point of noticing how it worked when closed—at night, it would be locked only from the outside, not for those leaving. It was an important bonus; not that I couldn't have climbed over it if necessary. I smiled casually at the guard as I left the marina. I would return tomorrow during their 'temple.' The next time I entered Devon's suite I would be carrying a gun.

My clothes were drenched. On the way back to my hotel I picked up shorts and a t-shirt.

That evening in Georgetown, I glanced constantly over my shoulder. Not far from the Tanjong City Marina, waterfront signs advertised tours and fishing expeditions. A young Malay with a speed boat looked me over—a guy with a brand new Tiger Beer t-shirt. Why on earth would I need a boat in the middle of the night? he wanted to know.

"My father is sick," I told him. "My mother will call me tomorrow, late. If he takes a turn for the worse, I want to leave right away." He tried to delve into the logistics of it but I passed him a wad of Malaysian rand that ended the argument.

"You Canada?" he asked. I nodded. He told me how to wake him up if I had to.

Morning came early and I waited for the world to catch up.

I wanted my 'face of respectability' clothes dry-cleaned. My preference was to look like I'd just gotten off a cruise ship rather than a hungry dog when I returned to the pier. Defying the most basic of ethnic clichés, my Chinese neighborhood did not have a laundry; at least not one that dry-cleaned. The woman at the desk of my hovel told me of a place in Georgetown. "Little bit esspensive but good," she said.

My impatience at the drycleaner's was excessive. After all, it was morning and I didn't need to be back on the *Aceso* until the late afternoon. But I was good and edgy. I pleaded with the woman at the counter, "Your signs says '*one-hour.*'"

"Today no one-hour," she replied. "Big order. Big, big, you seeing now." I could see a huge mass of laundry being sorted behind her.

"Please tell me I can get it by noon."

"Trying hard for two o'clock. Trying hard for you," she said.

"I very much appreciate that. Here's for your extra trouble."

The woman waved dismissively at the cash. "Two o'clock, ready." I thanked her again and left.

It was just nerves. 'Temple' didn't start until deep afternoon. Time was abundant. Too abundant. I went back to my room and tried to relax.

&

I was back at the drycleaner's just before 2 p.m. The place bustled. I fell into the rear of a line of customers. A massive order was being assembled by the counter; towels and sheets were wrapped in sheer protective plastic. Chinese boys were loading the laundry onto carts, helping with the big order. Though I tried not to, I felt impatient. The Big Task was looming. I was about sixth in line.

I felt a sense of rising unease. Something was wrong. *What was it?*

Why was I so impatient? But it wasn't just impatience. *Something was wrong.* Adrenaline pumped. Laundry was coming from the shop's rear; the boys in front handled it efficiently. I couldn't understand my feeling of panic. I told myself, *it's just jitters.*

The woman from the morning was at the counter, calling out a name, "Mistah Smith…" It took me a moment to realize that it was me she wanted—that was the name I'd given. I recognized my slacks and shirt. A trickle of anticipation dampened my forehead. The woman with my small bundle called again, looking at me, I lurched forward—

Then stopped dead.

It was the stack of lime-green towels—they were from the *Aceso*! A man at the counter turned around—it was Benoit, the devotee—

"Magnus!" he gasped. I bolted in shock. I stood outside the door, my back against a wall, not knowing what to say or do. Benoit was suddenly outside. He stared at me, wide-eyed.

"Hello, Benoit."

He shouted inside, "Get the laundry! Quick!" He began to run toward the marina. I took off after him.

"Hey, Benoit!"

I grabbed him on a busy street, spinning him around, holding him by the shirt. "What the fuck?" I said, pretending not to understand why he was running away. He looked at me like I was the devil then broke loose. I watched him jogging through the street, driven by fear—and devotion to Dadaram. My stomach sank to my knees. What the hell could I have said? *Gee, what a coincidence, I'm on holiday here too.*

Through my binoculars I watched the entrance point to the pier; guards had been posted, some of them devotees I recognized, like Samuel and Evan. An hour and a half after I saw Benoit, the *Aceso* left port, ripping out my guts as she went.

Chapter Forty-One

I teetered on the edge of an abyss. Without knowing where to find Devon Clarke, my *raison d'être* had been suspended. My legs could move but they had no ground to run on. Hell had shades and layers and a seemingly infinite number of little compartments.

The *Aceso* did not want to be found. I'd made an attempt to discover the next port of call from the dock authority in Tanjong City when I was still in Penang—but that was a military secret after they'd learned about me.

Here in Bangkok I'd contacted AMVER, a division of the U.S. Coast Guard that tracks marine vessels worldwide for the purpose of helping ships in distress. The *Aceso* was not registered, probably because she was a private vessel. They had no record of her. I wandered through Bangkok's hot poison air for days, thinking and sinking ... despair taking root like gangrene.

One afternoon, fate's wind blew differently. I was moving past booths of clothing and handbags and an endless repetition of voices: 'Come sir, just looking...' when I passed a hut with music tapes and movies on VHS. Devon Clarke's face stopped me dead.

Dadaram was on the cover of a VHS tape, lit to look as though his head was emanating light. Feverishly, I began reading the jacket notes: it was one of a series of lectures produced by The Children of a Living God in Boston. In the description of the speech, Dadaram was called a 'divine being,' a term I had once heard Mariel use. Most importantly, there was an address and a phone number. If I remembered correctly, Devon communicated with an office in the States, probably in Boston, I was now thinking. There were six episodes in the lecture series. The seller had just one of the others. The nonchalance of a good bargainer was completely abandoned as I bought both tapes, one and three in the series.

In the lobby of my little hotel, I watched the tapes with a cold fascination. Devon, as Dadaram, spoke of 'pathways' and of 'access to God.' In the first speech, he told the auditorium of followers that God had begun sending him visions of his own path sometime after the death of his son. I played the speech twice. A small crowd began to gather by the TV, captivated by his message, or maybe just by him.

That night I was at the Worldwide Overseas Phone Office, enthusing with a devotee in Boston about Dadaram's message. I gushed, calling it 'spirituality unrestrained by dogma'—a phrase I'd stolen from one of the folks in my hotel lobby. I said my name was Jim Douglas, that I'd come to Thailand to study Buddhism, and that I wrote for a Washington State journal called *The Chinook*. As I bubbled with fake enthusiasm, the devotee bubbled with real enthusiasm. How could I interview Dadaram? I asked. Hear him speak live?

The perky young man in Boston began providing me with the *Aceso*'s route and schedule throughout the Southeast Asian Pacific. It was a lengthy tour, and Dadaram was speaking at some of the stops that included Singapore, Melaka, Jakarta and Bali. The Children of a Living God were also going to Sri Lanka, the Andaman Islands, then on to Bombay. I wrote the entire schedule down with its approximate dates, though I believed Devon would be dead early in the tour.

"Thank you so much," I pulsed, my excitement now sincere.

"It's my pleasure, Jim … I'll tell Dadaram you'd like an interview."

"Uh … better give me a chance to get out of the monastery first—then I'll know my timeframe to catch up with him … I'd be thrilled to see him speak in person."

When the conversation ended, I felt like a drowning man who'd been thrown a life preserver.

I itched to leave. The big clock never stopped ticking—it just got louder. But my practical situation demanded strategic assessment. I couldn't fly due to airport security; x-ray machines would've detected my gun. That meant that I was stuck with buses, trains and boats—which in turn meant that I had to get ahead of the *Aceso*, get to one of her future stops, otherwise I would always be running behind. Screwing up was not an option. Each time I failed to kill Devon, it would get harder to do it the next time.

Presently, the *Aceso* would be in Singapore, then shortly en route to Jakarta, then Bali. I wanted to catch her in Bali. I thought I could.

I'd arrived in Bangkok with about 6,200 dollars when I'd first left Sally-Sue's. After a month's living and my ill-fated trip to Penang, I now had just under 4,700. It was decent coin in cheap Thailand, but I was watching expenses closely. I knew I might need cash to buy me out of a jam somewhere. And there was another outlay I couldn't escape: I needed fake ID, not a student card, the good stuff—especially since I'd been spotted in Penang. It could save me from the gallows. I wanted no record of Magnus Larsen ever having been in Bali when I killed Devon there.

None of the little fraud factories along Khao San Road could help out with the real prize: a passport. But when I let the King of Thailand's face on a stack of baht notes do the talking for me, I got a lead.

A few boat stops down the Chaophraya River, I found my way to a little semi-subterranean shop with a sign that read, 'Tattoos here are good, not cheap.' I pushed open the door.

An electric needle buzzed. Walls were plastered with photos and drawn images. Beyond a counter, a white guy was concentrating through thick glasses as he worked on a woman's exposed back. His crew cut was barely more than stubble on his skull, and he had piercings and tats of his own. A classical image was taking shape on the woman's skin; a cherub. Even from a distance, I could see the guy was good. For a moment I thought of Anna.

I heard an Australian accent. "There's a book on the counter if you don't know what you want."

"I'm here for a talk."

The hum of the needle stopped. He lowered his glasses, looking right at me, a flash of adrenaline in his eyes. A laugh escaped from me. "No, I'm not a cop," I said.

For a moment, he looked at me hard. "Come back later. An hour," he said without mirth.

Sharp on an hour I was back, facing the wary artist over his counter. Some pack of dogs was on his tail.

"This is a tattoo shop. You wanna get decorated, I can help you out."

"I heard it was a consulate."

"What's that mean?"

"I need a passport."

After the obligatory dance of paranoia he took me into the rear of his place and showed me a sample of his work, a Swiss passport with immigration stamps. I'd never seen a Swiss passport before but it looked damn good to me. Then he tried to tell me that something like this cost more than four thousand dollars in Sydney, and I had to point out that we're not in fucking Sydney, we're in Bangkok where your rent is seventy bucks a month. We finally agreed on 360 dollars for a Canadian passport, and he complained that his rent was actually eighty-five dollars a month. "Must be a nice place," I said.

The Aussie never once asked me what my story was, or why I needed fake ID. I figured it was probably because he didn't want to be asked about *his* story. He watched me as I opened up my new document. Staring back at me was James Arthur Douglas from Vancouver, British Columbia. He was born on April 18, 1962 in a place called Kamloops. I flipped the page to the immigration stamp—I had entered the Kingdom of Thailand just three days ago. *Lovely.*

"Nice work," I said. "I hope to avoid trouble."

"Shit, mate, what troubles'll you have? You look like the fuckin' FBI."

"Next to you, everyone looks like the FBI." I handed him 360 bucks.

"Got you a present—free of charge." He reached into a drawer and handed me a red and white cloth patch. "Get that sewn on, mate. A Canadian without a red maple leaf on his bag stands out like a Hindu without a red dot on his face."

Chapter Forty-Two

December 2, 1992

Lombok, Indonesia.

In the mega-light of midday, the *Aceso* looked like a dream. The bay was tranquil, and she rose from a translucent turquoise sea like a shimmering white alcazar. Colors burned like flares in the heavy equatorial air; lush green palms swayed in the eternal blue above a circle of bleached sand. I stood hidden in the shade of trees that contradicted the halcyon grace of my vision with a violent buzz of life.

Finding her that day brought a rare moment of peace. I had none of the jitters that I'd suffered in Penang. At least not for now. Days of stress on trains, ships and buses were alleviated for a breath of time. There she was.

Due to the machinations of the third world, which is particularly susceptible to Murphy's Law, I had arrived in Bali too late. Dadaram had given two nights of lectures in Ubud, a Balinese town, then the *Aceso* left port. A mooring at Lombok, the island east of Bali, was not on the schedule that I'd obtained from the Boston office. But for two days, devotees of Dadaram, The Children of a Living God, had permeated Ubud—and they had talked to the travelers and artists and seekers there about the excursion to a place of perfect beauty on the next island over. And those travelers and artists had in turn spoken to one James Arthur (call me Jim) Douglas, a fellow seeker, crestfallen to have missed Dadaram.

The circle of beach was vast, and there were tiny dots of humans infesting paradise. Some of them may have even been devotees from the *Aceso*. Since I had just arrived, I didn't know. The yacht's dinghy was tied to her hanging ramp. I was as prepared as I could be; my plans for escape from Lombok had been set.

I was so paranoid about being spotted by a devotee again that I'd lined up my ducks before I'd seen the *Aceso*. As before, I'd thought through the process that would commence upon Dadaram's death. The local authorities would be on the lookout for a U.S. citizen named Magnus Larsen. With a jacket, slacks and a briefcase, I would look like someone who wasn't me—I'd look like Jim Douglas, a Canadian businessman, a buyer of art. If there was ever any doubt, a glance at my passport would confirm it.

Along with the gun in my daypack was a coil of rope, and leaning on a tree was a bamboo pole I'd rigged with a hook. If they were on the lookout for me, most likely they'd be watching the hanging ramp on the port side. I figured it was safer to sneak up on the starboard side. I could secure the rope and climb it.

My plan had some risk. Death would be better than an Indonesian jail. I laid low, eating bananas and drinking water. After a few hours, the skiff began to ferry devotees from the beach to the *Aceso*. The engine hummed. Samuel's dark shape was at the rudder. The activity had my adrenal glands dripping.

When the skiff was secured to the *Aceso*, I jogged into the woods, away from the beach. As I passed certain shrubs, angry insects screamed at my presence as if they knew what I was up to. I neared a battered piece of pavement. My boatman was a teenager with a piece of dugout wood.

When 'temple' began and hymns from the ashram rode the soft waves, we launched the dugout. I'd chosen a point of land that wouldn't be visible to a portside watch. There may not have been a watch but I wasn't taking chances. Anchored in a serene bay, I doubted anyone would be watching the radar. As the tiny bow sliced through the water, the boatman began to sing the tune of the hymn. His voice was extraordinarily rich and melodic, and it was a strange sensation to hear the sound coming from both directions.

As we approached the *Aceso*'s hull, I put my finger to my lips, requesting silence. I sensed his fear rising. He spoke no English so I couldn't even lie to him about what I was doing. He tried to indicate he wanted no part of it. I shook my head calmly. "It's okay," I whispered, "*Bagus.*" It was an Indonesian word that meant 'good,' as in 'thumbs up,' or okay. Not ideal but the only communication I had. There was something about his fear that seemed to compensate for mine—my adrenaline was pumping but I wasn't shitting the same sized bricks as I had in Penang.

I lifted the rope up to the second deck on my bamboo pole, playing with it until it threaded through the *Aceso*'s railing. When I was set, I thanked the boatman, gave him some extra money and showed him which way to paddle to shore. The gun was in my backpack. I gripped the rope and climbed it easily, my muscles powered by excitement. As I unhooked the rope from the rail, I glanced at the boy paddling away. He was no longer singing.

I settled nervously, tucking the rope away where it wouldn't be seen. I moved with stealth. If anyone at all saw me, I was doomed. I circled quietly to the portside deck, pausing. I shot a long glance toward the bow—the corridor was empty. Stepping forward, I continued along to the stairs for the upper deck. Again I stopped, deciding to peer down over the hanging ramp—

The skiff was tethered by a leash of rope that was tucked into the hanging stairs—that was good news; if I needed to leave quickly I could jump in the boat and yank the rope rather than having to untie it. But with good luck—I'd suffered enough of Murphy's Law, I was due—I wouldn't need to leave in a hurry; I'd sneak away in the dark of night.

Fortune felt fair; serenaded by singers from the ashram, I ascended to the *Aceso*'s highest level. I stood in a furnace of heavy, windless air, sweat from my forehead falling between my shoes. Hyper-aware, my eyes searched the garden foliage for a sign of anyone. Confident that I was alone, I moved toward the living quarters. I stared at the handle for the door, expecting it to be locked—the latch clicked in my hand, and I pushed the door open. I stepped inside, closing the door as secretly as I could.

The exterior sound subsided to a whisper. The crescent room was cool and quiet; its ghosts felt more distant than they had in Penang. With a hint of antiseptic, it could've conjured the lair of Dr. Mengele. I took a deep breath. And then another.

I passed through the dining room … to the corridor that led to Devon's suite. I followed it to the patch of luminance from a skylight, then turned a sharp left and opened his double doors of carved black teak. Inside Devon's bedroom, I closed them gently behind me.

The scream hit me like a shotgun blast.

A blur of movement—a body bolted upright from the bed—it was Margaret, the young devotee, screaming hysterically—a towel had fallen away from her face; maybe she'd been sick or resting.

Her wail was blood-curdling, her face wild and hysterical—

Pushed back against the wall, I was trapped, her shriek like a malevolent swinging chainsaw—

All I could do was turn and run. I banged through the doors, past the skylight, shock and outrage chasing me through the hallway. I crashed through the dining room, onto the deck. The singing had stopped. Margaret's fury howled after me.

I ran to the stairs.

Devotees were already arriving at the bottom, blocking my escape route, and more were coming out of the ashram, running to join them. I didn't hesitate; the gun in my backpack and false identity meant going to jail if I was captured. I needed to go through them to get to the hanging ramp and the skiff. I flew down the stairs—men and women of all ages, people I knew and recognized, were bravely assembled to stop me. I launched myself airborne.

Through the screaming voices, the grasping arms, I intended to power over and through them, anything to get to the skiff—get off the yacht.

My body smashed through the crowd, fighting for the ramp-way. Arms and bodies pulled on me, women as well as men. My legs crashed to the deck. Evan hit me low like a football player and suddenly I was fighting with everything I had. Devotees were screaming and yelling.

I fought like a cornered animal. They were hanging on my arms, and my feet and elbows battered violently against anything I could hit; faces, torsos—

Dadaram's protectors smothered me. I tried to break loose, grappling with Evan, the strongest, in front of me, but the mass of people was growing, some hammering at me with blows. I slid in blood on the deck, fought like hell to stay up, pushed one way against the masses, then the other way, trying to break Evan's grip. I was smashed against the deck rail—pressed by a mountain of people, gasping for air, feeling the gush of blood over my chin—

Then Samuel was in my peripheral vision, mid-air, over the others, hitting me broadside, knocking me back against the railing. The screaming never stopped. Samuel was now on my back, his arm pressing my windpipe. Gasping for breath, I bucked and fought as hard as I could to shake him loose, but I was sinking—

Samuel's hard arm choked off my air—I couldn't breathe—I had one last desperate maneuver—I thrust violently into a direction they weren't expecting, hard into the portside tilt, flipping my weight over the rail with Samuel on my back.

Suddenly we were falling, hurtling through the skiff's rope, breaking the water, plunging below—

Underwater, Samuel let go of my throat. I kicked to the surface but he was holding on to me, now just grasping, just trying to get above water himself. I was holding a breath I didn't have—blacking out. I pushed on his body, getting my head above water for a gasp.

I sunk again, fought harder—choking with water for another gasp.

On the verge of the death process, time had a strange suspension. I heard a voice: *"You don't need to believe in oxygen either, but if you ever find yourself without it, you'll know something's wrong."*

I broke the surface again, sucking desperately for air. I kept Samuel below me, pushing his head and body down when I had the chance—he was now panicking, trying to get himself above water, but I established dominance, keeping him below me. My gasping was desperate.

Devotees were yelling, shouting. Evan was hanging off of the ramp; the *Aceso* had an extreme portside pitch with all of the bodies on one side.

The dingy was adrift; our fall had set it free from the ramp. Someone was yelling, "Get in the boat!" It was only a couple of yards away but it might as well have been a mile with Samuel hanging on to me. Christ, my backpack was still on, and Samuel was clinging to it.

A life preserver landed in the water. I flapped a desperate arm, catching it—and adjusted myself above it. With Samuel dragging on me, I fought my way to the dingy. I grasped the gunwale but I was helpless to climb into the boat with Samuel on my back. With one hand on the boat I pushed and fought him. He was under water and getting weaker. When I finally kicked him loose, devotees screamed like banshees.

Expended, I tried to pull myself into the dingy. With a massive effort I got the top of my body over the gunwale, and hung there in graceless exhaustion, face down in the boat, legs hanging in the water. The throng was screaming at me to help Samuel but I was gasping, too weak to even get in the boat.

The screams were getting hysterical—I couldn't even look up—I had not an ounce of strength left.

Then another voice cut through the rest like a knife.

"Magnus, get him out of the water!" It was Devon. "He's drowning!"

I forced myself up and into the boat. A bloody-faced Evan was leaning off the hanging ramp with a pole, but Samuel was too far away from him, and he was underwater.

I grabbed a paddle off the bottom of the skiff and began to pull desperately to where I'd seen Samuel going down. I could see his body below the surface. His fight was gone and the screams of the devotees were desperate.

I hung over the side, plunging the paddle down. I wanted him to grab it, but he didn't.

I stripped my wet backpack and dove over the side again.

I had no energy or breath to go down, yet I kicked and pulled straight into the depths and grasped his shirt. Pulling him toward me, I fought for the surface. He was no longer fighting but some instinct in his body took over, and he clung to me desperately, grabbing my arm, my shirt, pulling me down. My air was gone, I kicked like hell for the light above.

I broke through, inhaling violently. My arm leapt for the dinghy's gunwale, missed it, sinking again, and Samuel's body was pulling me down.

One final effort was all I had. I kicked and swam for the boat above us.

I broke the surface. I couldn't grasp the gunwale but the life preserver was adrift. I lunged for it, at first pulling it below surface, then getting it under me.

My priority now was keeping Samuel's head above water. Another life preserver hit the water but it was too far, the boat was closer. I reached the dingy with Samuel attached to me, the life preserver keeping us both afloat. I tried for the dinghy's railing, and this time I had it. Samuel was still pulling against me and I feared we'd capsize the boat.

It wasn't over yet. Getting Samuel to let go of *me*, and take the life preserver so I could get into the boat was no easy task; animal instinct had taken over and he was grasping, clinging to life. I couldn't speak, only gasp.

"Take!—life! –preserv—" I finally got his arms off of me and onto the float. I hung in the water, one hand on the skiff. It was at least two minutes before I could try to get in the boat. When I had at last hauled myself over the railing, I heard the deep grind of a motor—the *Aceso* was pulling up her anchor.

When I found the strength and balance, I pulled Samuel into the skiff.

My chest heaving, I watched the *Aceso* depart. I scanned the crowded second deck for Devon. He wasn't there. His presence—vivid as it was—had only been in sound. I'd felt him clearly above me just as if I'd seen him. And I'd obeyed his command instantly.

For the moment I was too exhausted to feel the full devastation of my failure. Samuel hung over the side of the skiff vomiting amid deep heavy breaths. I found myself patting his back almost unconsciously, as if he was a buddy who'd had too much.

I started the engine and aimed for land, veering away from a gaggle of onlookers, mostly youths and children, that had gathered. The boat slid thickly into sand and the little gang came running over. The long beach held a sparse dotting of Westerners as well, but they were more reticent about approaching us. Maybe a brawl on a yacht wasn't to their taste. I grasped my little pack, abandoned the dingy, and collapsed on some ground beyond the sand. I watched Samuel diligently secure the little boat and lift the engine.

A crushing weight spoke to me. Chalk up another loss for Magnus Larsen. The sun was an inferno. Some kids came running up, asking, "Why you fight?" Samuel fell down not far from me.

We had a time of silence, ignoring the chatter of the locals around us. I noticed that one of them was my boatman. I wondered about Margaret—why hadn't she been at temple? Was she a guard? A maid who fell ill and needed a rest? Or Devon's lover? The questions never seemed to end.

Samuel spoke. "Where's your dignity as a man? Lying here with blood on your face and hate in your heart?"

"I loved Anna and Amy."

"Then why can't you respect their choice?"

I felt a surge of rage. "It wasn't their fucking choice. Your divine shitbag is a murderer."

Samuel shook his head slowly, knowingly. "They agreed to participate in the destruction of their bodies."

I wanted to smash his fucking head in.

"I feel sorry for you, Magnus—you don't understand that these bodies," he gestured to us both, "are not who we are. The Schott sisters are not dead. *You* are dead on earth. Like all people who don't know their spirit."

His speech seemed a little ironic since only moments earlier his earthly body was fighting desperately for life. The *Aceso* disappeared as she cleared a contour of the coast.

"How are you getting back to the ship?" I asked.

"What's in your bag?" he taunted. Another depressing thought—my gun and ammunition would be wet, maybe ruined. "Something to kill with?"

"My toothbrush," I said. I was in no position to dog Samuel—not if I wanted stay out of jail.

Chapter Forty-Three

Bali, Indonesia.

I stared at a piece of paper, searching for the words to write to my family. They deserved a phone call—but I lacked the courage. This would be the first year of my life that I hadn't spent Christmas at home. We weren't the kind of people who ever went to Hawaii; it was always home on the farm with Bill and Ingrid, bring your friends or sweethearts. Each December, the homing instinct had called to me in Ao Lai, and I'd returned like a spawning salmon to my point of origin for a reunion with family, old friends, and America.

Whatever story I invented now, I had to believe it, just for a moment. A special project, secret and wonderful—*altruistic*. God, it would sound like bullshit, but the truth was much worse; hunting a man to kill him—they'd never understand. I remembered my mother's tears in the first phone call I'd made from Bangkok, the one Sally-Sue had badgered me into.

I owed Sally-Sue so much more than silence. I wondered about her performance piece and hoped it was going well. And she wasn't the only one; I had quite a list of folks when it came right down to it. I thought of Anna's parents and felt the hole that must be in their hearts.

Though I rarely drank even a beer these days, I stepped away from my blank page to buy some arak, the local grog. Alcohol was a god for some writers and I thought it might help me get my work of fiction started. *Dear Mom, Dad and Jason…*

I was deep in Bali's interior, as far from humans as I could get when I test-fired the Chinese gun. The shot blasted into the cushion of foliage. I breathed a sigh of relief. It still worked. I'd been more concerned about the shells than the gun itself, which I had taken apart, dried and oiled. I now had eight bullets left, two of which had not gotten wet. Those two were placed at the top of the clip and would enter the chamber first.

As I walked back to my rented scooter, I thought about practical issues. The one facing me now was whether to follow the *Aceso* to Australia. The schedule was a blank until February 8th and 9th, when Dadaram was speaking in Darwin. The thought of getting a ship seemed daunting. Flights were cheap from Bali but I wouldn't risk flying with my gun. I supposed I could try to buy another one in Australia but I had no idea what my chances would be.

Bali was a cheap place to ruminate. I took a room in Ubud, an arty tourist enclave. Sometimes people would try to 'connect' with me. I found casual sex a couple of times, though 'casual' is the wrong word and really it found me. One girl told me, "You're exactly the opposite in bed as you are out of it. I never expected such passion."

Mostly I was alone, the way I liked it, and heavy with thought and burden. I lived with my enemy every day. My mind played back my time with Dadaram in minute details. I burned with questions that had no answers—at least not for me. I recalled a history class in which my teacher had pointed out that a great many persons admired Adolf Hitler prior to World War II, even Charles Lindbergh. *How could I have not seen it?* was the remonstration that grated endlessly inside me.

By now I knew all too well about Devon's cunning and brutality. I even wondered if Anna and Amy had ended up in Bang Khen Prison by accident—or was it the machinations of an invisible Devon Clarke that set them up with the purpose of snaring me? Probably an accident, I thought—but I wasn't sure. There were so many things that I just didn't know.

More than ever before, I pondered Anna's miraculous healing. A piece of my past floated up to me. A guy called Mort the Magnificent traveled through west coast towns when I was a kid with a hypnotism show. Under Mort's control, shy girls necked passionately with nerdy guys in front of his roaring crowd; he awoke people to announce alien invasions. I'd seen Devon's hypnotism books in his study on the *Aceso*. I wondered if there were conditions that caused a temporary paralysis that could be exploited by an unscrupulous doctor. If I survived killing Devon, I would certainly investigate that.

And then there was the question that grew in mystery and power. Why had Devon Clarke chosen *me?* Why had he read my essay and given me a gun? Why had he sent me Anna? Why was I the chosen one? *From all the human beings on earth,* as Anna had put it. Did the answer matter? Or do answers cease to be important in the realm of an insane sociopath? I didn't know. But the question persisted.

Why me? Like a resilient stain, it persisted.

Chapter Forty-Four

July 18, 1993

Elle, Sri Lanka.

I was hiding out in the highlands, in the vast interior backbone of Sri Lanka's tea plantations. The land was gripped by civil war.

The *Aceso* would be arriving in Colombo, the capital city, in a matter of days. Dadaram was giving a speech in a venue called Vihara Hall. In the previous weeks I'd attended two concerts there, allowing me to get inside knowledge of the passageways and exits. Security was heavy throughout the city with military police on the lookout for Tamil fighters. But I'd walked and studied every street, path and alley that led to my escape. I knew which arteries were safe and which labyrinth would lose my pursuers. I knew where I could stash a bicycle. I had a paid connection into a non-public entrance to the hall.

Some thought it brave that the esteemed guru would visit their country during a time of bloody conflict. But Devon feared me far more than any Tamil Tiger. The Children of a Living God would be on the lookout early, scouring the cheap hotels, paying locals to be their eyes.

So here I was, in the high hills that produced tea for the world, hoping to remain invisible to The Children of a Living God until the very last seconds of their guru's life. Until the moment that I stepped out of the shadows backstage, or rose from my seat in the audience and said, "Hello, Devon," with a squeeze of the trigger.

I wore my string of failures. Each one had made me a smarter, tougher assassin. But with each near miss, with each new strategy employed, Devon had become a smarter, tougher target. With each frustration, my despair deepened.

My money was getting low, Dadaram's pockets were a pit. I was alone, he had an army of devotees. He crossed the seas in luxury, I slept on the decks of working ships. He was an exalted guru. I was a mariner with a rotting albatross around my neck. Only when Devon lay dead before me would I be free of the bird and its stench. I was so far from being the me I knew and from the world I knew.

I'd become a liar, a fiction called Jim Douglas. Avoiding other travelers, except when I needed information, was a part of my daily life. I'd burned my bridges to the sane world. Failure was not an option. Death was an option, but not failure. Who was I? Not Magnus. Not the Magnus I knew.

Perhaps human pain has a saturation point. Then the endorphins come. That's the only way I can account for what happened to me in a Sri Lankan village, when I started getting high without drugs.

It was near dusk when I walked from my guest house into the fresh, picturesque hills, dark green with native foliage and tea plantations. The elevation was a reprieve from the relentless heat and humidity of the lowlands. The birds here seemed lighter and happier, the insects less agitated. This was the country that the colonizing British had retreated to each summer when the coast became unbearable for their European constitutions, back when Sri Lanka was called Ceylon.

I came to a rough wooden bridge that spanned a river. Instead of crossing, I decided to sit. I found a downstream rock with an open view of the dimming yellow sky, an elegant curtsey of dying sunlight in the hills. I closed my eyes and listened without thought. The river had distinct layers of sound; closest to me it bubbled like a brook, but farther on it had a sibilant hiss as it dropped into a steeper chasm. Embedded in the harmonies of water were the chirps and squeaks of insects and birds. I listened, each sound distinct and integrated. It was there and then, in the garden of music, that I felt her beside me. Like a warm, beautiful liquid that radiated comfort.

My eyes opened and I looked to my left. Even before I saw her I knew who it was.

"Hello, Anna."

"Hey baby…"

Strands of hair drifted across her cheek. She sat on a nearby rock.

"I'm just imagining you."

"That's not very romantic."

I laughed. My God, she was beautiful. If there were flaws embedded in my vision I sure as hell wasn't going to go looking for them—I loved her and there she was.

"In a sense, honey, I am real. You're creating me from the woman you knew, the woman who became part of your history, your life…"

"Good of you to admit that. It proves I'm still sane."

"If I happen to be an angel, you would therefore be *in*sane?"

"If I happen to *believe* you're an angel, then I'm insane."

I had an overwhelming feeling of happiness. She breathed before me with the vividness of a dream, a living texture in her eyes and skin, in the soft fabric she wore.

"If I was Anna, I'd be telling you that I'm a spirit, not a manifestation of your mind."

I played along. "A ghost."

"I prefer 'angel.'" Her eyes filled with tears. She rose from her rock and my heart fluttered. Fantasies are ruled by their makers—but it was profoundly exhilarating that I had no sense of controlling her.

"Oh baby, look at you, you've suffered so much…"

"Hey, hey…" I soothed, with the alien feeling of being human.

She stood above me, tears rolling from her cheeks. Her radiance was nearly light. Her hands and fingers touched my face.

"Magnus, I want you to stop." She held my face firmly, lovingly, looking into my eyes. "Enough. You've done enough."

No.

"I know you love me, I know you love us…"

Don't. Don't ask me to stop.

She spoke over top of me. "Dadaram has hurt you so much … *I've* hurt you so much…" Suddenly she was sobbing. "If I'd known…"

"If you'd known *what*?"

"I didn't know what he was going to put you through."

Fear tightened my stomach. "You're not telling me…" I stared at her. She nodded, sniffled. "You agreed to die?"

"You know that I was a part of it." I shook my head, refusing to believe it. "I told you—I was loyal to Dadaram." I turned away, choking on tears.

"Thank God you're not real."

Anna sat next to me and we listened to the river. All the sounds were now one. The ochreous twinkle of fireflies had begun. Anna laid her head on me. Her fingers squeezed my shoulder.

"I know what you need," she said.

Anna got behind me, and I felt her fingers delving into my shoulders. Her body had a fragrance that was familiar and delicious. Comforting. Her touch, painful as it was some moments, felt so good. I moaned as my muscles surrendered.

"As far as apparitions go, you're pretty damn sweet."

"*Angel*," she corrected, jabbing me in the ribs. "We don't like being called apparitions—it's a slur in the spirit world." I was laughing. Her breath was on my neck. Her hands slid slowly around and over my thighs; fingertips stroked me seductively. "Does that feel like an apparition to you?"

"I guess not," I conceded. Her lips touched my ear as she whispered,

"You're fucking right it doesn't—it feels like an *angel.*"

The funny thing was, the next morning I felt lighter and looser than I had in long time.

I stepped outside my room onto a patio with a sweeping view of the valleys, dotted with pockets of orange and purple blooms, and a scattering and chattering of birds. Such exquisite creation seemed somehow incongruous with my dark task, or with the messy violence of civil war. I said good morning to a brave, happy French couple a few rooms over, apparently unshaken by conflict. In four days Jim Douglas had not introduced himself to his neighbors. Anna's presence had reminded me that Magnus would've.

The visitation came again that evening. We held hands, walking through the enchanting countryside. Next to her I felt no pain or worry, conditions I otherwise lived with. It was one well-needed holiday from reality. Technically I wasn't insane because I knew she wasn't real.

Sometimes I'd try to trick her into revealing that herself—but she was good. She enjoyed her little game.

"What's the afterlife like?"

"Like mortal life, it's different for everyone."

"So what's it like for you?"

She pondered for a moment. "You don't have a vocabulary that can accept my description. Imagine trying to describe the color blue to someone who's been completely blind their whole life; someone with the same ability to see as one of your fingers."

"Well, isn't that a clever evasion. You're oily, Anna Schott."

"Since you're the one inventing me, I would say that you're the one who's oily."

I snorted. "At least you admit that I'm inventing you."

"Magnus…" she said softly, moving into me with all her sensual grace, "sometimes I fear that *I'm* inventing *you*."

See what I mean? She liked playing with me.

&

The following afternoon in my room, I stood over a dressing table with a warped mirror, breaking small chunks of charred wood into a jar with a drizzle of coconut oil.

"What's that?" The voice surprised me. I glanced into the mirror; Anna was distorted in the bend of the glass.

I stirred the mixture. "It's makeup. In Vihara Hall only the stage is bright, everywhere else is dark. If I turn my skin black I won't stand out."

"It won't work. They'll catch you and hang you."

I stopped, swallowed. "This isn't an entirely psychotic episode, I can make you disappear."

She ignored the threat. "You're on the edge of a precipice," she said with eerie authority. "The risks you take to kill Dadaram get greater all the time. You're reckless."

By necessity, I'd become bolder. I knew that.

"Will your parents attend your execution?"

"Now you're being evil."

"Dada's blood is a monument I don't want."

"Maybe it's not about you, Anna."

"Then what would it be about?"

I couldn't speak. It *was* about her.

"Your consciousness is precious … it's all you've got, atheist. You should know what you're trading it for."

Her essence crowded the room and rendered me silent.

&

As early dusk lit upon the vast amphitheater of tea country, Anna's verdant eyes twinkled with life. Tonight she unsettled me. Her calm had a fierceness. I feared losing her.

We sat on the patio outside my room; her eyes and lips turned black as the stars came out. There were swarms of fireflies, the color of Mars but bigger, each little body turning on and off, in the high branches of trees. In the valleys, clouds of them swept like schools of tiny fish, pulsating in little dots of orange.

"I love you, Anna."

Her whisper uncoiled. "Then let me release your bonds."

"Tell Amy I love her. I miss her tons."

"I'm here to end your suffering."

"Anna, please don't do this to me."

"Your soul is sick. You're in danger of losing the other world, the real world, the world that loves you and the people that love you."

She was gentleness and compassion personified. "I'm here because without me, you won't survive your pain."

I started to cry. "For fuck's sake, you don't exist."

"You'll die with blood on your soul…"

I sobbed pathetically. "I want to go home … I can't take this anymore."

"That's what I'm telling you, sweetheart … it's over."

Her arms moved around me and held me tight. I felt her skin underneath the fabric of her blouse. I inhaled her hair and felt my wet cheek against hers. She stroked my hair. Her breath was deep and gentle, soporific. "It's okay, baby … it's over … you can go home now."

For a moment she rocked me like a child and cooed softly, "Anna loves you…"

I took her beautiful, radiant face in my hands. Before me was the very image of grace and compassion.

"You're not Anna," I said. "You're the same snake … that Jesus met in the desert."

And with that I banished the vision and went inside. The real Anna would've teased me about the metaphor.

My curtains parted, revealing a bright day. Dadaram and the devotees would already be in Colombo. Tonight was a game night, and I felt my proximity to another battle. I slid the clip into my gun, checked that the safety was on, and tucked it into my luggage.

I had breakfast on the patio outside my room. I drank tea and inhaled the fragrances of the vast green undulating hills. Just after 8:30 a.m., I heard a blast in the distance. An hour later, the entire village of Elle knew the facts. Tamil fighters had driven a car laden with explosives into a police outpost. Six Sinhalese officers and one Tamil were dead. As I waited for my driver, machine gun fire raked the hills.

Two hours later I was crammed into an old Mercedes sedan with a gaggle of other travelers, all of them locals. We came upon a military checkpoint, backed up with trucks and oxen carts. My heart sank. I could see the military police were thoroughly searching bodies and tearing through vehicles. I'd had only a cursory glance on the way up but this morning's bombing had changed everything.

I had to get rid of my gun. We were some way from the front of the line, and it gave me time to surreptitiously reach into my pack and withdraw the gun, sliding it under the seat while the focus was on the scene in front of us.

When our turn came we were all ordered out and Sinhalese soldiers went through our bags and pockets. They examined my passport, noting the Indonesian stamps and asking questions. Jim Douglas had his story down; buying art for a gallery in Vancouver, thought he'd pop into Sri Lanka on his way home, had heard it's a beautiful country, so sorry about the civil war, et cetera. The soldier gave me back the passport—I wasn't a serious suspect.

They found the gun under the seat. A soldier whooped, holding it up like a prize as he hauled it out. I'd never seen it before; neither had anyone else. The driver was dumbfounded. Thanks to me, we were interrogated for five hours. And they kept my gun. With my schedule ruined and my weapon gone, I'd lost again.

I thought of all the struggle and planning that it had taken me to get to this point. It was as if I was a tiny little bug, who with a monumental effort had climbed up out of a coffee cup, only to be knocked back to the bottom by some giant's finger. Time and time again. It was as if all the forces I didn't believe in—God, Fate—were conspiring against me. As if the universe itself hated Magnus Larsen.

Chapter Forty-Five

Singapore wasn't the obvious choice for a dwindling supply of money, but I figured I could teach some English under the table and build up enough cash to take another run at the *Aceso*.

I'd first seen the city of lush gardens in January 1987, while en route to Serapang, the island destination of my honors thesis. Like then, blocks of posh hotels and shining shopping centers had massive Christmas displays for affluent visitors. But I was hardly the eager drinker of life that had walked the streets wide-eyed and excited eight years ago with my lab partner, Peter Weller. Today, poverty added to my stress and frustration. My real horror, the demon *du jour*, was calling home.

Days of dread had infected me as I'd trodden streets with towering Santas, summoning my optimistic voice, auditioning different stories in my head. I imagined the various people that might pick up the phone at my parents' home. *My* home.

I walked to the international call center, a man trying to remain upbeat on his way to the gallows. On Orchard Road, well-heeled hordes from cruise ships and five-star resorts buzzed with the thrill of Christmas in the tropics and air-conditioned shopping. I passed a monstrous tree of electric pink and silver, while a Bollywood star glowed with skin of perfect amber on a L'Oréal billboard. The haunting nostalgia of Yuletide carols filtered through the din of people and traffic. Baby Jesus and His Holy Mother were in a manger with all the trimmings amid stores displaying Revlon's pouty-lipped women and the half-naked boys of Calvin Klein. I'd happily have traded places with even Joseph of the nativity scene, his somber face reflecting the pain in his blue testicles.

Though it was Christmas Eve Day in Singapore, my call would arrive home at 7 p.m. on December 23 in Copper Creek, Oregon, a time chosen for its proximity to Christmas, yet lacking the full emotional punch of Christmas Eve or Christmas Day.

Inside a little booth, the receiver was pressed to my ear, each faint ring booming in my stomach. My mother's voice said, "Hello," not Merry Christmas.

"Hi Mom, Merry Christmas," I replied. Despite the gush of emotion and the tears that followed, the first part of the call wasn't as agonizing as in my fantasies. There was something pleasing and comforting in hearing my mom's voice, reassuring me that the other world still existed. She soon learned that I was not just down the way, or even in Los Angeles or any place that she could easily imagine.

The story I settled on was no story at all—simply a project that I couldn't talk about, something classified. She wasn't buying any of it, nor was she accepting my confident assertion that all was well with me. "*Why haven't you called?*" was a brutal accusation. She reeled off a list of people who were worried about me. She relinquished the phone to my dad, who wasn't quite so raw but had his own version of harsh, understated judgment. I got passed to my Uncle Arnie and then to his wife, Bev, then back to Dad and then to Mom again.

My mother asked about Anna and Amy—a subject unbearably tender. I tried to deflect any real discussion as gently as I could, and she pounced on that as well. "There's a lot you don't talk about." She asked if I'd phoned the Schotts, their parents.

"Not yet," I said.

Just as Sally-Sue had, she jumped on me. "You need to call, Magnus."

My excuse for not calling was valid—I couldn't afford it. We were going on forty-five minutes now and this was costing me a large portion of my shrinking cash. And of course I couldn't say that or it would've caused more worry.

It was getting worse and worse with my mother begging me, demanding, that I come home. A friend of theirs, Sheldon, had become a counselor in Portland and they wanted me to go see him, the clear implication being that I was a mental case. It got to the point where I felt like I was standing taking punches, unable to respond or duck.

Like Sugar Ray Leonard in the late rounds of a title fight, Mom came on with her most vicious flurry yet: Jason was engaged and I hadn't even met his wife-to-be, Cindy. The wedding was at the end of May and of course I would be there, my mother told me. Sheer terror twisted in my guts at the thought that it might not be possible. "Don't worry if you have no money for the ticket," she said.

"Stop worrying about me," I said.

"And call your brother, sweetheart, he needs to speak to you. He loves you..."

I ended it as gracefully as I could, telling my parents I loved them. I exhaled with relief when the receiver was finally back down.

As I slogged back to my hostel through the grand artificial happiness of Christmas pomp, my resentment and anger grew. I was sorry that I'd called at all—they had not a clue of what I was going through, not a clue of what it felt like to come home to find your family slaughtered by a sociopath, to walk this ugly earth alone, an alien from humanity while the decency of justice is pursued. I recalled the images of Anna and Amy in the ashes and felt hell inside of me. *Fury.* I especially hated my mother, who accused me without a clue—without a fucking clue.

Back in my room, my rage subsided; I was glad that I'd called, glad that I hadn't unloaded any of my agony onto them. How could they know? I thought of my brother Jason and his fiancée and was once again felled by grief and regret.

How I ached to kill Devon. Sometimes it seemed as if my hunger to slay him was as impossible as bringing the Schott sisters back to life.

For two days I'd fought the quicksand of a deep depression. I was near broke and gunless. I stared hell in the eye and dusted myself off—if I didn't make some money soon, I would be sleeping in the street. I began seeking employment. Most Singaporeans speak English, even more than speak Mandarin, but I hoped to tap into the large population of migrant and foreign workers. Hell, anything would be fine at this point.

Monday after Christmas, I left the Sleepy Backpacker Inn on Mosque Street for a day of serious job hunting. I'd moved barely a block when I was stopped dead—by my own image on a posted handbill. It was a picture that Anna had taken of me in the garden on the *Aceso*. Amy was in the original photo as well but here she was cropped out. Up the street I saw two more—it seemed the entire neighborhood was plastered with them. *URGENT, Magnus Larsen please call…* I stared at the phone number of an Indian law firm and a blurb about the importance of me being contacted. What the hell was up?

The number was local, and I had the hostel dial it for me. I was routed to a man named David Singh. "Ah, Magnus..." said Singh pleasantly, "I have a package for you."

I paused. "It's not a bomb, is it?"

"Heavens no," laughed Singh. "Take my address, I look forward to meeting such a suspicious fellow."

Thirty-five minutes later, I was handed a white manila envelope doubled over to make a compact package. It was taped securely. "What's in it?" I asked as David Singh passed me a pen to sign for it.

"That's a secret that I share with only Santa Claus," he said. I smiled at the friendly cherubic man, despite a tickle of excitement mixed with fear.

Back in my room, I tore open the package. My mouth dropped as U.S. dollars fell out; mostly twenty-dollar bills; I knew it would be in the thousands. The cash scattered on my bed as I grabbed for a letter inside the ripped envelope. It was a single page, handwritten.

> *I am weary. How must you feel?*
>
> *If ever there was a deluded man who believed himself to be a knight in shining armor, it is you. You are attempting to compete with me for Anna's affection after her departure from your life. Go home and see a good psychologist—he or she will explain it to you.*
>
> *There are spiritual aspects to events that are inaccessible to you.*
>
> *Go home, Magnus. Take the money and go home.*
>
> *I could've stopped you long ago—I have that power.*
>
> *But I bear you no malice.*
>
> *Go home.*
>
> *Belated yes, but Merry Christmas.*
>
> *Devon.*
>
> *PS—if you ever truly look for God, He will help you to understand.*

The cash added up to four thousand dollars. I appreciated it. Within twenty-eight hours I had another handgun.

Chapter Forty-Six

The fact is, I lost the scent of the *Aceso* and was broke five months after Devon's infusion of cash. I was tired and humiliated by my failures. I had turned thirty-two. My brother, Jason, was now a married man. The world glittered without a shred of beauty. Knowing that I'd missed my brother's wedding left a hollow place where self-hatred now dwelled. The shame added to the weight around my neck.

The *Aceso* had been through the Andamans and along the east coast of India, to Madras and Pondicherry. The details aren't important. The places of discovery were now within myself.

Once upon a hot night, I walked the pavement of a city by a sea, where a power outage had rendered the streets lightless and stray dogs congregated in snarling packs. And out of the blackness stepped the hungry wolf within me, a beast so vivid and present and homicidal that I wondered if I'd ever been able to kill before. Could I have blown a hole through human flesh and destroyed consciousness? Would I have faced Devon and wavered? Maybe. Maybe not. Magnus had always struggled with his fear, summoning all his courage to stand up to it. But that night the hunger to kill was in my cells, salivating without fear or philosophy.

Another time I sat outside my room, my pain emanating into a black and yellow night. The physical facts of place and time fell away as I imagined my gun at my own head. My eyes closed and I felt the huge, aching consciousness in me and all around me. It could be over with just a squeeze of a trigger. Just a movement of my finger. Gone like Devon's little boy. Roger.

Ending the pain, ending the pain … I imagined someone else holding the gun, a life form above me, pulling the trigger, giving me release. Oh, it felt good. Despite the seductiveness of the thought, I wasn't suicidal. *No?* you say. No, not then. *To be or not to be* was not a question but a choice. That was in April—it would be four more months before death at my own hand beckoned as a viable path.

Those mad, altered states taught me more about myself than I'd learned in any other part of my hunt. To eat or not to eat, to kill or not to kill—*choices*. To know that hunger was just a feeling, bloodlust just a feeling, fear just a feeling. If I gained nothing of my quest, if my desperate hunger was never to be sated, if the albatross was never to be cut from my neck, at least I learned something. Consciousness and desire were separate.

I never stopped believing that I could kill Devon. I kept the faith. I returned to the basic truth, the source of the river: Anna and Amy were sacred.

August 8, 1994

Please bear with me while I place a bouquet of red roses before Yunsi. The morning I tiptoed out of her life, I couldn't have named the flowers that I left for her. There were pretty; I couldn't find roses.

Call her Yuni if you wish—her name is tonal and means 'beautiful rhythm,' but spoken in the wrong tone it can mean 'dizzy.' And that she wasn't. Her story belongs in its own book, or better, a poem. She's not crucial to my hunt for Devon, and yet … I just can't pass by her without a whisper, a blown kiss, a stroke of her cheek.

She was at first a student in my English conversation class in Toa Payoh, a district that saw few tourists, then a friend. A migrant worker from the Guangdong Province of China, she was not one of Singapore's wealthy children. One day, sensing with an animal-like genius that my defenses were down, she climbed into my bed and reminded me that I was still human. Yunsi was a lovely interval during a dark time. Especially with what was coming.

Chapter Forty-Seven

It was 4:30 a.m. as we moved north from the open Arabian Sea into Bombay Harbour. The lights of a port were sunken jewels aglow in the distance. The deck's railing felt vaguely warm. We were in tandem with the wind as the air was dead still and humid. For thirty-six hours, two nights and a day, I'd ridden with a community of strangers and their cargo on this island of floating steel. A layer of sweat moistened my forehead.

We passed through the massive shapes of dark islands. A chorus of Muslim devotion rose from a mosque on the highest deck, just above me, emanating into the night like the inky jet of an octopus.

I'd met my wolf within; it was time to set him loose. How difficult could it be to simply step out of a crowd, or the shadows, and shoot a public figure? If I was pulled down by a mob or surrounded by police—could I turn the gun on myself? My fear of capture arose from a lack of money; I had little, not like the old days. I couldn't buy a motorcycle and tuck it away in a dark corner for my escape. Even in a cheap country like India, bribes would be limited.

I was coming late to Bombay, a symptom of traveling with a gun on a tight budget. I should've been here days ago. Dadaram had a three-night speaking engagement at a place called the Nehru Centre, and tonight was his last night. I had to make it work.

A slight breeze stirred … smells from within the waking vessel, pungent and Asian, wafted pleasantly down the deck. The lights of port cast a thick orange haze as we crept past well-worn tankers and freighters, huge industrial vessels that hauled the world's goods, monsters to even the *Aceso*.

The devotional hymns from the mosque above made me think of Anna and her devotion. And also of Amy and the innocence of her belief, the happy sense of herself as a member of The Children of a Living God. And how that innocence was plundered. Raped. Some of it I couldn't comprehend. Anna Schott was an intelligent woman, and she was a devotee through and through. She'd managed to intertwine Christianity with something mystical, like the Sufis had done with Islam. I had avoided her spirituality and now I regretted it. I also regretted one other thing—that I'd never put a bullet into her guru's head when she'd asked me to honor his wishes.

The battleground approached. The sleeping giant, Bombay, encircled the harbor. I had an awareness of possessing a gun, the physical manifestation of that which separated me from humanity. The magic carpet of floating steel carried me above the sea, to my date with destiny.

Dark had just fallen as I inched my way along a wide boulevard, scanning the pedestrians for any familiar faces or searching eyes. Blocks away, a white cylinder rose from an architecturally sculpted cluster of buildings, surrounded by open green-space. Somewhere within was the auditorium in which Dadaram would speak. It may have looked graceful to the tourists and citizens drawn to its art gallery or planetarium or speakers' hall, but to me it looked like a fortress. As I moved toward it, another force pulled at me from within, saying, 'No, don't go, it's not right.' I feared that the devotees would be waiting to deny my chance to martyr their guru. No, I didn't like it. Here the sidewalk had no beggars or hawkers. In this neighborhood all the streetlights glowed. I'd hoped for a dense maze of third world confusion.

It was worse than not liking it; a sense of doom hovered like a low cloud. This Nehru Centre was no place for an assassin—of course devotees would be posted. These bright, wide streets with their taxis and police officers were no place to disappear. So nervous about being seen, I hadn't even scoped it out earlier. My other chance was to wait at the marina where Devon Clarke would be returning to the *Aceso* later that night. But I'd already crossed it off my list. The marina itself was heavily armed, and the soldiers there sported machine guns. The ugly truth was, I had no good plan. If I didn't kill him tonight—*Jesus*—then what?

It was my desperate feeling that I had but one match left to strike that kept me moving forward, watchful and hyper-alert. Headlights from the center lanes swept by without cessation. Middle class families and students, couples, tourists from the West and Japan, filtered past me. Taxis lined the boulevard densely by the Nehru Centre. Up ahead were also several police cars, also along the curb. A few officers congregated, looking relaxed, with the truncheons called *latis* secured at their waists.

The cops didn't worry me—it was the familiar faces of The Children of a Living God that were my phobia. A policeman sipped from a paper cup as he engaged with a couple of colleagues. My gait was slower than usual but I tried to appear natural.

"Magnus…" The Indian voice came from my right, injecting a pinprick of panic. From the corner of my eye I could see it was a cop. The voice repeated, "Magnus." I must've reacted. Suddenly, police with swinging *latis* were appearing like ninjas on all sides of me. The first blow struck behind my right knee, collapsing my leg. Another hit my arm, my back. They leapt on me, hammering me to the sidewalk, holding me down—I was yelling, "No, no, no…" into the void that some people filled with God.

My daypack was wrenched off me, and a heavy knee forced my face into the concrete while I was shackled with heavier chains than handcuffs. My weapon was pulled from my pack amid excited chatter. I carried no ID, but the gun was enough to confirm my identity. I was hauled to my feet; a policeman was speaking to me unintelligibly. I can't tell you how little I cared what he was saying. A bright flashlight was shone onto my face, then onto a piece of paper with my picture. The same one as on the handbill in Singapore.

My head hung miserably. The head cop jabbered into a radio. I heard my name in a blur of Hindi. My pockets were emptied. I had about forty-five dollars worth of rupees on me and a room key with no name on it. I cared not that I was an attraction for passersby.

A paddy wagon arrived and I was stuffed into a mass of bodies reeking of alcohol and sweat. They were shackled together—I alone was chained to a bar in the structure. It was the shared taxi to hell; for two or three hours the cluster of the damned jostled in the dark, picking up more prisoners until we choked for air. Some of the new men were covered in blood. From within the pile came little bursts of conversation and sometimes cries of pain or despair.

At last the doors opened on a prison yard; I could see barbed wire and guards, and a huge locked gate behind us. The human cargo was pulled out. Some were unchained to facilitate the evacuation. One of the unfortunates wore a stained and bloody t-shirt that sported the Stars and Stripes. I wasn't sure what that meant to me in my sorry state. When the van was emptied and it was my turn, the doors slammed shut. They left me in the dark chained up.

My agony throbbed into a timeless void. Sometime later we headed out again for what I thought would be another round of collection. I was still alone when the traveling ended and the engine turned off. The doors opened to reveal another prison, but with a smaller, darker yard. I was unchained from the bar, still wearing my original shackles as I was pulled out. I could hear some city life beyond the high walls topped with barbed wire.

Inside, four guards, two with their hands on me, escorted me down a shabby corridor, its flaws laid naked by overhead fluorescents.

"Bathroom—toilet—I have to take a piss," I told them. I knew no Hindi or even if they spoke Hindi—India has a lot of languages. They let me take my leak, two of them holding me over a squat toilet. I noticed it was fairly clean, like the women's jail in Bangkok had been, the free labor benefit of prison.

That theory was shot to shit, pun possibly intended, as they brought me into a tight little cell block that reeked of urine, feces, terror and God-knows-what else. Inspired by my entrance with a quadrant of handlers, a dog in the pack said, "Prince Charles," and some others sniggered. I was stuffed into a full cage and shackled to two other inmates, one on either side of me. The distant sounds of screaming and beatings seeped through the walls like an extra dimension of suffering injected into the stench and despair.

I retched. Drawing air was like taking in poison gas. There was an overflowing bucket of shit and piss in a corner of the cell—this I discovered when we all had to move as one shackled organism whenever someone needed to relieve himself. An older man chained to my right coughed constantly and dribbled phlegm. A long-haired boy to my left asked my name. "Magnus," I said. I forced myself to say, "You?"

I heard, "Vishnu."

I replied, "Lord Vishnu."

"No lord," he said.

The screams of the punished went in cycles but were of substantial duration. Shortly after the howls and shrieks of pain ended, the guards would return a battered, broken, whimpering body to the cellblock. Then the torture team would choose the next, unchain him from the density of torsos and haul his wailing body away. For those who balked at the journey, the blows of the *lati* came earlier.

I filled with dread knowing that my turn was coming. The boy next to me, Vishnu, laid his head on my shoulder. Chained to my fellow damned, misery was a smorgasbord; the choking stench, the confinement, the impending beating…

The loss of my gun was heartbreaking, soul-destroying. That little killing machine represented hope, a chance, a lottery ticket—that shit which springs eternal within the human breast. Another defeat was more than I could fathom. As a man screamed in an unseen room, Dadaram would be signing autographs after his speech.

A key broke me loose from my circle of men. Dread pushed at my chest from the inside. With my original arm chains still attached, guards yanked me out of the cell. Passing through the corridors I tried to surrender to the inevitable. Suddenly it wasn't what I'd expected.

I was pushed into a room with more guards and a man behind a desk, a head honcho. The room was as plain as a room can be, with bare walls and a few chairs. Most of the guards stood. They unshackled me. I was led to a chair in front of the desk. The honcho appraised me for a second or two, as if he was vaguely amused.

"Can I trouble you to furnish your good name, sir?"

A few things passed through my head but I said, "Magnus."

"Magnus Larsen, I am thinking." He smiled. Then said more gravely, "To carry a firearm in India hidden on your person is a serious crime." He waited for me to speak. I sniffed a chance to avoid a beating if I said the right things—I just didn't know what they were. He continued.

"Do not go to Kuala Lumpur. We have notified Malaysian police. This time is compassion. Next time is prison." I was stunned, almost disbelieving. "Prison in Malaysia is worse than India."

I floundered through the turn of events—first of all, I didn't know what the next stop was. Now I did. The office in Boston no longer spoke to me, and The Children of a Living God had gotten secretive. *Kuala Lumpur, Malaysia.* Another chance?

The bossman before me had a thick mustache—it was moving. "Compassion, compassion, compassion. The guru Dadaram offers you compassion."

Huh? *Compassion?* Suddenly I didn't feel so good.

"His heart is as big as the world."

Who was this prick, *Gandhi?* Unlikely, since he was surrounded by men with screams fresh in their ears.

Two years of hatred rose and stood like a brick wall inside of me. *Compassion?* This motherfucker was still speaking—

"*Fuck his compassion*," seethed out of me.

The sound beneath the mustache stopped. The man looked at me coldly, deeply. My defiance was surrender to a beating. Oh, I feared it. But *compassion?* No, not from Dadaram would I take it. The captain, or whoever the fuck he was, head-wobbled ever so slightly and the men pounced on me, taking my arms, my shirt—pulling me up and away.

Hauled down a hallway, my shirt ripping, I tripped over my feet in the tight mob holding me. An involuntary moan, a cry, was escaping my throat at the terror of what was coming. The overhead fluorescents flooded the corridors of hell; I was dragged in one direction, then another. The boots of my handlers tramped a scuffed floor; the lights died out through a dark stretch of walls—I felt my body being smashed through a heavy set of double doors—

Released, ejected from the multitude of hands and arms holding me, I fell over outside, on a concrete landing just off a city street. The men closed the double doors. They were done with me.

I had no idea where I was. I limped down steep stairs. Just up the street, sleeping bodies, some of them in groups, crowded the narrow strip between buildings and the broken concrete of sidewalks. I walked away from the jail, stepping over arms and torsos when necessary. Some of the sleeping souls were children. The pains in various parts of my body rose. An innocuous looking cardboard box was splayed on the sidewalk—as I dragged myself past it, my foot caught the corner and dozens of large rats came running out.

Compassion. My God I hated him. I don't have words.

Let me share the true story of a young British couple in Bombay. I'll call them Ilona and Tim.

They were staying in Murugan House, a cheap hostel not far from the rails of Victoria Station. They'd risen for an early breakfast and checkout because they had a morning train to catch. Standing by their backpacks, they waited at the reception as the clerk had stepped away, when suddenly, a man as foreign to India as they were came stumbling into the lobby from the street. Ilona gasped and Tim stiffened—he looked as if he'd been dragged behind horses; his shirt was torn and hanging off of his back, there was a line of dried blood coming from a scrape on his cheek and he moved as if in pain.

Ilona burst out, "Are you alright?"

The bedraggled man had a strange intensity.

"My God, were you attacked?" Tim asked.

"I'm fine," an American voice said, as if that explained it all. Their eyes followed him as he moved behind the counter. His odor was distinctly unpleasant, like he'd been dipped in a sewer.

"What happened?"

"Was it muggers?"

"There's bruises on your wrists…"

"Mistaken identity, some cops over by the Nehru Centre thought I was someone else." A bottle of water was plucked from the counter and a room key taken from the wall. "Can you tell them Jim Douglas took his key and a water?" The man began heading for the rooms.

Tim spoke. "Police attacked you at the *Nehru Centre*?"

"That's horrible," Ilona said. "We were there last night, for Dadaram's speech…"

The American creature stopped—and turned to look at Ilona. Long seconds hung in the air. There was something stirring in the man's eyes. Tim and Ilona were puzzled.

"Do you know of Dadaram? The guru?" Ilona asked, trying to decipher the strange response.

For seconds none of them moved.

"Do I *know* him? Do I know of Dadaram…?" the man replied as though seeking the answer himself. Then a smile broke across his face. He started laughing. "Do I know of Dadaram?" He began laughing harder. And then harder.

They stared, dumbfounded and unsettled, as the American's laughter became hysterical. He dropped into a lobby chair and the water bottle slipped from his hand, his entire torso shook—he held his face, tears falling through his fingers. He then fell to the floor, laughing so hard he struggled for breath.

The harder he laughed, the more frightened Tim and Ilona became. And when he looked at them and saw the fear in their eyes, he laughed even harder. And they became even more terrified. And he laughed harder still. It was as if he was on an acid trip and never coming back.

Stripped of my gun, air travel was once again an option for Jim Douglas. Or it would've been without poverty panting in my ear. I had 228 dollars left. Needless to say, I wouldn't be flying to Kuala Lumpur first class.

Bombay, a footnote

What else could possibly be worth noting after my night of hell? Just one other thing: an encounter with a beggar near Victoria Station. The desperate woman dropped to her knees, pleading then crawling—and an old specter came back. It struck me that whenever I flipped through my gangrened memories of life on the *Aceso*, I no longer recalled the night where Devon begged me to kill him. That very image had been the most haunting and reoccurring for a while. But the last time it had crossed my mind was in the embassy in Bangkok nearly two years ago. Until the sight of the beggar brought it back.

Remember? Devon Clarke kneeling in the moonlight, begging me to kill him.

Chapter Forty-Eight

I'd come overland from Bombay to Madras and found passage on a vessel called *Sirimau*. Here I mopped decks, cleaned heads (that means toilets) and did dishes. During my simple tasks I imagined every possible way to kill someone without a gun, from the plausible to the absurd. As I scrubbed pots I thought of poison darts; as I wiped off a meat cleaver, I paused, hefting it in my hand, assessing its lethal quality. I dreamed of ways to kill. But without actually seeing the *Aceso* or knowing the venue where Devon would speak, it was hard to make firm plans.

I spoke my silent mantra, 'Where there's a will, there's a way.' My endless mantra.

One night, when we were beyond the sight of land in any direction, my traveling mind tripped a switch wire—an epiphany flashed through me like an x-ray:

Devon wanted me to know about Kuala Lumpur. He needed me to know he'd be there. There was no way it was an accident that the cop in the Bombay jail had told me about it. And the money… the money in Singapore—did he really think I'd go home? No. *No.* He was enjoying this. The realization went through my guts like a hiss of frozen gas.

Kuala Lumpur presented some challenges, above and beyond the obvious pile. For one thing, I didn't realize until I got to the city that it wasn't exactly on the ocean. There was Port Dickson on the coast, the most likely mooring because of the luxurious marina, and also busy Port Klang to its north. The Klang River was a waterway that wound from Port Klang into the city, but there didn't seem to be any likely resting spots for a vessel like the *Aceso*. I didn't feel comfortable sleeping near either of the ports; I was too easy to spot, and my choices for a cheap bed were nonexistent. Jim Douglas preferred to hide in the great metropolis of Kuala Lumpur.

I was tucked away in a little slum, an old Chinese neighborhood that had not yet been devoured by the city's surging growth. Much of downtown was skyscrapers and shopping malls; here poverty still festered like an open wound. My room was a dump but it didn't cost much.

Were the Malaysian police really looking for me? I didn't know.

I started out early each morning taking city buses to the coast. Due to the time and cost, I alternated days between checking Port Klang and Port Dickson. The routine was tedious by local transit but I had no choice. I generally finished my circuit by early afternoon. In the city I scoured every discarded English newspaper for any notice of Dadaram's engagement. I counted every penny.

I spent nights in my room, sharpening knives of different sizes to their full lethal capacity. After carrying a gun for so long it felt primitive, even somewhat silly—but knives could kill, and unlike guns they didn't shout out noise when they tore through bone and tissue.

The simple truth was—I was scared. The eternal fire of Hope was a dying ember.

&

I shaved before sunrise, looking beyond the mirror's grime to my face—my eyes sat in dark hollows. It was hard to recognize the man I saw. Was that really me?

My day trip to Port Dickson yielded no sign of the *Aceso*. Had Devon duped me in Bombay? Reality was a rapidly invading force. I begged a silent god for a glimpse of the yacht, a chance. With brains and caution lost to the wind, I'd swim to it with a knife in my teeth, willing to trade my own life for a successful mission.

I returned to KL as usual, getting off my bus at a Presbyterian church. As my fear deepened, so did my sense of alienation—I saw myself as a cold white ghost that drifted among the warmth and bustle of mostly brown masses, Malays, Chinese, Indians, the occasional European face … through the docks with industry, marinas with their smell of world money, the skyscrapers of a modern city and the decay that they towered over.

At the window of my third floor room, I looked down on an alley with naked dirty children and mange-encrusted dogs; and old people, shriveled by time and opium, who spat on the concrete.

My money was gone. After two horrible, fruitless years, I was estranged from my family, my friends and my country. I'd never once written to Sally-Sue to see how her play turned out. How hollow and empty I was. I couldn't see a future beyond a Kuala Lumpur slum.

Tomorrow was a final day—then even my bus fare was gone. A million dress rehearsals and never a performance.

That night I lay in bed with a body that refused to recognize its fatigue.

I was on a plastic stool on the street before sunrise. Wafts of pungent steam from street carts passed over me. I forced myself to eat breakfast:

an egg, rice, orange juice from a man who squeezed it fresh. I forced myself to chew.

By early afternoon I had completed my familiar circuit, including the stop at the office of the port authority. There, the Malaysian clerk recognized me. He smiled without malice, knowing the question before it was asked.

Lurches of movement shifted me with a packed throng on the crowded local bus. I felt distant from the heat, the stares, the screeching, honking street noise just beyond. Mine was a world, an environment, that I refused to be present in. I didn't want to be present at all. I got off at St. Andrews Church on Jalan Raja Chulan as always before, threading my way through a density of bodies, back toward the slums, to The New World Palace. Not because I wanted to go back there—I didn't—but there was nowhere else I wanted go. There was nowhere I wanted to be.

My legs were leaden. I didn't give a shit that my stomach growled. Smoking food carts, humidity, sewers, made the air rich. I followed the tiny streets and dirty little alleys that led to my hotel. I was exhausted. Deeply, deeply, exhausted. It wasn't my body. A huge ball of agony was lodged below my throat, inside my chest. It was a pain that would not move—it would not eject, it would not detonate. It was a constipation of all the despair and sadness inside of me.

I followed the reek of another sewer. Visions flared like taunting demons: I saw my mother, Ingrid, informed by a state trooper that I had been found hanged in a dingy hotel room.

I entered The New World Palace, the remaining rot of another era. A greasy-haired, pockmarked Chinese boy, skinny as a junkie, played solitaire in the pit of reception. I climbed one stair after another, rising through stained yellowed walls. Stale air was tinged with the scent of mothballs. Behind a first floor door, someone old was hawking up phlegm. I'd given everything inside of me for two long years. Everything.

There was no path forward, nor backward, or any such thing as sideways. Anna and Amy were gone. They had not been honored with justice.

After the climb, I entered room 302 and shut the door on the squalor of the hallway. I crossed to the window and pulled the curtain closed; then I collapsed on the bed under a fan. I watched the dark spinning twirl on the ceiling. I couldn't face my failure. I couldn't escape my failure. Checkmate for Devon Clarke. I lay in the dark wanting existence to stop, the fan whirring above me, dull, ugly noise rising from the street. Come tomorrow, I had no money to pay for my four-dollar room. I had no plan for tomorrow. I had no need for tomorrow.

The afternoon sun glowed at the edges of the curtains.

There was a pounding. I ignored it. It persisted. It was at my door, the outer shell of my tomb. It added a voice, "Mistah Lahsan … Mistah Lahsan…"

Finally I called, "What?"

"Pahsal for you, Mistah Lahsan."

"It's not for me."

No one knew I was here. I had no parcels coming. The rap on the door kept up.

"Pahsal for Mannas Lahsan."

A wave of something cold and invigorating passed through my body. There was no 'Magnus Larsen' here—I was James Douglas. I rose from my sarcophagus like a mummy waking up.

I floated through the dim room, to the door—it emitted a long, rough squeak as I pulled it open.

It was like a dream. A very small Chinese man was holding a package. A dinner jacket hung loosely on his bird-like frame; his face seemed to belong to an older, dustier decade. My eyes fell to the parcel, the size of a shoebox … my name was on it, handwritten in felt pen.

It moved delicately from his hands into mine. As I fumbled into the reality before me, the man disappeared.

I shut the door, crossing to the window—I yanked the curtain, and sunlight flooded the crypt.

I set the box on a dresser scarred with cigarette burns. I began to peel away the paper wrapping, picking up pace, tearing through my printed name. Inside of that was a shoebox, marked with the address of a marina and a hand-drawn map. My brain was now fully awake, my heart racing. I removed two pieces of tape encircling the lid and box. For a long second I paused—

Then I lifted the top from the box. My breath stopped.

A 9mm Glock handgun was lying on a small pile of Malaysian rand and U.S. dollars. *My* 9mm Glock.

The thud in my chest hammered. I reached into the box; amid the gun and the money was a small piece of white paper, folded just once. It opened in my fingers. The message was handwritten.

Let's get it done.

D.

Part Four

Chapter Forty-Nine

I paced the room, ablaze with excitement. For moments, minutes, I was lost. I washed my face automatically, cleaned my hands with no thought to the task. Then I lifted the gun for the first time and opened the clip. It was loaded. I took out a bullet and examined it. It wasn't a blank. I slid the magazine back into the gun, feeling it click into place.

Was it a trap? Was Devon taunting me? Planning to kill me? It really didn't matter; I had no choice, no other options. Rational thought came with fear—not for myself, but for the feeling that there was no trap, no trick. Poison trickled into my gut. I stuffed a comfortable handful of cash into my pants, and felt the gun in my hand with another pulse of terror—then I tucked it into a daypack and tore off the address of the marina. I bounded down the stairs and into the street.

The taxi crept west through heavy traffic. Exhaust dirtied the air, but I needed an open window; the backseat felt like a cage. The gun was in my small backpack on the seat beside me. I was weak. Sweating. I forced myself to breathe slowly and deeply. I tried to summon the cold killer within me, the hungry wolf I'd met one dark night in a city by the sea. But that bloodless assassin was nowhere to be found.

We broke loose from urban arteries and traveled on a wider thoroughfare, driving forward into the sun. The taxi driver juggled for advantage, ducking in and out of lanes as he passed trucks, jostling the poison inside me. Perhaps I was being called to my own execution. But something told me that this was the real deal. I had the strange sensation that I was now awake, and that all the previous approaches to my prey had been a dream. I wondered if the ball of sickness in my stomach was cowardice.

We went north along the coast, and the taxi driver had to stop and show someone local the address. Knowing that I had surrendered to my fate wasn't making it any easier.

The lush drip of rainforest plants crowded our road as we approached the ocean. Tires crunched slowly over gravel as we crept along a series of jetties. The final pier was my destination, number nine. I swallowed—even before we stopped, I could see the *Aceso* offshore. For better or for worse, the end was nigh. Another surge of poison kicked through me as I passed cash to the front seat. It wasn't fear for my own life.

The sun had dipped into my eyes and the humans at the far end of the pier were silhouettes. Samuel and Evan. The backpack felt like an unfastened gun-belt in my hand as I approached the wharf. I stopped for a moment and summoned strength. A question with immortal resilience appeared.

Why me?

I walked down the gangway and onto the planks of the dock. Weak legs carried me past sampans and fishing boats. Rivulets of sweat moved down my skin under my shirt. As the devotees grew closer, and the boats thinned out, the sublime shape of the *Aceso* was unobstructed. She sat as if on a great stage, with the sun's golden glow behind her sultry shadows.

Samuel and Evan bowed as I approached. "Dadaram is waiting," Samuel said. Evan smiled softly, solemnly. I thought of our last meeting and the irony went unspoken. We loaded into a small power boat. As Samuel piloted through little waves, I kept my hand on my little pack with the gun. Tears streamed down Evan's cheeks.

We motored around the *Aceso*, where the hanging ramp was on the sunny side, unseen from the shore. For the first time, I was clearly cognizant that I was coming to kill a man, and that in Malaysia I could hang for it. At this point that was no deterrent.

Samuel tethered the boat to the hanging ramp, a ramp I'd climbed many times before. A cloud of devotees hovered above us. I stood, finding my legs uneasily. Samuel and Evan waited for me, the guest of honor, to go first.

My stomach was now a radiant ball of nuclear waste. I slid my pack over a shoulder and gripped the ramp's metal bars. I had no strength. My chest was constricted. My arms and legs didn't want to draw me upwards. I just stood while the world waited. I took a deep breath. Exhaled … and then again. Every eye was on me. How many times had I imagined killing Devon? Hundreds or thousands? In not one of those fantasies was I weak or fearful—I was cold, efficient. Pulling the trigger or wielding the axe was always executed with less concern than setting a mousetrap. This was the last thing I'd expected; you could've rung the sweat out of my shirt. I was dying.

I pulled myself up—rung by rung. When I neared the top, the devotees reached out to try to help me. I fought their touch, and they withdrew.

I found my legs on the deck. The Children of a Living God gave me space. I became aware that some of them were singing softly, chanting. Configurations of candles and flowers were dotted over the deck like miniature shrines. For a moment I felt a little stronger.

Mariel stepped out of the throng. "Hello Magnus, welcome," she said as if I were a teenage boy about to be shown his dead father in a casket. "He's waiting for you."

"Do you have a drink of water?" My mouth was as dry as chalk. I stood, looking at no one, taking deep breaths until Evan brought me a glass of water. When I handed the empty glass back, Mariel stepped forward gently to guide me—but I knew where I was going. As I moved for the stairs to the upper deck, the toxic ball in my stomach flared, radiating through my being, and I had to steady myself.

A tortured climb began. With a savage stab of emotion, I recalled my first day on the *Aceso* and how I'd ascended these stairs with Devon, enchanted and as light as air. Visions of the past threatened to consume me. I concentrated on moving up—one step at a time, each its own little marathon.

When I finally stood before the guru's door, the sun burned at my back. The handle clicked down, and I crossed the threshold. I shut the door behind me, confining myself, not daring to look above the floor. The curtains in the crescent room were drawn but I could see well enough. In here it was cooler. I dared a glance. Devon was sitting cross-legged amongst cushions on the floor on the far side of the sunken room.

My heart thumped. I tore at my daypack. First I fought to find the zipper—my fingers couldn't grasp it, it kept slipping away. Then I squeezed the zipper and pulled—it didn't want to open. My arm, my hand was shaking—nothing wanted to cooperate. Devon must've seen a madman fighting to open a simple zipper. Finally the meshed steel parted, and I reached in for the gun.

The pack fell to the floor.

The steel was in my hand. I turned off the safety. I still wasn't looking up as I went down the couple of steps into the sunken room.

I allowed myself to see Devon. He was much calmer than me, barefoot and dressed in loose clothes. He never met my eyes. He rose slowly and moved to a blanket on the floor. He knelt. He interlaced his fingers and looked toward me but not at me.

My arm rose with the gun. I shook just a little. I aimed at his forehead. *Pull the trigger.* I didn't move but for the involuntary tremor in my arm. After a moment Devon's eyes dropped submissively to the floor. I took a step forward. And then another. Now I felt too close. Awkward. The gun was aimed at his head. *Just pull the trigger,* I told myself again. Devon remained still. *Pull the trigger,* I demanded.

Pull the fucking trigger.

I was frozen. What the fuck was going on? Why couldn't I do it?

Shoot, motherfucker! I screamed silently. I didn't move. I shook. I lowered the gun to his chest. I ordered myself to squeeze the trigger—*just shoot!*

The force holding me inert seemed supernatural—time—time seemed to have stopped—*God help me!*

An explosion blasted out of the end of my arm—I squeezed again, focusing on his chest just to the left of center. He winced in shock as the bullets entered. By the third shot, I'd stopped shaking. I hit the targeted spot on his chest precisely where I wanted to—

I lowered the gun. He was looking at me. For a moment I felt relieved, but then his eyes—*Jesus Christ, they were different*—I couldn't process what I was seeing. Devon smiled, tears rolling down his cheeks. His eyes were radiant and alive. And so warm … the heat of his gaze was under my skin, inside of me. Words choked out: "I love—you—Magnus…" He looked so *happy.*

He said it again, "I love you."

I dropped the gun and started bawling. His body fell backwards and his head hit the floor. As Devon Clarke lay dying, I fell into a chair and sobs wracked my body. I couldn't stop. It went on and on.

Devon was gone. After a time alone, I went outside; a crimson sun was just above the horizon. I didn't try to fathom what had just happened. I moved to a deck rail, light and drained. What a vision hung before me: the ocean was a deep teal green and the crest of each wave was tinged electric pink with the setting sun. The pattern went out to sea for eternity. Peaceful like a tomb, it was exquisitely beautiful.

I thought of Devon inside; he had finally lain on his side to die. And here was insanity's *coup de grâce*—I wanted to go back and hold him in my arms.

I turned to meet a cluster of eyes in the garden and laughed unexpectedly. It reminded me of a scene in *Apocalypse Now* when Kilgore (Martin Sheen) emerged from the dark place covered in the blood of Colonel Kurtz to find an army of worshippers.

They were respectfully distant. There was no hostility from the people whose master I had just killed. Quite the opposite. Once again it was Mariel who stepped out of the group. "Would you like to join us?"

"No… " Some of the devotees entered Devon's quarters, with sadness settled into their faces. I began moving down to the lower deck with Mariel. More of The Children of a Living God were coming up. Faces floated by in the fading light: John and Benoit, Margaret and Suvita… and people whose names I'd lost. Some bowed their heads as we passed, others touched me. Song swelled from above as voices joined in mourning.

A few devotees, including Samuel and Evan, stayed with me, my entourage for the trip back to shore. We packed the boat. I knew they were there for *me*. Mariel held a parcel on her lap, bound with a ribbon that spoke more of academia than of someone's birthday. As we buzzed toward the pier, I thought of Anna and Amy and my emotion surged. I fought to swallow it, but suddenly hands and arms began to touch, then encircle me. There we were at the dock, still in the boat, a tangled ball of sad humans. Saturated with emotion, the irony of the devotees comforting me was lost. Of course, they had never been my enemy, only my obstacle.

On the wharf, I promised Mariel that I'd leave my forwarding address at The New World Palace. Then she passed me the box. "From Dadaram," she said.

The ride back to KL could not have been more different than the journey over. I'd never felt more expended. It brought a soothing relaxation to my body. Images of Southeast Asia moved past the window of my taxi. I couldn't begin to process what had just happened. All at once, my prey had not only capitulated, he had honored his assassin. I knew then that Devon had wished me to execute him all along. The 'why' of it was unfathomable. Yes, the question still persisted. But thank God it was over.

I sat with my mystery box. Thoughts of Anna and Amy surfaced again. There was a lot of grief that I hadn't faced.

Back at The New World Palace that night, I figured out that I had a couple hundred bucks from the handgun delivery. I needed to get back to the States but at least I could pay for my room. After a shower, I decided to splurge on a beer and eat like a horse. The box that Mariel had given me was unopened. Something told me that a package from Devon Clarke was bound to be a little rich for my exhausted spirit.

As it turned out, my instincts were right on the money.

Chapter Fifty

I awoke before dawn from a deep pit of dreamless sleep. This was the hour when I'd usually risen to begin my search for the *Aceso*. But now the great task of my life was done, and I had no immediate objective. I preferred to light a candle than to suffer the dull bulb that revealed my room for what it was. I sat on the edge of the bed, feeling clear and free in the flicker of burning wax. The parcel with its serious ribbon sat on the dresser.

Devon's victory over me was absolute. I saw him in Ao Lai, kneeling in the dirt, begging me to kill him. And just as he had threatened, he'd done the 'unspeakable.' For two years he'd had me on a string, his assassin in training. Still, I had no hate left. I was just so glad it was finally over.

Noise and daylight crept into the outer world hand in hand. The previous day was beyond deciphering. I didn't try. For that morning, that little slice of time, *why me?* didn't matter. Thank God it was over.

When the alley below me came to life, I opened the curtain by the dresser. I looked at Devon's box with a tickle of trepidation. What could the man who had welcomed and orchestrated his own death have for me? The ribbon slipped off and I raised the lid. For a solid moment I just stared. I'd never seen so much cash in my life. There had to be tens of thousands of U.S. dollars, a veritable fortune in Southeast Asia. I should've been thrilled. But I wasn't sure how I felt about it. Was Devon paying me for executing him? Was it compensation for Anna and Amy? There was no such thing as compensation for that. But it certainly had my attention—a huge pile of U.S. dollars was an elephant in the room in a dump like The New World Palace.

Another item was more ominous; a large, thick envelope was addressed 'Magnus Larsen' in Devon's handwriting. My stomach churned as I stared at it.

I ate breakfast in an open-air restaurant on the street, trying not to look at the large envelope. For a soft, inanimate object it held an inordinate power. As I swallowed orange juice, I sensed that it grinned. A beggar with eyes only for me came to my table and we exchanged a smile as I passed him a couple of rand. After breakfast I ordered a coffee and faced the monster.

I withdrew a folded letter and another envelope labeled 'Part 2.' Part two was much thicker than the letter I unfolded. And so it began:

Magnus, my dear boy, my sweet angel,

You will not soon imagine how much I have come to love you.

Spent of wrath I may have been, but these were the words of a man who had selfishly taken the lives of those I loved. Yesterday was a trip to the Twilight Zone, today I had a good footing back in reality. What was this shit about loving me? *I shot you dead, murderer!* The waiter delivered my coffee. A breath was breathed and my eyes returned to Devon's handwriting.

As I write this I find hope in my fingers and buoyancy in my heart. I believe you are ready. The fact that you are reading this indicates that I am correct. You have earned your honors. There is much to be explained and I will broach the

> *greater subject in a second letter. Today hope has lightened me, and as my death impends, I am anything but somber. I miss you. That doesn't mean I'm not enjoying the thought of your head spinning as you read this. And spin it will. That girl from The Exorcist can't spin her head like yours is about to.*
>
> *I recall some arrogant prick telling me that he can't get conned by charlatans like me. Remember that? Getting sucked in, fooled—that was for other folks, lesser beings, I suppose. I suggest you think back to the night where you arrived home in Ao Lai to see charred bodies being pulled out of your smoldering bungalow. Those bodies were purchased from mortuaries in another part of Thailand. If it makes you feel better, the families were well compensated. You have no idea what I went through to find a Thai woman of Anna's height who had recently died. The body we eventually used was a touch shorter but it worked—it fooled you, the guy who couldn't be fooled.*

The cocktail of emotions surging through me was indescribable—*did I dare to believe this?* The single most traumatic event of my life was … *fraud? Trickery?* As I gasped and fought for control of what was rising inside of me, Devon's words were flippant.

> *So yes, they're alive. In part 2 of this letter, Magnus, you'll find a different tone, considerably so. I suggest you do two things before you read it; if you haven't already, say goodbye to your friends at The New World Shithole and get yourself a decent room. If you haven't spent all your money on marijuana, get up to Lot 10, the mall in the Golden Triangle downtown, and find a shop called Wing Wong's. He's got a bottle of Glen Grant 1950. Don't forget your wallet.*

Go to your nice new room and take a glass of scotch before you read the letter.

Trust me, you'll need the drink.

Love, Devon

I ran. And ran. No one runs down crowded streets in Asian slums. I was mad, drunk with the notion that Anna and Amy were alive. *Did I dare believe it?* My head was spinning. *Yeah, you got that part right, motherfucker.*

Two hours later I was in a large, clean room with a balcony overlooking the street. It wasn't posh but its high ceilings and scent of jasmine paid a decent homage to the colonial glory from which it came. On a coffee table, the envelope labeled 'Part 2' awaited me next to a forty-four-year-old bottle of scotch whiskey. I drew the curtains to shut out the world.

Taking my orders from a dead man, I poured golden liquid into a glass. *Trust me, you'll need the drink.* Devon's warning was certainly ominous—but what could trump finding that Anna and Amy were alive?

Opening the envelope, I found a thick letter, typed. The tone of 'Part 2' was different indeed.

I fell into the pages, entranced. Several months after Devon had killed Roger, he was a deeply troubled man, suicidal. He began to have dreams, visions, about me. About Magic Larsen. I would've been in my mid-twenties then, but in his dreams I was always eleven or twelve, an age when my name was Magic. These visions were like no dreams he'd ever known, and he was certain they came from God. He saw idyllic, happy scenes that always ended with me taking his life—a bullet to the head as he knelt before me. When Devon had told me of these visions on the *Aceso*, I thought he was lying, playing the conman. Now I was spellbound.

The glass of scotch was untouched hours later. I'd read the long letter several times. A deception had begun long before I'd ever set eyes on Dr. Clarke. And it had begun with the last person on earth that I had ever expected to deceive me.

When I rose and opened the curtains, I knew why it was me—and me alone—that was the Angel of Death for Devon Clarke.

&

The next two days were stupidly, joyously wonderful. I kept having to laugh at myself—*you even don't like Kuala Lumpur.* The Indian food was delicious. The Indians could cook the ass off the Malays and the Chinese any day. But there was a trade-off—due to them being Muslim you couldn't enjoy a cold beer with a mouth-burning curry, which for me was an ideal combination. I couldn't help but think of my crooked old friend General Bukit and his pig-like son Arnold. They certainly didn't mind having a drink. Once, as I refilled Arnold's glass with Kentucky bourbon, I had inquired about the apparent contradiction of him being a Muslim and drinking. With a thirsty smile he informed me, "I'm a little bit Christian." But these Malaysian guys seemed to suckhole a whole lot more vigorously to Allah than Arnold and his dad. While my thoughts lingered on my old friends I wondered just how much Devon had paid Bukit. I remembered that new jeep.

By the time I had finished Devon's second letter, there was not a hint of doubt that Anna and Amy were alive. Regardless of what I was doing, that knowledge was always alive and buzzing through my head like a swarm of hummingbirds, gushing through my veins like gold and carrying its arteries of terror. Like the Anna in my imagination, the real one had been complicit in the hardest, cruelest time of my life. Would she understand what I'd been through? As much as I burned with desire to see her, I feared it as well. I didn't know if I could still be a part of her life.

The task of the moment was to get home and hug my family: Mom,

Dad, Jason and a shitload of friends. I decided not to call first. I'd been gone long enough—what difference would a couple more days make?

My new heart showed me another side of Kuala Lumpur, a place where space age towers hung over slums. Thick air was pungent with the odors of smoky food carts and mingled with the diesel of buses. Crowded boulevards had a musical bustle, and in simple neighborhoods colorful laundry hung off balconies like upside-down rainbows. What beauty. I was in a perfect mood to say goodbye to Southeast Asia.

Now that James Douglas was just a name in a forged passport, I no longer avoided creatures of my own ilk. At dinner, Kim and Carla, pretty young Americans, bubbled with their wild backpacking adventures. Like the time they hitchhiked a truck into an isolated region that was devoutly Muslim. With her feet on the ground, Kim felt an uncommon intensity to the stares of young men in a nearby field. In the following second she registered that, to her horror, they were all masturbating. Since they'd come to no harm, I was laughing. "How many times in your life are you going to be such a hot babe that a guy just can't help himself?"

I was mocked with charm, *nasi lemak* was consumed, and then they challenged me with a tough question—one that would dog me in the days and months to come. So ... what was *I* doing, what had Magnus been up to down here?

I thought you'd never ask. I've been hunting a man down to kill him, and I just bagged him a couple of days ago.

For a moment I struggled; their eyes were on me like a field full of masturbating farm boys. When I found words, I managed to skip over two years of my personal history and went back to Ao Lai, pre-Devon. That wasn't going to work with the folks back home.

That evening I treated Kim and Carla to a swanky joint called the Royal Chinese Spa and Massage Palace for a herbal sauna, hot oil massage and body scrub. The night was still young when our kneaded flesh glowed and tingled on the street outside. They knew of a bar with music that was popular with backpackers and expats. As tempting as it was, my flight left at 3:55 a.m., which meant I had to leave for the airport within a few hours. I already had a foot out of this world. So, like a hungry beggar passing on a sandwich, I hugged them goodbye on the street.

As I meandered back to my hotel, pieces of Devon's letter came back to me. His excuse for prolonging my suffering was that he didn't want to see me hanged, and also to be sure that I wasn't going to jam out (my words, not his). I was still sorting through various elements of that life-changing document when the desk clerk of The Queen's Garden Hotel caught my attention in the lobby. He indicated toward a furnished alcove. The devotee, Mariel, was waiting. She rose as I approached and I warned her, "Bow and there's gonna be trouble."

She smiled and we hugged. "Dadaram wanted you to move to a *nice* hotel," she said. I guess she hadn't seen the last one.

Mariel had a box that contained an urn with Devon's ashes. An alcoholic drink wasn't part of her discipline, so forty-four-year-old scotch went untouched in my room while we had herbal tea in the hotel restaurant. "Will you accompany the ashes to Los Angeles?" she asked. I nodded. She explained that Olivia Clarke would have someone there to meet me.

I wondered out loud, without Dadaram, what would be the future of The Children of a Living God?

"Without Jesus, what was the future of Christianity?" she said. I didn't know if she was comparing Devon Clarke to Jesus Christ or if it was just an analogy.

Since I haven't revealed the essence of Devon's letter, the devastating illumination of the question, *why me?* I won't say more of our conversation that night, except that I was transfixed through her description of Dadaram's funeral. We must walk a little farther yet before the great mystery is put to rest.

Chapter Fifty-One

In the reception lounge of a private hospital, butterflies sung in my stomach as I leafed shallowly through the latest dose of Americana, a copy of *Time* with a finger-wagging Fidel Castro drawn on the cover. The receptionist kept trying my mother, who was on the line in her office. It was my second September 8 since we'd crossed the international dateline a few hours out of Narita Airport.

At dawn in Los Angeles, Olivia Clarke's men had taken possession of the urn that cradled Devon's ashes. Professionally somber in grays and blacks, they'd passed on Olivia's regards and her desire to meet me.

"Your son is here, Ingrid..." The receptionist lowered the receiver. "Jason..."

"I'm Magnus," I said, dropping the magazine and bounding for the stairs to her office.

My mom had stepped into the hallway, expecting my brother. My approaching smile jolted her, and she went good and apeshit.

We stood in her office hugging. As she reached for a Kleenex she kept saying, "You look wonderful ... you look wonderful..." as though in some kind of shock. "Oh we were scared ... we went to Sheldon, he said you were a heroin addict."

"*What?*" I cried. Sheldon Kennay was a friend of my parents, a former nurse who had completed a psych degree, come out of the closet and set up shop in Portland.

My mom had picked up a few gray hairs and a couple of extra pounds. "There were all the signs," she sniffled.

"Is he a psychologist or a psychic?" I asked.

My mother exploded into a smile. "You look wonderful," she said again. "You never took drugs?"

"Got anything good locked up around here?"

Ignoring my wit, she grabbed me for another hug. "You look wonderful, God you look wonderful."

My mom got on the phone, an attempt to hunt down my father. "A bit too skinny though," she added as she tried my dad's cell phone.

On her desk, I noticed that her pens, a note pad and a ledger were all marked *Vali Pharmaceutical.* "Mom, you're bought and paid for … Vali gave you an award, and now you dutifully buy their products."

"They've always been a progressive company, sweetheart." Mom reached for another Kleenex.

"What happened to the Ingrid Larsen that stood up to corporate America?"

"You be quiet," she said, blowing her nose. "You know your father won't answer his cellular phone—your brother's wife has convinced him they cause cancer." My mom hung up. "He'll be at Henry's…"

Whatever my mother's next action was to be—grab her coat, call her secretary, ask me what I'd been doing—it was derailed by a small package sitting on her desk, roughly the shape of a tiny coffin.

"That's your present," I said.

Despite a little dance of protest, my mother was thrilled. Her son was back without a track mark in sight and he'd thoughtfully brought her a gift.

That was before she saw it, that is.

I sat down and watched her pleasure as she delicately removed the paper. Behind her, a window revealed a sunny afternoon; seventy-six degrees, the pilot had informed us prior to our descent into Portland.

Seeing the joy in my mom's face gave me a sense of peace. My nerves relaxed. I realized that I had nothing to say to her, nothing to get off my chest. For a moment in Kuala Lumpur I had felt betrayed—but that feeling was all gone now. I was just happy to see her. Happy to be home. It was suddenly that simple. Ingrid was my mother and Bill was my father.

But that moment of peace was short-lived.

The box Devon had given me with the letters also contained 60,000 dollars in cash. In the distinctly foreign territory of Lot 10, Kuala Lumpur's priciest shopping mall, I had perused necklaces. One in particular held a seductive power: a mouth-watering blue sapphire with an understated elegance, artistry that whispered rather than screamed. The price tag, however, screamed rather than whispered. My mother would've been happy with a rock I'd found on a beach, but Devon's voice played in my head, "Get her the *sapphire*."

The little coffin opened in Ingrid's hands. She stared, transfixed. "What is it?" she asked with an undercurrent of sheer terror.

"It's a sapphire," I said. I began to explain the silver setting ... but my mother was shaken. She placed the jewelry box on her desk.

"We thought you were ... starving..." she said quietly.

I was fairly certain that her image of me as a junkie had just been replaced with an image of me surrounded by Asian gangsters, awash in kilos of white powder.

"How can you afford something like this?"

"I don't know, Mom, maybe you want to call Sheldon and ask him."

After a moment of silent rebuke, my mother made an effort to be gracious. "It's beautiful, sweetheart." She lifted it out of the box. "My God, Magnus..."

"I picked it out, but really it's from Devon." It just slipped out.

My mother continued to stare at the necklace. The silence in the room was now different; it had a pitch, a quality. A self-consciousness.

She finally asked, "Who—who's Devon?"

"You know, Devon Clarke," I said innocently. My mother placed the necklace back in the open box and seemed to stroke it for a second, as if she was putting it to bed.

"Who's that, honey?"

"*Devon Clarke.* He was at your conference, Mom," I said as if trying to casually jog her memory. Again she wasn't speaking.

"In Massachusetts … where you won the speaking award."

My mother was very calm and very controlled when she said, "There were one hundred forty medical students at that conference."

"You don't remember *Devon Clarke*?"

My mother stared straight into my eyes, the ice melting under her feet. I said it as gently as I could.

"He remembered *you*."

Book of Devon 11

July 9, 1961

Newton, Massachusetts.

Ingrid Mulestadder was twenty-three years old when she arrived at the Vali Conference on a Sunday afternoon. A taxi driver pulled bags from his trunk for both her and Wendy Carlisle, another young nurse she'd met on the train. The campus had large, manicured grounds and the air was full with summer. "Is this what they call Ivy League?" Wendy asked.

The Van Derman Life Company had recently changed its name to Vali Pharmaceutical. Some said the shortening was due to students calling the company VD Life, a reference to the fact that it manufactured drugs for chlamydia and gonorrhea. Ingrid had mixed feelings about the week-long junket. She wasn't so naïve as to think that drug companies wined and dined medical students and nurses simply because they liked them so much. Ultimately, they were here to get an education about using and prescribing Vali products.

Despite her concerns, she had come for two reasons: first, Vali was a company with a strong, compassionate presence in the South. Not only did they have a Negro on their board of directors, they supported programs that helped Negroes get access to quality education both through project grants and generous funding for the United Negro College Fund. Ingrid had taught briefly under a Vali grant in rural

Alabama. It mattered not that the pay was terrible; she was thrilled and grateful for the opportunity. The second reason was more pragmatic; attendance at a Vali conference looked good on a job application. Only nurses and medical students with the highest marks were invited. All expenses were paid for what the Vali brochure described as "the bright lights of our American future."

After Ingrid had registered and freshened up, she pinned her nametag to her blouse, and set out to meet Wendy in the Student Union Building pub. She joined her new friend in a room that was filling up. "Such a nice place," Wendy said, lighting a cigarette. Ingrid had to agree—the pool tables and dartboard were familiar fare, but this was roomy for a college pub and even had an alcove with furniture that faced a television set. "Look where we dine on Thursday … The Atlantic Charter in Boston," beamed Wendy, passing Ingrid the Vali Conference menu of the weekly events. Ingrid felt a tickle of excitement.

The room buzzed. A nearby table of young men had drawn a coterie of nurses, slightly more made up than the average. In those days, doctors were virtually all male and nurses were female. Ingrid noticed bursts of bravado; they were bantering over a competitive test later in the week. "…you'll never break my record … but since I'm a good sport, I'm wishing you luck..."

"Unfortunately for you, Harv, I'll be taking the test sober this year." Peals of laughter that Ingrid found fawning erupted from the nurses.

She glanced over at their neighbors, and Wendy leaned in. "They're already doctors, studying for specialties. Vali scholarships probably."

The men were of a genre that she had rarely, if ever, encountered—a combination of ego and erudition, brains and braggadocio. Someone, somewhere, in some ancient speech, may have described them as the 'best and the brightest.' Ingrid would've conceded some respect for 'the brightest' but certainly not 'the best.' Not with the opinions she could hear. A doctor with a hint of the South in his voice complained that Uncle Sam had 'fleeced him' after his first year of private practice.

The poor bastard claimed that he'd only gotten to keep 32,000 dollars. Ingrid almost choked—she'd earned 228 dollars a month teaching in Alabama. Together with her fiancé they'd barely made 4,000 dollars for the entire year. Did this man have no idea how selfish he sounded?

"Cheers." Glasses of draft beer clinked together. Wendy was impressed that Ingrid was going to enter the oration contest—she could never get up publicly. "I'm not here to win, just to participate and share ideas." Ingrid sparkled thinking of it.

Before long, Ingrid heard their neighbors discussing the need to avenge the Bay of Pigs, with one doctor advocating an invasion of Cuba. She tried hard to ignore the other table, but it was like a flaw on a new carpet, that once noticed, was always drawing the eye. Her own beliefs often fell well outside of the mainstream, so she was used to hearing ideas that she didn't personally agree with. But what continually grated on Ingrid, far worse than the politics, was the automatic agreement of certain nurses to whatever was said, no matter how ridiculous. The young doctors spoke with a diversity of opinion; even when in general agreement among themselves there were unique threads to each viewpoint or pebbles of contrarianism. But the nurses were cloying and acquiescent to every notion that was expressed, especially by the doctor with the Southern hint in his voice.

Ingrid's eyes were on Wendy, who'd read an article about dressing successfully for job interviews. Wendy's cigarette waved in her hands as she expressed, "…interviewed by a woman, no cleavage … by a man, a *little* cleavage…" But Ingrid's ears were stuck on the next table.

A particular nurse, who had only moments earlier supported a moderate position on Cuba, was now all for an invasion—and Ingrid couldn't take any more. She interrupted Wendy. "Please excuse me."

The doctor was saying, "Dinner does taste better without missiles pointed at your head…" when Ingrid loomed, clearly confrontational.

"If you don't want to turn Cuba into a Soviet military base, then show some respect for the will of the people. Don't drive them into Khrushchev's arms."

The entire table recoiled, particularly the nurses, as if Ingrid was a pathogen and they were unprepared antibodies. The man she faced was inordinately, maybe even heroically, handsome. He had gray-blue eyes, and if he hadn't been speaking such nonsense she may have been able to imagine him as some classical hero. It disturbed Ingrid, that of the entire table, he alone, *the accused*, looked pleasantly pleased to see her.

He smiled, reading her nametag. "A Miss Mulestadder, representing the Fair Play for Cuba Committee." The table broke into laughter at the reference to a group of Castro supporters. (A medley that included Norman Mailer; later, Lee Harvey Oswald was secretary of the New Orleans chapter.)

And thus, Miss Mulestadder and Dr. Clarke began a battle of ideology that drew other voices into the fray. When Ingrid finally remembered her abandoned friend, she began to move away from the fire she'd started, with a parting word. "And don't complain about your taxes, Dr. Clarke—be happy you can afford them."

Devon referred to the doctor across from him. "One day I'd like to do for my son what Harvey's father has done for him. Is that offensive?"

"Only when other Americans don't have the same opportunity."

When Ingrid at last sat down she apologized. There was no need; Wendy was titillated. "I bet *you'll* have a good speech."

July 12, 1961

It was pushing midnight when Ingrid stepped away from writing her speech to meet Wendy in the pub. The room was darker and sparsely patronized. The doctors were huddled in the TV alcove and no women accompanied them. Their conversation was rougher, drunker and more humorous—at least to them.

As Ingrid took a seat, Wendy whispered across the table, "You should hear them, the Jewish fellow and *your friend* worked as waiters in some snooty restaurant in Boston where they rated every woman who came in. One of them would walk by the other and say a number from one to ten, like 'table 4, six.' Then the other one would check her over and come back with a number of his own."

Ingrid gave a dull shake of her head as if to say, 'Why doesn't that surprise me?'

Wendy dropped her voice even lower. "They never agreed. When Haskell liked one, Devon thought she was a dog, when Devon liked one, Haskell thought she was a dog. *And* the owner of the restaurant owns another business with the blond one's father. *Interesting*. Lotsa moola there I bet."

Ingrid tried to pull Wendy away from her fascination with the doctors. She beamed, "I've almost finished my speech." But her effort was derailed by a rising voice from the little alcove.

Haskell Grund, a babyface with longer locks, was stating emphatically, "I never fucked her…"

Devon could be heard laughing while the one called Harvey was trying to get it straight in his head: "This gentleman wanted you … to fuck his wife?"

Devon interjected with delight, "You were close to those people, Haskell."

"I never fucked her, I had problems with those people." Haskell turned to the others. "They would show up near the end of my shift. Devon knows that."

Devon breathed fresh life into Haskell's embarrassment. "They loved you, they came in twice a week sometimes. They fucking loved you!" Devon howled, and a level of intrigue gripped the others.

Harvey asked, "Was she hot, this woman?"

To which Devon's laughter rose, and Haskell replied, "They were good tippers but I never touched her … and *he* knows that."

No discussion of a speech was going to compete for Wendy's attention against this. Ingrid's friend had a shocked grin frozen onto her face.

"No gigolo offers for you, Dev?"

The young Dr. Clarke was still merry. "I avoided that couple like an open sewer. Christ, I'm *Catholic* and that's too perverted for me." More laughter ensued.

Wendy's jaw dropped in a grand show of disbelief—then, to Ingrid's horror, she rose, marching over to face the culprit. Ingrid sensed a layer of absolute delight in Wendy's indignation as she zeroed in on Devon.

"So Catholics are *perverts*, is that what you're saying…?"

Laughter burst with applause as the others thrilled to see Devon busted.

"No, no, I said I'm *not* a pervert."

Wendy wouldn't let up. "Well it sounded like you were implying that Catholics are perverts. Do *I* look like a pervert?"

Harvey stepped in kindly. "It's only the men. You're a lovely girl."

Devon continued, "If you'd have been eavesdropping a little more closely you would've discerned that Haskell here, who happens to be a Jew, is the pervert."

Through another wave of merriment Ingrid heard someone threatening to report Devon to the ADL for maligning Jewish perverts. Wendy enjoyed the commotion she was causing, though Ingrid was quite certain that she had no idea what the ADL was. "Well, I still think you need to buy me and my friend a drink to make up for your slur."

Ingrid quietly cringed. She did not want to deal with *that* doctor tonight.

"My pleasure," said Devon, glancing over at Ingrid, "though it appears that Miss Mulestadder is waiting for Karl Marx to buy her a drink." The doctors laughed, but it was a little more subdued out of politeness. Ingrid smiled as well, assuring herself that the absurdity of the comment was what she found amusing and not Devon's wit.

A blond doctor opined, "He'd have to buy us all a drink, and no one could get a better drink than anyone else." That caused more alcohol-fuelled chuckles in the little alcove.

Wendy, eager to get past jokes she didn't get, called over, "Come on, Ingrid … Devon's going to pay up for his rude remarks. Come on, even if you're Protestant you can be offended."

Ingrid rose as if her body was slightly heavy, picking up Wendy's cigarettes for her. Devon grinned as she approached. Ingrid stated, "I'm done drinking, thank you."

Wendy beamed in, "I'll bet Ingrid's a Protestant."

"I'm not religious," Ingrid said, pulling in a chair. There was a moment of quiet as the medical students and Wendy absorbed what she had just said.

Harvey asked, "You don't believe in God?"

"No, I don't."

Haskell nodded and raised his glass to her. "The opiate of the masses is not for Ingrid." Wendy looked borderline shocked.

Devon addressed Wendy. "It appears that your friend may get Karl Marx to buy her a drink one day after all—though it will no doubt be a flaming cocktail since he's burning in hell." Ingrid took no offence to the chuckles as Devon turned to her. "And not because he's a communist, Miss Mulestadder—but because he's an atheist." Then he added, "I learned that from my parish priest when I was twelve."

Harvey laughed. "Damn, the Catholics deliver a full education."

A waiter delivered drinks as Wendy defended her friend. "God won't send Ingrid to hell—she's a good person, she even taught underprivileged Negroes in Alabama."

Devon paid the waiter as he remarked, "Then Miss Mulestadder will be pleased to learn that in this state Negroes have more rights than I do."

It was then and there that Ingrid lost it.

"How dare you imply that you're underprivileged!"

Under siege, Devon replied that he simply meant that some scholarships were open to Negroes but not to him, whereas his were open to all. Just when Ingrid's fury seemed ready to abate, Devon said, "If a Negro student had my athletic scholarship and my academic record, the United Negro College Fund would have to rent an extra-large truck to carry all the money over to him." That set Ingrid off again. She could not believe this man.

Ingrid was still hot when she and Wendy approached the women's dormitories. "Never in my life have I suffered such arrogance … from someone educated, who should know better—"

"Ssh," Wendy warned, referring to the darkened buildings.

Ingrid dropped her voice, "May I?" She rarely smoked but she wanted one tonight. Ingrid lit a cigarette and exhaled smoke. "He's perfectly and horribly selfish."

"Harvey said he'll be a great surgeon."

Ingrid replied, "So what? A man like him is not going to live his life, he's going to achieve it."

"Harvey's really nice," Wendy glowed. "He told me that Italian and Irish is a lovely combination."

That night Ingrid was on fire. She rewrote her entire speech.

Ingrid's speech was a hit with the nurses, or at least enough of a hit to become one of the six finalists. Tomorrow she would give it again, not in a classroom like today, but in a lecture arena, where the final jurists would be medical students. Ingrid flushed with excitement, thanking the other nurses as they complimented her speech. That was the good news.

In the dormitory hallway, Wendy bubbled that Devon Clarke had broken Harvey Cook's record on Vali's notoriously difficult test. At ninety-six points, his score was now the highest ever. Ingrid managed to squeeze out, with no small effort, a gracious response. But his victory bothered her, violating her notion of justice. She rebuked herself, *Why am I being so petty? Why do I care?* Finally, she prepared herself to congratulate Devon if they should happen to cross paths—something that she wouldn't be going out of her way to do.

That night in Boston, the French wine, the lobster, the rare beef were all superb. Ingrid had to hand it to Vali Pharmaceutical. At her table the talk ranged from fashion to family to politics. Ingrid enthused about her impending marriage and the plans that she and Bill had for their future. She was happy that Wendy had decided to sit with her—though she'd encouraged her to sit with the doctors if that's what she wanted.

A sole glimpse of Devon came near the end of their evening as Ingrid was leaving the ladies room. She recognized the voices talking about getting a bottle to go. Haskell was on his feet, teetering slightly as he stared down at a handful of cash that Harvey was trying to pass him. "What's that for?" he asked.

"Good stuff," said Harvey.

Devon butted in, "It's from that guy over there, Haskell, he wants you to fuck his wife." The men exploded in drunken hilarity.

Haskell fell back into his chair, shaking with laughter. "You fucking prick, Devon, you've only got morals when a woman is ugly."

Ingrid tried to imagine her sweetheart, Bill, in a conversation like that. Fortunately, she couldn't.

Her nerves fluttered as Ingrid approached the podium. She wondered how many of the medical students in the darkened seats would be nursing hangovers. Soon after she began, her words and her heart connected. For nineteen of her twenty allotted minutes she gave an impassioned plea for true and equal opportunity for all of America's citizens. When she had finished, there was a hearty round of applause for Ingrid Mulestadder from Gray Glen Nursing Academy in Minnesota. Ironically, her clash with Devon Clarke had sharpened her speech.

Up last was an intelligent nurse from Engels College in Vermont. She reached out to a Vali executive's own heart when she talked about drugs for the future and the human suffering they would one day alleviate. She spoke well and her ovation reflected it.

Carrie Evans and Ingrid Mulestadder together claimed over seventy percent of the total vote, with Carrie getting fifty nods to Ingrid's forty-nine. But since each student's vote was recorded as the result of their test score from the previous day, the final result was 2,315 to 2,289 for the nurse from Minnesota. The winner of the Vali Oration Award for 1961 was Ingrid Mulestadder.

She swooned with the unexpected thrill. Less than an hour after she'd accepted her trophy and congratulated all the other speakers, she was stuffing a payphone with coins. She oozed excitement as she told Bill and her parents about the award.

It was late Friday afternoon when Ingrid entered the Student Union Building. The mood in the pub was buoyant; a sense of relief that the pressure was off, that the tests and serious presentations were over. The next two days would be largely recreational, with food, entertainment and a dance. Vali was determined to send their young charges off with a positive glow. And Ingrid certainly had that as she moved through the hum of bodies, continually stopped and congratulated on her victory.

Wendy was amid the throng of doctors that drew her. At that point, Ingrid cared not. This time when beer glasses clinked there was a squeal of excitement. Devon Clarke was nearby among the buzzing crowd. Ingrid could see, at a glance she did not hold, that he was captivated by one of the other speaking finalists, a pretty and buxom brunette. More nurses squeezed through to join Wendy and the winner of the oration award. The room was light and bright with conversation. Then it happened. In an instant. And the ensuing consequences of that instant would change Ingrid's life forever.

In a moment when overlapping conversations abate and lone sentences rise, Ingrid heard Devon's voice—they all did. It was clear that he meant to console or flatter the pretty nurse over the fact that she had not won. He was telling her with a flirtatious warmth, "I never listen to those speeches anyway. I vote for the most beautiful woman."

The words stabbed Ingrid in a vulnerable place. For a horrible moment, she could've burst into tears. But that was unthinkable. She swallowed the emotion, and swallowed it again—until it returned as something else.

Ingrid interrupted Devon, keeping the hurt beneath her surface, or trying to. "That's not just an insult to me, Devon … it's an insult to all of us." She spoke simply without anger but there was a weight in the air that stopped the other conversations. "You've just told every woman … that our thoughts … our beliefs, and our labor … are *meaningless*." Ingrid paused for a second, and more pain oozed out than she intended. "That doesn't leave much of us."

Ingrid's open wound held the sympathy of the nurses and medical students watching her. Only the pretty nurse, the object of Devon's attention, eyed her warily.

Devon stood quietly for a second, caught off guard. "This time you're being hard on me. If you took away the vote from women, Richard Nixon would be the president."

Again, there was a terrible fragility in the feelings Ingrid swallowed. "It wasn't a beauty contest … it was a *speaking* contest. Some of us put our…" she controlled her emotion, "…*hearts* into that."

There was an uncomfortable silence. Harvey Cook broke it. "I loved your speech, it was very nice…" Ingrid thanked him, and turned back to her friends. But it wasn't over just yet.

A buried Southern drawl followed Ingrid like a lasso, pulling her back to the gray-blue eyes. "You're absolutely right to chastise me," Devon said softly. "Women of wonderful intelligence put their hearts into those speeches … and I'm the lesser man, the lesser being … not to honor that."

Ingrid stared at him. She, and probably no one else, had ever seen a humbled Devon Clarke before.

"Please forgive me," he said.

Ingrid, slightly stunned, nodded. "Thank you for saying that."

Devon kept on with a complete lack of hubris. "To be perfectly honest, I *did* listen to most of the speeches. Nearly all. Yours was the only one I never listened to, Ingrid," and then he said, "I voted for you because you're beautiful."

He added, "I know that was wrong."

Ingrid was trapped without speech or movement. All the other conversations in their vicinity had now stopped. "You won by twenty-six points, am I correct?"

The implication hung in the air like a recently exploded ordinance. Dr. Clarke's vote was worth ninety-six points. Everyone who had passed third grade arithmetic understood what was being said.

Ingrid was locked into the pale eyes. Finally she sputtered, "I don't believe you … I'm not beautiful…"

"Then I suggest you check the record … only one vote was worth ninety-six points, and that vote was cast for Miss Mulestadder."

The world was now upside down. Just outside of the little circle where time had stopped, 'Please Stay' by The Drifters was winding its way through a tangle of voices.

"You could've been talking about making ceramics out of cow patties with Chairman Mao…" He paused cruelly, then said it again.

"I voted for you because you're beautiful, Ingrid."

Blood pounded through Ingrid's face. A blur of male bravado and laughter began to rise; a hero had risen from the dust—but Devon displayed no recognition of his victory.

"If you wish, we can go together and I will retract my vote."

All eyes were on Ingrid. And now enjoying her distress. The pretty nurse asked gleefully, "What do you say, Ingrid, are you going to return your trophy?"

Ingrid was still looking at Devon. And he was still looking at her. She knew he was an evil son of a bitch and she had no adequate response. Finally, with a slight smile, she just turned away.

Wendy was agape with a look that said, 'Wooow…'

Well after dinner, students had returned to the pub, now ripened with smoky air. Ingrid was near the bar, engaged with her fellow nurses. Devon was suddenly there, handing her one of his martini glasses. "Hope you like it dry. Where I come from the classy drinkers say 'fuck the vermouth.'" Though none of the women stared, they were all keenly aware that Devon had chosen Ingrid and drawn her attention away.

The thick air was hot. Ingrid pulled the olive out her glass and sucked it a little. She watched his lips move. "You know, Ingrid … I'm pleased to find that we're not all that different, you and I…" The olive fell back into her glass as he spoke. "At first you intimidated me. I felt morally diminished in your presence. But now … I believe we have the basis for a true friendship." Ingrid laughed a little and shook her head.

Devon said, "Let's get some air."

In just a few weeks Ingrid Mulestadder would stand before a God that she did not believe in and vow to love and honor William Larsen until such time as they were parted by death. For Ingrid, there was no question that it was the right thing to do. But she wasn't married yet, and tonight, with alcohol and endorphins swirling through her head, stepping into the sweet night air of Newton, Massachusetts with Devon Clarke seemed not exactly the right thing to do—but the unavoidable.

Chapter Fifty-Two

My mom sobbed. Her blinds were drawn on the glorious September afternoon and her phone calls held, as if some terrible secret needed to be isolated from the outside world.

Devon was only a sperm donor, she said.

I assured her, "I know who I am … Bill's *my dad*, I know that."

Devon had become a hell of lot more than a sperm donor, but I spared her that information. What left her in near paralytic shock was the fortune that Devon had left me. I skipped the fact that I now owned a yacht with a swimming pool on the upper deck. Details like that would've been a little rough on the poor old socialist.

Corny as it may sound, I knew that my real fortune was the one that Bill and Ingrid had given me.

My happy, raucous homecoming had faded into night, and all was quiet in my childhood home. Before bed, I stepped outside for a moment. The air was clean with a distant tease of mint, and it felt cool on my Southeast Asian skin. A crescent burned white in a deep blue twinkling sky. I marveled at the quiet.

My true journey was far stranger than the made-up story I had told my family that night. Even my mom would never know the real facts of Devon's death. How could I ever explain that I had been an assassin with the wings of an angel? I wondered if I could ever tell anyone, and the thought of Anna suddenly flashed through me like a blow on an unhealed wound. Despite all the joy I'd found in recent days, that pain was always lurking nearby.

I wandered out toward our barn, a stoic silhouette in the moonlight, and it reminded me of Magic Larsen, the boy I once was. But I also thought of Magic Larsen, the vision that flickered inside of Dr. Clarke. It mattered not whether Devon's dreams arose from a swirl of cells in a distant galaxy of his brain, or if they came from a place beyond his own being—they had charged him with a task to redeem his soul.

He needed to die at the hand of his *other* son—as little Roger had died at his.

His God drove a hard bargain. He couldn't make Magic a murderer, and it couldn't be a mercy killing. A killing of intent that wasn't murder or mercy. A near impossible task.

Against all odds, Devon tendered the fee.

Chapter Fifty-Three

A motorcade of black limousines proceeded through Boston's South End, twisting left onto Washington Street, toward the towering glory of St. Francis of Assisi Cathedral. In each car was a board member of Clarke Surgical Centers and his or her family. I was in the first car with the chairman of the board. Under her coat she wore a black dress with a single red rose. As we approached the church, she reached over and held my arm without looking at me. I'd spent a day with Olivia in Houston, home of the company's head offices, and we'd flown up together for the funeral.

The early afternoon was overcast. A crowd was beginning to amass. Some stood outside smoking or talking while others trickled into a venerated old Catholic church. As we moved through the people, Olivia introduced me as 'Magnus Larsen' with no additional description—I could've been her boyfriend or her nephew—but when a woman named Brigitte asked me how I knew her, Olivia replied for me, "He's Devon's son." Brigitte's mouth froze half-open as we moved along.

Olivia was a VIP who drew her own crowd, and as they circled her, I saw an older woman, a short distance away, staring at me. Lean and well-dressed, she was surrounded by a coterie of mostly elderly people. Her gray eyes were fierce—I felt the gaze in my stomach. I suddenly realized that she was my grandmother. Olivia stepped in to break the spell. She led me over to the woman whose eyes never left my face.

"Fiona, this is Magnus…" The woman grasped my hand rather than shook it, an unexpected strength in her grip. Neither her gaze nor her hold on my hand wavered.

"What do you make of *this*, Olivia?"

Olivia told Fiona that we would come by and visit her during the coming week.

Approaching the steps, Olivia Clarke was once again swallowed by a sea of greetings. I paused, looking up at the Baroque architecture against the textured clouds, the tribute to the Holy Trinity that towered above us. How magnificent this would've looked to the poor immigrants massed into Boston's early slums.

I then noticed a man smoking a pipe on the steps of the church. He appeared scholarly, with a gray goatee that looked more manicured than his longish hair. I absorbed his appearance for a moment, and decided to prove once and for all that I'm still in touch with my lower self. After he tamped out the ashes of his pipe, he turned, to find me standing in front of him—holding out a wad of cash.

The man looked at me blankly. "What's that?"

In my dead perfect imitation of Devon Clarke, I replied, "It's from that guy over there, Haskell … he wants you to fuck his wife."

A hurricane hit the man's face. It was as if Devon had reached out from the grave and given him a smack. As the poor man twisted with shock, I said, "I'm Magnus Larsen, I've heard a lot about you."

"You're a real prick, Magnus," he said, apparently on the road to recovery.

My smile radiated.

"I'll tell you this," he said, still ogling me with disbelief, "someone's got some fucking explaining to do."

As the pews filled up I found myself standing under the elegant curves of the church dome with Haskell and his girlfriend, Annette.

Instantly likeable, she had quickly described herself as an aging hippie. Olivia alighted to chat with Annette for a moment as politeness dictated. As she moved on to Haskell, I sensed a vast history, not without complications.

When Olivia moved up the aisle, Haskell said, "Devon was a brilliant man but when it came to her ... blind as a bat." The note of dissent surprised me; Devon had always spoken of his former wife with the utmost respect.

An explosion of flowers surrounded a casket that contained the urn of ashes I had brought to America. As I took my seat next to Olivia, it seemed that more people were eyeing me, as if I was the object of a strange rumor. (Imagine that.) Just down the pew were Fiona and her people. A great mass of bodies pressed behind me. Were they here for Dr. Clarke or for Dadaram? Or drawn by the intrigue of controversial celebrity? It was standing room only behind the pews.

The priest was portly and solemn. The official version of Devon's expiration was death by fever, though I think most of the congregation suspected that 'fever' was a euphemism for suicide.

As my heathen socialist parents had brought me up outside of the church, my entire experience in places of worship was from weddings and funerals. I was struck by how adept the priest was at dancing over spiritually tricky areas—like leaving your wife to start your own cult. His practiced voice also spoke of the terrible loss of little Roger, that had shaken his parents so. He had no idea.

Moving into standard territory, we were reminded of Christ's sacrifice. It struck me that my little brother Roger had also sacrificed his body for me. Had it not been for Roger's tragedy, I never would've met the defining challenge of my life. The Catholics like their saints, and succumbing to the plague of superstition that infects the human race, I decided to adopt my little brother, Roger, as mine.

A choir of white-robed angels sang. Then a man with a statesman's presence rose to the podium. Haskell's voice played in my head: "You're going to do that imitation for Harvey." As Harvey Cook spoke of his lifelong friend, I could hear fierce old Fiona choking with sobs.

After the final prayer, organ music swept in and the pews began to empty. There was a reception to follow at a hotel downtown. Olivia was caught up in another wave of people so I went to the back of the church to get our coats.

A line had begun by the coat check, and I joined the rear. I was suddenly struck by a feeling that was both strange and familiar: the sense that I was being *watched*, not just looked at. It was the same sensation that I'd had on the dock in Ao Lai, the day I'd turned to find Devon Clarke staring at me.

The feeling pulled me slowly around … my breath stopped—

Barely beyond an arm's length away was the most exquisite pair of eyes—as if glass, the color of a deep forest, had been broken into sunlight, turning it into shades and hues of green and gold. The hair around the woman's face was darker and shorter than I remembered it, and her skin was paler. But it was her bearing that held my breath at bay—she looked ready to break—

I recalled a moment on a dock in Ao Lai, when she'd stood before me, holding out twelve tickets with the most naked vulnerability … but here she was a tower of crystal so fine … a single word, a whisper, could destroy it. Somewhere in a distant land, a dragonfly flitted in and out of long shadows.

The woman's companion was a young woman with a distinctive lilt to her features. She stared off, not at the floor as she had once upon a time, but into an undefined space. There was a dignity about her, but it was her reticence that made her appear arrogant and noble. It may have intimidated a suitor. One who didn't know her better.

My lungs found air, first in bits and stops, then in a long, deep, invading breath, beautiful and terrifying. I moved, ever so slowly, into the realm of the woman's aura. Her lips and skin drew me to her cheek … where I hovered, fearing the intensity of touch. Then I whispered, so softly that only she could hear.

When my voice stopped, I withdrew. For a moment she held my eyes. Then she turned to the girl who refused to look at me, and spoke.

"Magnus says he's a little bit shy … he wants to know if he can have a hug."

Somewhere in the world, a colored bird screamed in a jungle. And somewhere beyond the world, a man with a newly acquired soul passed into Infinity.

Or so the myth goes.

Author's Acknowledgements

It is to my early readers that I owe the greatest debt. For a first-time novelist, nothing is more uplifting than the excitement of real people. The very first eyes to fall upon this story belonged to Eleanor Fussey and Kinga, Donna Yamamoto, and Lisa and Frank Samko. They all have my profound gratitude.

Editors Sylvia McConnell and Allister Thompson have also contributed to these pages. Allister performed the copyedit with a sharp eye for errors. I thank them both.

During the creation of this book, I often felt a sense of gratitude to the great invisible mass of humans who have shared their knowledge on the internet. Whether checking a fact or learning the proper format for a novel, the internet was my resource time and time again. How did we ever survive without these people? My hat is off to them all.

Author's Notes

Death of a Guru is fiction. There is no such place as Ao Lai on the Andaman Coast or Copper Creek, Oregon. Wamathani Station is north of Bangkok, not south. *Et cetera.* While the facts in the story often fit with the real world, at times the real world has been altered to fit the story.

Somewhere within the pages of this book there is a blurb that contains the phrase, *any similarity to persons living or dead is entirely coincidental,* and in all instances we shall defer to that truth. If you have recognized yourself, and feel as if I have reached into your life and stolen from it—like an early explorer capturing a savage's soul with his Brownie camera—I suggest you take it as a compliment. If you see me, you can buy me a drink and thank me for immortalizing you—or send me a poem that you've written yourself (nothing too brilliant or I might be tempted to steal from it).

Most of all, thank you for reading my story. That's from my heart.

Doug Greenall

www.ingramcontent.com/pod-product-compliance
Lightning Source LLC
Chambersburg PA
CBHW021621030826
48979CB00035B/1341/J

* 9 7 8 0 9 9 0 8 7 8 2 0 9 *